The Lord of Castle Black

BOOKS BY STEVEN BRUST

THE VISCOUNT OF ADRILANKHA ADVENTURES
The Paths of the Dead
The Lord of Castle Black

THE KHAAVREN ROMANCES
The Phoenix Guards
Five Hundred Years After

To Reign in Hell
Brokedown Palace
The Sun, the Moon, and the Stars
Cowboy Feng's Space Bar and Grille
The Gypsy (with Megan Lindholm)
Agyar
Freedom and Necessity (with Emma Bull)

THE VLAD TALTOS NOVELS
Jhereg
Yendi
Teckla
Taltos
Phoenix
Athyra
Orca
Dragon
Issola

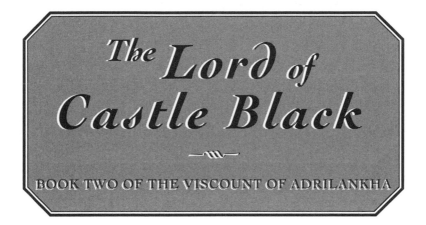

The Lord of Castle Black

—⚬⚬⚬—

BOOK TWO OF THE VISCOUNT OF ADRILANKHA

STEVEN BRUST, P.J.F.

TOR®

A TOM DOHERTY ASSOCIATES BOOK
NEW YORK

THE LORD OF CASTLE BLACK: BOOK TWO OF THE VISCOUNT OF ADRILANKHA

Copyright © 2003 by Steven Brust

Afterword copyright © 2003 by Neil Gaiman

This book is printed on acid-free paper.

Edited by Teresa Nielsen Hayden

A Tor Book
Published by Tom Doherty Associates, LLC
175 Fifth Avenue
New York, NY 10010

www.tor.com

Tor® is a registered trademark of Tom Doherty Associates, LLC.

ISBN: 0-312-85582-6

First Edition: August 2003

Printed in the United States of America

0 9 8 7 6 5 4 3 2 1

The Viscount of Adrilankha

BOOK TWO

The Lord of Castle Black

Describing Certain Events Which Occurred
Between the 247th Year of the Interregnum
And the 1st Year of the Reign
of Empress Zerika the First

Submitted to the Imperial Library
By Springsign Manor
House of the Hawk
On this 3 day the Month of the Athyra
Of the Year of the Vallista
Of the Turn of the Jhereg
Of the Phase of the Phoenix
Of the Reign of the Dragon
In the Cycle of the Phoenix
In the Great Cycle of the Dragon
Or, in the 179 Year
Of the Glorious Reign
Of the Empress Norathar the Second

By Sir Paarfi of Roundwood
House of the Hawk
(His Arms, Seal, Lineage Block)

Presented, as Always,
To Marchioness Poorborn
With Gratitude and Affection

Cast of Characters

Blackchapel and Castle Black
Morrolan — An Apprentice witch
Erik — A fool
Miska — A coachman
Arra — A Priestess
Teldra — An Issola
Fentor e'Mondaar — A Dragonlord
Fineol — A Vallista from Nacine
Oidwa — A Tsalmoth
Esteban — An Eastern witch

The Kanefthali Mountains
Skinter — A Count, afterward Duke
Marchioness of Habil — His cousin and strategist
Betraan e'Lanya — His tactician
Tsanaali — A lieutenant in Skinter's army
Izak — A general in Skinter's army
Brawre — A general in Skinter's army
Saakrew — An officer in Skinter's army
Udaar — An adviser and diplomatist
Hirtrinkneff — His assistant

The Society of the Porker Poker
Piro — The Viscount of Adrilankha
Lewchin — An Issola
Shant — A Dzurlord
Zivra — House unknown

CAST OF CHARACTERS

Whitecrest and Environs
Daro — The Countess of Whitecrest
Khaavren — Her husband
Lar — A lackey
Cook — A cook
Maid — A maid

Dzur Mountain and Environs
Kytraan — The son of an old friend
Sethra Lavode — The Enchantress of Dzur Mountain
Tukko — Sethra's servant
Sethra the Younger — Sethra's apprentice
The Necromancer — A demon
Tazendra — A Dzurlord wizard
Mica — Her lackey
The Sorceress in Green — A sorceress
Berigner — A general serving Sethra Lavode
Taasra — A brigadier serving under Berigner
Karla e'Baritt — A military engineer

Arylle and Environs
Aerich Temma — Duke of Arylle
Fawnd — His servant
Steward — His other servant

On the Road
Orlaan/Grita — A sorceress in training
Wadre — A brigand leader
Mora — His lieutenant
Grassfog — A bandit
Iatha — A bandit
Thong — A bandit
Ritt — A bandit
Belly — A bandit
Ryunac e'Terics — A lieutenant in Skinter's army
Magra e'Lanya — Ryunac's sergeant
Brimford — An Easterner and Warlock
Tsani — Grassfog's sister
Tevna — A pyrologist

"Ah, I am reassured. Here, may I offer you these figs? I have made trial of them upon myself and found them excellent."

"You are very courteous. For my part, I have managed to save a little wine, and, by the Gods, you are welcome to the half of it."

"I am deeply in your debt, my friend. Tell me, if you would, how you happen to be out here alone, if, as you say, you ply your trade in a band?"

"I met with misfortune, and became separated from my companions. But you, what brings you to these mountains alone, if you will forgive my curiosity?"

"I am on a mission."

"A mission?"

"Yes, exactly, and of the most serious kind."

"Ah! You say, 'serious.'"

"And if I do?"

"That is to say, rewarding?"

"Rewarding? Well, it is not impossible that, at its end, there will be a certain recompense."

"In that case, well, do you have any need of a confederate?"

"How, a confederate?"

"Well, you perceive I have a sword, and I give you my word I am tolerably well acquainted with its use. If this would be useful to you, we could perhaps consider a partnership of some sort. I tell you frankly that I have been unable to decide upon my course of action, after losing my companions; indeed, I have been sitting in this very spot trying to come to some sort of decision, and, as I have sat here, I have watched my few provisions gradually disappear. You have already given me some aid, in that you have brought food just as I was coming to a most unwelcome understanding of hunger. In short, I am, just now, meeting severe circumstances, and I look to you for rescue. You perceive I hold back nothing; I hope that, even if you cannot use my services, you will love me a little for my honesty."

"You interest me exceedingly, young man, and I must say that I am considering your offer in all earnestness."

"I am glad you are considering my offer, because I certainly made it with no question of joking."

"What of your companions?"

"Well, what of them?"

"Do you speak for them as well?"

"Only under a certain condition."

"A condition? Let us hear this famous condition, then."

"Feathers! It is that I find them again!"

"Ah. Well, I understand how this could be necessary."

"And if I find them, are we agreed?"

"Permit me to consider."

"Oh," said Wadre, "please believe that I would never question a gentleman's right to consider. Even when I was with my band, and we would come upon a stranger and I would offer him his life in exchange for whatever he possessed of value, well, even then I would not begrudge him some time to consider."

"And you were right not to. In this case, there are many things to consider, but, above all, I must consider whether my objectives will be aided by having a swordsman, or perhaps, indeed, a few swordsmen, near at hand; or whether these objectives will be hindered. As I consider, perhaps you will tell me what you have been doing in these regions, and how you happened to become separated from your associates."

"Oh, that is easily enough explained."

"Well, I am listening, then."

"We were hired for a mission by a sorceress, which mission proved to be overly difficult for us."

"Well, but you must understand that this answer, laconic as it is, only produces more questions."

"How, does it?"

"I promise you it does."

"Well, I cannot help that."

"But can you answer them?"

"My dear sir," said Wadre, "should you but ask, I will turn my entire attention to doing so."

"Very well, let me begin then."

"You perceive that I am listening."

"You say you were hired by a sorceress?"

"I say so, and I even repeat it."

"Tell me, then, about this sorceress, for it is unusual to meet someone with such skills in these days when the Orb is no longer whirling merrily about the head of an Emperor."

And in this way, Pel very soon had extracted from the bandit the entire history of the recent encounter between Orlaan and Piro in all significant details. And, although Wadre mentioned nothing that might divulge the identity of Zerika or her friends, he did happen to include Tazendra's remark about having known the sorceress by another name.

"Grita?" said Pel. "That was the name of the sorceress? Grita? You are certain?"

"It is as I have had the honor to say, my dear sir."

"And the name of the Dzurlord?"

"This name I never heard pronounced."

"But she was wearing a uniform of sorts, mostly of black, yet with hints of silver as a Dragonlord might wear, similar to the old uniform of the Lavodes?"

"Yes, indeed."

"And she was the one who called the sorceress by the name Grita?"

"It was none other; indeed, there is no question in my mind that the Dzurlord and the sorceress knew each other."

"Well, that is more than a little interesting," said Pel, considering the matter deeply.

"You think so?"

"Believe me, my friend, I am captivated by your tale."

Wadre bowed. "I am glad that you are."

"But it does make me wonder one thing, my dear brigand."

"What is that?"

"It concerns loyalty."

"How, loyalty?"

"Exactly. Suppose that my mission were to conflict with that of this Grita, or Orlaan, or whatever her name is. Where would your loyalty lie?"

"Why, I am always utterly loyal to whoever pays me, at least for a while."

"For a while?"

"Yes. For example, if we were to fight with Orlaan—"

"Yes, if we were to fight her, what then?"

"Why then, as you had hired me, I should fight for you at least until the end of the battle."

"So then, you are not fanatical in your loyalty."

"Oh, I think I am fanatical in nothing. And, as for loyalty—"

"Well?"

Wadre shrugged. "I am a highwayman. You perceive, loyalty is not of great value in my profession."

"Yes, there is some justice in what you say. But I must know if I can depend upon you to remain loyal for a certain period of time."

"If you have engaged me for it, and I have agreed, you can depend upon me."

Pel nodded. "I will take you at your word," he said.

"You may do so with confidence," said the brigand. "But, what is it you would have me do?"

"In the first place, you must find your confederates, because we may require them."

"That may be difficult."

"The reward will be commensurate with the difficulty."

Wadre bowed. "I will take you at your word."

"You may do so with confidence," said Pel.

The highwayman made a respectful salute and set off. When Wadre had departed to begin looking for his associates, Pel spent some few moments in deep consideration; as he considered, he frowned, then briefly shook his head as if to dispel a stray or distracting thought that had intruded upon his contemplations. Sometime later he permitted himself a brief smile, after which he nodded abruptly, as if he had at last come to a decision. The results of this decision we will see presently.

Chapter the Thirty-Sixth

How Khaavren At Last
Set Out from Adrilankha
With the Intention of
Visiting an Old Friend

The reader may recall that Khaavren had determined that, rather than permitting history to wash over him as if he were a piece of driftwood by the banks of the Laughing River, he would prepare himself to take an active part in it. He had further determined that he was in no condition to do anything useful; therefore, he reasoned, he must remedy this condition at once.

He thus began to attempt to recover some of the form and physical situation he had enjoyed years before—driving his agèd body (or, at any rate, what felt to him like an agèd body) as hard as he could. He rose before dawn, and, before even so much as taking a glass of klava, he would slowly run through a series of motions he had learned of Aerich and which were designed to put his muscles into such a state that they could suffer certain abuse without being damaged—these were very slow actions, taking each joint in the body in turn and slowly causing it to extend, stretch, or turn; the result, though Khaavren didn't know this, was very similar to the motions and gyrations of an Issola snake-dancer.

These motions and actions took rather more than half an hour, and, when they were done, Khaavren took himself out of doors and ran in a regular route that took him some three miles to complete. We must say that he had begun by walking this route, and then, after some weeks, he had begun to trot through parts of it, and so on; but now he was running the entire distance, and, indeed, was beginning to run it at a good speed.

Having completed the run, he would pause long enough to drink a glass of water and another glass of a certain combination of fruit juices that he had learned of years before from Tazendra, who pretended it replenished resources of the body which running tended to consume. Then, having taken this sustenance, he would retire to the weapons room and there spend two hours running through the sword training that he had begun learning as a child, and that had never entirely deserted him. He would thrust, parry, advance, retreat, circle, and go through complex combinations and patterns that had been handed down from Tiassa swordsmen of antiquity, improved by practice in combat, refined by theoretical studies, and tempered by experience. To these traditional maneuvers, Khaavren, like the Tiassa he was, would add in his own techniques, taken from his observations of Aerich's coolness, Tazendra's aggressiveness, and Pel's ferocity.

When finished with these exercises—and the reader must understand that, as Khaavren drove himself through these with all of the enthusiasm of a Tiassa, he was by now exhausted, and trembling in all of his parts—he was not yet done. Next came the part where he worked to make his muscles stronger. On certain days, he would work on lifting heavy objects; on other days, he would attempt to increase his flexibility by straining his various limbs to the limits of their movements. On other days, he would combine these activities.

Often, his wife, Daro, would come to him when he had concluded his regime and with her own hands rub and massage his muscles. Whether this aided Khaavren in his efforts to return his body to what he called "fighting trim" we cannot know; but there is no question that it was enjoyable for both of them.

We should say that, when he had first begun to subject himself to this regimen, he had discovered in terms that left no room for doubt how far his physical state had deteriorated. He would quickly find himself covered with perspiration, and note that his breath was coming in gasps, and sometimes he could barely sustain himself upright for the trembling in his limbs; whereas at night it would seem as if he were, as he put it to himself, "trying to sleep in a pool of my own aches and pains."

But he was a Tiassa, and he had made a decision; nothing was going to shake his resolve. The more his body seemed to object to the treatment to which he subjected it, the more determined he was to do more. He played mental games with himself, saying that if he could push himself a little harder to-day, he would ease off to-morrow (which agreement with himself he would promptly break the next day), or else he would try to convince himself that it was easier than it had been the day before, or sometimes pretend that he was displaying his prowess before a host of admirers who had never seen such a display of strength and endurance, and were cheering him on.

But, most of all, he simply gritted his teeth and carried on, pushing himself for no other reason than that he had decided to do so, and his self-love would permit no failure, no cessation, no easing up in the effort.

In all, he would spend five hours at these activities, at the end of which time he would bathe and then break his fast—and break it well, for by this time he would have built up a prodigious hunger. He would drink more of Tazendra's juice combination, as well as eating hot bread, butter, and certain fresh fish that the Countess caused to be brought to Whitecrest Manor directly from the piers. In addition, he would have kethna procured from smokehouses in South Adrilankha, and various vegetables that Daro, the Countess, pretended would help improve his hearing and eyesight.

His repast would be in the company not only of his wife, but often of their guest Röaana as well, and, as the weeks became months, both of these women were unable to help but notice certain changes in our old friend, as this physical training caused not only physical, but also mental, or, if the reader prefers, emotional improvements. His eyes began to recover their old glint; his voice became at once more firm and more gentle; his conversation both more precise and more intriguing. It need hardly be added that Daro was no less than delighted with these changes, and, if she understood that it meant he would be leaving her for a more or less prolonged period, and to go into greater or lesser danger, well, that was still some weeks or months away, and the Countess of Whitecrest, being herself a Tiassa, understood how to live fully in the moment.

As for their guest, she had, within the first few days of her visit, become part of the household. She had at once made friends with the cook, and could often be found in the kitchen, snacking on cinnamon crusts and chatting with her about almost any subject. And she had entirely won the heart of Daro because the girl's enthusiasm had quite reminded the Countess of herself at that age, and Röaana had almost immediately discovered that it was completely natural to confide in Daro, telling her much about her life and her hopes for the future, and, indeed, as is the way with such conversation, many things that she, Röaana, had not herself realized before speaking of them. With a sensitivity that is, alas, rare in a Tiassa, she had recognized at once that Khaavren rarely wished to be entertained by bright conversation, but had rather respected his reticence and desire for quiet, and so she often amused herself when in his presence by reading from Whitecrest Manor's rather extensive library of works historical and poetic.

A little later, as Khaavren began to feel some of his old power returning, the girl volunteered to spar with him, an offer which he accepted at first grudgingly, then more willingly upon finding that she had, in fact, some skill as a swordsman, and so after this the two of them would fight with buttoned foils for an hour each day, at the end of Khaavren's exercise period. If he was able to teach her much of the technique that made him such a formidable adversary, she, in turn, was able to give him a great deal of practice in fighting against younger and less disciplined swordsmen; practice that he was convinced would be useful to him. In this way, as we have said, she endeared herself to all of the house, and, between her influence and the improvement in Khaavren's disposition, there was a period of some months when Whitecrest Manor was a happy household. If there was no small worry on behalf of the young viscount, and yet more worry regarding Khaavren's future departure, we hope the reader will comprehend that, in a time of such fear and sorrow as the Interregnum, families and individuals grasped at such joy as they were able to, keeping well in the back of their thoughts such fears as concerned matters over which they had no control.

And so it was a smiling, happy Countess of Whitecrest who greeted Khaavren and Röaana early one afternoon on the terrace overlooking the ocean-sea. Khaavren rose as she appeared, and kissed her hand tenderly as she seated herself. She smiled at their guest, who had fit so well into the household, and said, "A very pleasant day to you both."

"It is," said Khaavren. "Though I perceive the sea is troubled below us; no doubt there is a storm to the southwest, beyond the range of our vision."

Daro said to Röaana, "It is hard to believe that my lord Khaavren was raised far inland, hundreds of leagues from the ocean-sea, for, in the short time he has dwelt here, he has come to know the sea as well as any of us born to it. Indeed, my lord has predicted storms that old, old men could not sense, and I have never known him to be wrong."

Khaavren smiled. "I must say that I love the ocean-sea as much as if I'd been born to it. It is peaceful, yet never inducing of ennui."

"Indeed," said Röaana, "the waves have been dancing for us. I find that I never tire of watching them."

"It does soothe the heart," said Daro. "My lord Khaavren and I have spent many a troubled hour staring out at the sea." Daro gave Röaana a friendly smile as Cook appeared with cool drinks hinting of mint and lime.

Khaavren sipped his, then permitted his gaze to drift eastward for a time. Neither of the others spoke, nor needed to; they were well aware that his thoughts were following his eyes out toward where his son was, wondering, and worried. Daro watched him, and Röaana watched Daro.

Khaavren let his gaze return to the ocean-sea. After a time he said, "My dear, I must tell you that I believe it is at last time to set out. Today I completed the Form of the Six Valleys in the proper time, and, upon completing it, was able to do so again, and then yet a third time, with no greater result than a rapid pulse, a need for deep breaths, and a slight trembling in my forearm. I cannot recall a time when I was able to do more with milder effects, therefore I conclude I have reached a state of conditioning that I must deem sufficient."

Daro nodded slowly, as if she had received a message that she had been dreading, but knew was to come sooner or later. After a moment, she said, "Where you will go, my lord?"

"Arylle," said Khaavren.

"Of course," said Daro, nodding, and even managing a smile. "It will be good for you to see your friend."

"Yes," said Khaavren. "And, of course, he is not far from Dzur Mountain."

"Yes," said the Countess. She sighed then. "I wish I could accompany you."

Khaavren nodded. "I should like that very much."

"Alas," she said. "It is impossible. With the breakdown in municipal government, everything must be done by the county, and I am the county."

Khaavren nodded. "If Piro were here, why, he could require the city to better manage its affairs. But then, if Piro were here, we would not be setting out after him in the first place."

Daro nodded, struck by the extreme justice of this remark.

"I should very much like to accompany you, sir," said Röaana.

Khaavren smiled. "Thank you, my dear, but, of course, that is impossible."

"Is it, my lord?" said the girl. "But —"

"Yes?"

"Why is it impossible? It seems to me that it would be, not only possible, but a matter of the greatest simplicity."

Khaavren turned to look at her, feeling his eyes become wide. "How, you are serious about this?"

"My lord, you may perceive by my countenance if I am jesting."

"You wish to accompany me?"

"Yes, my lord. If I may."

Khaavren continued looking at her. "For what reason?"

Röaana raised her eyebrows. "My lord? You wish to know the reason?"

"Why yes, I do. And the proof is that I asked."

"Well, that is true. Then I will tell you. The reason, then, is simply the same reason that you, yourself, set out from home when you were very much my age."

"How, you pretend that I set out from home at your age? And that I did so for a certain reason? How is it you know that?" Khaavren accompanied this question with a look at Daro, who replied to him with the least shrug of her shoulders, as if to say that any such information as the girl might possess had not come from her.

Röaana said, "I did not exactly know, my lord, I merely assumed. Was I correct?"

Khaavren cleared his throat. "Well, in fact, you are not far from wrong."

"And my lord, if I may ask, did you have a reason?"

Khaavren chuckled as he understood what the young Tiassa was telling him. "I see. But perhaps, if you have understood all of this, you could explain—"

"Yes?"

"—what we are to tell your mother and your father if you decide to have an adventure and manage to get yourself killed in the process."

"Oh, as to that—?"

"Well?"

"They would understand."

"How, they would understand?"

"Certainly."

"I beg leave to doubt that they would understand, my dear girl. On the contrary, I am convinced that they would not understand at all, but, rather, would be entirely displeased with how we had exercised care of the young lady whom they entrusted to us. I believe that, had I a daughter of your age, and sent her somewhere to be safe, I would take it amiss were her guardians to send her off into the wilds in search of exactly the sort of danger from which I had hoped to have her protected. Indeed, I should find myself more than a little annoyed at this behavior. That is my opinion, and if you think it wrong, well, tell me so at once."

Röaana set her countenance in an expression both unyielding and unhappy, and said nothing, looking at the floor of the terrace. Khaavren looked at the young lady in question, and, when she did not speak, he turned his gaze out to the ocean-sea once more. The Countess, for her part, looked at the girl for some few moments, as if reading her thoughts by the expression on her face.

"My lord husband," said Daro with a slight smile. "I must admit that there is, I believe, something that you have not considered."

"Well," said Khaavren, "if there is something I have not considered, then tell me what it is, and, well, I will consider it."

"I ask for nothing more," said Daro.

"And then?"

"It is this: Our guest's mother and father—that is, Röaanac and Malypon—will be displeased to learn that their daughter has been held in chains."

"How, chains?"

"Assuredly."

"But, why should she be held in chains?"

"Because," said Daro at once, "I am convinced she would soon bite or rub through any ropes we could find."

Khaavren frowned. "And yet," he said, "I fail to see—"

Daro chuckled. "My lord, I am implying that, unless she is secured, she will certainly set out after you, and it is safer for her to travel with you than on her own, following."

Khaavren considered this for some few moments, still frowning. Then suddenly he smiled. "You are right, madam, as you usually are."

Daro smiled back at him.

"But my dear," said Khaavren. "Should anything happen to her—"

"I will explain to them."

"But will they understand an explanation? Consider—"

"My lord—"

"Yes?"

"It is difficult to make such a decision, but, yes, I believe they will understand."

Khaavren nodded slowly, then, at last, he said, "Very well, then, it will be as you say."

"Which means?" said Röaana, looking up with an expression of one who hardly dares to hope.

"Yes," said Khaavren. "You may come with me."

The young Tiassa beamed, and was about to speak when she was interrupted by Cook, who arrived with a bow and the news that a messenger was at the servants' entrance.

"Well?" said Daro. "For whom is this famous message? Is it for my lord Khaavren, or is it for me?"

"My lady," said the cook, "it is for our guest."

"A message for Röaana?" said Khaavren.

"A message for me?" said Röaana.

"That is it exactly," said Cook.

"Well, but then," said Daro. "Let this messenger come to us here."

The cook bowed and left, to return in a few moments with a Teckla dressed in the livery of the House of the Dzur. This worthy bowed to all present, and then addressed himself to the youngest of them, saying, "You are, then, my lady, Röaana, of the House of the Tiassa?"

"Well, that is my name," she said. "And you have a message for me?"

The Teckla bowed once more in sign of assent, saying, "Your Ladyship has understood exactly. I have a message." With this, he produced a small, rolled-up piece of parchment, tied up with a silver ribbon. The girl at once took the message, untied the ribbon, unrolled the parchment, and said, "Ah! It is from my dear friend, Ibronka, of whom I have told you so much."

"Yes, indeed," said Daro. "But, what does she say?"

Röaana laughed. "She says, in fact, that she is nearly dying of ennui, and begs me to find an amusement for her."

"Is there a reply?" asked the Teckla.

"Oh, a reply?" said the young Tiassa. "Well—" She frowned and looked at Daro, then at Khaavren.

Daro said, "Your friend, as I recall, is a Dzurlord, and is of your own age?"

"Nearly," said Röaana.

Khaavren and Daro exchanged glances, whereupon Khaavren sighed and said, "Very well, then. She may accompany us as well."

Röaana smiled.

"Well," said Daro, smiling. "You will certainly be the envy of all you behold, traveling with such companions."

"Bah. You are pleased to jest with me," said Khaavren, smiling in his turn.

"Well."

"When shall we set out?" said Röaana, betraying an understandable eagerness.

"Early to-morrow morning," said Khaavren.

"Well then," said Röaana, addressing the messenger. "Tell my dear friend Ibronka to prepare herself for a long journey, and to be here by first light in the morning. And be certain to tell her not to forget to bring a sword of good length."

"I will not fail to convey your message," said the Teckla, bowing first to Röaana, then to the others, after which he took his leave.

After the messenger had left, Khaavren turned to Daro and said, "We must begin preparations at once."

"Yes," she said. "I understand this. Where shall we begin?"

"I shall begin at the stables, and attempt to determine which horses to bring, and, in addition, which equipage."

"Very well," said Daro. "And I will instruct Cook to prepare such comestibles as are suited for traveling."

Khaavren nodded, and cast his gaze once more to the reddish ocean-sea before him.

"Are you looking for ships, my lord?" said Daro, smiling.

"I always do, madam," said Khaavren.

"Someday you will see one."

"Yes."

Khaavren stood up and extended his hand. The Countess placed her hand in his, and Khaavren bent over and tenderly kissed her hand; then, with a nod to Röaana, he set off for the stables, leaving Daro smiling fondly after him. Röaana, for her part, blushed in confusion at this display of conjugal affection, and rose in turn, explaining that she would begin her packing.

Ibronka arrived early the next morning, just before dawn, in fact, as Khaavren was completing his preparations for departure, and Daro and Röaana were on the terrace taking klava. Cook announced her arrival, and shortly after she appeared, clad in black traveling garb and carrying a sword in a baldric slung over her shoulder. Röaana stood, and introduced her friend to Daro, who received her with a graciousness that would have done credit to an Issola.

"And where?" said Röaana, "is our dear Clari?"

"Outside, awaiting us, and causing another horse to be saddled."

Ibronka was seated and given klava and warm butterfly rolls with honey. At around this time Khaavren entered to say that all was now ready.

"My lord," said Röaana, "you know that we are now four?"

"So I have been informed," said Khaavren. "Quite a pretty troop we will make, too—me and three young girls. As the Countess has said, I shall excite no small amount of envy as we pass."

He was, we should add, dressed in his old, worn traveling clothes, very like those that he had worn when we first had the honor to bring him to the reader's attention in the town of Newmarket, nearly eight hundred years before. At his side was a sword that, like himself, was beaten and scarred, but still strong, flexible, and able to give a good cut or two.

Khaavren took a glass of klava and a roll, though he declined the honey because he pretended that it would delay them several hours if he had to wash it off his hands. Daro smiled at this, and adjusted the long, tapering collars of his blouse, as if it were important that he look his best as he set out into the wilderness—an attention to which our friend could not help but respond with an affectionate smile.

He was introduced to Ibronka, to whom he bowed solemnly, then said, "I perceive you have a Nelshet."

Ibronka frowned and said, "My lord, I do not understand what you have done me the honor to tell me."

"Your sword," said Khaavren. "It was made by Nelshet."

"Ah. That may be. You perceive, I am not familiar with the maker of the weapon."

"It is good steel that comes from the best iron taken from the northern-most reaches of the Kanefthali Mountains, and smelted by a special process known only to the masters in Krethtown, and then crafted by Nelshet or his offspring. I identified it at once by the curve of the hilt and the heart-shape of the guard, which are always the marks of a Nelshet weapon. You will, moreover, find an ornate 'N' on the strong of the blade, very near to the guard. It is one of the very best of blades. I had one myself for a number of years, but lost it during a skirmish before the Three Hands Road campaign, when I was forced to leave it in the possession of an officer in the service of Count Rockway, because I could not afford the time to extract it from his person. I have always regretted the loss, the more-so because this officer had no use for it."

"This one," said Ibronka, "was a gift of my mother, and I treasure it for that reason, if no other."

"Well, but you are Dzur."

"I am, sir. And then?"

"There is no doubt that, sooner or later, you will come to appreciate its other qualities as well."

Ibronka bowed.

"And you, Röaana," continued Khaavren. "I perceive you also have a tolerably long stick with you, and I know well enough that you can play with it. Be certain to check your sheath each time we stop, for the fit of the weapon into it is not perfect. I have known pebbles kicked up from the road to become stuck in a sheath, causing the weapon to be wedged into it, to the embarrassment of the player."

"I will not fail to do so," said Röaana.

"That is good, then." He then turned to Daro and said, "Come, my dear, and embrace me. It is time that we left."

Daro came into his arms, and, upon being given a glance by Röaana, Ibronka permitted herself to be led from the terrace to permit the Count and Countess a little privacy to say farewell to each other.

"Madam," said Khaavren, "I am not insensitive to your wish to accompany us."

"Ah, sir, do you hear me complain?"

"Not in the least."

"Well then?"

"Nevertheless, I know this is difficult for you. Should it be you leaving on such an errand, and I required to remain, well, I should not care for it."

Daro smiled. "My lord, you must understand that my delight in seeing you active again overcomes any trifling annoyances caused by inaction."

"And yet, I well know that you are not cut from a fabric suited to looking on while others act."

"My lord, it has often been remarked that you are unusually reticent for a Tiassa."

"And then?"

"Then permit me to be unusually patient. My time will come."

"Then I have nothing more to say. Embrace me, madam."

"Gladly."

Khaavren met Ibronka and Röaana near the side door of the manor, and led them out to the stables, where three horses were saddled and ready. Clari was already mounted upon a fourth, and awaiting them. Khaavren looked around, observing the fine weather—warm, but not hot—and nodded, as if satisfied that it would be a satisfactory day for travel. Anyone who knew him well would have seen a certain light come into his eyes—the warrior once more returning to arms after having felt himself useless and finished with life for long years. He set his hand upon the hilt of his sword and his eyes upon the path they were to take, then returned his attention to his companions.

"We will travel light," said Khaavren. "That is, we are not taking a pack animal. This means that, alas, we will not be eating as well as we should like."

Both of the ladies indicated that this would not upset them to any great degree. They mounted their horses with the aid of the night-groom, while Khaavren himself used the mounting post. His thoughts as he looked at the manor are impossible to describe. It had been hundreds of years since he had set out on a mission of any sort, or since he had left his home without the expectation of returning to it by nightfall. He bit his lip and frowned, and then, seeing Daro standing in the front door, he raised his gloved hand in a salute to her, then directed his horse's head away from the manor, lightly touched his spurs to its flanks, and and set out upon the road, the two girls riding knee to knee behind him, Clari coming last.

They took the long path down to Kieron Road, and took this eastward across the canal, both Röaana and Ibronka recognizing places they knew from their arrival in the city. They were, we should say, quite remarked upon as they passed through Adrilankha. Some of these remarks expressed curiosity, others surprise, and a few amusement; while there were one or two that nearly passed the bounds of what a gentleman could tolerate regarding ladies in his company. We say "nearly" because, in the first place, this was no longer the Khaavren of old, who welcomed any opportunity to test his steel against another's, and, in the second, because the merest glance from the Tiassa was sufficient to cause the comments to be bitten back into the mouths from which they nearly emerged. Ibronka and Röaana, of course, did not deign to give notice to any remarks or comments of any kind, and Clari quite wisely kept her own thoughts or reactions entirely to herself, and so in this way they at length passed out of the city along what was still called the Eastgate Road in spite of the fact that there had not been an East Gate since the city walls had been taken down, which had happened thousands upon thousands of years before (at least, according to those who claim the city was once walled; the prevailing opinion among historians is that Adrilankha had never been a walled city, in which case the name "Eastgate Road" presents its own puzzle, but one which we hope the reader will forgive us for merely making an observation upon without following it with the careful exploration that, perhaps, it merits).

Although keeping a careful watch for brigands, they nevertheless made moderately good time, achieving fifteen miles on the first day, and nearly twenty on each of the next two. They slept out in the open, under the sky, taking turns watching. There being only four of them, and there being as well a need to keep one on watch at all times as they slept, by the fourth day they were all sufficiently exhausted as to get a late start, and to decide to retire early; which they repeated on the sixth day. If Khaavren was annoyed at this delay, he gave no signs of it.

In this way, then, it happened that by early evening of the sixth day they had passed the Collier Hills, and, riding down in the twilight, Khaavren at last was able to see, with a pleasure that can hardly be described, the lights of Brachington's Moor twinkling in the deepening gloom ahead.

Chapter the Thirty-Seventh

How Morrolan Came to
An Interesting Town
And Had a Vision

It was on a Firstday in the summer of the two hundred and forty-seventh year of the Interregnum that Morrolan arrived in the county of Southmoor, and, more particularly, a small barony called Bellows, located along its eastern border. We should say that, although the county was named Southmoor, this appellation was largely unearned. Although there are moors, swamps, and marshes in plentiful supply in the deltas and wetlands to the north, Southmoor in general consists of jungles, tropical rain forests, and some land suitable, although just barely, for maize and certain grains, as well as for the raising of a few kethna. The name, we should add, came from the one moor to be found in the region, a small one in its northeastern corner, but the first area to be settled. As for the barony of Bellows, it should be added that the last Baron of Bellows had fallen prey to an unspecified illness some eighty years before, and the barony was, therefore, vacant.

Morrolan, Teldra, Arra, and the warlock discovered where they were in the simplest possible way: They happened to meet a peasant as they followed the road from Chorbis, the village where they had managed to find an inn the night before. This worthy Teckla had stopped upon seeing the two aristocrats riding proudly along with two Easterners, a dog, and a cat. As he gawked, he had been asked to name the place where they were. "Bellows" had been the answer, more squeaked than pronounced.

The Teckla being dismissed, they continued on their way. "Welcome home," said Teldra.

"Well, and this is my home?" said Morrolan.

"You are now within the confines of Southmoor, and, were there an Empire to recognize titles, you would be recognized as its Count."

Morrolan considered, then said, "I believe we should look for a place to spend the night."

"Your first night in your own domain," said Teldra.

"Well, yes," said Morrolan. "And I should be less than honest if I did not admit that this notion pleases me."

"And well it should," said Arra.

In the event, they were unable to locate an inn, and so once more slept out in the open, just off the road under a few trees, guarded by the warlock's "friends" as he called them. Teldra, Arra, and the warlock awoke early the next morning to find Morrolan already awake, and staring to the west. Arra took his hand in her own and said, "Yes, my lord. In that direction, as far as you can see."

"Once, and perhaps again. And yet, there is no Empire, so what then?"

"What the Goddess wills," said Arra.

Morrolan nodded. "Perhaps," he said, "she wills that I take back what is mine. Soon several hundred witches will make their way here, and, after that, who knows? Perhaps I can find warriors as well."

"Hundreds now," said Arra, "and a thousand to-morrow. And with warriors as well, yes, you could reclaim your land."

"I will do so, then," said Morrolan.

"I should be glad," said Teldra, who came up next to him, "to offer whatever assistance I might be capable of."

Morrolan said, "I had another dream last night."

Arra looked at him quickly. "Tell me of it," she said.

"It was another occasion when I was looking for something."

"But then, for what were you looking?"

"I don't know."

"You don't remember?"

"I remember that, in the dream, I didn't know, yet I was determined to find it, nevertheless."

"That is right," said the warlock. "I know many people who do not know what they want, yet are ready to kill for it, and that is in the waking world. So much the more should you be willing to look for it in a dream."

"And yet, when I awoke, I had a vision before me, as of a staff, or wand, that was all black, and had a jewel, also black, on the top of it, and I wonder if that is not what I was seeking in my dream."

"Well, it is possible," said the warlock.

"Was there more?" said Arra.

"Just before I woke up, I seemed to be looking upon water, but it was all black."

"But," said Arra, "where did you look from?"

"From a great height."

"You seemed to be above the sea, looking down, as from a mountain?"

"No, I seemed to be floating."

"And you saw black water?"

"Only for a moment, as I have said, just before waking. Before that, well, I saw only the ground, but as from a great height."

Teldra said, "I have spoken to you of the floating castles that many of your line had before Adron's Disaster."

"Yes, that is true," said Morrolan, "although I had not considered that until this moment."

"It may be that there is some connection," said Arra.

"Perhaps," said Morrolan, "there are the ruins of such a castle nearby."

"I am certain there is at least one," said the warlock. "At any rate, I have heard of such a thing."

"Where?"

"Perhaps sixty or seventy miles west of here."

"Then let us go there."

"Very well," said Arra.

"I agree," said Teldra.

The warlock indicated he would be willing to accompany them, and so, after saddling and then mounting their horses, they set out. The day was uncomfortably warm, forcing them to stop often to water the horses in the ponds or streams they passed, with the result that ten or eleven hours after setting out, they had traveled some fifteen leagues, bringing them, at the end of that time, to the wall that circled the village of Nacine, on the Hightower Brook. Nacine, we should say, was not, by any means, a normal village, for Southmoor or anywhere else. To begin with, its name, Nacine, was a mispronunciation of *Nerise Séteen*, or "High Tower" in the ancient language of the House of the Dragon, which House had first reached the district in the Dragon Reign of the Third Cycle. In fact, there was not, and never had been, a high tower near-by; rather, the town, and, for that matter, the river that ran near-by, were both named for a guard tower that Lord Drien had intended to build there.

Lord Drien was known to have favored extravagant plans of all sorts, and was better than usual in carrying them out. In this case, his idea was for a series of towers, anchored in that spot, to serve as a center of communication between the coast to the south, the Shallow Sea to the east, the Adrilankha River to the west, and Dzur Mountain to the north. For this reason, he had not only planned the line of towers, beginning with High Tower, but brought in (at considerable expense, we might add) a number of artisans from the House of the Vallista to aid in the construction. The Vallista arrived in droves, prepared to begin the well-conceived if ambitious project, and prepared a list of materials they pretended were required. These materials were then gathered, along with armies of Teckla to perform the menial labor as well as to provide food as best they could where conditions permitted little to grow except sugarcane and wetcorn.

The Vallista, however, had barely begun their work when Dzur Mountain, some seventy or eighty miles north, had unexpectedly erupted, either because of the arcane activities of the Enchantress or in spite of them. The eruption had resulted in a remarkable flow of lava, which, in turn, resulted in the river becoming blocked to such an extent that it was no longer suitable for navigation; indeed, as the astute reader may have observed, it came to be called a brook, rather than a river; and we should add that the intervening years have done nothing to increase the flow of water, but rather the reverse: the brook is now sometimes dry for months at a time, in spite of the prodigious amount of rainfall generally received in the region.

For a number of years, those who lived there expected the reduced flow of the river to reverse itself—that is to say, they thought the river would regain its former majesty. When it became clear that this would not happen, there was some consideration by the Vallista engineers over the possibility of unblocking or re-routing it, but before any decision could be reached, Drien had been taken to Deathgate Falls and the Cycle had turned, bringing to preeminence a Lyorn Emperor less interested in expansion, and so the project was, ultimately, abandoned.

However, the Vallista had, by this time, become so well settled into their new homes that it appeared never to have occurred to them to leave, and, moreover, the peasants of the district somehow contrived to not only wrest a living from the land, but to positively flourish (a condition, it must be admitted, that was no doubt aided by the fact that the nominal baron of the district was involved at the court and had never paid sufficient attention to the holding to receive his due). The end result, however, was a tiny area centered around the village of Nacine where the Vallista had built, and built, and built. Around the village was a wall of blue and green mosaic tiles. Within the village itself, every building was constructed of stonework; in some cases of marble imported millennia before from quarries near the southern tip of the Eastern Mountains, in other cases of granite brought north from the coast. The lowliest keeper of the poorest livery stable had a house of granite with a marble fountain in front of it; the Speaker's house, though there had not been a Speaker for ten thousand years, would stand for another ten thousand even if no Speaker were appointed.

The reader can well imagine, then, the amazement our friends felt upon passing the gate as evening fell and they came upon these surroundings as if they had crossed a necromantic gate into another world. None of them spoke at first, being too astonished to find words; and for their part, the villagers found the visitors no less startling as they rode down the main street—which street, we should add, had been paved by carefully crafted rectagonal stones, so that the horses made an extraordinarily loud sound as they walked, which sound not only alerted the villagers of new arrivals, but served as well to disquiet the horses.

"Let us," said Morrolan, controlling his mount with an effort, "endeavor to find an inn."

The warlock wordlessly pointed out a sign, on which, beneath a symbol they could not yet make out, was printed in large, bold script: "Inn."

"I hadn't realized," said Morrolan, "that you knew your symbols."
The warlock shrugged.

"Well then, do you also see a livery stable?"

It was Arra who pointed out a sign depicting a horse, curled up in a bale of hay and sleeping soundly, with a feed bag hanging over it.

"Well," said Morrolan, "that seems clear enough."

They went to the livery stable, and Teldra entered (they having discovered that, especially when dealing with humans, she was by far the best at negotiating the rate with the coinage they had) while the rest of them dismounted and waited. She returned shortly thereafter along with a groom who, notwithstanding the unusual makeup of the group before him, agreed to tend their horses with all due care. This accomplished, they proceeded to the inn, where Morrolan, feeling expansive, arranged for a separate room for each of them, after a meal consisting of the local fish, called freshwater whitefish, which they prepared by a system they called "double-cooking." This peculiarity of the region required them to sauté the fish with slivered rednuts and toe mushrooms, and then, after sprinkling them with sesame seeds, to cook them briefly in a large baking oven. The consensus among Morrolan and his friends was that this procedure was successful, but not worth the amount of time they were required to wait.

The beds were soft, and, moreover, of solid construction—these, too, showing signs of Vallista craftsmanship. Needless to say, they slept well, and were up early the next day, prepared to start on their way once more. Of them all, the warlock was up earliest; Morrolan found him in the jug-room of the inn, breaking his fast on fresh bread with honey, goat's milk, and thick slabs of bacon. While he ate, he was simultaneously in deep conversation with a Vallista with a bony face and a pronounced forehead. The warlock rose and bowed when Morrolan appeared; the Vallista did the same.

"My lord Morrolan e'Drien," said the warlock, "permit me to name Sir Fineol, a Vallista who is willing to speak with Easterners."

The two humans exchanged salutes and, at a gesture from the Vallista, they sat down.

"Sir Fineol," said the warlock, "pretends that he knows where, not fifteen miles from here, are the ruins of a castle that once floated above this district."

"Indeed?" said Morrolan. "Well, I should be grateful if you would take me there."

"I should be glad to do so," said the Vallista. "Yet it is just as easy to tell you as to show you. Once past the west gate continue for three or four leagues until the road curves left to avoid a pond. After following it to the left, you will almost at once see a smaller trail also going to the left. Take this trail up into the hills, and, from the top of the hills, you will see the ruins of the castle spreading out before you."

"Well, that seems easy enough," said Morrolan.

"It is," said the Vallista. "Nevertheless, if you wish, I will take you there myself."

Morrolan shrugged to signify that this offer, while courteous, was unnecessary.

The others joined them and broke their fast, eating quickly because it was apparent that Morrolan, though he said nothing, was anxious to be on his way. When they had finished, Morrolan paid the shot—including that of the agreeable Vallista—with the local coins he had acquired in change from the livery stable. As he was doing so, Arra said, "A moment, my lord."

"Well?"

"May I see that coin?"

Morrolan shrugged and passed it over. It was a silver orb—showing, in fact, a representation of the Imperial Orb on one side, and, as was customary with moneys of the Empire, a throne and a face on the reverse side. Arra examined it, then showed it to Morrolan. "Consider the features of the face, my lord."

Morrolan did so, and said, "What of it?"

Teldra looked over Arra's shoulder, and said, "Yes, I see it. There is a resemblance to you, my lord."

"How, is there?"

"Indeed. And a strong one, too. I would venture to guess that this coin was minted nearby, and that this is a picture of your father, Lord Rollondar e'Drien."

Morrolan took the coin back and examined it carefully. There was not only the face imprinted in it, but, on the orb side, there was stamped the Serioli symbol for "17," indicating that it was a product of the Seventeenth Cycle, and a minuscule glyph that, upon close examination, appeared to be a jhegaala.

"It is recent," said Morrolan.

Teldra nodded.

Morrolan stared at the first image of his father he had ever seen, and, if this was accompanied by certain emotions, we hope the reader will understand if we permit him some measure of privacy regarding these feelings.

After some few moments, Morrolan pocketed the coin and handed a different one to the host, and said, "Come. It is time to go."

They retrieved their horses from the livery stable, the proprietor of which helped them saddle the beasts and then mount, and made their way to the west gate of Nacine and the road beyond.

The Vallista's directions were sound, and following them brought Morrolan and his friends, after some hours of riding, to a low series of hills. They climbed the tallest of these hills, stopped, and looked down.

Morrolan had not been certain what he expected—perhaps a mound of rubble, or maybe something that appeared to have once been a castle, only now collapsed upon itself. What he saw, instead, was a wide area, roughly circular in shape, over which pieces of stone and brick were liberally spread. There was no sign of anything resembling any part of a structure, nor was the rubble even piled upon itself; just pieces with no indication that there had ever been anything built by man.

Morrolan looked it over for some time with none of his companions venturing to comment. At length, Morrolan gave his horse a nudge, and made his way down the hill. The others followed behind in single file, maintaining their silence.

When he reached the bottom of the hill, surrounded by rubble, Morrolan dismounted and stood amid the ruins, looking about. After a while, he took a deep breath, closed his eyes, and remained in this attitude until, at length, Arra ventured to say, "My lord, you seem to be deep in thought."

Morrolan nodded. "Yes, I have come to a decision."

"If my lord would be pleased to tell me this decision, well, I should be glad to hear it."

"I have decided," said Morrolan without further preamble, "that I have come home."

Chapter the Thirty-Eighth

How Grita Collected Information
And Left Some to Be Collected

As Wadre attempts to gather his band and Pel attempts to gather information, we assume the reader is not so naïve as to believe that Grita has, upon receiving the setback at Deathgate Falls, abandoned her schemes for power and revenge. In this, the reader would be entirely correct; far from abandoning them, she in fact redoubled her determination. Making her way some distance from what had been the scene of battle, she looked for a place from which she would be able to remain concealed while observing anyone who returned along the Blood River. As the mountainous terrain was ideally suited to such clandestine activities, she found such a place easily enough, and waited there with the patience of someone who has already waited hundreds of years for her opportunity and is determined to wait hundreds of years more if necessary.

The reader should understand that this quality, this ability to remain patient even when burning with anger and the desire for vengeance, is an uncommon trait, and one that, in another context, might be considered a virtue; and it is exactly this that made her dangerous. With this patience, then—patience cultivated by decade after decade of nurturing her hatred—she took her position and waited for Piro and his friends to pass by. How long was she prepared to wait? This we cannot know—perhaps weeks, perhaps years. But in this case, it was a little more than a day, because her quarry stopped to rest for the night in a place a kilometer or so north of her, then proceeded directly past where she awaited them early the next morning. After permitting them to pass her by, she began following them at a good distance, so there would be no chance of being observed. And it must be admitted that she exercised a degree of skill in this activity; at any rate, she was not detected as she followed them, nor even, late that night, when she drew up near their camp hoping to overhear somewhat of their conversation.

And in this, we must say she was successful: She heard Mica explain to Lar how well his saddle-sores had healed, while Lar, on his part, held forth upon the proper way to "season" cast-iron cook-pots. While this was not what Grita wished to hear, it was, nevertheless, what was said, and she was required to accept it as much as the reader—although the reader is perhaps more fortunate insofar as he is not required to hear the entire conversation, but only a summary of it. It is well known by those who make a career of listening in on private conversations—by which we refer to those who do so for the Empire, as well as those who do so for personal reasons of one sort or another—that one must often listen to a considerable amount of wearying, trivial discourse before hearing anything of interest.

Grita moved around, hoping to hear conversations by others of her enemies. Indeed, she was able to hear Tazendra speak, but the subject of Tazendra's conversation involved speculation on what sorts of changes in fashion might have occurred had the Interregnum not intervened—speculation with which we will not tire our readers. This monologue—for it cannot be called a conversation—was listened to by Kytraan; Piro held himself apart and stared out into the night (of which, because the campfire was behind him, he could see nothing) and spoke to no one, evidently occupied by his own thoughts.

We need hardly add that Grita learned nothing that night. She was, however, not in the least discouraged, but, with that patience we have already mentioned, followed them again the next day as they retraced their path along the Blood River. Once again, after a day's travel they made camp, and once again Grita crept as close as she dared, hoping to hear something to her advantage. This time, the conversation between Lar and Mica had to do with the best way to open a wine bottle if one didn't have wine tongs, as well as about certain incidents each had heard of in which a lady of the aristocracy had been known to lower her standards and engage in dalliances with a servant, combined with notes on the dangers of such liaisons. Grita worked her way around once more, and this time heard

Kytraan saying, ". . . am worried about what we are going to tell Sethra Lavode."

"How," replied Piro. "What we will tell her? Why, we will tell her what happened."

"And then?"

"And then she will know."

"Pah. I do not like it."

"What is it you mislike?"

"To return thus, having utterly failed."

"And so, Kytraan, what do you suggest? Would you prefer not to return?"

"No, that was not the meaning I intended to convey."

"Well, then?"

"Rather this: I should like to accomplish something first, and then return."

"Accomplish something? But, what do you pretend we can accomplish?"

At which time another voice, which Grita recognized as that of Tazendra, entered the conversation, saying, "Cha! as your father would say, good Viscount. I know the answer to that!"

"And cha yourself," said Piro. "I am well enough aware of what you would do!"

"Well, and?"

"And I say," said Piro, "what I have said all along: We ought at once to inform the Enchantress of what has occurred. After we have done so, if we choose to run our own errand, well, I will say nothing against it."

"By the time we have returned to Dzur Mountain," said Kytraan, "it will be too late."

"That may be true."

"And then?"

"Nevertheless, it is what we ought to do."

"Perhaps," said Kytraan, "we could send one of the lackeys back to tell the Enchantress what has happened, while we continue with our business."

"Why now," said Tazendra. "There is an idea. What do you think of Kytraan's idea, Piro?"

"It is one I had not thought of," admitted Piro.

"And do you think it a good one?" said Kytraan.

"I must consider it."

"Oh," said Tazendra, "we have nothing against considering."

"No, indeed," said Kytraan. "I, myself, have been known to consider on occasion, and would scarcely begrudge another's chance to consider."

"That is good, then; I will do so."

"And will you do so now?" said Tazendra.

"I am considering this very instant," said Piro.

"That is good," said Kytraan.

"Yes. I could not tell, or I should not have asked," said Tazendra.

"Then it is right that you asked."

"Do you think so?"

"I am certain of it."

"Well, then I am pleased."

"And you should be. But, your pardon, I am considering."

"Of course," said Tazendra, falling silent.

"Very well," said Piro, after a moment. "I agree. We will send one of the lackeys back with the message."

Grita then heard a sound which, after some consideration on her part, she concluded was one of them clapping his hands together.

"Then," said Tazendra, "it is decided. Only—"

"Yes?"

"Which one shall we send?"

"Oh," said Kytraan, "it doesn't matter."

"How, doesn't matter?" said Piro. "Well, neither one is your lackey."

"That is true," said Kytraan. "Then I shall say no more about it."

"Oh, on the contrary," said Tazendra. "You must say a great deal more about it."

"Indeed?" said Kytraan. "Well, what must I say?"

"Why, you must choose which one goes."

"Who, I?"

"Yes, you. What is your opinion, Piro?"

"I am entirely in agreement with you, my dear Tazendra. You,

Kytraan, have no lackey, therefore you are the one to choose which one takes the errand."

"Very well," said Kytraan. "Let Mica go, because he has more experience, and a better chance to arrive safely."

"Agreed," said Tazendra.

"Agreed," said Piro.

"I will instruct him to set out in the morning."

"Yes," said Kytraan. "And we, well, we will set off on our own errand, and, if Fortune favors us, well, we will take the vengeance we wish."

"Indeed we will," said Tazendra.

"Indeed they will," said Grita to herself, smiling grimly and stealing off into the night.

Mica, when informed of this mission (the reader will understand if, even though Grita has left, we continue to follow Piro and his friends for a time), was of two minds on the subject. To the right, he was flattered by the confidence that was shown in him by entrusting to him such an important assignment. But, to the left, he considered a journey of months, on his own and through dangerous country, to be a matter of some concern. But, as he was given no choice in the matter, and, moreover, as the look on Tazendra's countenance made it clear that there was no question of joking, then to be sure, was there to be no question of arguing; he therefore made plans to depart early the next morning.

As he made these preparations, Lar said, "I wish you good fortune upon your journey, my friend."

"I thank you for your kind wishes."

"Does the mission frighten you?"

"Frighten me? You ask if it frightens me?"

"Yes, I do, because I am curious."

"Well, I nearly think it does!" said Mica with great enthusiasm.

"It would frighten me," said Lar.

"Yes," said Mica.

"In addition to bandits, there are various beasts, after all."

"I know."

"Or dangers of simple accidents, which are an inconvenience when traveling with a group, but can be fatal when alone."

"Yes, but—"

"Or starvation, on such a long trip."

"If you—"

"Even dying of thirst is possible."

"Wouldn't mind—"

"Or you might become ill—"

"Will you have done?"

Lar paused. "Ah. I beg your pardon. I perceive I have discomposed you."

Mica glared at him. Lar swallowed with some difficulty and said, "Well, is there some help I can give you in your preparations for departure?"

"No," said Mica coldly.

"Oh, come now, my friend. I have apologized. There must be a great deal yet undone. Permit me to help you."

Mica relented, and the two of them set about selecting what Mica would need to begin his long, solo journey on the morrow. In the meantime, Piro, Tazendra, and Kytraan sat around their fire, each lost in his own thoughts, and unaware that their conversation had been overheard by her whom they hoped to hunt down. At length the fire burned down, and Mica's preparations were finished, and they fell asleep.

Early the next morning, as the first light was just beginning to brighten the Enclouding, Tazendra pulled Mica aside in order to be certain he understood his mission. "You must reach Dzur Mountain as quickly as you can manage, and you must give the Enchantress this letter which Piro has done you the honor to entrust to you."

"Yes, mistress."

"To this," she continued, "I add this purse, which contains seventy good silver orbs, which are still in use, and one gold imperial, which ought to be plenty to see you through any emergencies, as well as purchasing any food and supplies you may need from whatever mountain villages you may pass. Apropos, you must be careful in bringing out the purse, because some of those who live in the mountains are not particular about differentiating between coins that are their own and coins they can acquire by some means or another."

"I understand, mistress. I will be careful."

Tazendra nodded and continued, "If, by chance, something happens to the letter, you must tell the Enchantress what has happened—that is, that Zerika leapt over Deathgate Falls to her death, that we were treacherously attacked by a certain Grita of whom she has heard me speak in the past, and that we are now in pursuit of this Grita, as well as the brigands she has hired while calling herself Orlaan. Be certain to tell her this name, as she may use it again. Do you understand all this?"

"You will see, mistress: The letter first, failing that, Zerika has leapt, Grita has attacked, and you are pursuing Grita, Grita is called Orlaan."

"That is it. And, if you can do so without compromising your mission in other ways—"

"Yes, mistress?"

"Have a care for your skin."

Mica bowed as if, in fact, he had intended all along to do nothing exceptionally rash with regards to his life, though whether as a favor to his mistress, out of duty for the mission, or for his own reasons, we will not speculate.

These last instructions given, then, and with a backward glance to Lar, who raised his hand in salute, Mica continued as they had been going, following the Blood River, mounted on his pony, his faithful bar-stool strapped to its side.

Lar watched him disappear, then turned back to Piro as if to say, "And now, what of us?" though, of course, he did not actually utter these words.

Piro shrugged and, as if in answer, turned to Kytraan. "Well, my friend, it was your wish to find this Orlaan, or Grita. Have you a plan as to how to go about it?"

"I? Not the least in the world. In my opinion we should ask Tazendra."

"Who, I?" said the Dzurlord. "Well, if truth be told, I have never been gifted in regard to plans. That is to say, in *making* them. In carrying them out, well, that is a different matter entirely."

"Yes," said Kytraan, "I understand that. But in the old days, well, who was it to whom you turned for plans?"

"Who was it? Why, we had a Tiassa with us, and so felt no need to look further."

Piro sighed, as if he had been expecting no other answer but this.

"Well," he said after reflecting for a moment, "we cannot know where she has gone—whether back the way she came, or following us, or in another direction entirely; and so—"

"How," said Kytraan. "You think she may be following us?"

Piro shrugged. "How are we to know?"

"Bah!" said Tazendra. "Do you think she would have the audacity?"

"You know her best of all of us," said Piro. "Would she?"

"Well," said Tazendra, "that is to say—" She broke off and frowned. "It is not impossible," she said at last.

"And then?" said Piro.

Tazendra frowned and fell silent in evident contemplation. Piro and Kytraan (and of course Lar) maintained their silence, aware that contemplation was not Tazendra's special skill and that therefore she should be given all of the assistance she might require.

At length, Tazendra stood up and said, "If you, my friends, would be so good as to wait here, I shall return directly."

"We will do so," said the Dragon and the Tiassa.

Tazendra walked out from the fire and began a careful inspection of the ground surrounding the camp while Piro and Kytraan, as promised, waited quietly, exchanging glances but making no remarks.

After some time, the Dzurlord returned.

"Well?" said Piro anxiously, observing she had acquired a certain paleness.

"Well," said Tazendra. "You are right. She has been here, outside of our camp."

"Shards!" said Kytraan.

"Indeed," said Piro, a grim expression stealing over his countenance.

"But, how can you be sure?" said Kytraan.

"How?" said Tazendra. "Because I looked."

"Very well, I understand that you looked. But, what did you see?"

"Oh, you wish to know that? Well, I will tell you. There are foot-prints in the area outside of our camp."

"Well then," said Kytraan, "there are footprints."

"But then," continued Tazendra patiently, "it would seem that someone was there."

"Oh, I agree that *someone* was there. Only, how can you know it was Grita?"

"I am explaining that very thing," said Tazendra, a trifle impatiently.

"Very well, then, I will listen."

"That will be best. So then, there are footprints. But you perceive that, although we traveled this way two days ago, our own footprints are no longer visible, nor are there any signs of the prints which our horses must have made, which means that rain or wind has effaced them. If the footprints I observed are still there, it seems probable that these were made by someone who was here more recently, which I would think to be last night."

"Well, there is something in that."

"Moreover—"

"Yes?"

"—why else would someone—whoever made the footprints, because I am convinced that, if there are footprints, there are feet to make them, and these must be attached to legs, and so to a body— why else would this someone be so careful to remain around the edge of our camp other than to observe us?"

"Your logic is inarguable," observed Piro. "Especially the matter of footprints requiring feet, and so on."

"And in addition," said Tazendra, who, now that she had begun her train of logic, was no more able to prevent it from reaching its conclusion than a boulder, once it begins rolling, is able to stop before it has exhausted itself, "the footprints were made by a pair of boots with a small, square heel and with a peculiar texturing on the sole—in other words, boots made for walking through a variety of terrain, rather than one made for the city street or for riding. Now I happened to observe Grita's boots when we saw her, and they were just of this type."

"Well observed," murmured Kytraan.

"Moreover, if one were to study the marks, as I have done, one might observe the peculiar impression made by someone standing in one spot and shifting his weight back and forth, as will happen when remaining in place over a long period of time, as if listening. Therefore, I conclude that it was Grita who was sneaking around our camp last night, and that she was attempting to hear our plans, and, moreover, may well have done so."

Tazendra finished, and Kytraan and Piro stared at her in silent astonishment, as they had never had cause to suspect that the Dzurlord was capable of this sort of observation, not to mention the reasoning that accompanied it. At length, Piro said, "Well, I understand."

"As do I," said Kytraan.

"We must, then, remain on our guard at all times," said Piro. "Do you agree, Kytraan?"

"Nearly."

"And you, Tazendra?"

"Oh, I am convinced of it," said the Dzurlord, grimly bringing her fine hand with its long fingers to wrap around the hilt of her sword.

"Or—" said Piro.

Kytraan turned to look at him. "Yes? Or, you said?"

"Or, instead of being on our guard—"

Tazendra frowned. Kytraan said, "Yes?"

"Well, perhaps we could follow her from her tracks."

Tazendra's eyes widened. "Follow her from her tracks?"

"Perhaps," said Piro.

"It *is* a thought," said Kytraan.

"And yet," said Tazendra, "could her tracks not lead into an ambuscade?"

Piro shrugged. "It is not impossible. And then?"

"Splinters!" said Kytraan. "Why, then we should be killed!"

"Well, that is possible," admitted Piro.

"But then," said Tazendra, "perhaps we will turn the ambuscade back upon those who attempt to snare us. It is what we used to do in the old days, you know; it became something of a habit."

"It is a good habit," agreed Kytraan. "And yet—"

"Well?"

"I am not convinced that we can do it."

Tazendra shrugged. "Well, and if we fail, what will happen? We will die, that is all."

"That is true," said Kytraan. "Your argument is a good one."

"And then?" said Piro, who was, if truth be known, a little dubious about Tazendra's proposition, but who did not want to lose the opportunity. "Besides," he told himself, "more than likely there will be no ambuscade."

"Very well," said Tazendra. "I agree to following her tracks."

"As do I," said Kytraan.

"Then let us pack up and be about it," said Piro.

We should add, in case the reader has not noticed, that there was one member of the party, by which we mean the worthy Teckla, Lar, who had not been consulted. But this, of course, was only to be expected.

Lar packed up the camp, thinking his own thoughts, and they set out to follow Grita's tracks, as the hunted became the hunters, and the hunter, the hunted. As to whether this transition will occur one or more times again in the future, we do not, at this moment, choose to reveal.

Chapter the Thirty-Ninth

How Kâna Learned What Zerika
Had Been Doing, and Took Steps

On the other side of the continent—that is, in the Kanefthali
Mountains—as these events were unfolding, certain
other matters were occurring which cannot be ignored by
the prudent historian. To be precise, Habil found her cousin—that is
to say, Skinter, the Duke of Kâna, or the Emperor of Dragaera as he
now styled himself—in the library, and at once said, "My dear
cousin, there is a problem."

Skinter looked up from the map he was studying—a map which
detailed certain areas to the northeast of Suntra—and said, "Not in
the least."

Habil stopped, her mouth open. Whatever she had expected to
hear, it was not this; and, whatever she had been about to say, she
instead emerged with, "I beg your pardon?"

"I have said, my dear cousin, that you are wrong. We do not have
a problem."

"And yet, I am convinced—"

"Rather, we have many problems."

"Ah! I comprehend."

"Yes. In addition to whatever you are about to tell me, we have
the matter of supplying our army that is only now extracting itself
from the desert, and has nearly run out of fodder for its horses, not to
mention hardtack for its personnel."

"Very well," said Habil. "What else?"

"Next, we have the matter of the Houses, who have failed to
come along with us quite as readily as we had hoped they would.
There are, to say the least, holdouts. To be more precise, we have
three sorts of responses: those who have said they will not support
us, those who have said they are considering the matter, and those
who have given us no reply whatsoever."

"I understand about the Houses," said his cousin. "Next?"

"After that, there is the matter of transport. We cannot go to Adrilankha, for the simple reason that we have not secured it. And our ships that were intended to run between Hartre and Candletown are afraid of the reavers from Elde Island."

"That is transportation. Is there more?"

"Nearly. There is discontent in the rear areas. Indeed, there have been murmurings of revolt from Brightstone, not a hundred leagues from where we stand."

"I understand your concern about discontent, my dear cousin. Is there anything else?"

"There is. Do not forget intelligence. With our brave Yendi off on his mission, well, reports have been arriving less regularly, with fewer details, and they have been imprecise and unreliable, which means that, in addition to all of the other problems, we cannot be certain how bad they actually are, how best to address them, or what problems we do not yet actually know about.

"For this reason, my dear cousin, I insist that, rather than a problem, we have many problems. That understood, tell me about this new difficulty you have discovered."

Habil sat down across from him and said, "Well, but before I do, let us discuss these other matters that occupy your mind."

"Very well, if you wish, we will discuss them."

"To begin, then, you have mentioned supply problems for the Third Imperial Army, as we have named it, under the command of Lady Suura. It is true that matters are serious, but I received a message from her yester-day, and she believes that, although it will not be easy, she will succeed in extricating herself from the desert, and it is well known that she intends next to cross the Pushta, where there is no shortage of grain, water, and even grass for the horses. In my opinion, and Suura's, they will manage."

"If you say so, then I believe you. What next?"

"Next, you spoke about the Great Houses. It is true that the response we have received is not all we would have wished for."

"Feathers! That is true!"

"But neither is it as bad as you believe."

"How, it is not?"

"No. Consider Casement, for example. She is a Yendi. Her 'no' can almost certainly be taken as a 'yes,' particularly since we know that her half-brother has been organizing against us, and there is no doubt that Casement quite hates her half-brother. And then there is the Dzurlord Sennya, who indicated that she thought little of us, but has failed to take any steps, and has even spoken in our favor among certain other Dzurlords. Röaanac is weak, and can be swayed easily. Mistyvale is ready to agree, requiring only confirmation from certain scryings and other arcane sources. Newell has not replied because he is fighting on our behalf within his House, and, in his opinion, nearly about to carry the day. Indeed, I think that soon the Lyorn, Ritsak, will be alone in opposing us. If so, he can be brought around. He has not sufficient strength to stand against us all."

Kâna frowned, but did not otherwise respond.

"So much," said Habil, "for the matter of the Houses. Now, as to transport, well, are we not building a navy? Do we not have the cooperation of the Orca in this endeavor? To be sure, their cooperation is not under the seal of the House, but it is none the less useful for that. It may take time, but I am convinced that we will soon be able to answer each of the reaver's ships with two of our own, and then we will have transport."

Kâna continued frowning, but didn't speak, instead gesturing for his cousin to continue.

"As to Brightstone, well, so long as the murmurs remain murmurs, I am not worried. But, in any case, you have dispatched a brigade of Home Guard under Marchioness Wunra, have you not? That should be sufficient even if the reports be true. Which leaves the matter of intelligence. And as to that—"

"Yes," said the Duke. "As to that?"

"Well, my dear cousin, I beg leave to submit that, were our intelligence in as poor condition as you contend, I would not have the information needed to bring to your awareness the problem to which I referred on entering your presence an hour ago."

Kâna thought all of this over, then said, "Very well. Let us hear of this problem, then, and perhaps I will be able to address it as easily as you have addressed all of those I mentioned."

"I should like nothing better," said Habil.

"Tell me, then."

Habil held up a scrap of parchment. "This has just arrived by the post from our clever Yendi."

"Well, and?"

"Everything he mentioned before, that he feared, seems to be true."

"Be specific, please."

"I will do so. In fact, I will be more than specific, I will be precise."

"Precision is good, my dear cousin."

"Here it is, then: There is a Phoenix Heir."

"Shards! Is he certain?"

"Listen: 'I have confirmed beyond doubt the existence of a Phoenix Heir.'"

"Well, it seems he is certain."

"So much so that I believe him."

"Then I must as well. Well, what next?"

"Next, it seems this Phoenix, whose name is Zerika, is daring nothing less than attempting to retrieve the Orb from the Halls of Judgment itself."

"Bah! Is such a thing possible?"

"Galstan believes it must be, because the effort is being sponsored by Sethra Lavode."

"Blood of the Horse! Her again!"

"I'm afraid so. Now, Galstan is not certain she will succeed—the attempt is fraught with peril. First, she must negotiate the Paths of the Dead, next she must convince the Gods to give her the Orb, and, last, she must leave the Halls of Judgment still living and still holding it. None of these are easy."

"Well, that is good, at any rate. But if she were to succeed?"

"Yes, my dear cousin. That would be a problem. Indeed, so much so that I have brought it to your attention."

"Well, but what is Galstan doing?"

"He is attempting to locate those who traveled with the Phoenix, in hopes of learning more of what has become of her mission."

Kâna nodded. "And while he is doing that, we, for our part, must be prepared for the worst."

"I agree," said Habil. "And yet, how do we prepare?"

"In the simplest possible manner. We attempt to take the Orb ourselves."

"How, take it?"

"Precisely."

"Your pardon, my dear cousin. But how does one 'take' the Orb? And, moreover, how can we take it when we do not even know where it is?"

"The Orb, by itself, can do little; it requires someone to defend it. And so the answer to your first question is: with an army. And, my dear cousin, it so happens that we have one; and a tolerably formidable one at that."

"Very well, then, I accept it that we have an army. But still we do not know where the Orb will be, if and when it appears."

"We do not know where it will be, but we can be certain of its first destination."

Habil frowned. "Dzur Mountain?"

"You have it exactly."

"You may be right."

"I am convinced I am. This Phoenix has no strength—that is, no army—otherwise, we should have heard of it. Where else can she go?"

"I accept it, then. She will attempt to reach Dzur Mountain. And so?"

"We at once gather our forces, and we march to Dzur Mountain to intercept the Orb."

"With our army?"

"Yes. In fact, with two armies, because, I assure you, there is nothing more important than this."

"And yet—"

"Well?"

"To get them in position will take months, will it not?"

"Certainly."

"Do we have months to spare?"

"My dear cousin—"

"Yes?"

"You know as much as I do about Deathgate Falls and what lies beyond it. We cannot know how much time we have. We may have years, or it may already be too late."

Habil considered this for some few moments, at the end of which time she said, "It is a plan fraught with peril. Consider that it involves declaring open hostility with the Enchantress, who has we know not what power. And consider that, if Zerika manages to retrieve the Orb, she will have all of the power of sorcery at her disposal."

"That is true. There is, to be sure, one other choice."

"How, another choice? And what is that?"

"To surrender at once."

"Unthinkable!"

"I agree. And then?"

"There are no other choices?"

"None that I can see."

"Well, my dear cousin, you are right. We must march to Dzur Mountain."

"Yes. Dispatch a message at once to Suura, and another to—hmmm—who commands our armies to the southwest?"

"Tonchin."

"Yes, Tonchin."

"In the first place, Suura is to be replaced by Izak—"

"How, Izak?" said Habil. "And yet, it seems that he is rather young for such a post."

"That is true. And so is Brawre."

"Brawre? Who is Brawre? You cannot mean the young captain of cavalry who led the exploratory expedition to the south."

"None other."

"But, she is only a captain, and is now merely in command of a cavalry expedition under Tonchin."

"No, she has now replaced him. Brawre will henceforth command our southwestern forces."

"And yet, I fail to see—"

"Trust me, cousin," said Kâna. "I will explain to your satisfaction in a moment."

"Very well. Orders to Suura to give her command to Izak, and to Tonchin to give his command to Brawre. Will there also be orders to Izak and Brawre?"

Kâna nodded. "Draft orders for them both to rendezvous at

Dzur Mountain with the intention of attacking it without delay. And, moreover—"

"Yes?

"Here are additional orders."

Kâna explained the other orders to be given, which explanation we hope the reader will permit us to delay, for the sake of heightening the drama and the sense of surprise which we confidently expect the reader to feel when this matter is, in its proper time, revealed.

Habil, upon hearing these orders, bowed and said, "Very well, it will be done. And yet—"

"Well?"

"I do not yet understand why you wish to replace our experienced generals with inexperienced ones."

"Do you not? Then I will explain in two words."

"I am listening."

"What goes with experience?"

"Age."

"And what determines age?"

"Why, date of birth, what else?"

"So then, consider the date of birth of our experienced generals, and those I am replacing them with."

"Why, I confess, I do not know their dates of birth."

"Well, but you must know one thing about them: Those we are replacing were born before Adron's Disaster. The younger ones were born after. And consider that this Phoenix might succeed."

"Ah! Now I understand. Should the Orb return, we can no longer depend upon the loyalty of those who feel its effect."

"That is exactly my thought, dear Habil. And do you agree?"

"Entirely."

"Very good. Then do you see to those dispatches. And as for me—"

"Yes? What will you do?"

"I will take the post directly to Suura's—that is to say, Izak's—army, with only a small escort, so that, once there, I can take personal command both of the attack on Dzur Mountain and of the effort to locate the Orb. You will remain behind, and act to aid my efforts."

"Very well, to this I agree. But what of our Yendi?"

"Let him know the plan so that he is able to second our efforts."

"Agreed."

"Good. Then let us begin at once. There is no way to know when the Orb will suddenly appear, and it is vital that we reach Dzur Mountain before it does."

"I will begin composing the messages at once. You will review them?"

"And sign them myself, yes."

"That is good. It will take me an hour."

"Until then."

"Until then."

And yet Habil, as she left her cousin's presence, was already considering, not only the carrying out of her part of Kâna's plan, but certain alternative ideas of her own. Whether any of these ideas had any effect on the unfolding of history we will see in due time.

How Morrolan Learned What Kâna
Had Been Doing, and Took Steps

Now, at nearly the same time as this discussion was taking place, there was another conversation occurring which resonated with it in an interesting manner. That is, at just about the same time that Kâna was learning of Zerika, Morrolan was learning of Kâna. It happened in this way:

By this time, what could almost be considered a small village had grown up around the site of the ruined castle. Dwelling here were, in the first place, Morrolan, and the warlock, and Arra, and Teldra, along with the animals that the warlock kept with him. However, from there, Morrolan began to hire laborers from Nacine to help him go through the rubble, looking for any artifacts that might have survived the destruction of the castle. At first, he had two young Teckla lads helping him — just to scour the ground. He did, in fact, find several items of greater or lesser interest, including a surprising quantity of silver that had somehow escaped detection until that time. These laborers soon found it easier to construct temporary residences around the ruins than to return to Nacine.

But Morrolan soon realized that he could not do a thorough job without moving some of the larger stones, and so he hired a few larger and stronger and older Teckla to assist. Within a few days, these Teckla, as well, found it more convenient to bring makeshift tents with them and to simply sleep on the grounds, and so Morrolan hired a cook and had supplies brought in.

The mere fact that Morrolan was a Dragonlord — and a young Dragonlord at that — was sufficient to command for him most of what he needed from Nacine with no difficulty. The presence of the Easterners was, perhaps, not pleasing to the locals, but none of them had any intention of disputing Morrolan's right to associate with whomever he chose, or do whatever he wanted; and so when he announced one day that the blocks of stone were to be put to use in the building of a temple to his patron Goddess, and that therefore he would require still more laborers (and that, moreover, he would continue to pay in good, hard silver for work that was done), this was greeted with little muttering and no small measure of cooperation.

We should add that the tales which have been told of Morrolan having found a temple, fully built and having survived the fall of the castle, have, in fact, a certain basis in fact: during the excavation of the region, portions of two walls had been found to be intact, and Morrolan, considering how strongly these were built, calculated to use these as the basis of the temple—that is, to rebuild, as closely as possible, the chamber as it had once been. There are various theories as to what the original chamber had been: ranging from a dungeon, because of the nature of its construction, which suggested a lower or basement area; to a banquet hall, because of its size, and moreover, because the castles of many Dragonlords of the period had large banquet halls on the upper stories, and, for reasons which ought to be obvious, a chamber on an upper story was more likely to survive a fall. This latter theory is the one to which the author subscribes, but it must be insisted upon that there is no conclusive evidence.

But, as the reader is, no doubt, aware from experience with his own projects, be they as great as excavating a castle or as small as rearranging the furnishings in a favorite room, one problem cannot be solved without two more appearing in its place. In Morrolan's case, the next problem to appear before him came when Teldra felt obliged to point out to him that his funds would not last for-ever—in fact, they would scarcely last a year at the rate at which they were being expended, and, as is well known, for-ever is much longer than a year, however it may seem to an individual who is awaiting a lover's return from a long journey.

"Well, then," said Morrolan, "I must find a way to gain the funds I need. Can you think of any?"

"Certainly, my lord. As rightful lord of these domains, you may legally exact tribute from all who live here."

"I may?"

"Yes, provided you have the means to enforce your decree."

"Oh, as to that, well, I must consider the matter. I do not believe

I would care to go, myself, from place to place with my hand out. It, well, it would not feel right."

"No, it would not."

"And then?"

"You must hire tax collectors to do this for you."

"Well, but then I must pay the tax collectors."

"You will pay them with a portion of what they collect."

"Will they not rob me?"

"Certainly. But this has, nevertheless, the advantage that you will gain income without needing to take it into your own hands, and, in addition, the people's hatred will be directed against the tax collectors, rather than against you."

"I see. And, well, where might I find these tax collectors?"

"That is easily done, my lord. Simply look in Nacine for those who seem least likely to be able to pay tribute, and set them to collecting it."

Morrolan found nothing wrong with this plan and wasted little time putting it into practice, with the result that, although there was some grumbling about the tribute, it was very little, because Morrolan's demands were not excessive, and because the oldest representatives of the local population, although they would not admit it, were actually glad to see some semblance of order returning to the district, and the collection of tribute represented order. And what annoyance was occasioned by the collection was most often directed at the collectors, rather than at Morrolan.

The temple progressed quickly once the coinage began to flow into Morrolan's coffers—in part because no time was wasted in planning it: Morrolan wanted a structure that resembled what he had known in Blackchapel, and so he would point and say, "Put that block there, on top of that one." The broken blocks were fitted together by cunning and industrious Vallista—whom he began to employ more and more around this time—and the temple grew. As an afterthought, he added a small section in back for himself and his companions to sleep in, and certain alcoves that Arra, as priestess, said would be indispensable for private consultations. A basement was dug beneath, and rudely completed, some of which would be used for storage, but most of it intended as the living and working quarters for Morrolan's Circle of Witches (which Circle, at this time, continued to arrive in small groups, and to meet, and to send eastward signals that they hoped would draw other witches in their direction). When at length a roof was placed over the temple, Morrolan felt as if he had accomplished a great deal indeed.

He spoke with Arra about the temple, considering what to use for an altar. "I have been considering returning to Blackchapel to take that altar. Have you any opinions on the idea?"

"My lord," said Arra, "is that the only reason you wish to return there?"

"You know it is not," said Morrolan. "There are other matters to attend to." As he said this, he touched the hilt of his sword.

Arra nodded. "My lord, I must beg leave to doubt the wisdom of returning to give battle; I do not believe you are ready yet. And, as to the altar, it is my opinion that it should remain where it is."

"Very well, then," said Morrolan, accepting her judgment. "But, nevertheless, I must find something to use as an altar."

"With this I agree," said the priestess.

"And then? How am I to find it?"

Arra frowned. "I will consider this matter. I will ask the Goddess, and perhaps she will send one of us a dream."

"That would be like her," agreed Morrolan. "She has done so before. And, as to the other matter—"

"Well?"

"More witches for the Circle have already begun arriving. You perceive, there are nearly an additional score here already. Soon there will be more."

"That is inarguable, my lord."

"Well, I shall use them."

"Use them? In what way, my lord?"

"You must devise a way to use the power of the Circle to help me begin to gather an army."

Arra considered this for a moment, then said, "Yes, my lord. It shall be as you wish."

Morrolan nodded.

The Circle at once began its new task, and, within a few days, strangers began drifting into the little village, having heard somehow that an army was forming, and these being persons who had nothing to sell except their sword arms. The growth of Morrolan's army was slow, but steady; in a month he had gathered together thirty or thirty-five men-at-arms, and had been fortunate enough to find a Dragonlord named Fentor e'Mondaar.

Fentor had been born some two hundred years before Adron's Disaster to a family which had fallen on hard times. Upon reaching sufficient age, he had, in order to aid his family, enlisted in a small mercenary army. This army, identified by a symbol of three crossed spears, set out from Dragaera City on a long campaign in the service of a certain Dzurlord who sent them west to the city of Thalew in the Pushta. We have said that the campaign was a long one; in fact, it reached such proportions that additional troops, many of them Teckla, were required to be enlisted and trained. Fentor had, it seemed, a certain aptitude in the training and drilling of raw troops, and so this became his duty, along with his secondary duty, which involved sorting and classifying such intelligence reports as might come in from time to time.

After Adron's Disaster, the Army of the Three Spears disbanded, and, while many of them set up as road agents, Fentor was able to procure employment with a warlord who hoped to expand his holdings much as Kâna was doing in the west. This employment sharpened his skills in the drilling of troops as well as in intelligence gathering, and, in addition, gave him some experience in commanding small units in battle.

This continued until the warlord with whom he had allied himself was defeated by the army under the command of Suura. Fentor escaped from this defeat, and might have taken service with Kâna except that, as he was considering doing so, he had a dream in which he was traveling south toward a mountain of gold. While not the most superstitious of Dragonlords, neither was Fentor the least, and so he determined to follow this dream, which became stronger each day, until, after several weeks, he wandered into Morrolan's encampment. After a brief discussion with Morrolan, to whom he explained his experience and abilities, he was put in charge of the training of Morrolan's slowly growing army.

While this was going on, Morrolan also purchased a great

amount of black paint, which he used on the temple, having the opinion that if the last temple to Verra had been black, then this one should be as well. We should also add—because it is the truth—that Morrolan also spent some time drilling as if he were merely a private soldier. If Fentor felt any discomfort in treating Morrolan as he treated all of the other recruits, we can only say that he hid this discomfort entirely; Morrolan received the same instructions and the same treatment—as harsh, rigorous, and unyielding as it was—as anyone else during this process.

The Circle of Witches, the temple, and the army all gradually increased in size during this period, until a day came when a particular man came into the collection of tents that we have already had the honor of comparing to a small village. Now this man did not, in appearance, seem any different from any of the others who had come before him—a Teckla with all the appearance of having been a road agent for a time. And in this, we must say appearances did not deceive: in and of himself, apart from all of the multitude of individual characteristics that makes each of us unique, he was not, in fact, a terribly distinctive individual. What makes him of interest to our history is not who he was, but, rather, what he brought. And what he brought was that most valuable, most priceless of articles in any time of doubt and uncertainty: information.

He arrived and introduced himself to the first soldier he met, and asked what was required to sign up. He was directed to the tent that Fentor (who was doing duty as recruiter, as well as drillmaster) made his day-quarters, and, when facing this worthy, repeated his question.

"You wish, then to become part of the Lord Morrolan's private army?"

The newcomer (whose name, alas, has not come down to us) nodded as assent.

"You understand that this is not a mercenary army, but, rather, the standing army of a Dragonlord anxious to protect his rightful properties?"

The other signified that this fine distinction held no interest for him.

"You heard, then, that you will be paid three pennies each day, as well as food that is, if not imaginative, at least plentiful, and a bed that is, if not comfortable, at least warm?"

The Teckla bowed.

"And a daily ration of wine amounting to three pints?"

The Teckla smiled.

"And that is sufficient?"

"It is, my lord."

"Sergeant. Call me Sergeant."

"Yes, Sergeant."

"What brought you here?"

The Teckla shrugged. "It was a choice of you or Kâna, and he only pays two pennies a day, and the daily ration of wine is not so generous."

Fentor frowned. "Who?"

"Kâna, my lord. That is to say, Sergeant."

"From Kanefthali?"

"Exactly, Sergeant."

"He is recruiting?"

The Teckla nodded.

"He is recruiting around *here*?"

"Oh no, Sergeant. Not here."

"Where, then?"

"Stable Point."

"How, Stable Point? You idiot, that is scarcely fifty leagues from here!"

"That is true, Sergeant."

Fentor glared at the Teckla, then said, "Corporal, sign this man in. I must find the Lord Morrolan at once."

The corporal arrived even as Fentor left, the latter going at once in search of Morrolan. Morrolan, for his part, was at this time holding conference with Arra about another extension onto the temple to permit a fixed location for a lockable supply area for the wine stores of the gathering army. In the midst of this discussion, Fentor presented himself, bowed, and said, "I beg your pardon, my lord."

"What is it, Sergeant?" said Morrolan, giving the soldier all of his attention, aware that for Fentor to have interrupted his conversation it must be for a good reason.

Fentor bowed and said, "My lord, I have just learned that Kâna is approaching this region."

"How, coming here?"

"Yes, my lord. I came to you at once."

"And you were right to do so!" said Morrolan. "Come with me, and we will talk."

"I am at Your Lordship's service."

Morrolan led him away from everyone else, and, still walking, said, "Come, my dear Sergeant, I perceive there is no question of joking."

"None, my lord."

"Then you are quite certain that Kâna is approaching?"

"There can be no doubt of it, my lord."

"Well then. But there are certain things I must know."

"Very well, I will answer, if I can."

"I ask for no more. My first question is this —"

"Well?"

"Who is Kâna?"

"How, Your Lordship doesn't know?"

"Not the least in the world, I assure you. If I had known, you must believe I would not have asked."

"Well, that is true."

"And then?"

"He is a warlord who believes he is re-creating the Empire, with himself as Emperor. He comes from the Kanefthali Mountains. There have been many such, but he has swallowed most of them, including, most recently, the warlord with whom I had taken employment before I had the extraordinary good fortune to find you, my lord."

"This Kâna — he is a Dragon?"

"Yes, my lord."

"I see. How large are his forces?"

"My lord, they are terrifying."

"Has he any just claim on the throne?"

"Only if he succeeds, my lord."

"Then, you believe he will attempt to swallow me up, as he has swallowed up the others?"

"My lord, I am convinced of it."

"Well, I shall not permit this to happen."

Fentor bowed his head, but said nothing.

"How," said Morrolan. "You doubt me?"

"My lord—"

"Come, come. You doubt me. Say so at once."

"My lord, I do not see how you have the resources to resist an army such as Kâna can bring against you."

"Do I not have an army as well, and is it not growing?"

"Not enough, my lord."

"And have I not my Circle of Witches, and is it not growing as well?"

"Not enough, my lord."

"And am I not of the House of the Dragon?"

"Not enough, my lord."

"Bah!"

"It is as I have the honor to tell you."

"Sergeant, I am becoming annoyed with this conversation."

"I am sorry to hear that, my lord. But, you perceive, your annoyance will not change the facts, and it is my duty to acquaint you with the facts, however unpleasant they may be, or unwelcome to your ears."

Morrolan glared at him, which glare Fentor withstood coolly. At length, Morrolan said, "And then, what will you do?"

"I, my lord? I will do as I am ordered, until I fall in battle. What Dragonlord could ask for more?"

"I can, my dear Sergeant. I do not wish us to die gallantly, I wish us to win!"

"My lord, I beg you to believe that I would like nothing better."

"Well, then, tell me what is required for me to do so."

"I will consider the matter, my lord."

Upon returning to overseeing the construction of the temple, Morrolan spoke to Arra, saying, "What we have is insufficient."

"How, insufficient in what way, my lord?"

"We require a structure that can be defended: hence, we must have a wall, with guard towers. And we must begin to build it at once."

"We are to be attacked, my lord?"

"It is my intention, my dear Arra, to do the attacking. Yet I must consider the possibility that I will not be ready in time, and we therefore must plan to withstand a siege, or an assault, or a combination of both of these circumstances."

"It will need to be carefully designed, then, my lord."

"Yes."

"I will send for a Vallista architect."

"Do so at once."

"Yes, my lord."

"And we will require more stone than is presently here."

"The Vallista will, no doubt, know where to procure it, my lord."

"Then let him be found."

The Vallista was found, and spent some days in close consultation with Morrolan, Arra, Teldra, and the warlock.

Chapter the Forty-First

How Khaavren and Aerich
Met Each Other Again At Last
And At Once Got to Work

Aerich met Khaavren and his traveling companions outside of his front door, and only one who knew Aerich as well as Khaavren did would have understood how rare was the expression of joy on the old Lyorn's face. The instant Khaavren had dismounted, they embraced for some few moments. During this time, without a word being spoken, servants came and took the horses away to be groomed and fed.

"Ah, my dear Khaavren! I should say I was astonished to see you, but I am too old to begin lying now, so instead, I will merely say I am delighted."

"No more so than am I, old friend. It makes me feel a hundred years younger just to see you! But, you say you are not astonished?"

"Not the least in the world, dear Khaavren," said Aerich, still holding him. "Because I knew you would eventually take a hand in all that is happening, and I suspected that this would bring you, eventually, to my door."

"Well, in this you were not incorrect, it seems to me," said Khaavren, smiling—nay, *grinning*—as he had seven hundred years before.

At last they separated, and Aerich said, "You are looking well."

"Perhaps," said Khaavren. "Better, at any rate, than I must have looked a year ago. But what of you? You seem as fit as you were the day we met in that charming little town of—what was it?"

"Newmarket. But come, who are these young ladies with whom you are traveling?"

Khaavren performed the introductions. Aerich kissed Röaana's hand respectfully, then greeted Ibronka in the same way, after which he led the way into the house. Clari, meanwhile, was shown to the kitchen.

The reader will, we believe, not be astonished to learn that within five minutes of meeting Aerich, both the young Dzur and the young Tiassa—that is to say, Röaana and Ibronka—had been thoroughly captivated by him—his natural charm, his old-fashioned courtesy, his warmth, and his air of nobility—and to such an extent that were Aerich less of a nobleman than he was, we would find ourselves obliged to be writing an entirely different sort of story than that which we have the honor to set before the reader. They sat in the Lyorn's study, and for three or four hours he and Khaavren spoke quietly of their past experiences, and of their friends, especially Pel and Tazendra. They spoke of their friend Uttrik, who had perished in Adron's Disaster and whose son now traveled with Piro (much to Aerich's astonishment and delight), and of Adron himself, and of Sethra Lavode. During this conversation, in which much more was implied than actually stated between the two old friends, the two girls sat and listened, drinking it in, fascinated by the hints of adventure from what seemed to them a lost age, and of great figures out of history whose names were mentioned as casually as those of one's favorite uncle or closest neighbor.

Soon, however, the conversation took a more serious turn, as Khaavren spoke to Aerich of Piro's mission, and Aerich spoke of Pel's visit (omitting, of course, the discussion of Khaavren himself).

"So then," said Aerich, "you do not, in fact, know what Piro's mission is?"

"Not the least in the world, I assure you. And you, do you know anything of what Pel is up to?"

Aerich sighed. "I do not know, but—"

"Yes, Aerich? But?"

Aerich shook his head. "You know that he is always up to something—"

"Oh, yes."

"And, as to what it is this time, well, I am not sanguine."

Khaavren knew the Lyorn well enough to require no explanations—that Aerich had this suspicion was sufficient for him. He said, "And Tazendra?"

"I do not know."

"Well," said the Tiassa, "as far as Pel is concerned, I know more than you. You mentioned stirrings in the west. You know of Kâna?"

"I have the heard the name pronounced. Rumors have reached Arylle."

"Well, Pel is now Kâna's creature."

Aerich nodded. "It is as I feared, then."

"And that will bring Pel into conflict with Sethra Lavode, and, moreover, with my son."

"Yes."

"Something must be done, Aerich."

"And soon," said the Lyorn.

"Yes. We must find Pel, and convince him."

"Do you think we can?"

"I do not know. It is a matter of ambition to the left, and friendship to the right. With you, or with Tazendra, there could be no question. But with Pel—"

"Yes, I comprehend perfectly."

"We will set out at dawn to-morrow."

Khaavren smiled. "I expected no less from you. We must consider what to say in order to convince him."

Aerich shook his head. "No. He will be convinced upon seeing us—or he will not. Nothing we say will have any influence."

Khaavren bowed his head in mute agreement.

Aerich stood up and said, "You will, I trust, excuse me for a moment while I make arrangements to leave?"

Aerich left to be about the business of making preparations. While he was gone, Ibronka said, "My lord?"

"Well?" said Khaavren.

"Can you tell me what it is we are setting out to do?"

"No," said Khaavren. "In fact, I fear that I cannot. Or, rather, I can tell you we are going to be searching for our old friend Pel. I cannot tell you how we are hoping to find him, or, indeed, what will happen when we do."

Aerich caused a meal to be prepared, featuring a suckling kethna that had been fed on onions and chives, and which was stuffed with partridges snared in the woods behind his pond, as well as radishes from his garden and lurker mushrooms grown in the shadows of the Collier Hills, the whole served with the dry, white wine from his own vineyards. Khaavren, for his part, could not stop praising the food; while Aerich made no effort to conceal how pleased he was to receive the compliments.

After the meal, each of the guests was shown to a bed-chamber — for by this time it was quite late — where they passed a night that was all the better for not only the meal, but the comfort of sleeping in a bed for the first time in more than a week, and the last time in, they were all certain, even longer. Aerich, after spending some time explaining to Steward what ought to be done and not done while he was away, and arranging the papers and documents that would become important if he failed to return, also retired for a very sound night's sleep. Instructions were given not to awaken any of them until well into the morning, which, to be sure, occasioned a certain delay, but as a result of this they all awoke refreshed, and ready to travel.

Khaavren greeted Fawnd (whom he had not seen the evening before, as this worthy had been busy preparing for his own and Aerich's departure) as an old friend, which greeting the Teckla returned respectfully and with unfeigned pleasure. Then Aerich appeared, and Khaavren's face broke into a smile, because Aerich was dressed in his brown ankle-length skirt, his old vambraces, his plain blouse, and, over all, the old gold half-cloak that had been the mark of the Phoenix Guard. Beneath the cloak was the hilt of the plain but very serviceable rapier that the Lyorn had purchased when he had enlisted in the guards so long before.

Aerich saw the smile on Khaavren's face, and gave his friend a small bow — no words were required. Soon Clari appeared, and they made their way out to the stables, where six horses and a pack animal waited, all of them saddled and ready for the journey. With no ceremony, the horses were mounted, and the small troop made its way through the gates and at once turned northward.

Khaavren said, "It is still warm. We dare not push the horses too hard."

"That is true. We will make short stages, then."

"Agreed."

"And you know where you are leading us?"

"As to direction, we will go north, of course. Directly north, toward Deathgate. If we have seen nothing when we reach the mountains, we will continue northward, with the mountains always to our right hand. We will keep our eyes and ears open, and hope to hear word of our elusive Yendi."

Khaavren and Aerich, of course, rode in front, with Röaana and Ibronka behind them, and Clari bringing up the rear. As they rode, Ibronka turned to her friend and said, "I have thought a thought and see a thing."

Röaana smiled and laughed. "Then let us see what it will bring. Is it something living?"

"The answer 'no' I am giving, and it is not the sky."

"I have to wonder why. Will it fit into my hand?"

"You can hold it while you stand. But it is not a stone."

"And it cannot be a bone. Is there only one?" asked Röaana.

"There are many, that's the fun. And you see them every day."

"Then the answer's on the way. Are they found near the sea?"

"You are much too good for me! But it is not the water."

"My mother raised no foolish daughter. Is it a shell?"

"You did that very well. Yes, you have guessed it. That was too easy."

"Well, I shall think of the next one and will attempt to make it more difficult, while you, on your part, can make better rhymes than what I could manage, I think."

"Very well, let us do so."

"All right," said Röaana after a moment. "I have thought a thought and see a thing."

"Then let us see what it will bring. . . ."

And, in this way—along with an assortment of other road games, such games as "Pig in the Tree" and "Rope or String"—the two girls passed the hours as they traveled. And, as the hours became days, and the days became weeks, Clari was brought into the game, astonishing them all with her ability to make clever rhymes, and sometimes even Khaavren and Aerich would join in with them for a while.

Eventually, the country became more and more hilly, and then they saw in the distance South Mountain, where the Eastern Mountains begin, and knew that soon riding would become more difficult, although the ground where they were was, as yet, easy enough.

The next day, they saw a lone rider on horseback. After a short time, it became apparent that the rider was approaching them, and, as this was the first person they had seen, Khaavren determined to bespeak the rider to see if anything could be learned, or if any of those they sought had been seen. As the rider approached, however, it seemed they would not in fact meet, and so Khaavren led the troop a little more to the west.

After some few moments, the rider changed direction to the eastward. Khaavren adjusted accordingly.

"He does not wish to meet us," remarked Khaavren.

"That is apparent," said Aerich.

"Which makes me all the more determined to say two words to him."

Aerich nodded.

The rider, now only a quarter of a mile away, stopped, and appeared to consider the matter. Khaavren brought his mount up to a trot, Aerich riding with him knee to knee, the others close behind him. The lone rider ahead of them reached back behind him, and pulled out something which he held in his hand—probably, deduced Khaavren, a weapon.

As the rider now appeared to wish to play, Khaavren prepared to oblige, drawing his own weapon, and was aware of the girls doing the same behind him, although, as yet, Aerich had not drawn. He approached the stranger, and the first thing he noticed was the oddity of the weapon he was confronting. In fact, his first words, as he came within twenty feet or so of the stranger, were, "Cha! Are you going to hit me with a bar-stool?" Even as he said this, however, the term "bar-stool" brought back to him a memory, and he looked closely at the other's face.

At almost the same moment, Aerich said, "Mica!" and the stranger said, "My lord Khaavren? Your Venerance Arylle? Feathers of the Phoenix, I am saved!"

"How, saved?" said Khaavren, smiling and sheathing his weapon. "You were never in danger from us!"

"Well, but to never have been in danger, that is just as good as being saved, is it not?"

"At least as good," agreed Khaavren. "But come, my dear fellow, be a good lad and tell us what you are doing here, and, moreover, where your mistress, Tazendra, is."

The Teckla tied his bar-stool to his horse's saddle once more, and said, "My lord, I shall tell you all you wish to know, I assure you, if for no other reason than because I am so delighted to see you when I had feared I should have to contend with brigands of the worst sort, and would be required to die valiantly, which, you perceive, does not suit my inclinations, as I am only a Teckla."

"Yes, I understand that," said Khaavren, amused. "But then, what of Tazendra?"

"She was unhurt when last I saw her. She is some distance behind me along with Piro and Kytraan."

Khaavren took in and then let out a deep breath, relieved in no small measure at the news that his son was unhurt. Then he said, "Some distance is not, you perceive, very exact."

"My lord, I am unable to be more precise. It has been months since I have seen them. They were coming, I believe, in this direction, but traveling much slower, having sent me on ahead. However, I happened to become entangled with a darr, who chased me no small distance, after which I became quite turned around, and then, after that—"

"There is more?" said Khaavren.

"Oh, much more. After that, when purchasing food (for you must know that I am not a mountaineer, and cannot forage for myself) I noticed certain ill-favored individuals looking at me in a way I liked not at all after I was so indiscreet as to permit them to see my purse. I therefore avoided them, which caused a further delay, as it involved a detour far to the east. Then in getting back on my proper path, I found myself in a charming valley, with a charming village, entirely surrounded by snow that was not at all charming, and had there not been an unseasonable thaw, I should be there yet, with the result that I am some months behind on my errand."

"It seems there is some news here," said Khaavren, chuckling. "Let us dismount, and we can speak together."

"My lord," said Mica, "I beg you to believe that I would like nothing better, but, alas, I have been given to understand that my errand is of the most urgent sort, and will not wait."

"Ah, you are on an errand then?"

"Precisely, my lord."

"From your mistress, Tazendra?"

"From her, yes, and from my lord Piro, and my lord Kytraan as well."

"They all gave you this errand?"

"They all seemed to think it of the greatest urgency, my lord."

"Well, can you tell me what this famous errand is?"

Mica considered, then said, "I do not see why I cannot."

"How, you can tell me?"

"I can, my lord, and, if you wish, I will even do so."

"If I wish? It seems to me it is an hour since I wished for anything else!"

"Well, this is it, then: I am to report to the Enchantress of Dzur Mountain."

"To Sethra Lavode?"

"Yes, my lord. I am to report to Sethra Lavode."

"But, upon what subject are you going to report to her?"

"My lord, on the failure of our mission."

"How, it was a failure?"

Mica bowed.

"The mission failed then?"

"It grieves me to say it, my lord."

"But, what happened?"

"We were attacked at the top of Deathgate Falls, and Zerika—"

"Who?"

"Zerika. The Phoenix."

Khaavren stared for a moment, then said, "There is a Phoenix named Zerika?"

"Yes, my lord. That is to say, there was."

"There was?"

"Yes, my lord."

"But—go on."

"In the course of the battle, she—that is to say, Zerika—leapt from Deathgate Falls. As our—"

"She leapt?"

"Yes, my lord. That is, she caused her horse to leap from the very lip of the Falls. And, as our mission was to deliver her safely—"

"Yes, I see. And the battle?"

"We had the honor to send them flying, my lord."

"So you won?"

"Entirely."

"So, she need not have leapt from the Falls?"

"Well, my lord, it is true that, after her leap, some of the enemy lost interest in continuing to play."

"Well, and my son? How did he acquit himself in battle?"

"My lord, I have the pleasure of assuring you he did well enough, bringing his enemy to the ground with a good cut, and, moreover, at no time did he show the least hesitation."

Khaavren gave the Teckla a smile full of affection, then said, "Well, and who was it who attacked you?"

"It was a band of brigands, along with our old enemy, Grita."

"Grita? Greycat's daughter?"

"The same, my lord."

Khaavren exchanged with Aerich a glance full of meaning. Aerich furrowed his brows and turned to Mica, saying, "I wish to hear the entire story."

"Your Venerance," said Mica, "my mission was given to me as most urgent."

Khaavren cut off his words with a gesture. "You have mentioned Grita. I know her, and I know her blood. There is no question of joking. Moreover, this might have far-reaching consequences that go beyond my concern for my son and for your mistress. Do you agree, Aerich?"

"I assure you, my dear Khaavren, in all the years I have known you, you have never spoken words more full of wisdom and perspicacity."

Khaavren turned back to the Teckla and said, "There. What more testimony do you require? However much of a hurry you are in, you must take whatever time is necessary to tell us everything that has happened."

Mica bowed. "Very well, my lord. I will do so at once."

With this, Mica instantly launched into the tale of their journey, while Khaavren, Aerich, Röaana, Ibronka, and Clari all listened carefully, none of them interrupting. When he had at length finished, Khaavren grunted and said, "Yes. As I have said, we must find Pel."

"That is true," said Aerich. "But it is more important that we find your son and his friends."

"How, you think so?"

"I am convinced of it."

"But, why is that, my friend?"

"In the first place, because of Grita. I am uncertain if they will survive another attack without assistance."

"Well, there is something in what you say. What next?"

"Next, there is their mission."

"Well, it has failed, has it not?"

"I am not convinced."

"How, you are not convinced? And yet, Mica has said—"

"Then we will say no more about it. There is, however, the matter of Kâna."

"Well, of a certainty. That is why I believe we must find Pel."

"Well, and what will Kâna be doing?"

"Oh, as to that, who can say?"

"It may be, my dear Khaavren, that I can."

"Can you?" said the Tiassa, smiling. "Well, that doesn't startle me. What is it, then?"

"He must prepare to attack Dzur Mountain."

"How, you think so, Aerich?"

"I am convinced of it."

"But why?"

"Because that is where Zerika will bring the Orb."

"And yet, Zerika is dead, and can thus bring the Orb nowhere."

"That may be true, and may not be true, my dear friend. But, even if Zerika cannot bring the Orb, can Kâna know this?"

Khaavren considered this for some few moments, then said, "If this is true—and I give you my word, I am very nearly convinced—

then, even more, we must, instead of seeking Piro, return at once to Dzur Mountain to warn Sethra."

"As for warning Sethra," said Aerich, "Mica is on his way to her anyway, and can easily carry another message."

"Well, that is true."

"And then?"

"Well, I agree we should find Piro. But how can we do so?"

"Oh, as to that."

"Well?"

Aerich frowned. "I am not yet certain."

"I could lead you," said Mica. "But, alas, I must continue to Dzur Mountain."

"Can you," said Aerich, "describe where they are?"

Mica frowned and, after some thought, shook his head to indicate that he could not.

"Then," said Khaavren, "perhaps we should continue with our plan of finding Pel after all?"

"No," said Aerich, frowning in concentration. "We must find a way to discover where Piro is."

"I am told," said Mica, "that Eastern witches can sometimes locate a man from—"

He abruptly broke off his speech upon seeing Aerich's look in response to what he had begun to say.

Khaavren said, "Well, if we must hunt these mountains, then we should be about it."

"But what about Pel?" said Röaana suddenly.

Khaavren turned to her. "You must not have heard. We have decided we must find Piro; it has become more urgent."

"Yes, my lord. I understand that. But is it not the case that Pel is, most likely, looking for your son and the others as well, and to find him is to find them?"

"Yes," said Khaavren. "That may well be true. But it does not help us."

"But my lord, you have not asked Mica if he had seen Pel."

Khaavren blinked. "Well, but that is true. Mica, have you seen any sign of Pel?"

"Oh, of a certainty my lord. And that, not two days ago."

"How, you saw him?"

"I more than saw him, my lord. I spoke with him."

"Cha! You did?"

"It is as I have had the honor to tell you."

"Well, but what was he doing?"

"Oh, as to that, I cannot say, my lord."

"But, what did he ask you?"

"Why, the very thing you did. He asked what I was doing."

"And you told him?"

"Of a certainty I told him."

Khaavren and Aerich exchanged a look. "And," said Khaavren to the Teckla, "what did he do after you had told him?"

"What did he do? Why, he wished me a pleasant journey."

"And then went on his way?"

"Exactly."

"And, what way was that?"

"Why, as I recall, he went north, back the way I had come."

"And had that been the direction he had been going when you met him?"

Mica frowned. "Well, that is to say—"

"Yes?"

"Not precisely, but close."

"So that, when he left you, he turned to follow the trail you had taken?"

"Well, that is to say, yes."

Once again, Khaavren and Aerich exchanged looks, after which it was the Lyorn who spoke. "Your message to Sethra Lavode must be delayed, my friend."

"How, delayed? And yet, I have been given instructions—"

"Your mistress and the others are in great danger, Mica, and only you can save them."

"Who, I?"

"Exactly."

"And yet—"

"No," said Khaavren. "We have no time to argue. Turn your horse around and lead us to the place where you met Pel. And hurry."

Mica seemed caught for a moment between his orders from his

mistress and these new instructions, but, in the end, he could not deny the combined will of Khaavren and Aerich, and so, without another word, he turned his horse around and began leading them back the way he had come. As they started toward the mountains once more, Khaavren glanced back at Röaana and gave her a nod of approval, which made the girl flush with pride.

They rode that night until both their own exhaustion and that of their horses threatened them with a longer delay than stopping would cause, at which time they found a narrow stream to camp beside. Khaavren took the first watch, and as he was about to do so, Aerich said, "What do you think, old friend?"

"Nothing good," said Khaavren. "Pel is two days closer than we are. How can we catch him?"

Aerich shook his head. "I do not know. But we must try."

Khaavren stared into the distance, knowing there were mountains there, but quite unable to see them. "They are out there, somewhere."

"Yes. All of them. Our friends, our enemies—and Pel."

Khaavren nodded. "Get some sleep, my friend. I will wake you soon enough."

Aerich nodded, clasped Khaavren by the shoulder, and went off to sleep. Khaavren stared into the night.

It was near the end of the last watch—which is to say, it was only a short time before they had planned to rise, when Clari awoke Khaavren.

"Well?" said the Tiassa. "What is it?"

"My lord," said the Teckla. "Ibronka has asked me to awaken you."

"How, Ibronka? And yet, is it not you that are on watch?"

"Yes, my lord. But she wishes to speak to you on a matter that, she pretends, is of great urgency."

Khaavren sighed and rose. "Very well, then."

He found the Dzurlord staring to the west, which Khaavren thought odd for two reasons: first because it was too dark to see anything; and, second, because it was not the direction in which they planned to travel.

"What is it?" said Khaavren, trying to keep annoyance from his voice.

"My lord," said Ibronka. "Someone is coming."

"How, coming?"

"Approaching us."

"I see. Who?"

"As to that, I cannot say. But they are on horseback, and there are a good number of them. Scores."

"And you say they are coming toward us?"

"Yes, my lord. It began some twenty minutes ago, and it woke me."

"But what woke you?"

"The sound, my lord. Of the horses."

"Ah! Ah! You are a Dzurlord."

Ibronka bowed.

"Do you know how far away they are?"

"I am sorry, my lord, but I do not. Perhaps ten miles, perhaps twenty."

Khaavren had heard enough. He turned to Clari and said, "Wake everyone up. We leave at once."

Aerich, one of the first to be ready, turned to Khaavren and said, "What is it?"

"Kâna. His forces are behind us, and approaching."

"You believe it is Kâna?"

"I must assume it is, until I have some reason to believe otherwise."

"Well, that is true. And then?"

"We have, perhaps," said Khaavren, "an hour. Possibly two hours. And then, at this rate, they will undoubtedly overtake us."

Aerich's eyes narrowed and he nodded.

In a very short time they were on their way once more, riding through the darkness. Khaavren, be it understood, would have preferred not to travel at night because of the risk of a mishap and difficulty in maintaining the proper direction; yet he was made anxious by the thought of scores of riders who seemed themselves willing to travel under such conditions, and preferred to stay ahead of this pursuit, if pursuit it was.

They kept their pace to a walk until there was enough light for Mica to pick out, by certain landmarks, whence he had come, after which they began to travel rather faster. Also, at about this same time, Khaavren began looking over his shoulder, but, as of yet, saw no signs of pursuit.

"You realize," said Aerich, "that, as we must pay attention to our path, they can travel faster than we."

"And yet, if they are pursuing us, they must pay attention to *our* path. And if not, then no doubt they must pay attention to a path of their own."

"Well, that is true. Apropos, if they are pursuing us, and they catch us, shall we fight them?"

"Probably," said Khaavren.

"Very good," said Aerich.

The mountains were now noticeably closer, and Mica appeared to know where he was going. Khaavren strained his eyes to look ahead, hoping to see a figure, or figures, but as yet saw nothing and no one.

After an hour or so, Clari called, "There is a dust cloud behind us."

"Well," said Aerich.

Khaavren shrugged.

The South Mountain had grown considerably, but was, as yet, some distance away. At just this moment, however, Mica turned around and said, "There!"

"What is it?" said Khaavren.

"That is where I made my camp," said the Teckla. "Beneath those trees. There is a river on the other side of them. This river, whose name I do not know, is fed by various streams out of various of the mountains, but it runs as a brook for a considerable distance alongside of South Mountain, which I recall because I followed that brook for days and days. It was along that brook, in fact, that I exchanged words with Pel."

"Well," said Khaavren, "then as long as we stay with that brook, we will not stray from our path. It is well. We can go faster now."

"Not only can we," said Aerich, "but I suggest we do so. You perceive, the cloud of dust behind us is growing."

"I had noticed the same thing, my dear Aerich," said Khaavren. "And it seems to me that this can mean only one of two things. The first, that the numbers of our pursuers are growing, seems unlikely.

This leaves the second, which is that they are getting closer. For this reason, then, I am in complete agreement with you. We must move faster."

As no one had any disagreements with either Khaavren's calculation or his proposal, his idea was put into action at once—that is to say, they made their way toward the mountain with redoubled haste. In this way, after some time, they did, in fact, succeed in pulling away from those who were either pursuing them, or perhaps, simply riding in the same direction, and who were, as Khaavren thought, troops of Kâna, or else another troop of horsemen entirely. They continued in this way for several hours, trotting their horses when they could, walking them when necessary, and stopping as little as possible. Khaavren, for his part, chewed his lip until it bled and attempted to watch both in front and behind as he rode. They made good time, although they had to slow down for Mica and Clari, whose horses didn't have the endurance of the others, and whom Khaavren was unwilling to leave behind.

It was around noon when he suddenly said, "Hullo!" and drew rein.

"Well?" said Aerich coolly, coming up beside him. By this time, we should say, they were riding due north, on the west bank of the stream to which Mica had referred, and with the South Mountain looming over them further to the east.

"A horseman," said Khaavren.

"Where?"

Khaavren pointed across the stream and slightly behind them. "There—you can still see him a little. Riding like the wind away from us."

Aerich squinted. "Yes. I see him. Whence came he?"

"From there," said Khaavren, to a dark place in the mountains. "It was as if he emerged from a cave."

"Is this possible?" asked Aerich. "You know these mountains better than I; are there caves in them?"

"There are, and it is certainly possible."

"Could he have seen us?"

"Perhaps. If he had a touch-it glass, he could certainly have seen us."

"You saw nothing?"

"Little enough," said the Tiassa. "Only a figure upon a horse. It seemed to be a roan horse, however, with white markings upon its chest and flank. I mention this so that we will recognize it should we see it again."

"And that was well thought," said Aerich.

"How," said Mica, who had come up during this conversation. "The horse, you say, is a roan?"

"Precisely."

"With markings as if white paint had been thrown on a place high on its flank, and again, dripped down its chest?"

Khaavren turned to the lackey and nodded. "You have described it exactly. It remains, then, for me to ask, what do you know?"

"Oh," said the lackey. "I know nothing, except—"

"Yes? Except?"

"Grita rode a horse very like that."

"I see," said Khaavren grimly.

Chapter the Forty-Second

How Everyone Was Placed
And What Everyone Was Doing
When the Interregnum Ended,
With Some Discussion of the Effects
Of the Orb as It Emerged

Having now brought each of those persons with whom we have concerned ourselves nearly to the point in time when Zerika emerged from the Halls of Judgment, it remains only to go the last step—that is, to describe how these people were placed at the exact moment, and, where appropriate, how they responded to the beckoning call that the Orb produced, upon its emergence, in those who were familiar with it from having once been citizens.

Zerika, as we have already had the honor to inform the reader, knew where Piro was the moment she emerged; but Piro, for his part, did not know where Zerika was—indeed, Piro was convinced that Zerika had perished at Deathgate Falls. In order to help the reader fully appreciate this situation, it is our wish to begin at a point a few short hours before Zerika's emergence once more into the mundane world. At this time, we can find Piro easily enough, for he is standing upon a shelf near the base of the South Mountain. We should point out for those who do not travel, that South Mountain is not the southernmost of the Eastern Mountains—Tiren's Peak has that distinction—but is, rather, a large mountain *near* the southern tail of the chain, and one that actually marks the westernmost extremity of the mountains. It achieved its name, in all probability, because it is the first mountain one will encounter when traveling from the southwest, or the last one will see when traveling from the northeast.

From his vantage point on the small shelf to which we have already alluded, Piro looked out to the north and the east, where mountains still loomed over him majestically, and said, "My dear Kytraan, do you have the feeling that we have been going in circles?"

"Eh? Not at all, my dear Viscount. We have been going south."

"Well, I know that, my friend. And, if truth be told, we have been going south at far greater speed than I should have thought we were capable of, with all that has happened and all we have been doing, first traveling along the feet of these mountains, then venturing into them, then down once more. But what I meant was this: It seems to me that Grita has been leading us by the nose. We see signs of her—a silhouette against the mountain, a boot-print, a hoof-print of her horse—but we can never seem to catch her."

Kytraan frowned. "How long have we been in these mountains?"

"In all, it as been very nearly a year."

"And how much of that time have we spent chasing her?"

"All of summer, all of autumn, and much of this winter which, thank the Lords of Judgment, is a mild one."

"Well, but she must, by now, know that we are after her."

"Precisely."

"So then, it is hardly surprising that she has been difficult to catch."

"But my question is, is she simply avoiding us, or is she leading us somewhere?"

"You mean, an ambuscade?"

"Exactly."

"Well, had she wished to snare us, would she not have done so in the weeks we have been following her?"

"Perhaps. And yet—"

"Well?"

"It may be that she has tried on more than one occasion, and we have avoided the traps."

"Ah. You refer to the brushfire?"

"Yes. If Lar had not looked back and seen the thin trail of smoke, we would very likely have been caught between the fire and the cliff."

"Well, that is true. What else?"

"What else? Do you forget the rockslide?"

"How, you think she may have been responsible for that?"

"Well, it came very close to us. So close, in fact, that we would have been caught by it had you not noticed the birds suddenly taking flight, and caused us to halt our progress, for which I must compliment you."

"You have already done so, my dear Piro."

"Well, I do so again. And then there was the dragon."

"Yes, that is true, only I do not see how she could have set that upon us."

"Bah!" said Piro. "You don't? It would have been simple enough, if she had known we were following her trail, to have led us past its lair."

"Without the risk of becoming entangled with it herself?"

"If she was able to muffle the sounds of her horse's hoofs, and find a way to hide her horse's scent, then I believe it could be done. After all, we *did* follow her trail past its lair."

"Yes, that is true, Viscount. And I should say that only your quick thinking with our pack animal saved us."

"Well, but it cost us the animal."

"Better it than one of us."

"That is true, although it gave us some hungry days until we were able to stop in a village and purchase another and more supplies. But then, consider, those are three incidents where she might have attempted to kill us. What will the fourth be?"

"You ask a valid question," admitted the Dragonlord, "and one that deserves serious consideration."

"Do you think so? Well, that is good, then. I do not like my questions to reflect light-mindedness."

"Oh, they do not, I assure you. Only—"

"Yes?"

"I am unable to answer this one."

"Tazendra, what is your opinion?"

"How, you wish my opinion?"

"Yes, exactly. And the proof is: I asked."

"Well, that is true, you did."

"And then?"

"Well, in the first place, my opinion is that I should very much like to find Grita and run my sword through her body, as we should have done two and a half hundreds of years ago."

"Well, we are all in agreement with this; indeed, it is exactly to accomplish this that we have spent so much time chasing her. But have you a second opinion, to go with your first?"

"I do."

"And that is?"

"I believe it doesn't matter."

"How, it doesn't matter?"

"Not the least in the world."

"Well, but, why does it not matter. You perceive, you have said something that puzzles me."

"Because she is no longer in the mountains."

"How, not in the mountains? Well, but where is she?"

"There," said Tazendra, pointing off to the west.

They followed the direction of her finger, and, indeed, they saw a rider on a horse that quite resembled Grita's dashing off at a good speed.

"She is going to meet those riders who are approaching us," remarked Kytraan.

"On the contrary," said Piro, observing closely. "She is avoiding them, and going off in another direction entirely."

"On reflection," said Kytraan, "I believe you are correct. But, wherever she is going, she is certainly going there quickly."

"With this I agree."

"As do I," said Tazendra.

"Then, for now, we've lost her," said Piro.

"So it seems," said Kytraan.

"But I wonder," said Tazendra.

"Yes?" said Kytraan.

"You just made a reference to a group on horseback."

"Yes, some riders who seem to be traveling generally in this direction."

"Yes. Well, I wonder who they are. There are six of them, and as you have said, they seem to be coming directly toward us—or, rather, they were. Now they have stopped."

"Well," said Piro grimly. "If they are looking for us, we will not be hard to find." He put his hand on the hilt of his sword as he spoke.

"So then?" said Kytraan.

"So let us remain quiet and await them here."

"Is this a good place?" asked Kytraan. "Consider that there is a cave at our back, which I do not like."

"On the contrary," said Tazendra. "I explored the cave earlier, while you were attending to the horses. It is scarcely fifteen feet deep, and quite empty."

"Well, that is good as far as the cave is concerned. But are we not rather exposed here?" said Kytraan.

"Not," said Piro, "if we remain crouching, and keep our horses hobbled where they are now."

"Well then," said Kytraan, "that is good as far as being exposed. But can we form an adequate defense here?"

Piro shrugged. "We have height, and the ability to observe. Moreover, they cannot bring their horses up this slope."

"Very well, then," said Kytraan. "I have no more objections to make, and I agree with waiting here and remaining quiet."

"As do I," said Tazendra.

Lar bowed but, already putting the orders into execution, said nothing.

As Piro stood on a low ledge of the South Mountain and looked at the small troop that, had he but known it, was led by his none other than his father—that is to say, Khaavren—there was another who was standing upon a slightly higher bluff and looking at Piro. This was Wadre, who had, after months of searching, at last come across their tracks in the snow, and had been following them ever since, catching up to them the night before. Now that he had found them, however, he was uncertain what to do. He had completely failed in his effort to locate his band, and without them he felt as if he were unarmed. Moreover, it was certainly the case that, by himself, he was unable to do anything about the Dzur, the Dragon, and the Tiassa below him, all of whom were well armed, and all of whom had demonstrated a certain facility in games when he had met them before.

He wondered, as he had many times, where his band was, and how it happened that he had not been able to find them in the months he had been in and near these mountains, traveling south into the heat, and surviving through the season of storms, huddled inside of caves or beneath overhangs, and now the winter, which, mild as it might have been, was always brutal in the mountains, forcing him to sometimes kill game, other times to steal, or, when desperate, to even buy food from the few villages the mountains boasted. And now, at last, he had found what he was looking for—but, where was the man who had employed him, who, though his House was uncertain, seemed so like an aristocrat? And why had he seen no sign of his band in all of this time?

He was, of course, unable to answer these questions, and so he watched, and waited, and considered what to do, which activities he carried out so well that, at the expiration of an hour, he had not moved by so much as an inch from his position, cold as it was to lie upon the snow-covered ground, still watching those below him, who, although moving more freely than Wadre did, continued to do little except to wait. What it was they were waiting for, Wadre could not have said.

He had just reached this point in his thoughts when he was startled by hearing the sound of boots on stone behind him, which sound startled him so much he very nearly cried out, and did, in fact, go so far as to reach for a weapon. He arrested this action, however, upon seeing who it was who stood behind him, a cynical smile tugging at the corners of her mouth.

"Orlaan!" he cried. "That is to say, Grita!" He scrambled to his feet.

"Well met," said Grita, in a voice in which a listener could not have failed to detect considerable irony. "What brings you here?"

"How, you wish to know that?"

"Well, I think I do," said Grita.

"It is simple enough. I have been following your old enemies."

"Oh, have you then? And for what reason?"

"For what reason? Why, to find them!"

"Do not play the fool with me, brigand. Remember what I can do."

"I have not forgotten."

"Well?"

Wadre considered for a moment, then decided that, for lack of any better idea, he would see what would happen if he told the truth. "I was asked to by Galstan."

"Ah. Galstan."

"You know him?"

"Nearly. He is another of those enemies I spoke to you about long ago."

"Ah. I had not, you perceive, been aware of this circumstance when I agreed to assist him. And, moreover, you were, at that time, nowhere to be found."

"And if you could have found me, then what?"

"Oh, as to that —"

Grita cut him off with a gesture and said, "Well, if that were not enough, I believe I had an encounter with him this very day."

"How, an encounter?"

"Yes. I had just seen you, and made up my mind to speak with you. As I approached you—this was an hour and a half ago, I believe—I thought I caught a glimpse of him. I at once determined to follow him, and I did."

"Ah. And did you find him?"

"No, but I found the place where, upon setting out down this rather steep path to find you, I had tethered my horse."

"The place where —"

"Yes. My horse was gone. I am convinced he stole it."

"How, stole your horse?"

"I am certain that he did."

"That is remarkable."

"In what way?"

"I had just convinced myself that he must be an aristocrat, and now you tell me that he is, instead, a horse thief."

"You think the two are incompatible?"

"I had thought so."

"Now you have learned better."

"Well, it seems I have. Then it must have been his horse I found with its throat slit yesterday. It seemed to have broken a leg."

"Yes, that would explain it."

"And then?"

"Well, Galstan's horse broke a leg, and so he stole mine, so I will take yours."

Wadre started to protest, reconsidered, sighed, and nodded. "Very well, then," he said.

Grita nodded. "And, by chance, do you know where this Galstan is now?"

"He has just ridden out in that direction," he said, pointing to the west. "The proof is, in fact, that I thought it was you, having recognized the horse."

"Has he indeed?" said Grita, drawing forth a touch-it glass, which she brought to her eye. That she made good use of this glass we can prove by her next words, which were, "Well, it seems that he is speaking with a good troop of horsemen."

"Then he has allies," said Wadre. "I had some once, but I do not know where they are."

"They are with me," said Grita.

"How, with you?"

"Yes, now they serve me."

"Well, but they are mine."

"No," said Grita. "They are mine."

"And yet—"

"Where is your horse?"

Wadre sighed. "It is on the other side of that copse of trees."

"That is good," said Grita, and replaced her touch-it glass in the pouch at her side, from which pouch she, at the same time, produced what seem to be a narrow rod of some metallic substance, perhaps copper, as it had a reddish-golden hue.

Wadre frowned. "May I inquire as to the item you now hold in your hand?"

Grita nodded. "It is something of my own devising. Its function is not unlike that of a flashstone, but it is far more complex, as I was required to draw directly upon the Sea of Amorphia, rather than upon the power of the Orb. I have, however, made certain tests upon it, and I am convinced it will do what I wish it to in every way."

"So then, it causes explosions?"

"Yes. You see this end, marked with small black stripes, I hold in my hand. And the other end—"

"Yes, the other end?"

"Why, that indicates where I wish to have its destructive powers directed."

"Well, but you are pointing it at me."

"You are most observant."

"Do you, then, intend to make use of it upon my person?"

"I confess, that is exactly my intention."

"I beg you to reconsider."

"Alas, my dear bandit, it is quite impossible. I have stolen your band, and I am about to steal your horse. You perceive, to leave you alive at this point would be utterly unthinkable."

"So you are going to kill me?"

"Exactly. And this very instant, too."

"I should like to find a way to change your mind."

"Alas," said Grita. "That is unlikely."

Wadre sighed.

At about this time, Khaavren said, "I see something."

"What do you see?" said Aerich.

"I saw, or, that is to say, I believe I saw movement upon that bluff."

Aerich frowned and looked carefully, then shrugged and said, "I see nothing, but I do not doubt you."

"I see nothing now, and I quite doubt myself, Aerich." Khaavren chuckled a little. "But, still, let us go in that direction."

"With this plan, I agree."

Khaavren nodded, and led his small troop forward.

As he did so, some distance behind him, Pel spoke to a Dragonlord named Tsanaali e'Lanya, saying, "An hour ago, they were upon that bluff, there."

Tsanaali said, "Then that is where we will go."

"They may have moved."

"That is natural. But then, they may not have. And, if they have, they may have left tracks, as you perceive the mountainside is covered with snow."

"Yes," said Pel. "I have been hunting them for some time. I do not wish to lose them now."

Tsanaali gave him a look of distaste, then said, "I do not understand why these people are important to my lady Suura."

"They are not."

"They are not? But yet, her orders—"

"Your lady Suura has been replaced by your lord Izak."

"Who is Izak? It cannot be the subaltern on Suura's staff; he is scarcely two hundred years old."

"As to that, I cannot say. But it is the case, whoever it is."

The captain spread his palms. "Then why are they important to Izak, whoever he is?"

"Well, in fact, they are important to your lord Kâna."

"His Majesty!"

"Very well, then," said Pel, shrugging. "His Majesty."

"Why, then, are these people important to His Majesty?"

"Because they have been assisting a lady whom — His Majesty — wishes stopped at all costs."

The lieutenant (for this was nominally Tsanaali's rank) nodded and said, "Then, is it your opinion that we should follow them, hoping they'll lead us to her, or should we destroy them?"

"They do not know where she is."

"Are you certain of this?"

"Yes."

"How?"

"How?"

"Yes. How can you be certain?"

Pel said, "And what would you do with your cavalry troop if you were threatened by a spear phalanx?"

"Eh? Why, I should cause them to spread out, remaining on horseback, and sweep around both flanks."

"How do you know that is the right thing to do?"

"It is my business to know such things."

"Exactly," said Pel, bowing.

Tsanaali scowled and said, "Well, what then should we do, now that we have found them?"

"Destroy them, of course, if you can."

"Well."

"And, my dear Lieutenant, there is another matter."

"And that is?"

"If I am to give His Majesty his proper title, then you may do the same regarding me."

Tsanaali clenched his jaws, then said, "I was given the order to follow your instructions, Your Venerance—" This last term seemed to emerge with some effort on the Dragonlord's part. "—therefore I will do as you say."

"That will be the best thing to do, believe me."

"And will Your Venerance remain with us?"

"I? Not the least in the world, I assure you. I am going forward to attempt to ascertain if they are still there, and, if they are not, where they have gone."

"Well," said the Dragonlord, who clearly thought the Yendi intended to do nothing more than avoid the battle.

Pel tilted his head to the side. "My dear Lieutenant," he said.

"Yes, Your Venerance?"

"This is likely to be a rather difficult battle, followed by other matters in which the future is uncertain. You know that Izak is approaching Dzur Mountain from the north, while Brawre approaches from the west."

"Brawre?"

"A certain Lady Brawre, who has replaced Tonchin."

"I do not know who this is."

"Nor do I. But, nevertheless, that is what is going to happen."

"Well? What of it?"

"Well, it may be that you will not survive these battles."

"That is always possible for a soldier."

"And it is possible that I will not survive these battles."

"That is always possible for a spy."

"But," continued Pel coolly, "if it should happen that we both survive, then, when all is over, I give you my word I will cut your heart out."

"You think so?"

"Yes. I will cut out your heart, and I will feed it to you past those lips with which you do me the honor to sneer."

"We will see, then."

"Yes, we will."

Tsanaali responded to this compliment by nodding brusquely, after which he turned to his troop and gave them the signal to move forward. Pel, for his part, turned the head of his horse and rode back toward the foot of South Mountain.

Khaavren and his friends were, at this same time, riding toward the same place. They were closer, but riding more slowly.

Grita found Wadre's horse, and, leading it, went to gather together the remainder of what had been Wadre's band, but was now hers. She led them toward where Piro and his friends waited, looking out at the dust cloud that was the advance of the troop led by Tsanaali. In fact, so intent on them were they, that for a time they forgot the smaller band—that is to say, Khaavren's—until they were nearly upon them, scarcely a hundred yards away.

It was Tazendra who eventually noticed this latter group, at which time she nudged Piro and pointed.

"Now who is that?" said Piro, frowning and drawing his sword. Tazendra and Kytraan also drew their swords, and Lar came forward, brandishing a stout cast-iron cooking pan. "I had been observing them for a time, and then they escaped my attention," Piro concluded.

"I don't know who they are," said Kytraan, peering forward.

Tazendra shrugged. "Perhaps it is that road agent, Wadre, with whom we have already had dealings. I will tell you frankly that I have not trusted him since he allied himself with Grita and attempted to kill us."

"If you will permit me, my lady," said Lar. "At any rate, it is not him."

"How," said Piro. "It is not?"

Lar shook his head.

"But," said Kytraan, "how can you be sure?"

"Because the road agent is dead," said Lar.

"How, dead?"

"Entirely."

"But," said Piro, "how can you know that?"

"In the simplest way," said Lar. "Because his body is lying not thirty feet behind us."

"The Horse!" said Tazendra. "It is?"

Lar bowed an assent.

"But, how did it arrive there?" said Kytraan.

"It fell."

"It fell?"

Lar nodded.

"When?" demanded Piro.

"Half an hour ago, my lord."

"But," said Tazendra, "why didn't you acquaint us with this circumstance?"

"Because," said Lar, "my lord the Viscount said I was to remain silent."

Piro looked at Lar, but found nothing to say. Kytraan went back and looked at the body that had almost fallen upon their heads and said, "Well, it is certainly Wadre."

"And that," said Piro, still staring forward, "very nearly looks like my father."

"And that," said Tazendra, looking in a slightly different direction, "appears very much like my old friend Pel."

"Impossible," said Kytraan, although it was impossible to determine to which of them he was speaking, if not both.

"And yet," said Lar.

"Well?" said Kytraan.

"If Wadre fell from above—and I give you my word he did—then I wonder what is up there that causes someone to fall."

Kytraan took a step backward and stared up at the ledge, which was thirty or thirty-five feet over his head, then turned to Piro and Tazendra and said, "Do you know, I think what he says is full of wisdom. I believe I will keep an eye on that cliff above us."

"Yes," said Piro. "Do that."

Piro stared forward, frowning, and Tazendra stared forward, also frowning, and Kytraan and Lar stared upward, grimacing, and they all waited, knowing the next few moments would give the answers.

Meanwhile, some thirty or thirty-five feet above them Grita turned to her band of brigands—now numbering ten or twelve—and said, "We will go down the cliff and kill them all, at once. Do not waste time, nor give them a chance to defend themselves. Do you understand?"

The various bandits indicated that this was clear.

"Are the ropes ready?" said Grita

In answer, the ropes, well secured to certain trees, were shown to her.

"Then," she said, "let us have at them."

And it was at this moment that Khaavren, riding toward the small rise near the foot of the South Mountain, suddenly stopped in his tracks, overwhelmed by a feeling that was most peculiar because of its familiarity.

Aerich looked at him, eyes wide, because he felt the same thing, and it is a measure of the magnitude of the occurrence that Aerich was unable to prevent himself from showing astonishment.

Just a score of yards away, and at almost this same instant, Tazendra said, "It has returned, or I'm a norska!"

"What has returned?" said Piro.

"The Orb," said Tazendra.

"That is not likely," said Piro.

"Impossible," said Kytraan.

"Not the least in the world," said Zerika, emerging from the darkness of the cave, the Orb slowly circling her head and emitting a soft green glow.

Kytraan stared at her, Piro turned around an instant later, then Tazendra, who not only turned, but, upon seeing Zerika, dropped to one knee, eyes wide. Piro and Kytraan, seeing her, did the same an instant later. Lar, for his part, dropped his cooking pan and prostrated himself on the snowy ground.

Some historians have placed this day, the thirteenth of the month of the Jhegaala in the two hundred and forty-seventh year of the Interregnum, and this moment, the fifth hour after noon, as the end of the Interregnum and the beginning of Zerika's Reign. Others claim that the placing of the cornerstone of the new Imperial Palace is the moment; whereas, to others, it is the end of either the Battle of South Mountain, or sometimes the Battle of Dzur Mountain (that is, the Ninth Battle of Dzur Mountain, or the Tenth as some historians call it). Still others do not consider the Empire to have truly existed until Zerika actually took possession of the Imperial Palace, whereas some think it did not exist until the last of the serious opposition to it was crushed—which, in turn, leads to many debates over what might be considered serious opposition. Volumes have been written defending and attacking these various times and dates.

Of course, there is no question that the dates do matter; the question is more than academic because of the many calculations to be made by seers and oracles that depend on the exact moment at which the Empire existed once more. Therefore, it is worth taking a moment to consider the matter. Be assured, our consideration will be brief, because, in the opinion of this historian, the matter is far less complex than it is often made out to be.

Expressed in the simplest terms: What is the Empire? It is the political and economic organization of states united under the Orb—an artifact that is both symbolic and functional. While the Orb did not function, there was no Empire; or, there was that condition which has come to be called the Interregnum. As to such matters of just how many of these lesser states—principalities, duchies, and so on—must acknowledge and pay homage to the Empire for the Empire to "exist," this historian will not venture an opinion. It might be that Zerika's Reign actually began at one of these later dates, or, more likely, at the moment she ascended the "throne" in her temporary palace and began to conduct business there. But, even if this is the case, the Interregnum ended at the instant she emerged from the Paths of the Dead—that is, at exactly the place where we have interrupted our story.

Certainly, it was the opinion of those present at that moment—the first to feel the effects of the Orb—that this was the case. The reader has seen that Khaavren, Aerich, and Tazendra were all aware of it at once—that is, they felt the echoes of the Orb in their minds.

We should add that there has, in fact, been some confusion on this issue over the years: In what manner, and how quickly, were those who had once been citizens aware of, and affected by the emergence of, the Orb? As we are now discussing the moment of its emergence, this would seem to be the most expeditious place to make this regrettable but necessary digression.

The confusion over this question is understandable, and, of itself, a part of the answer: Of millions who still lived who were once citizens, there are thousands of different experiences of its return, these differences based on the individual's distance from the Orb, and, to a degree, his sensitivity, personality, and attitude toward the Empire in general and the Orb in particular.

To a few, such as Sethra Lavode, it was as if the Orb had never been away: In an instant she had fully assimilated it, along with all of its capabilities and its connections to Zerika. To others, such as Aerich, this connection came, but a little more slowly: he reports that he knew at once what had happened, but there was a period lasting several minutes while it settled itself fully into his mind. For Khaavren, it was a shock, and it took him some seconds to recognize what it was, after which he, too, permitted it, by a conscious choice, to take its place—that familiar, comforting presence that we all know so well that we become aware of it only if it vanishes, or if we deliberately pay attention to it (the reader is invited to do so now, for his own education).

Others became aware of it more slowly, or refused to recognize it, or recognized it but refused its call—this latter including Kâna and his cousin, as well as Tsanaali. If there was one reaction that was most frequent, it seems to have been a certain confusion and disorientation, as those who were once citizens became aware of a peculiar sensation, perhaps a familiar one, but one which left them unable to concentrate for a length of time more or less prolonged.

Those who had been conceived or born after Adron's Disaster had no experience of the Orb, and were unaware of its return, and so had to recapitulate the experience of those of our ancestors who lived at the time of the formation of the Empire: they had to make a conscious choice to become citizens, and, as they were as yet unaware of it, they could not yet make that choice.

We should add that by using the locution "conceived or born" we have avoided one of the controversies upon which hundreds of magical philosophers have been debating ceaselessly: Where between conception and birth falls the moment when the Orb insinuates itself from a mother who is a citizen to an infant who is to become one? We cannot, in this brief work, take the time to explore this question with the thoroughness it deserves, so we will say only that it *seems* to be the case that the connection comes somewhere toward the end of the mother's term of pregnancy. We hope the reader will be satisfied with this explanation, because it the only one we are offering. Our point remains that those who had never known the experience of citizenship would be required, at some point in the future, to make the decision as to whether to accept this connection, and that those who had known it were able to make at the very instant of awareness.

That is, at this moment, the question of citizenship in the Empire was once more up to the individual.

And this, then, is the answer to the question we did ourselves the honor of asking above, and the historian humbly suggests that it is inarguable. The Interregnum ended upon that well-known winter's day in the two hundred and forty-seventh year, when Zerika emerged from the Halls of Judgment bearing the Orb (not, as many have it, having found it upon the ground after leaving the Halls of Judgment, or, as others have it, having searched the Paths of the Dead far and wide for where it had accidentally fallen after being blasted from the domain of men by Adron's Disaster, or having been handed it by someone else who retrieved it from the Paths—the candidates for this nonexistent honor being as diverse as Lady Ithanor and Lord Morrolan—or, indeed, having carried it within her all of her life, at last giving birth to it as if to a child, as a few ludicrous mystics have suggested).

That day, that moment, all past and potential citizens of the Empire had the choice to become so again, and, therefore, at that moment the Interregnum ended, and if there are words to mark the event, as there often are in moments of high historic drama, they would have to be Tazendra's remark, "It has returned, or I'm a norska."

The proof that these words marked the event, and the beginning of the spread of the influence of the Orb over all of those who had once been citizens of the Empire, is the very fact that no other words have ever been recorded; and it is well known that "historians" of the popular school dearly love to mark great events by the words which accompanied them. What reason would they have for ignoring words to mark the occasion except that these words fail, in their judgment, to convey the proper sense of the occasion?

This does not trouble us for the simple reason that we have set as our goal the reporting of what occurred, not the pandering to public taste that corrupts and defiles the work of some of our fellows.

That the words uttered by the brave Tazendra are not as grandiose and full of pomp as Kieron the Conqueror's, "The sea has brought our salvation," or Undauntra the First's, "Let him who doubts the victory wrest the banner from my hand," or Sethra Lavode's, "I speak for the Mountain, and the Mountain speaks for the Orb," or Lord Kuinu's, "By all the Lords of Judgment, it is proved at last," or expressive of the elegant understatement of Tigarrae's famous "Turn around, my lord; I am behind you," or Deo's "Welcome, my lady, to my home"; still they are what was said, and so our duty as historian places before us the necessity of laying them before the reader. "It has returned, or I'm a norska" are the words that ushered in the end of the Interregnum, if not the restoration of the Empire and the reign of Zerika the Fourth.

They also ushered in certain events of more immediate concern to the reader who has done us the honor of following the unfolding of this story; which events we now propose, without further delay, to describe.

Chapter the Forty-Third

How Four Old Friends Met
After Being Apart for a Long Time

Some historians have expressed the belief that Grita would have given the order to halt the attack if she had been able to—that is, if there had been time for her to issue an order of any sort. The author, for his part, has no way of knowing for certain if this is true, but begs to submit that none of his brother historians has any way of knowing either. It must be the case that Grita, having at one time been a citizen, and being, moreover, in close proximity to the emerging Orb, was aware that it had returned; yet, it is worth considering that three hundred years earlier she had shown no especial loyalty to the Empire of which she was a citizen; why, then, should she now?

But, as the matter cannot be proven one way or another, there is no reason to dwell upon it—the moreso as we know, if not how she was thinking, at least what she did. The command had been given, and the two or three ropes went over the bluff, and Grita's small troop went sliding down these ropes, each holding a weapon at the ready. The surprise was complete: Piro, Kytraan, and Tazendra were all on bended knee, and Lar was actually prostrate upon the ground. The brigands landed with the additional advantage of numbers— there were ten or twelve of them, compared to four of our friends with the addition of a lackey.

It should, from all of this, have been over quickly—a most appalling slaughter.

But there was one thing that changed the entire nature of the battle, and, in the event, determined its outcome: the Orb. That most vital of all artifacts wasted no time in making its presence felt; indeed, it began to play a role in its own defense within seconds of its reappearance. It did so, to begin with, in the simplest possible way: merely by existing.

That is, several of the attackers were old enough to have been citizens before the Interregnum, and, even as they were going down the
rope, they, each in his own way, became aware of the sensation of the
Orb's return—a sensation to which each, of course, reacted in his
own way. And, when they reached the ground and the first thing
they saw was Zerika, with the Orb sedately circling her head, well,
the reader can understand that some of them became more than a little agitated. Indeed, two or three of them, upon seeing her, at once
dropped their weapons and prostrated themselves, even as Lar,
alarmed by the sudden intrusion of briganded ropes, began to rise
and reach once more for his cooking pan. Some of the others, while
not going so far as to take themselves entirely out of the fight, were,
at least for a while, sufficiently discomfited to impair their ability to
mount an attack.

Of the remainder, the reader should recall that these were the
younger ones—that is, those who had not yet been born at the time
of Adron's Disaster, and so had no connection to the Orb, nor awareness of it; and the reader should understand that Grita, in planning
her battle, had placed the older and more experienced brigands in
such a position as to land first, on the theory that they had cooler
heads, and would thus be better able to handle effectually any
unforeseen circumstances. Unfortunately for Grita and her force, the
particular unforeseen circumstance that occurred tended to remove
from combat those upon whom she had depended to handle any
emergencies. With several of these individuals shocked into immobil-
ity, the others, coming down the rope, became entangled with them,
with the result that, instead of being confronted by an overwhelming
force, our friends were, in the event, confronted only by three of
their enemy in any condition to pose an immediate threat—a number
which very quickly became two when Tazendra, the first to recover,
stood up and neatly took the head off the one who was nearest her.

Kytraan and Piro recovered at almost the same instant, which
might have been an instant too late, except that their opponents
found themselves distracted by observing their companion's head fly
from its shoulders, which delayed them just long enough for the
Dragon and the Tiassa to assume their guard positions and engage
those who were about to attack them.

Of them, Kytraan struck first, at once giving his opponent a good cut on her sword arm, causing her to drop her sword and retire from the contest in confusion. Piro took a defensive posture and received the attack with good style, first parrying a cut for his shoulder, then leaning back to avoid a cut for his head, and then slipping sideways away from a thrust at his chest, after which, his enemy being slightly off-balance, he gave this worthy a thrust through the upper part of his thigh which left him stretched out on the ground unable to rise, and which forced him to surrender his sword, declaring himself beaten.

Another of the brigands, disentangling himself from the others at the base of the rope, attempted to rise, but was met unexpectedly by a heavy, cast-iron object in the form of a cooking pot, wielding by Lar's strong right arm; after receiving this, the bandit exercised the only option then available to him: he fell like a dead mass.

Tazendra stepped forward, looking for another — but this was too much for the brigands. One of them, a man named Grassfog, ran past Zerika into the cave, only to emerge a moment later, hands raised in token of surrender. Two or three others dropped their weapons and declared themselves unwilling to continue the contest. The remainder ran, picking the direction away from Tazendra and her greatsword, running to the southeast, leaving, in all, five uninjured prisoners to have their weapons collected, these being, in addition to Grassfog, a woman named Iatha, a woman named Thong, a man named Ritt, and a man called Belly, named for a rather remarkable paunch that he had developed from living a sedentary life and in eating, as his friends said, "Like an Easterner."

It is worth asking why Tazendra had not, in this battle, used the remarkable powers she had been developing under the tutelage of Sethra Lavode. Alas, we cannot answer this for certain. It is possible that it was her innate sense of fair play that prevented it; that is to say, she feared to take unfair advantage of her opponents. It is also possible that matters developed too quickly for her mind to organize itself into the necessary patterns required by wizardry. In the opinion of this author, the reason is more simple: it didn't occur to her. In any case, the fact remains that she did not, and the reader is welcome to draw his own conclusions as to the reason.

"Well," said Tazendra, lowering her sword and frowning. "That was hardly worth the trouble."

"You think not?" said Piro, staring out to the west once more. "But perhaps there is more to come. If all of those horsemen are to attack us, well, I nearly think we will be required to break a sweat in order to defeat them."

Tazendra looked in that direction and said, "You may be right. But first, while we have the time, I must bow once more to my Empress."

"With this plan," said Piro, "I agree. Only, I beg leave to observe that we cannot all do so at once while still maintaining a watch on our prisoners."

"That is true," said Kytraan. "But then, in what order shall we go?"

"Tazendra first," decided Piro. "You next, and I shall go last."

"But what of Lar?" said Kytraan

"Oh, Lar can make his obeisance after me."

"Very well," said Kytraan. "I have no more arguments to make."

"Nor have I," said Tazendra, who then, without further delay, made a courtesy to Her Majesty, which salute the Phoenix acknowledged with a grace and aplomb which belied a certain discomfort she felt in accepting such a gesture, not being used to it. Kytraan went next, and then Piro, and finally Lar, while Zerika did her best to accept the reverences, reminding herself that it was to the Orb and to the Empire it represented, not to her, that the honor was being done. The only sign betraying her distress was a slight orange cast that crept into the Orb.

At this point, Zerika cleared her throat, in order to make her first speech as Empress, or, at any rate, to respond to the obeisances done her. She was prevented, however, by a voice saying, "Our arrival appears, on this occasion, to have been rather less timely, but not so urgently required." We hasten to add that, just as it was the last time we referred to a voice, rather than a person, as if it could speak, the speaker was none other than Aerich. This time, instead of rescuing Khaavren in the company of Tazendra, he was rescuing Tazendra in the company of Khaavren—although, as he himself said, their arrival was not as urgently required as it had been on that day more than two hundred years before to which we have done ourselves the honor to refer.

These words having been spoken, everyone at once looked in the direction of the voice, and there were gasps of astonishment from several of those present.

"Father!" cried Piro.

"My lord!" said Kytraan.

"Ah, it is Khaavren and Aerich," said Tazendra, rushing forward and throwing herself into their arms.

"Bah!" said Khaavren. "It could not be you! You have not changed by so much as a hair."

"On the contrary, my dear Khaavren," said Aerich. "It must be she, for who else would prevent us from paying our respects to Her Majesty?"

"Ah, how you take on!" said Tazendra. "Empires come and go, but friendship is rare."

Khaavren, still holding her, chuckled and said, "No, it cannot be Tazendra. The Dzurlord I know is incapable of such profundity."

"Ah, you jest with me! Well, there is no doubt that you are Khaavren!"

We should add that Röaana and Ibronka hung back rather shyly, unsure of what they should do or say. At last the embrace ended, and Tazendra stepped back and looked at her two friends, while Piro rushed forward, in his turn, to embrace his father. As he did so, Tazendra remarked, "Well, that is three of us. I wonder where Pel is?"

"Why, my dear, I am behind you," said the Yendi, coolly standing on the bluff from which the brigands had just launched their attack.

We hope the reader will permit us, even as these words are pronounced, to say two words about our ineffable friend, the Duke of Galstan. We do not know, in fact, when he realized that it was Khaavren's son he had been following with malicious intent. We do not know what went on in his heart upon realizing that he was faced with conflict between his unquenchable ambition and the friendship that he treasured more than he was capable of admitting, even to himself.

But from all we know, we can be certain of this: When these two powerful emotions—ambition and friendship—at last faced each other in the crucible of his heart, the decisive push, as it were, came from the same source for him as for so many others: the Imperial Orb. He could not deny, even to himself, the flood of emotion that accompanied its return. And so, even as made the cool announcement to which we have alluded, "Why, my dear, I am behind you," the contest within his heart was over: ambition had surrendered, and friendship had triumphed.

Tazendra turned. "Pel! But, was it you who launched that attack upon us?"

"I?" said Pel. "Not the least in the world. My attack is coming from that direction, and will be more severe."

At these words, Tazendra, Khaavren, and Aerich, who had been staring at Pel open-mouthed, suddenly turned in the direction he had indicated, and realized that, in fact, there was a sizable group of riders bearing down on them, looking as if they had no intention of stopping.

"Cracks and Shards," said Tazendra.

"Who are they?" said Khaavren.

"They are a detachment of Kâna's army," said Pel. "Sent to intercept the Orb."

"How, they know of the Orb?" cried Piro. "And, Father, who is this man? And Zivra—that is to say, Zerika—how did you survive the fall from Deathgate? And who are these girls you have brought? And what shall we do about these forces about to descend upon us?"

Khaavren chuckled. "I believe, my son, that we should begin with the last question."

"You are, as always, full of wisdom," said Aerich.

"No, my friend, you are full of wisdom. I am merely clever on occasion."

Aerich smiled and didn't answer.

"And I agree as well," said the Yendi. "Only—this is the son you told me about?"

"Yes," said Khaavren, with a fond smile at the Viscount.

"The deuce! And I have been spending all of this time tracking him, and attempting to thwart his mission. And to make matters worse, there is Tazendra with him."

"How, you have?" said Khaavren, frowning.

"Yes, alas, it seems I have."

"Well, and now?"

"Ah, and now? Well, certainly, now it is different. We must find a way out of this. Give me a moment, and I will come down to you that we may consider the matter."

"Not the least in the world," said Piro.

"How? What do you mean?" said Pel.

"Instead of you coming down, I would suggest the rest of us go up. After all, the ropes are already there, and I think sufficiently strong to support us."

Aerich smiled. "Your son, my dear Khaavren, takes after his father."

"Then you agree?" said Khaavren.

"I nearly think I do."

"As do I," said Pel.

"And I," said Tazendra.

"Only—" said Aerich.

"Yes?" said Khaavren.

"What of Her Majesty?"

"Ah! That is true!" cried Khaavren. "We cannot require her to climb up a rope."

"And there is, in addition," said Aerich, "the question of whether Her Majesty will condescend to retreat."

"The easiest way to discover the answer," said Pel, "would be to ask her. Moreover, I think we should do so quickly, because I give you my word, those horsemen are not getting any further away."

"Permit me," said Piro. Then, turning to the Empress, he said, "Well, Your Majesty? Would you condescend to climb a rope with us? I promise you, from that position, you will be better defended."

Zerika smiled. "After jumping from Deathgate Falls, I assure you I have no objections to climbing thirty feet on a rope made of good hemp, and well secured. And it would seem that my duty to protect the Orb is of greater moment than any distaste I might feel for retreating a few steps."

"Then," said Pel, bowing from his position above them, "I would suggest Your Majesty do so at once, because we have very little time to waste."

Zerika nodded, and, without any further discussion, grabbed onto the nearest rope and easily and smoothly, hand over hand, climbed to the top, ignoring Pel's outstretched hand, instead simply pulling herself up to the ledge. Once on the top, she looked around at the shelf as if to judge it as a position from which to mount a defense, then gave Pel a brief nod.

Pel bowed low to Her Majesty, then looked down at the others and pointed to the late bandits. "What about those reprobates?"

Khaavren shrugged. Aerich frowned. Tazendra scowled.

The Viscount looked at them, and, stepping forward, stood over where they knelt. He put a hand to his sword and and said, "Do you all swear allegiance to Her Majesty, the Empress Zerika, and to the Dragaeran Empire?"

"We do!" they cried, with no hesitation, and, as these words died out, each them felt (some for the first time, some like a memory made real) the feeling of being, once more, in touch with the Orb and a part of the Empire.

Piro turned back and looked, first at Pel, then Her Majesty, and finally at his father, and shrugged.

"Very good," said Khaavren, giving Piro an approving look that filled the young man with pride. "Then have them pick up their weapons and climb up the rope they have so recently descended, and be certain they understand they are now sworn to the Empire, and thus to the person of the Empress."

These things were done, and, as the five new Imperial soldiers—who had just lately been highwaymen—made their way to the top, Khaavren looked at the approaching riders, and said, "We must hurry, if we are all to reach the bluff over our heads."

"I will remain until the last" was the response that met this remark; a response that came in two voices at once. Tazendra, who had been one of the speakers, turned to the other speaker and said, "Your name, madam?"

"I am Ibronka, my lady."

"Well, I perceive you are a Dzur."

"I have that honor, my lady. And I observe that you are, as well."

"That is true," remarked Tazendra. "Therefore, let these others go up the ropes, and, if there is a last defense to be done on this spot, well, we shall do it, you and I."

Piro and Röaana began to object, but Khaavren said, "No. When a Dzurlord falls into this mood, there is no arguing; we would only waste time. Piro, this is Röaana; Röaana, my son Piro, and his friend Kytraan. Now, up this rope, and Aerich and I will go up that one, because my place is near the person of Her Majesty. The servants will follow, and then our brave Dzurlords. Come. No arguing. On your way."

From these words, and, moreover, from the tone in which they were delivered, all who heard them knew without question who was now in charge of the defense and that nothing good would come of any disputes, and so they all made their way, as best they could, up the ropes. The one who had most trouble in this climb was Lar; not because of any weakness, but because he was unwilling to relinquish his cooking pot, and so had difficulty negotiating a hold upon the ropes. Eventually, Mica and Clari, who were already at the top, had him hold on as best he could, and pulled him up, after which they threw the ropes down again for the two Dzurlords, who, as it turned out, had time to scramble up before the approaching riders were upon them.

The leader of the riders—that is to say, Tsanaali—reached the place below the bluff upon which our friends waited, and drew rein, holding up his hand to indicate to his troop that they, too, should arrest the progress of their horses. When he had stopped, he looked up at the forces—such as they were—arrayed against him on the bluff. Tazendra, from her position on the top, bowed to him politely, which gesture he ignored. These forces—in case the reader has forgotten—consisted of Khaavren, Aerich, Tazendra, Pel, Piro, Kytraan, Ibronka, Röaana, Zerika, Grassfog, Iatha, Thong, Ritt, Belly, and three lackeys—for the reader must not forget Clari, although she has, we must admit, said little enough for some time that the reader could be excused this lapse. Arrayed against them was a force of some thirty-five or forty Dragon warriors, some of them appearing a little concerned as they looked upon the Orb, but, nevertheless, Dragonlords prepared to do their duty, under a commander who appeared to understand that there was to be no question of joking.

As Tsanaali looked, he identified (for the reader must understand that the distance was little more than a hundred feet) Pel as being among them, and he called up, "May I do myself the honor of wishing Your Venerance a pleasant day?"

Pel bowed to him, saying, "And I greet you as well, my dear Lieutenant, and am pleased to see you in good health."

"Well," said Tsanaali. "And has Your Venerance anything else to say?"

Pel called back, "You may return, Lieutenant; the mission has failed."

"Then," said Tsanaali, "that is not the Orb I see circling the head of that lady?"

"I have not asked her," said Pel, truthfully. "It did not seem proper to ask such a question."

"I admire your delicacy. Yet, you perceive, the question is important, because of the nature of the mission with which I have been entrusted."

"You may return, Lieutenant," repeated Pel. "The mission has failed."

"If Your Venerance will come down," called the Lieutenant, "we will discuss the matter."

"Come up here, then," called Pel. "I give you my word, you will receive a welcome you will not soon forget, and a discussion that will interest you greatly."

"How, you invite me up?"

"I do, and I give you my word that if you accept the invitation you will make me the happiest of men."

While none of them heard a reply from the officer to this proposal, they all saw the glint of his teeth as he smiled, and the crown of his hat as he bowed. He then turned away, and addressed some words to his command, after which they rode away in tight formation, moving to either side, with no attempt at concealing their intentions.

"I believe," said Pel, "that we are about to have the honor to receive a charge."

"It seems likely," said Tazendra.

"Well," said Khaavren.

"I still think," said Tazendra, "that you ought to introduce us to your traveling companions."

"In a little while," said Khaavren.

"Very well."

"Do you," said Zerika, "think that there is a way to avoid them?"

"Your Majesty," said Pel, "we dare not avoid them."

"How, we dare not?"

"No. On the contrary. If they do not attack us, we should be obliged to attack them."

"How, you think we could attack them?"

"Well, I should prefer not to. But, if Your Majesty would consider —"

"Yes?"

"If any of them escape, Your Majesty's whereabouts will be known."

"Well, and then?"

"And then Your Majesty will be attacked by a much larger force."

"By whom, then?"

"By Kâna, who has sent this detachment against Your Majesty."

"He would, then, make himself a traitor?"

"Your Majesty must understand that he considers himself to be the Emperor; therefore, he is not, in his own mind, a traitor."

Zerika frowned, and considered the matter carefully. "I see," she said at last. "Well then, there must be no attempt to escape."

"That is my opinion," said Pel. "I am delighted to find that it coincides with Your Majesty's."

At this point, Röaana turned to Ibronka and said, "How do you think they will attack?"

"I don't know," said the Dzur. "Are you frightened, Röaana?"

"Nearly. And you?"

"Oh, well, perhaps I am a little concerned."

"You were right to admit it to me, my friend, and you may be assured that I will tell no one."

"I am glad of that. It is difficult not to feel a certain trepidation, because we cannot know what we will do in battle until the first time we experience it."

"You are exactly right, Ibronka. But I will make you this bargain—I will stay and fight if you do."

"Oh, but that is easy, my dear, because you perceive I could never retreat while you are fighting; if I should, well, I believe the shame would kill me."

"Then we shall each guard the other's honor. Agreed?"

"Agreed. Here is my hand."

"And here is mine."

"And now I draw my sword."

"And I draw mine, and let who dares come against us."

A short distance away, Piro said to Kytraan, "Who are the girls?"

"I do not know, yet they came with your father."

"That is true. Can they get above us, do you think?"

"The girls?"

"No, the enemy. I beg your pardon, but I changed the subject of my discourse without informing you of my intentions."

"It is of no consequence."

Kytraan turned around, and studied the slopes behind them, frowned, and said, "It would take them hours, and we should see them well before they were in position to make a charge. No, I think they will occupy the position beneath us, climb up around our flanks, then attempt to coordinate an attack from both sides at once. It is, at any rate, what I should do."

"How many of them can attack us at once, then?"

"In close formation, perhaps five on that side, six on this side at one time. Thus, if they divide evenly, they will be three deep, with a few in reserve. Moreover, whoever takes the outermost position much watch his footing, lest he go over the edge of the bluff, which would, if not kill him, at least disturb him seriously."

"As to that, the same is true of us."

Kytraan shrugged. "I will take the edge."

"On the contrary. I claim that honor for myself."

Kytraan started to argue, then said, "No doubt we will be

assigned positions, which assignments we must agree to as dutiful soldiers of Her Majesty, which, you perceive, is what we now are."

Piro nodded his agreement and drew his sword; Kytraan echoed this action. The Dragonlord held the blade up, and said, "I was given this weapon of my father, you know." He studied its length critically. "It is called Reason, because my father always believed in the power of reasoned argument. And yours?"

"From my mother. She found it in the armory when I was very young, and it is one of the last weapons made by Ruthkor and Daughters before their business failed. It is the style my father has always preferred: light and quick, to strike like a snake. I call it Wit's End."

"Wit's End? Why?"

"Well, for much the same reason that yours is Reason."

Piro turned it in his hand, observing the blade—slender but strong, and the elegant curve of the bell guard. Then he turned to Kytraan and said, "May Reason triumph."

"It always does, at the end of the day," said Kytraan, smiling. "And as for you, well, you will always have a resort when you are at your wit's end."

"Indeed," said Piro with a smile, as they waited for the assault to commence.

As they were having this conversation, Aerich said softly to Khaavren, "My friend, if he has survived for nearly a year on his own, in the wild, facing brigands and running errands for Sethra Lavode, well, now is not the time to worry about him."

Khaavren smiled thinly. "Ah, you are reading my thoughts, good Aerich? Well, I do not deny that your reading is true. Still, after all of this, should I be here with him, and—"

"My dear friend, curb your imagination. Now is not the time, as you know well."

Khaavren nodded, started to speak, then closed his mouth again.

Aerich said, "No, you need not ask. I will take that side, with him, and do you take this side. I answer for him."

Khaavren smiled. "Thank you, old friend."

"It is nothing. But what of you, Tazendra? Why are you looking as if your best sword were notched?"

"Bah, think of it. There are no more than forty of them, and there are thirteen of us, with the addition of three lackeys. Why, what will be remembered of this battle? It is very nearly as if we had outnumbered them, especially when considering that we have the advantage of a strong position, where they cannot attack more than five abreast, whereas six of us can defend. You recall when the four of us fought off this many? It, well, it is irksome."

We should take a moment to explain that the bluff they prepared to defend was, as Pel had observed, well chosen for such games. The mountain was steep behind them, but the ledge upon which they positioned themselves was large enough to permit them some room to maneuver, yet could only be approached by relatively narrow paths on either side of it; it was along these paths that an enemy must attack them (unless the enemy chose to make a laborious climb to a position above them and hurl rocks down upon them; which activity they would be able to see in good season to avoid it).

Khaavren chuckled at Tazendra's remarks and shook his head, and then drew his sword, as he deemed it to be very nearly time to do so. Tazendra stood next to him, and drew her own weapon. Aerich did likewise, walking across to where Piro and Kytraan stood, presently joined by Pel. The two girls positioned themselves near Khaavren. Mica, of course, positioned himself near Tazendra, holding his trusty bar-stool, and Lar, wielding his cooking pot, stood next to Piro. Clari, though she had no weapon save a fist-sized rock which she thought to pick up, stood near Ibronka. Three of the new recruits—Belly, Iatha, and Thong—were positioned beyond Mica, the others behind them; Zerika stood alone in the middle, her head bowed and her eyes closed, the Orb glowing with a pale blue which occasionally pulsed a deep red, as if of a heartbeat.

And, in this position, they waited.

Chapter the Forty-Fourth

How the Battle of South Mountain
Was Fought

The Battle of South Mountain has been much neglected by our brother historians, who seem to have spent a considerable amount of ink and effort upon Zerika's time in the Paths, and her discussion with the Gods, and even the battle of the cliffs, as well as later events of considerable moment, but very little about the conflict that took place the very day upon which the Orb emerged into the world once more.

In some measure, we can understand this neglect—the battle was not large, nor was it, one must admit, conclusive. Yet the student of history ought not to forget that, in the first place, it was the first engagement in which Zerika was present with the Orb (we do not include the skirmish with the brigands, as this cannot count even as an engagement) and, in the second place, it was this battle that prepared the soil, as it were, for the larger battles and intrigues that were to be sown shortly thereafter.

This said, we propose to describe the Battle of South Mountain without further delay.

Our friends did not, in the event, have to wait long: The attack began within two or three minutes of the time when they had taken their defensive postures, and it came, as they had predicted, along the two sides of the semicircular bluff—these sides, as we have attempted to make clear, being the only directions from which an attack could be mounted without attempting to scale the heights above and behind, or, worse, climbing the face of the bluff.

Tazendra's confidence notwithstanding, the results of the conflict were far from certain. These were not brigands, but, as we have said, soldiers, and, moreover, Dragonlords, used to obeying orders, and knowing how to conduct themselves in battle. Their officer, Tsanaali, was, although young, well versed in the tactics of small-scale combat, and was determined to do exactly his duty as he understood it—not to mention that, by this time, he had evolved an emphatic grudge against Pel—which feeling was, to be sure, returned by the hot-tempered Yendi.

The attack began as Tsanaali had intended it, with both of his lines striking at the same instant. On the right side (for convenience, we will refer to direction as if from Zerika, so that the right side is where Khaavren and Tazendra stood, the left side, therefore, by process of elimination, being the other side, or, more precisely, the side occupied by Aerich and Piro), some sixteen or seventeen of them struck, under the command of the lieutenant himself, whereas on the other side were the remainder, perhaps twenty of them, led by an ensign whose name has come down to us as Marra. Khaavren took an overhand guard position as he often did in circumstances of limited lateral dimension—his blade perpendicular to the ground, his left foot forward, a poniard in his left hand, held low against his leg and also pointing forward, his eyes narrow and glinting. Tazendra held her large sword easily in her right hand; her left hand held a tall, thick piece of wood with a dark jewel on the top, and this staff was held out in front of her as if she intended to ward off blows with it; more intimidating to an opponent than the contents of either hand, however, was the fiendish grin on her countenance, as if there were no thought in her mind save for the rapture of a being devoted to battle, and anticipating blood and death as a lover anticipates the press of a sweetheart's lips upon a delicate hand.

However it may have appeared, the staff was the more fearsome weapon, as Tazendra wasted no time in proving. Even before the first clash of steel, she lifted it and sent the jeweled tip through a brief but complex motion, at the end of which action one of the attackers gave a strangled cry and pitched forward onto his face, although there was no mark upon him. Though not yet enhanced by sorcery—that is to say, Tazendra had not yet integrated the capabilities provided by the Orb into what she already knew—her skill in the art was, nevertheless, apparent at once. There can be little doubt that such an occurrence—that is, the collapse of this soldier—would have been sufficient by itself to have dismayed, or at least confused, some or all of the others, had they been brigands. But, as the reader is aware, these were not brigands—these were warriors of the House of the Dragon. While they certainly noticed the fall of their comrade, they continued their attack as if nothing had happened.

Tazendra at once found herself, to her annoyance, facing only one opponent, although it is true that others stood behind, waiting for their opportunity. Khaavren, standing near the edge of the cliff, also faced but one enemy. Indeed, it was entirely a match of one against one along that entire line, with the exception of Tsanaali, who was dueling with two of the recent brigands at once—these being Iatha and Thong. Mica found himself facing a Dragonlord who gave him a contemptuous gesture indicating he should retire if he wished to save himself. Mica, though too frightened to speak, declined this offer with a shake of his head. The soldier shrugged, as if to say that, having relieved his conscience, he had no more to say—and, indeed, he said nothing more, because in the next instant Mica had struck him fully in the head with his trusty bar-stool, knocking the warrior senseless. This having been accomplished, the stalwart Teckla prepared to assist his mistress, except that he was at once confronted by another warrior, and this one, it seemed, had no intention of taking her opponent as lightly as had her predecessor. This Dragonlord, therefore, cut and thrust in a very businesslike way, while Mica, who also took the matter entirely seriously, did his best to keep his bar-stool between his enemy's weapon and his own epidermis.

Tazendra, according to her custom, not only kept her own extremely large blade moving, but also her legs—that is, she continued to shift her ground, the position of her feet, and even the attitude of her body, so that her enemy was unable to get a clear strike at her. Moreover, this led her opponent to shift his own ground, and, in so doing, this worthy chanced to move a little too far to her left—his own right—where he rubbed shoulders with Khaavren's opponent, who, in turn, was pushed to the brink of the cliff. Khaavren, ever the opportunist when it came to matters of steel, took a step forward and struck down to his left a blow that was given with such force that, although parried, it promptly sent his enemy skittering over the embankment where this individual fell some thirty feet, with results upon which we can only speculate. Another soldier at once stepped forward to take his place, and Khaavren then dueled with her for two passes before giving her a thrust through the throat that ended her participation in the conflict, and shortly afterwards her life.

At almost this same instant, an apparently wild and uncontrolled swing by Tazendra at her opponent's head turned into a sudden thrust which penetrated the other's side deep enough to cause this Dragonlord to lose interest in anything except attempting to staunch the flow of blood from his body before all of it ran onto the ground.

As this was occurring, there were two recent recruits from Wadre's band, Thong and Iatha, who, while not at all enthused to be facing a Dragonlord—and the enemy lieutenant at that—neverthe-less took their recent oath seriously enough that, at any rate, they had not yet broken off fighting, but rather still maintained their positions and a good defensive posture. One had received a scratch on the back of his hand, the other a similar scratch on her right leg above the knee, but neither was seriously discommoded, and they continued defending themselves with all the earnestness the situation required.

That side of the battle being, for the moment, stable, let us discover what has happened on the other side. Aerich, who held the edge near the cliff, fought with his accustomed coolness and discipline, deflecting his enemy's thrusts with the tiniest motions of his blade or his vambraces while waiting for an opening that would permit a single attack that would end the affair. It chanced that his enemy was a sergeant named Lazzo who had seen military service for nearly two thousand years, and who had no intention of making the sort of mistake Aerich was looking for; it may also be the case that the Lyorn was distracted by his promise to look after Piro, who stood immediately to his right. But the result, in any case, was that Aerich and Lazzo continued dueling with each other for some time, both of them as cool as if engaged in training exercises.

In the event, Piro did not require any help. He had been trained in the science of defense by his father, of whom it can be said that there were few better instructors anywhere in the world. If Piro was lacking in experience, he nevertheless had not only a solid understanding, but also the physical training of his muscles which permits one to parry an attack and to then make a return thrust before one is even quite aware that the attack has been made. Under the circumstances, he knew that he should be fighting defensively, and so he took a peculiar stance, presenting mostly his side to his opponent and, as he had been taught to do under such circumstances, created with his blade a veritable shield of steel which could not be penetrated. His other hand held a long poniard, which he held ready to use should the opportunity present itself. He recited to himself various lessons that he had learned, and reminded himself of certain important sayings, such as, "maintain correct posture," and, "there must be some bend in the knees at all times," and, "the wrist must be strong, but must never lock," and so on, while, at the same time, keeping his eye focused on a spot in the middle of his enemy's chest, and attempting to keep the point of his blade always lined up with his opponent's eyes. In this way, the two of them made several passes at each other with no blood, as of yet, being drawn.

Next to him, Kytraan was, we must say, rapturous as only a Dragonlord can be when involved in a battle and facing another Dragonlord. His heart pounded, his eyes glowed, and his lips were drawn up in a delighted snarl as he thrust, cut, and parried as if no entertainment could be grander. His opponent, we should say, was older, and had a more businesslike attitude, yet, for all of that, neither could gain an advantage over the other.

Because of the size and shape of the bluff upon which this battle took place and the paths leading to it, it happened that there was room for five attackers, but six defenders; for this reason, the reader ought to understand that, by necessity, one of Tsanaali's soldiers would find himself in position against two opponents. In the event, it was a certain Dragonlord named Stonecutter, a veteran of more than a few battles, who found himself confronting Ibronka and Röaana. Experienced though Stonecutter was, and as inexperienced as were the two girls he faced, this circumstance could have presented certain difficulties for the Dragonlord, save for the fact that Ibronka, disdaining to be part of an attack of two against one, lowered her weapon with a shrug, thus giving the Tiassa the honor of sustaining the attack, which Röaana endeavored to do to the best of her ability. This ability, we must say, was not up to the task—while Röaana had trained as a swordsman, and had, indeed, a certain aptitude, she was no match for a warrior of Stonecutter's experience, ability, and temperament. The result, then, was predictable: in two passes, Stonecutter gave her a thrust through the thigh which caused her to give a small cry and to fall to her knees. Upon seeing this, Ibronka, in turn, gave a cry, but this was one of surprise and anger, and she raised her sword at once and, before Stonecutter had time to withdraw his weapon and resume a guard position, Ibronka had passed her sword entirely through his body, at which time Stonecutter said, "Do you know, I believe you have killed me, madam."

"Well," said Ibronka, shrugging, at which time the Dragonlord fell upon his face and didn't move. Ibronka began to kneel next to her friend, but before she could do so, another Dragonlord had stepped forward, standing over the prostrate Stonecutter, and the Dzurlord was thus required to defend herself to avoid having her head cloven in twain by a vicious overhand cut. She parried this in good style, and then set in to defend herself in all earnestness.

Pel looked for Tsanaali, whom he had promised to have words with, and was so incensed to be unable to find him, that he made up his mind to fight his way through all of the enemy troops until he could meet him. This decision made, he attacked with a ferocity that none of the Dragons, war-hardened as they were, had ever encountered before. His first thrust went into the eye of his amazed enemy, who at once dropped his sword and fell backward, holding his hands to his face. Pel did not even slow down, but, rather, took a step forward, into the thick of the opposing forces, and, with two quick cuts—low to the right, then high to the left—had wounded two of them, one seriously enough to cause him to retire from the contest with the side of his neck bleeding profusely.

The warrior who now stood directly in front of Pel was none other than Tsanaali's lieutenant, Marra, who had enough time to aim and execute a good cut at the Yendi's head, which cut Pel barely deflected with his thin rapier. While he did so, however, the soldier on Pel's right recovered from the wound he had inflected on the calf of her leg sufficiently to aim a furious thrust at the exposed middle of Pel's body. There can be no doubt that, at this moment, matters would have gone ill for the Duke of Galstan had not Röaana, observing the contest from her knees and her position on the Yendi's right, suddenly lunged forward with her poniard and thrust it into the stomach of the Dragonlord just as she was about to complete her attack on Pel. This was too much for the Dragonlord, who, wounded twice, the second time quite seriously, moaned and fell to the ground. Röaana, at the same time, was overcome by exertion as well as loss of blood, and fell forward onto her face next to the woman to whom she had just given such a hideous wound.

This created a certain confusion in the ranks of both sides. During this confusion, Pel was able to retreat a step, having come to the conclusion that he could not, by himself, penetrate through all the enemy forces to reach the one he wanted (and who was, had he known it, in fact on the other side of the clearing). At the same instant, there being a gap in the line where Röaana had fallen, it was, quite unexpectedly, filled by Lar, who stepped up holding his cast-iron cook-pot as if doing so were the most natural thing in the world. It was at just this moment that, at the other end of the line, Aerich found the opening he was looking for and passed his sword almost entirely through his opponent's heart, killing the man at once.

On the other side, after several passes, Tsanaali managed to inflict a good cut on the one called Thong, slicing past his defense and putting a terrible wound on the left side of his cheek. Upon receiving the wound, he dropped his sword and took two steps backward; however, his place was at once filled by one of his comrades, Ritt, who came in and attacked Tsanaali furiously, as if to extract revenge for the painful wound his friend had suffered. The Dragonlord parried strongly, and refused to give ground, even when the attack was joined by Iatha, the other recent recruit to the service of Her Majesty. Now Iatha wielded her oversized blade with sufficient abandon to cause some concern in Mica, who was next to her on the line, yet with sufficient skill that Tsanaali had never had a chance to wound her, yet she, on her end, had given the Dragonlord three or four shallow but annoying scratches—the more remarkable because it was not such a weapon as one would expect to be able to deliver an injury of that sort—one would think that it would either miss or strike deep. Nevertheless, that is what happened, and this duel continued for some time with none of them able to gain a clear advantage.

The same could be said for Mica, who required all of the skill he could muster to keep at bay the weapon that constantly snapped and struck at him from a hand that knew its business, and if Mica had had no chance to attempt to counterstrike, well, it is the author's opinion that he can be forgiven—it being an accomplishment of no small order merely to have remained so long with a whole skin.

Tazendra was no longer considering such matters of who was outnumbering whom, or whether this engagement would involve more or less of glory, but was rather, quite simply, fighting. That is, she was continuing to thrust, cut, parry, move in, move out, move sideways, duck, spin, and lean as if she had been made for nothing else in the world. In the course of this activity, she had placed another of her enemies out of action, by the expedient of striking him in the face with the hilt of her weapon, thus stunning him; and she was now well engaged with the warrior who had stepped up to replace him.

Khaavren continued fighting with his accustomed energy and coolness, protecting himself with efficient and precise parries that moved across his body much more quickly than they appeared to, and set up counterattacks that came without warning and on unexpected lines; while, at the same time, he moved to take advantage of the edge of the bluff on his left, which he knew his opponents could not be unaware of after seeing one of their number tumble from it. In this way, he managed to slip his weapon beneath his enemy's with a good thrust through the body that forced the Dragonlord to retire in pain and confusion.

During all of this, we should explain that Zerika was watching with a sort of fascinated horror, as if she had never before seen such a shedding of blood, and was appalled to consider that it was taking place, at least in part, in her name.

Another who was unhappy with the battle in its development was Tsanaali—at just about this time he made a sudden attack against his opponents, and then retreated a few steps, and used the brief space of time this maneuver gave him to survey the tactical situation as it had developed. It is very possible that, at this point, he would have broken off the engagement if he had been able to give the order—for it was clear that he was unable to make any progress against the stubborn defense mounted by Khaavren and his friends. However, he had no opportunity to give the order, as he was too closely pressed by his two opponents, these being Iatha and Ritt. The battle, therefore, continued.

Aerich, his face expressionless, continued fighting with complete coolness, waiting for opportunities to strike, and, at the same time, as a favor to Khaavren, keeping track of Piro to be certain the young Viscount did not find himself in any trouble from which he could not extricate himself.

In fact, the Viscount was having no trouble of any kind. More than surviving, he would have discovered, had he been able to take the time to make such an evaluation, he was enjoying himself tremendously. He had reached that state of mind where, on the one hand, every movement came automatically, without the need for thought, and yet, in apparent contradiction, his mind was fully engaged at the same time. He was, one might say, thinking in terms of tactics of defense; his eyes would register a low-line thrust, his body would move, his blade would adjust for a cut at his enemy's head, and, somewhere in his mind, he would, though not consciously aware of it, consider their relative positions after the other should parry the thrust, and where he might move to be in a good position to create an opening for a thrust or a cut. In this way, not too much time had passed before he found an opening, which, after he took it, resulted in a Dragonlord who had several inches of steel run through his throat. It would, no doubt, be useless to observe that, for this individual, the battle was now over.

Next to Piro was Kytraan, who, in a different way, was as much in his element as Piro was in his. This was battle, in exactly the way that he understood battle. It was, one could say, what he had been waiting for, if not his whole life, then at least since his earlier encounter with war, in which he had developed the taste that all Dragons eventually acquire for such games. The fact that it was Dragons he was facing, of course, only increased his delight. And the fact that he had neither given nor received much in the way of wounds did nothing to diminish his pleasure.

Ibronka, a scowl affixed to her pretty face, fought in a way—had she known it—that was much the way Tazendra had fought some eight hundred years before—wild, uncontained, presenting, now and then, some danger to those next to her as well as, we must admit, not inconsiderable danger to her opponent. Her opponent, however, was himself a battle-seasoned veteran, and had fought Dzurlords before, and was quite confident, based on this experience, that, if he fought defensively, remained alert, and did not permit himself to be either unduly distracted or unfortunately disabled, she would eventually make a mistake which he could exploit. Up to this moment, she had not done so, and so they continued their duel with the utmost seriousness on both sides.

But of all of them, it was Lar who, one might say, broke the battle open. Amidst the shuffling back and forth that will inevitably accompany such a confused battle in such difficult surroundings, it suddenly occurred that he found himself without an opponent—that is, while everyone else was engaged, he was not. It seemed to him, therefore, to be a splendid time to strike someone with his cooking pot, which plan he put into effect at once, aiming a terrific blow at the head of the Dragonlord to his right, who was exchanging passes with Pel. This warrior, catching the motion out of the corner of his eye, as it were, instinctively moved his blade to parry it as if it were a normal blade. This resulted in two distinct occurrences: The first was that Pel took the opportunity to deliver a furious thrust directly through the soldier's heart. The other was that Lar's cooking pot met the heavy sword of the Dragonlord with a screeching, crashing sound that made itself heard well above the clashing of blade against blade, along with the grunts of efforts, shouts of triumph, and cries of pain usual on a field of battle.

Moreover, there was Pel: Still determined to reach Tsanaali and settle matters with him, he thought he detected a chance to do this very thing, and so charged forward, a poniard suddenly in his hand. He bound the sword of the next warrior in his own, and plunged his poniard viciously into her stomach. Another turned to face Pel, completely ignoring Lar, who, seeing the opportunity, and with great deliberation, struck him three solid blows to the head; although one was probably sufficient, and two most certainly were enough.

After this, matters progressed quickly. Once Lar had so effectually dropped his man, and this coming on the heels of such a thunderous and unexpected sound, the warrior facing Ibronka permitted himself an instant's distraction, which instant was sufficient for the Dzurlord to catch his blade in hers, and, with a twist, disarm him. The warrior quickly retreated out of the way of Ibronka's oversized weapon, and, in so doing, stumbled over the feet of the woman behind him, upon which they both fell in a heap.

This was enough; the Dragonlords required no more to understand that the day was against them. These were soldiers, not fools. They understood when a battle was lost, and when there was no point throwing away their lives needlessly. Though they did not panic, they nevertheless, as if by a spoken order, retreated in some haste, making their way back the way they had come.

Tsanaali, seeing this, understood that his fight was lost for this instant, and called for a general retreat, and those on his side withdrew as well, leaving our friends alone on the field of battle.

Pel, now seeing Tsanaali, took two steps in the direction in which his enemy had left, but Aerich said, "Come, my dear, there is nothing to be gained in that."

"You are right," said Pel, sighing. "And yet, we have failed to kill them all."

Khaavren watched the retreating figures for a moment, then said, "Is anyone hurt?"

"I'm afraid," said Iatha, "that Thong is dead." The others of his friends gathered around him sadly, realizing that, by the flukes of combat, what had appeared to be a relatively benign cut on the cheek had somehow, in fact, caused the late brigand and now Imperial soldier to fall stone dead on the field.

"And Röaana is wounded," said Ibronka. "And that is my fault entirely." As she spoke, she knelt next to the Tiassa, saying, "My dear, are you hurt badly? I will never console myself!"

Röaana, who had not actually lost consciousness, opened her eyes and bravely attempted to give her friend a reassuring smile, which she accompanied by the whispered words, "I think it is not so bad."

The others quickly gathered over her, although Khaavren, Aerich, Tazendra, and Pel continued watching around them. Ibronka drew a knife, and, removing her cloak, began to make cuts in it.

Clari, who had not been involved in the battle itself, cried out, "Mistress! What are you doing?"

"Clari, you should be able to see that I am making a bandage, or have you failed to observe that poor Röaana has been injured?"

"Oh, I noticed that," said Clari. "Only—"

"Well?"

"Your good cloak! What will your mother say?"

"But then, it seems to me that Röaana requires bandaging more than I require a cloak."

"I do not dispute that, but you must observe, mistress, that there are dead people here. Cannot one of their cloaks be used?"

"How," said Kytraan, in a tone of outrage. "Strip the clothing of a warrior who fell in honorable combat?"

"Impossible," agreed Aerich.

"Unlikely," said Tazendra.

"Unthinkable," said Khaavren and Pel together.

"Well," said Mica softly to Lar, "I would offer my own cloak, but, alas, I do not have one."

"You do not?" said Lar. "Well, in fact, neither do I. We should find cloaks."

"I agree, my friend, but I think we ought not to strip the dead to do it. It would go hard with us if we did."

"I am convinced you are right."

As this conversation was taking place, Ibronka, aided by Piro, was binding up Röaana's leg.

"We ought to find a physicker," said Ibronka.

"In these mountains?" said Tazendra. "There is none. We must do the best we can. Someone should boil water."

"For what reason?" said Röaana, appearing somewhat more uneasy about the concept of boiling water than about the deep wound in her leg.

"I don't know," said Tazendra. "But it is something Sethra Lavode told me to do."

"We must also tend to the wounded of our enemies," said Zerika, speaking for the first time.

"As Your Majesty wishes," said Khaavren at once.

"Do you think they will return?" said Kytraan.

Khaavren shrugged. "Who can say?"

"Alas," said Pel, who was looking through his touch-it glass. "I fear they will not. They are re-forming, and appear about to ride away."

"And their wounded?" said Aerich.

Pel shrugged. "Perhaps they will leave horses for them. But we have greater concerns than that, I'm afraid."

Khaavren looked at him. "Well?"

Pel removed the glass from his eye and said, "Grita."

Chapter the Forty-Fifth

How Some Decisions Were Made
Following the Battle of South Mountain

Khaavren and Aerich frowned, and Tazendra turned quickly to look at the Yendi. "What of her?" they said.

"She is now speaking with Tsanaali, who is the captain who led the attack against us."

"Grita and Tsanaali," suggested Khaavren.

"Tsanaali and Kâna," observed Pel.

"Grita and Kâna," concluded Aerich grimly.

"What must be done?" said Tazendra.

Pel frowned. "That is a good question, Tazendra."

"Is it? Then I am gratified."

"And you are right to be. Alas, however, I do not know the answer."

"Well, don't be vexed at it," said the Dzurlord kindly.

"You perceive," continued Pel as if Tazendra hadn't spoken, "Kâna will now be told that the Orb has returned, and where it is, and he will send all of his forces against us."

"Not against us," said Khaavren. "Against Dzur Mountain."

"Dzur Mountain?" said Pel.

"Exactly. We must go to Dzur Mountain as quickly as possible, and I should be astonished if he were unable to make that calculation."

Tazendra looked around. "Must we go there? This is a strong position to defend," she said.

"Against tens of thousands?" said Pel, smiling.

"Why not?" said Tazendra naïvely. "We did before."

Pel stared at her, uncertain of how to respond to this enormity.

Zerika said, "I beg you to remember that we are not entirely without resources. That is to say, as you yourself have observed, the Orb has returned. Apropos," she added to Tazendra, "my dear, the next time you attempt sorcery, or wizardry, whatever it is you are doing, you may wish to remember that there is the Orb available to you now; it may make your work easier."

Tazendra looked startled at this remark Her Majesty had condescended to address to her, and then settled in to consider it. As she was doing so, Pel observed, "Well, what Your Majesty does us the honor to tell us is true. But then?"

"Bide," said Zerika. She then closed her eyes, as if to concentrate, and, at once, the Orb began to pulse with a color somewhere between a pale green and a faint orange, if such a thing can be imagined. After a moment, she opened her eyes again, and the Orb's color returned to a more pleasing azure.

"I believe," said the Empress, "that I will soon become better at this."

"If Your Majesty will permit a question—" said Pel.

Zerika nodded and, anticipating the Yendi's question, answered it. "I have informed Sethra Lavode of what has happened here, and what we expect to happen next."

"I see," said Pel. "But, Your Majesty, is there anything she can do?"

The Empress shrugged. "She is Sethra Lavode."

"Well, that is undeniable," said Pel, although he did not appear to be convinced.

Ibronka finished bandaging Röaana's leg, and said, "There. Let us see if you can stand."

"Bah. What does it matter if I can stand? I'm convinced that I can ride." Nevertheless, with the Dzurlord's help, she attempted to rise to her feet only to collapse again, not so much from the injury to her leg as from weakness caused by loss of blood.

"Well," said Khaavren, frowning, "it is not clear to me that you are able to ride after all. But this, you must see, is unimportant in any case, as I fear we have nothing to ride."

"Our horses?" said Tazendra.

"I believe that our late opponents in combat have chosen to take our horses with them."

"All of them?" cried Kytraan.

"So it seems," said the Tiassa coolly.

"I am not certain how well I can walk," said Röaana, whose position on the ground spoke more eloquently than her words. "You must leave me here."

"After you have recovered some of your strength, we will fashion you a crutch," said Ibronka, ignoring, as did all of the others, her offer to remain behind.

"We have no hope of catching them in any case," said Aerich.

"Nor," added Piro, "have we any hope of caring for their wounded."

Pel shrugged, as if this last detail were of no interest to him.

Khaavren looked around, frowned, then said, "With Her Majesty's permission, I think we will remain here for tonight, and rest. There is no reason to hurry, as we cannot catch them anyway. A good night's sleep will do us all good, and we will see how our brave Röaana feels in the morning."

"If that is your advice, Captain," said Zerika, "then that is what we will do."

Khaavren's nostrils flared and his eyes narrowed at hearing himself addressed by this title. He started to speak, but Zerika pretended not to notice, and turned away to say a few words of sympathy to Röaana.

Khaavren said, "Your Majesty—"

Zerika turned to him. "I am speaking with another. Do not interrupt your Empress, Captain."

As she gave him this title again, he once more opened his mouth to speak, but Zerika had already turned back to Ibronka, and was conversing with her. Khaavren turned toward Aerich, only to find that the Lyorn appeared to have become fascinated by the peculiar rock formations one can see on and from the South Mountain. Khaavren scowled and said nothing.

Piro turned to Lar. "You and Mica and . . . you," he said, indicating Clari, "set our camp up here."

Lar bowed and, collecting the other servants, set about doing as he was told. In the meantime, Grassfog, Iatha, Ritt, and Belly stood around their late companion, Thong, speaking in low tones. Brigands though they had been, they were offered condolences and sympathies by the others as they shared memories and respectfully divided Thong's belongings among themselves.

"It is sad," observed Grassfog, "that our friend here is dead, and we have no wine."

"It is your custom," inquired Piro, "to become drunk when a friend dies?"

"Not in the least," said Grassfog. "I was merely making an observation about two conditions that are both true, and both regrettable."

Aerich and Khaavren did what they could to see to the comfort of the Dragonlords who were wounded but alive, including Stonecutter, who, in spite of his opinion when struck, was not dead, although his wound was painful and Aerich thought nothing good of it.

As this chapter of our history concerns the process of decision-making that followed the skirmish, we hope the reader will not be alarmed if we move from the scene of the battle to the place where, as Pel had observed, Grita was engaged in conversation with Tsanaali. She approached the captain boldly, riding out at a cool walk to where the Dragonlord had assembled his troop, along with all of the horses they had gathered up on the way. When she came to him, she said simply, "So you failed."

Tsanaali shrugged. "Their position was strong, and their defense determined. We could not get through them."

"Bah. Outnumbering them three to one—"

"Madam, if you have something to say, you may do yourself the honor of saying it. And, if the thoughts in your head are those indicated by your countenance, you may go have words with the Yendi on yonder mountain, because he has those same thoughts, and the two of you may decide the order in which you should like me to entertain you. Until you have made this decision, madam, permit me to go about my business. There are matters I must attend to. These matters may or may not be important, but I give you my word, I care about them far more than I care about your evaluation of how I carry out my duties."

"You will be getting a message to K—to His Majesty?"

"I will."

"And you will tell him of my service to you? Of how I warned you of the perfidy of the Yendi, and told you where to find the Orb?"

"I will tell him."

"And, do you think he will be grateful?"

Tsanaali looked at Grita closely, thinking that she did not have the aspect of someone who would be likely to ask such a question. "Well, what is it you wish to know?"

"If I can accompany you."

"You wish to come along with my troop?"

"Yes."

"And why would you wish for such a thing?"

"Because you will be where the Orb goes, and where the Orb goes, my enemies go. And I wish to be there when they die."

"I see."

"And I hasten to add that it may be to—His Majesty's—advantage."

"Oh? In what way?"

"As to that, I will not now say, Captain, save there will be certain services that I shall ask of His Majesty, and that I know of, well, let us say of certain *resources* which I believe he will be grateful to have. And you may tell His Majesty that if I get what I want, I will gladly put these resources at his disposal, and I promise you he will not be the loser in such an exchange."

Tsanaali studied her carefully—disliking her intensely, yet aware that she could be of service to His Majesty Kâna. At last he said, "Very well," and, before she could say anything, he turned away from her. Then, calling his company into formation, he led the way, as quickly as he could, toward Dzur Mountain.

And, as we have brought up the subject of that enigmatic feature of the landscape, let us turn our attention thither and see what is passing in the home of Sethra Lavode.

With Tazendra having left on a mission, and the Necromancer having left on another, the Enchantress was, as we look upon her, alone save for her servant, Tukko. And yet, it is safe to say that she was never alone, because she always had with her the dagger whose name has come down to us as Iceflame, and, through this weapon, she had with her, at all times, Dzur Mountain. The exact nature of the relationship between mountain and enchantress is beyond the scope of this work, but it is fitting and proper that, as we look upon her, we remember that they were a part of each other in a way that is as undeniable as it is incomprehensible.

She walked through her home aimlessly, as if it didn't matter exactly where within her domain she happened to be. She walked with her head bowed and her eyes, in fact, closed—although it should be no surprise to the reader that, after as long as she had dwelt there, she did not need her sense of sight to know where she was or where she was going or what obstacles, if any, might be in her way. And, as she walked, her right hand would occasionally touch the hilt of Iceflame.

And, as she walked, she began to speak in very low tones, her lips barely moving, though there did not appear to be anyone in sight with whom to hold a conversation. At a certain point in this inaudible conversation with no one, she went so far as to draw her dagger from its place at her hip, holding it in the gentle but firm grip of one who knew its length, and with this grip, moved it in a manner that seemed to be meaningless, as if she were paying no attention to the arm, the hand at its end, or the poniard it held. She continued her apparently aimless walk, and apparently senseless utterances, and apparently meaningless gestures for some time, until, finding herself in the kitchen, she opened her eyes to see Tukko there.

"Well," she addressed this worthy. "I have done all that I can."

"The mountain?"

"Dzur Mountain is now protected, as well as it can be."

"And the Empire itself?"

"I attended to that over the last several days. As I have said, my friend, I have done what I can."

Tukko glanced up at her. "And what of the Gods? Have they done all they can?"

"They can do nothing until the crisis is at hand."

"Yes," said Tukko. "At which time, no doubt, they will be help-less."

Sethra chuckled. "That *is* their custom, isn't it? But you know they are more tightly bound than you are."

"That is as may be, madam," said Tukko severely. "But you know that I prefer not to discuss my own condition."

"And yet, if we do not discuss it —"

"Is now the time, madam?"

Sethra sighed. "No, my dear friend, I imagine it is not."

"Well then?"

"Well then, as I said, I believe I have done all that I can."

"What of the emissary the Gods have sent?"

"I have instructed her not to return. She will do more good with the little Dragon than she will here."

"Perhaps you are right, young one," said Tukko. "But the Dragon is unpredictable, and the demon is unknown. It is not good that they are all we have to depend on."

Sethra Lavode permitted an expression of annoyance to cross her countenance, no doubt at the appellation "young one," which she had never liked. "They are not *all* we have to depend on, as you know very well."

"Oh, you speak of steel."

"Do not disparage steel. The Empress, it seems, has just won a sort of victory against the forces who oppose her. And all of our arcane activities will be worthless if the Empress is defeated by an army. That would be the end of the Orb, and another fifty years without the Orb, and I do not think anything can keep them out. Indeed, with its reemergence, they must have become aware of my illusions, and it is unlikely we can keep them out for a week should it vanish again."

"Oh, I do not disparage steel. Yet that is not where the real threat lies. Something must be done."

Sethra said, "I should be delighted to learn more, if you have any suggestions as to what we can do."

"I have none."

"Well then, we are doing what we can. Above all the Orb must be protected. Once it is secure —"

"We both know," said Tukko, "that the Orb will be on our side. The question is, will it be enough?"

"We both know," said Sethra, with somewhat of a mocking edge to her voice, "that the Jenoine are a far greater threat than the upstart from the west. But—"

"Yes," said Tukko. "But. But the one from Kanefthali can open the way for the Makers. That is what I worry about."

"Yes, and it is against just this threat that I have put up safe-guards around the Great Sea, as well as around the mountain, as you know very well, *Dri'Chazik a Tukknaro Dzur.*"

Tukko shrugged, ignoring the use of his full title, which always meant the Enchantress was annoyed. "We both know you are more subtle and skilled than I am. But have you the skill to truly protect us from the Makers?"

"If I do not, who does?"

"The Necromancer."

"How, you think so?"

"I do."

"I had not thought such matters involved necromancy."

"How not, Enchantress? Is it not a matter of transfer from one world to another, one plane of existence to another? And is it not exactly at this that a Necromancer is skilled? In fact, I am convinced it is for this reason that this demon, and not another, was sent to us by the Gods."

"I had not considered it in this way."

"Well?"

The Enchantress thought about this for a long moment, at last saying, "Yes, Tukko, I believe you are right."

"I am convinced of it, Enchantress."

"Well then," said Sethra, "now that the Orb has returned, I will reach out to her through it, and speak to her of this, and see if she can manage these safeguards."

"That will be good."

"But, at the best, it will take time for her to do anything."

"Yes. I know. In the meantime, well, you must simply do the best you can."

"I always do."

"Yes, I know that, Enchantress. I know that you do."

Zerika, at this same time, was addressing herself to Khaavren, who had been sitting in silence with Aerich, Pel, and Tazendra. As she approached, the four of them rose to their feet as one and bowed to her, each in his own fashion, a salute which Zerika returned in a rather distracted way.

"Please, sit," she said.

Taking this as an order, they did so. Zerika, however, remained standing, and addressed herself to Khaavren.

"Tell me, Captain, what you conceive our tactical situation to be."

Khaavren ignored the title she had given him, although, as the reader has realized, he was not entirely at ease with it, and said, "Your Majesty, it is not good."

"Well?"

"We wish to reach Dzur Mountain, because there we can manage a certain degree of safety while Your Majesty gathers forces. But I am convinced that this pretender, Kâna, will stop at nothing to gain the Orb, and the army he has at his disposal is, to say the least, formidable. In a word, then, our situation is grim."

Having said this, Khaavren permitted his head to drop onto his breast, as if he were in deep contemplation. Zerika nodded, accepting his judgment, then glanced at Khaavren's friends, and said, "And do you, who among you have great experience, agree with my captain?"

"Oh, yes," said Tazendra, delighted. "The circumstances are so grim as to be nearly hopeless. It is a joy to me."

Aerich, for his part, said, "Your Majesty, it is true that there are considerable forces arrayed against us, in this I cannot disagree with the captain. In truth, I do not know how we can succeed. But I know that we must try, and that is sufficient."

"And you," said the Empress, addressing Pel. "You agree with the others."

"Not in the least," said the Yendi.

"How, you do not?"

"I do myself the honor of standing in disagreement with them, yes."

The others looked at Pel, who had accompanied these words with a graceful bow in their direction.

"In what way do you disagree? Please be specific."

"Oh, Your Majesty need not fear that I will speak in generalities.

And I do not dispute that there are tremendous forces at work against us. But—"

"Yes," said the Empress. "But?"

"But there is a circumstance upon which my friends have not reflected."

"I hope," said the Empress, "that, as you have reflected upon this circumstance, whereas they have not, you will do us the honor of sharing these reflections."

"I am about to do so."

"And then?"

"It is simply this," said the Yendi. "For the first time in hundreds of years, the four of us—that is, Aerich, Tazendra, Khaavren, and I—are together, united. Consider what we have done in the past. For my part, I can conceive of no force, of any kind, that can stand against us."

Zerika frowned, considering this, but made no response.

Aerich smiled a little.

Tazendra grinned and said, "Ah, my dear Pel. I recognize you so well in that!"

Khaavren slowly raised his head, looking at his friends with a kind of fire in his eyes, and said, "Do you know, my dear, I think you may be right."

Chapter the Forty-Sixth

How Morrolan Met an Intriguing
And Unique Individual, Who
Caused a Certain Amount of
Excitement at His Encampment

I t was in the middle of the morning on a Marketday in the first year of the reign of the Empress Zerika the Fourth that the Lord Morrolan became aware of a certain commotion in his encampment, by which we mean at the site of the temple and associated fortifications that he was in the process of building. At the time, he was inside the temple structure itself, consulting with Arra about the placement of sconces and other matters of decoration, Arra pretending that plain and simple was in keeping with the nature of the Goddess, whereas Morrolan favored more elaborate adornments. This discussion was interrupted by a young man of the House of the Teckla, who was one of many who assisted the builders in their work. This young man entered, made an obeisance to Morrolan, and said, "My lord, something has happened."

"Well? And what is it, then?" prompted Morrolan, who always preferred some degree of detail when hearing of an alarming event.

"You wish me to tell you what has happened?"

Morrolan frowned. "How, this was not clear to you from my question?"

"Oh, it was clear, my lord."

"Well then?"

"Then I will tell you."

"Well," said Morrolan, "I shall offer my thanks to Verra for that!"

"Shall I wait while you do so?"

"Speak!"

"This is it, then."

"Yes?"

"The first thing that happened, then, is that a wolf appeared."

"How, a wolf?"

"Yes, my lord."

"In the camp?"

"Yes, my lord."

"Well, what next?"

"Next, there was a dzur."

"Ah, ha!" said Morrolan, beginning to understand. "And was my friend the warlock near these animals?"

"Yes, my lord, he was. Right among them."

"Well, if that is all, then —"

"Your pardon, my lord, but that is not all."

"What, there is more? Tell me what it is, then."

"It is the warlock, my lord. He pretends that the wolf and the dzur appeared because of someone entering the encampment."

"Well, and have you seen a stranger?"

"No, my lord."

"And did the warlock say where this stranger was?"

"No, my lord."

"Well, but what did he say?"

"He said to bring you, my lord."

"Ah. Well, now I better comprehend why you have come."

"Then I have done my duty, my lord."

Morrolan shrugged his shoulders and threw a cloak over them, after which he went out into a day that was sufficiently bright, compared to the inside of the temple, that at first Morrolan could do nothing but squint. Presently, however, he saw the short figure of the warlock standing, along with the wolf and the dzur, in the midst of a small group of people who appeared to be engaged in some sort of animated conversation. Morrolan approached them directly.

As he came closer, he noted that Lady Teldra was there, as well as Fentor, his sergeant, whose hand was gripping his sword as if ready to draw it upon an instant. The remaining member of the party was a woman, very tall, very pale, and very thin. But what was most remarkable about this woman was that the two beasts who were the warlock's familiars, each in its own way, showed unmistakable signs of hostility toward this woman, as if they both but waited a word of command before tearing her to pieces.

As Morrolan approached, he observed that the stranger, whoever she was, seemed either oblivious of the threat posed by these animals, or, at the least, unworried by it. As he came near, Fentor turned and bowed, and made some remark to the stranger, who also gave a certain incline of her angular head. In many ways, she had the appearance of a Dragonlord, though her eyes were, perhaps, set a trifle too far apart, and her noble's point, though present, was not quite sufficiently pronounced.

"Well?" said Morrolan.

Fentor said, "My lord, this person appeared in the camp, and will not give her name, nor tell us whence she came. Do you agree with this, good warlock?"

"Nearly."

"Nearly?"

"You are incorrect on one count, my dear Sergeant."

"And, if you will, in what particular have I erred?"

"She is not a person," said the warlock coolly.

"How, not a person?" said Morrolan and Fentor.

"No, she is an undead."

"Ah," said Morrolan.

"More than that," continued the warlock, "she is also a Necromancer, and certainly the most powerful I have ever known, or, indeed, heard of."

"Bah," said Morrolan. "How can you know that?"

"Sireng told me," he said, indicated the dzur. "And, if that is not enough, she appeared suddenly, amid a shower of golden sparks, which is a means of travel that only a Necromancer is capable of."

"That is true, my lord," said Fentor. "The warlock alerted us to her impending arrival before she had appeared, and we were thus able to see her as she emerged from nothing, exactly as he has described."

Morrolan frowned, not entirely certain how to respond to this intelligence, and turned to the stranger, to whom he gave a polite bow. "I am Morrolan, Lord of Southmoor," he said. "And these are my lands."

"It is you I have come to see," said the Necromancer, speaking in a rather deep but not unpleasant voice, although one nearly devoid of inflection, and with a pronunciation that was quite as pure as that spoken in Dragaera City before the Disaster.

"Ah!" said Fentor. "She speaks! I had begun to wonder."

"If you please," said Teldra to Fentor, with a touch of severity in her voice. Fentor shrugged.

"Well," said Morrolan, "you have not only seen me, but you have spoken with me as well."

"That is true, but I have more things to tell you."

"How, more?"

"Exactly."

"Well, say it, then, I am listening."

"You wish me to tell you now?"

"I beg your pardon, but are you of the same family as the boy who—but no, it could not be. Well, to answer your question, yes, if you would, at this moment—by which, you perceive, I mean right now—do me the honor of saying what you wish to say, and that without taking any more time than should be required, well, I give you my word I would be very grateful."

"Then I will tell you."

"I am grateful."

"A large army of the Duke of Kâna is heading in this general direction, bent on what must be considered evil, and you have the only force in a position to stop it."

"Who, I?"

The Necromancer bowed assent.

Morrolan frowned. "On whose behalf am I to use this force?"

"On behalf of Her Majesty, Zerika, the Empress."

"An Empress named Zerika?" said Morrolan.

The Necromancer bowed once more.

"Someone different from the Emperor Kâna, and from the other pretenders of whom I have heard so much?"

The Necromancer signaled her agreement for the third time.

"So," said Morrolan with a shrug. "It is another Empress. What makes this Empress more legitimate than Kâna?"

"The Orb," said the Necromancer.

Morrolan turned to look at Teldra, whose eyes were wide. "It has returned?" cried the Issola, who, having been born after the Disaster, had no awareness of its presence.

"So I am informed," said the Necromancer.

Teldra stared at the Necromancer, while Morrolan stared at Teldra staring, and Fentor watched Morrolan for a hint of what action, if any, he ought to take. The Necromancer, we should add, for the sake of completeness, didn't appear to be looking at anyone or anything, though her eyes were pointed generally in Morrolan's direction.

"Well?" said Morrolan, addressing Teldra.

"My lord, I do not know."

"But, is it possible?"

"I, well, I imagine it *possible*, my lord."

"And then, is there a way to discover for certain?"

The Necromancer said, "Anyone who practiced sorcery at the time of what is called the Disaster will be able, with a small effort, to become aware of the return of the Orb."

Teldra nodded. "Yes, that would seem reasonable."

Morrolan nodded to Fentor. "Find such an individual."

"Yes, my lord."

In a very short time, the sergeant returned with a middle-aged Tsalmoth, who was involved in the construction. She bowed to Morrolan, and introduced herself as Oidwa.

"Oidwa," said Morrolan, "is it true that you are a sorcerer?"

She seemed startled. "My lord," she said. "It is true that I had some skill, but that was long ago."

"Before the Disaster?"

"Exactly, my lord. There has been no sorcery since then."

"But, if the Orb were to return, what then?"

"If it were to return, my lord? Oh, but that could never happen."

"Why could it not?"

"Because it was destroyed in the Disaster."

"Oh? And how is it you come to know this?"

"How? Well, but, if it was not, where is it?"

"It is not for you to question me," said Morrolan sternly.

"Yes, my lord."

"What could you use sorcery to do?"

"What could I . . . my lord, there are so many—"

"Could you light a fire with it?"

"Well, but, yes, surely."

"Do so."

"My lord?"

"Do so now. Start a fire, in that pit at which I am now pointing."

"With sorcery, my lord?"

"Yes, yes. With sorcery."

"But if—"

"Make the attempt, as if the Orb were back."

The Tsalmoth hesitated, then said, "My lord, I will do as you say, of course. But you must be aware that it is pointless. If, indeed, the Orb had returned, I would know it by simply sensing for . . ."

Her voice trailed off, and her eyes became as wide as flattened pennies.

Morrolan, who could not but observe the remarkable expression that crossed her countenance, and, moreover, the fact that she then fell to her knees, as one who has received a vision of divine origin, looked at her, then said simply, "Well?"

"I believe," said Teldra softly, "that the Orb has returned."

Oidwa, evidently hearing these words, looked at Teldra, focusing her eyes upon her with some difficulty, and nodded. Then she turned, and with a small gesture, started a fire in the place Morrolan had indicated. It is possible that this was the first use of the Orb for sorcery after the Interregnum, although this cannot be established with any certainty.

The Necromancer then said, "My lord," thus recalling Morrolan's attention to her.

Morrolan looked at her, and nodded abruptly. "Very well, I accept that the Orb has returned. And I accept that this—what is her name?"

"Zerika the Fourth," said Teldra, who of course knew her history, and was able to supply the proper numeral to associate with the name.

"Yes," continued Morrolan. "I accept that this Zerika has the Orb. But, what then?"

"Then," said Teldra, "it is the duty of a gentleman to support and defend the legitimate Empress."

Morrolan considered this for a long moment. "Very well. I must consider this matter. In any case, it is clear that I cannot permit this—what is his name?"

"Kâna."

"Yes, I cannot permit this Kâna to over-run me. Therefore, I will gather the army, such as it is. We will set out in the morning."

"My lord," said Fentor. "I do not believe sufficient preparations can be made between now and to-morrow."

"And why is that?"

"Well, Your Lordship must consider that provisions must be organized, order of march determined, weapons and supplies allo-cated —"

"How long will it take?"

Fentor hesitated. "I believe I could manage it in three days, my lord."

"Three days?"

"Well, perhaps it could be rushed —"

"The morning of the day after to-morrow."

Fentor winced, then nodded. "Very well, my lord. I will see to it at once."

Morrolan then turned to the warlock, who was now standing placidly next to his dog, with his cat sitting between his feet. Of the wolf and the dzur, of course, there was no sign. After taking a moment to recover his composure — he had, after all, just experi-enced several remarkable revelations — Morrolan said, "Do you leave now, and attempt to discover who they are, how many they are, and what they are doing."

The warlock bowed his agreement with this plan, and turned away to put it into action at once, his dog and his cat following behind him.

The warlock, we should say, wasted no time in gathering a sup-ply of provender for himself and his horse (his familiars, as he called them, were capable of hunting for themselves) and setting out on his mission — that is to say, he was gone within the hour. Fentor, for his part, began at once to prepare such an army as Morrolan had built — scarely three thousand, all told — for as quick a departure as possible.

Morrolan returned to the temple to hold conversation with Arra, whom he found standing at the altar, running her hands along its smooth, polished surface as if it were a pet she was stroking, or as if it was a precious treasure and she alone were responsible for its fate.

She looked up as Morrolan entered and bowed to him respectfully. Morrolan, without preamble, explained to her all that he had just learned, and the actions he had taken in response. "What is your opinion?" he concluded.

"I do not understand on what you do me the honor of asking my opinion," said the priestess.

"Do you believe them? About the Orb?"

"My lord, you must understand that this is not a matter with which I am conversant."

Morrolan sighed and nodded. "Well, I can only hope I have done the right thing, and that, moreover, I will continue to do it. You perceive, this matter of an Empress, a real Empress, has thrown me out of my reckoning, and I am not entirely certain how I ought to respond."

"My lord, what causes this confusion?"

"The notion of serving another. This idea is not pleasing to me."

"I understand."

"But then, Teldra, whom I trust, seems to feel I must do so, as a matter of course."

"If you wish, I can ask the Goddess for guidance."

"I can see no reason not to," said the Dragonlord.

"I shall set about doing so, then."

"Yes, and I will await the results, for you perceive it is no small matter that we consider. Indeed, a great more than my own fate may rest upon the decision I ultimately make."

"As to that," said Arra, "I have no doubt at all."

Chapter the Forty-Seventh

How Tazendra Put the Empress's
Suggestion into Action

Khaavren was awakened early the following morning by a remarkably loud sound, in the form of a "boom" similar to what a heavy log might make when dropped from a great height into a rocky valley of the sort that generates considerable echoes. He came at once to his feet, to find that everyone else was also rising, the entire camp having been startled by this sound. He wondered at once who was on watch, and, without thinking about it, consulted the Orb to learn the time—which action proved how quickly he had, in some ways at least, habituated himself to its return.

Having learned the time, he was able to quickly determine that it was the last watch, and that, therefore, it was being shared, according to the scheme that he had laid down, by Iatha and Tazendra, wherefore he at once called for the Dzurlord by name.

"I am here," she said coolly, emerging from behind a large stone, from which, Khaavren realized, a certain amount of heavy gray smoke was also emerging, as if a fire had been quickly smothered in that spot.

"The Horse!" cried Khaavren. "Are you injured?"

"Bah. It is nothing."

"How, nothing?" said Khaavren, as the others, now fully awake, also stared at her. "You perceive, your face is blackened, much of your clothing burned and torn to the point where your modesty is compromised, and, if I am not deceived, there is smoke still curling from your left hand."

"Well," shrugged Tazendra, endeavoring to adjust her clothing. "It is not so bad as it looks."

"But what happened?"

"Oh, as to that—"

"Yes?"

"Her Majesty—" Here she bowed in the direction of Zerika. "—was right."

"That doesn't startle me," said Khaavren. "But, in what way was she right?"

"My friend, you know that I have trained as a wizard."

"Well, yes, I am not unacquainted with this intelligence—my son has spoken to me of it, and, what is more, I had the honor of seeing you perform in that little entertainment we just enjoyed."

"And, moreover, I was a sorcerer in the old days."

"I cannot forget how often our lives were saved by the flash-stones you prepared for us. But what then?"

"Her Majesty did me the honor to suggest that, the next time I performed a spell, I ought to draw power from the Orb."

"Well, and?"

"I had bethought myself that, before attempting such a spell upon an enemy, I ought to make a test."

"You thought of that yourself, Tazendra?"

"Entirely."

"Well, it was a good thought."

"I am gratified to hear you say so, my friend."

"And so, then, you made this test?"

"Yes, and it is good that I did, because, well, the Orb has changed."

"How, changed?"

"Exactly."

"In what way has it changed?"

Tazendra frowned, as if looking for the words she required to clearly explain a difficult concept. "It is," she said at last, "as if you were attempting to lift a boulder, only to discover that it was made of paper."

"That is good, if you wish to lift it," observed Khaavren.

"I attempted to start a small fire. Instead of a fire igniting, however, the stick I was attempting to ignite quite exploded, making a considerable amount of smoke, and no small degree of noise."

"I had remarked upon the noise," said Khaavren. "And, moreover, I perceive the smoke. But what can account for this change?"

"Oh, as to that, I cannot say."

Khaavren turned to Zerika, as if to ask her opinion of this strange phenomenon, but the Empress merely shrugged, as if to say that, never having felt the presence of the Orb before the Interregnum, she had no standard against which to compare it.

"Is it possible," said Khaavren, "that, somehow, the Orb has changed, and that sorcery is more powerful?"

"If it is," said Ibronka suddenly, "then perhaps Röaana's leg can be healed."

The Tiassa, who had been sitting on the ground, looked up hopefully. Piro glanced at Ibronka, then at Röaana, then at Zerika, and finally at Tazendra as he considered the question, the potential, the unknown, and the possibilities.

"I know little of healing," said Tazendra, blushing a bit, as if ashamed of admitting to a limit to her knowledge.

"I believe," said Ibronka, "that you know more than any of the rest of us."

At this point, Grassfog hesitantly cleared his throat.

"Well?" said Ibronka, turning to look at him quickly.

"I was apprenticed to a physicker for a time, shortly before the Interregnum."

"How, you?" said Ibronka.

Grassfog bowed his head.

"And how did you go from physicker's apprentice to brigand?"

"Easily enough," said Grassfog. "My mistress died, and none of the spells I knew for healing were efficacious, and I had to eat, because I considered that, as every living thing must eat to live, and as I was a living thing, should I stop eating I would no longer live, and I wished to continue living."

"Yes, I understand that," said Ibronka, struck by the extreme justice of this explanation. "But, do you think you can heal my friend's leg, now that the Orb has returned?"

"It is possible," said Grassfog, with some hesitation. "You perceive, it has been a long time. Yet, I am not unwilling to make the attempt."

"Then, you are willing?" said Piro.

"Entirely," said Grassfog.

"In that case," said Khaavren. "Do so at once."

"I shall, I assure you. Come," he said to the Tiassa girl, "make yourself comfortable."

"Oh, I am comfortable."

"Then permit me to examine the wound."

"How," said Ibronka, "you wish to examine her leg? Here? In front of, well, here?"

Piro felt himself flushing, though he was not certain as to the cause of this reaction, and turned away in some confusion, remarking to his father that he would see how the servants were coming along on breakfast. Kytraan, for his part, at once agreed with this plan and pretended he could assist his friend in this difficult task.

Khaavren gave his son a look full of amusement, and suggested that Röaana be brought some distance away where considerations of modesty could be met as well as sorcerous and medical requirements. While this was taking place, Tazendra took herself to a stream at the foot of the mountain where she cleaned herself up, after which she returned to the encampment and, with Aerich's help, effected such repairs on her clothing as she could (the reader must understand that she was unable to change her clothing, as her valise had been carried away when her horse had been stolen). By the time she returned to the encampment, Röaana was standing, leaning against Ibronka and smiling at Grassfog.

"It is a marvel!" cried the young Tiassa.

"Well, it is true what was said," said the onetime brigand. "It does seem easier to draw upon the power of the Orb now than it did. It seems as if—"

But Röaana was not, in fact, interested in the details. She said, "Whatever caused it, it is wonderful. I believe that, with the help of a stick, I will be able to walk nearly as fast as anyone. There is no pain, and only a little weakness in my leg."

"Is there a scar?" said Ibronka.

"None at all," said Röaana.

"Ah! That is too bad," said the Dzur sympathetically.

Khaavren smiled slightly at this interchange, then said, "Come, let us break camp. We have a long way to travel, and we should be about it at once."

"My lord," said Grassfog. "Ought I to take the time to see what I can do for those of our enemies who are wounded?"

"No," said Pel, coolly.

"Yes," said Zerika, scowling at Pel.

"In my judgment, Your Majesty," said Khaavren, "he should do what he can to comfort anyone who is dying. And, for anyone who will live, well, consider that they are enemies, and it will do us no good to have them healthy and in our rear."

"I cannot always tell who will live and who will die," said Grassfog, "unless I make the attempt at healing."

"Moreover," said Zerika, "I believe that we can accept their parole."

"Will they give their parole?" said Khaavren.

"Kill anyone who doesn't," said the Empress coolly.

"Very well," said Khaavren. "With this plan, I agree. But work quickly," he added, looking to the west. "I wish to be on our way within the hour."

The others acknowledged this request, and at once set themselves to work. While they were busy "striking camp" as is said by those of a military bent, we must now, for the sake of completeness, make certain brief but important investigations into some of the other places where certain events are taking place. While these events are not of sufficient breadth, if we may use such a term, to justify devoting a chapter of our history to them, they are, nevertheless, too significant to ignore without the danger of leaving the reader confused as to how and why later events transpired as they did.

At just about the time the Empress was setting out, then, led by the intrepid Khaavren (whom Zerika continued to insist upon calling "Captain"), Kâna was receiving a messenger as he rode near the head of a column of infantry. He permitted the messenger to approach him, whereupon he said, "Well, and who has dispatched you?"

"General Brawre, Your Majesty."

"Ah. What is it that the general wishes to communicate to me?"

"Just this, Your Majesty: Everything is moving as you wish, and the advanced units will be in sight of Dzur Mountain in nine days at the present rate of march."

"Well, that is good. I am pleased."

"The general will be pleased that Your Majesty is pleased. But, are there any additional instructions I am to give?"

"Oh, as to that, I must consult with Izak about matters of coordination. Do you go and find him, and have him meet me here."

"As Your Majesty wishes."

In a short time, Izak, still not entirely certain how he felt about his recent promotion, had arrived and was speaking with Kâna.

"The question, my dear Izak," said the latter, "is, can we be at Dzur Mountain in nine days?"

"Your Majesty," said Izak, "I *think* so."

"How, you think so?"

"That is to say, if we do not have any unexpected delays."

"Hmmm," said His Majesty. "Well then, see that we do not."

Izak bowed, and returned to his duty, worry apparent on his brow.

We must now take the reader to a point a few hours later and some distance away, from an army to a small detachment of that army—to wit, Tsanaali's detachment. As we look upon them, making their way westward at a good speed, this very speed became the subject of conversation, when Marra said, "Captain, at this pace we will kill the horses."

Tsanaali frowned and looked behind him at the remainder of his troop, noticed how spread out they had become and the sweat evident on the horses close to him, and, sighing, signaled that they should slow down to a walk.

"You are right, Marra, and you were right to mention it. I am too anxious to arrive in a timely manner."

"I understand, Captain."

"At best," said Tsanaali, "it will take us eight more days to get there."

Marra nodded. "Nine is more likely, I think."

"Yes, perhaps nine. We must not permit it to take any longer than that, however."

"Yes, Captain. I understand. But—"

"Yes, Lieutenant?"

"When we get there, what will we do?"

"As to that, I cannot say for certain. We will fight, or be sent on patrols. But, more significantly, while we travel, we will be able to learn if there is any organized resistance to His Majesty, and give a report when we arrive."

"I understand, Captain. Then, in a few days, we will begin a careful watch."

"That is right, Lieutenant. Apropos, how are our supplies?"

"We have plenty, Captain. The horses of our late opponents, and their pack animals, were well supplied. We will have no need to stop before we arrive at Dzur Mountain."

The captain nodded, and stared into the distance. "Dzur Mountain," he repeated quietly.

Far away in space, and, as we have already suggested, an unknowable distance away in time, in the Halls of Judgment, Verra was sitting with what appeared to be a young child seated on her lap. But, instead of speaking or playing with this child, Verra was addressing the Gods, saying, "We are committed now. Not only has the Orb returned, but Sethra Lavode has sent an emissary to Morrolan—Morrolan being the Dragonlord of whom, you may recall, I spoke some time ago."

"Yes," said Ordwynac. "I, for one, am unable to forget. And what will this Dragonling do, now that an emissary has arrived? Is it not the case that his little force is not only untrained and poorly organized, but also outnumbered more than thirty to one?"

"Ah," said Verra. "I perceive you have been keeping a watch on matters in their progression."

"Well."

"As for how it will all develop, there is now contact between Dzur Mountain and the Orb, and between Dzur Mountain and Morrolan and his witches. And Morrolan, I think, will soon establish contact between himself and the Orb. Thus the three sides of the triangle will come together. A triangle is a strong structure and will be hard to break."

"You speak in abstractions. I speak of a discrepancy of forces of thirty to one."

"Abstractions, my love, are not always further from the truth than facts; sometimes they are closer."

"I am not convinced."

"Then let us observe. The true test of strategy is found on the battlefield, not in the mind of a strategist."

There was some murmuring among the others of the Gods at this observation, but none of them spoke against it.

"In this instance," said Trout, speaking for the first time. "Verra is right. We must wait and see."

As Trout spoke, the child on Verra's lap shifted a little to hold the Goddess closer, as if for protection.

Chapter the Forty-Eighth

How Morrolan Prepared for Battle
And Was Forced to Consider
The Considerations of Command
Insofar as They Involve Considering

Morrolan stood before the temple he was causing to be built and met there a lone rider, an Easterner who traveled in the company of a dog and a cat, and who had generally come to be known as the Warlock. The Warlock had been observed by a workman on the temple roof some ten minutes before, and word had been sent to Morrolan, who had rushed out to meet him, so that, by the time the rider dismounted, the Dragonlord was standing next to his stirrup, where, at a polite distance, out of earshot, gathered those always curious about seeing this enigmatic individual, as well as those who had been happily watching the workmen, with the idle pleasure that combines the joy of watching someone else work when one need not, with the more sublime delight that is always associated with observing the growth of a new structure.

"You are back quickly," said Morrolan.

"Well, that is true. You have not yet left."

"We were to have left yester-day, but, it seems, we will not be ready until morning to-morrow."

"Perhaps that is just as well."

"How, do you think so?"

"Nearly."

"From this remark, and, moreover, from the very fact that you have returned so quickly, I presume you have something to tell me that might cause me to change my plans."

"That is not impossible."

"Well, let us withdraw to within the temple, find a bottle of the local wine, which, though perhaps too spicy, is nevertheless palatable for all of that, and then, why, you will give me your news."

"I can find nothing to say against this plan."

"Then let us execute it."

And, arm in arm, the tall Dragonlord and the short Easterner repaired within the temple, followed by the ubiquitous dog and the cat, where Morrolan managed to find a cool bottle of wine and two cups. As Morrolan worked the tongs and feather as best he could (he had only recently been shown, by Teldra, how to use this equipment), the Warlock said, "Well, the first thing you must know is that, indeed, there are armies marching."

"Ah, you saw them?"

"I did, or Awtlá did; it is all the same."

"Very well, if that is what you say, I will accept it. So, there are armies marching. More than one?"

"Two. One from the west, the other from the north."

"And the numbers?"

"The one from the west has nearly forty thousand."

"Forty thousand!" cried Morrolan. "Perhaps I should turn my attention to the other!"

"Alas, the other has closer to sixty thousand, including infantry and cavalry."

"Verra!" said Morrolan.

"Moreover," said the Warlock.

"Yes?"

"The army that is advancing from the west seems, unless they change directions, to be heading directly for us."

"Hmm. So that, in fact, we could defend this position, rather than attacking."

"That is true, my lord."

"And yet, I should much prefer to attack."

"Well, as to that, you must decide. You perceive, I understand nothing of these matters."

"It is clear that I must consider the matter carefully. We are gaining troops every day; the longer we remain here, the more time we can spend drilling them, which Fentor pretends will make them more effective in combat. Apropos, when is the enemy likely to be in this region?"

"Two weeks, perhaps a month."

"How precisely can you calculate wither they are bound?"

"If they continue as they are marching, they will meet at a point somewhat north of here, but, of course, we cannot know exactly."

"Very well, I will consider—"

"There is more," the Warlock interrupted.

"How, more? What then?"

"A small troop, perhaps twenty or twenty-five in number, is coming from the east, and much more rapidly."

"Well, but there must be many of these."

"This one is special."

"In what way?"

"As to that, I do not know; but Sireng assures me that there is something about this troop that makes them important."

"Very well, I will consider this. Is there anything else?"

The Warlock nodded, and said, "Does the Necromancer remain with us?"

Morrolan nodded. "She remains, though I do not know why."

"I have learned a little of her."

"Oh? Tell me."

"There are rumors of her mysteriously appearing from nowhere, and making her way to a place called Dzur Mountain."

"I have heard of this mountain," said Morrolan. "It is, after all, part of my fief."

"How, is it? But you know that it is inhabited."

"Inhabited?" said Morrolan, startled. "I had not known of this circumstance."

"How, you had not? But then, those who are working for you are, perhaps, more willing to speak casually with me than with you. But there is no doubt that there is a presence of some sort there, and, I am told, a sinister one."

"And yet," said Morrolan, "I have seen no tribute."

"As to that," said the Warlock, "I cannot comment."

Morrolan frowned and seemed to consider for a moment, but then he merely shrugged, turned away, and called for Fentor, who was acting as his second-in-command. When this worthy arrived, Morrolan, in two words, explained what he had learned, and asked for suggestions.

"We are to bring our three thousand against forty thousand?"

"Yes, that is what we must do, my dear Colonel"—the reader may perceive that, as the numbers of Morrolan's army rose, so too did Fentor's rank—"unless, that is—"

"Yes, unless?"

"Unless you can think of a way to stop these forty thousand without the use of our three thousand."

"Well, in fact, I do not believe that I can."

"Then we are required to use our army. Although—"

"Yes?"

"We have our witches." The colonel looked uncomfortable at the mention of this practice, but did not take it upon himself to voice his objections, if, indeed, he had any, to his liege. "As to whether they will be sufficient," continued Morrolan, shrugging, "who can say?"

"Your Goddess," said Fentor.

Morrolan appeared startled, as if he had not expected an answer to the question. After consideration, however, he said, "Do you know, that may be true. It may be that we will ask her. And yet, she is not speaking to us as we would like. We asked her for a sign some days ago, when word came of the approaching army, and we have received nothing—or, at any rate, nothing we have recognized as a sign."

"Who can know of the Gods?" said Fentor dismissively. "But we can know of armies. What do you have it in mind to do?"

"I wish to attack them," said Morrolan. "Yet, it would seem that we would have a better chance if we arranged for a careful defense."

Fentor frowned, as if considering the defensive possibilities of the immediate terrain. At last he said, "We can defend this ground well enough, though hardly against such odds. And, as I have said before, the more time we have to drill and train the new recruits who are still arriving, the better it will be for us, and consequently, the worse for our enemy. Of course, it is possible that they will go around us."

"Yes, but if we are in their path—"

"Yes. This warlord does like to gobble up everyone he comes across."

"Then we have no choice but to assume, as we have been, that we are to be attacked."

"Exactly."

"Very well. See to it. Do you know —"

"Yes my lord?"

"It seems to me that I have been doing a great deal of considering, of late. I wonder, is this a natural consequence of command?"

"Yes, my lord. Indeed, the more you command —"

"Well?"

"The more you must consider."

"I am not certain that I care for it."

"You will become used to it, in time."

"Will I? That is good, then. I take your word for it."

"You may."

"Very well. You know what you must do?"

"Entirely."

"Very good. I must run an errand."

"An errand, my lord? Will it be a lengthy errand?"

"A day or two."

"But, my lord —"

"You must manage things here while I am away."

"Very well, my lord," said the colonel. "But, if I may ask whither are you bound?"

"Dzur Mountain," said Morrolan. "I must learn who is this person who dwells on my land without even giving me the courtesy of a welcome, much less whatever tribute I am owed."

"But, my lord, is now the time —"

"Yes," said Morrolan, and with this word, he turned away and called for a horse to be saddled. Once this was accomplished, Morrolan rode off at once, not even giving the colonel time to reply, but rather at once turning his horse's head to the north and setting off at good speed.

As he does so, we believe that is time to look back on him for whom this history is named, that is, the Viscount of Adrilankha.

Chapter the Forty-Ninth

How Zerika Acquired Horses
For Her Small Army

Though traveling slowly, and on foot, Piro and his friends have nevertheless managed to make a certain amount of progress in the time that has elapsed since we last saw them: South Mountain has, by this time, quite vanished behind them, and they are making their way along the vast plain occasionally dotted with forests between the Shallow Sea and the Laughing River.

Ibronka, Röaana, Kytraan, and Piro walked some distance behind their elders, which permitted them to engage more freely in discourse—for it is well known that the presence of a paternal or maternal figure will inhibit even the most innocent of conversations. And, by all measures, this was among the more innocent of conversations, because they spoke of techniques of defense—a subject of which their elders would have strongly approved.

"Certainly," Kytraan was saying, "that is one of the first techniques I learned of my master. Cut high, then low, then high, then low, then high, then high again."

"Or, then low then low again," said Ibronka, agreeing. "Yes, it is a beginner's technique, but it remains effective nevertheless."

"Oh, as to its effectiveness," said Piro, "I do not question that— my father speaks of it in terms that leave no room for doubt, and, like you, insisted that I not only learn it, but practice it regularly. But the question is—"

"There is a question?" said Röaana.

"There is about to be," said Piro.

"Well," said Ibronka, "ask it, then."

"The question is, what does this teach us?"

"How," said Ibronka. "You pretend it teaches us something?"

"Without doubt," said Piro. "Consider: I cut at your head, you parry. I cut at your side, you parry. I cut at your head again, then at your side again. Now, by this time, you know very well what I am doing—that is, you are aware that I will soon change my rhythm in hopes of catching you off guard."

"Well," said Ibronka carefully, "that is true; were you to do this, I should know what you were doing."

"And then? Do you think my plan would work?"

The others considered this for a moment, and then Kytraan said, "Do you know, it would still work. That is, even knowing what was happening, the arm quickly falls into the pattern so that it is difficult to break."

"Exactly," said Röaana. "That is what makes the technique so effective."

"I agree," said Piro. "And so, I repeat my question: What does this teach us?"

"Ah," said Ibronka. "So you speak of philosophy?"

"Well," said Piro, "or of defense. They are all the same."

"That is true," said Röaana.

"And then?" said Piro. "What is the answer?"

"I know," said Kytraan.

"Then tell us," said the others.

"It tells us that, in a fight, thinking—that is, what one knows—is not of as much importance as we might believe."

"Ah," said Piro. "Well, that is an answer. Are there others?"

"Yes, I have a different answer," said Ibronka.

"Well, we will listen to your answer," said the others.

"It is this: It shows the importance of aggression—that is, of being the one who initiates the attacks."

"Yes," said Piro. "I see truth in this, too. But are there other answers?"

"To me," said Röaana, "it shows the importance of timing. That is to say, the creation of a rhythm is a powerful thing."

"I think," said Piro, "that is also true."

"But come," said the others. "What is your answer?"

"How, you believe I have an answer?"

"I nearly think you do, or you should not have asked the question," said Kytraan, smiling.

"Well, you are nearly correct," said Piro, smiling in his turn.

"Although I must say that I agree with all of the answers I have heard hitherto."

"And yet," said Röaana, "you perceive we are most anxious to hear your own answer."

"My answer is this: If I were aware of what you were doing, I could break it myself, thus catching you off guard. In this way, I become the aggressor, and I control the timing, and suddenly, it is *your* thinking that is unimportant. Or, to put the matter differently, it demonstrates the importance of remaining flexible in both body and mind, and of being ready to adapt to changing circumstances."

"Well," said Ibronka, "I see a great deal of truth in what you say."

"Do you?" said Piro, feeling himself flushing for reasons of which he was unaware.

"Well, I am gratified that you do."

"Alas," said Röaana, "we have had, as yet, little chance to test our ideas of the defense. It is vexing."

Ibronka nodded. "Soon, however. In this company, well, it cannot be long before a sword is drawn from sheath with the intention of finding more than a whetstone!"

"Oh, as to that," said Kytraan. "There is no doubt you are right. It cannot be long."

Ibronka smiled at this thought, an expression which suited her countenance splendidly.

"Indeed," said Röaana, "we did not leave our homes with the notion of merely riding horses from one place to another, however estimable the company."

"But," said Kytraan, after bowing to acknowledge his share in this compliment, "why *did* you leave your homes?"

"Oh, as to that," said Röaana, glancing quickly at her friend.

"Well, the truth is," said Ibronka, flushing slightly, "we were told to. But Röaana will explain."

"I will?"

"Why not?"

Röaana did her best to answer this question, aided now and then by Ibronka, and with comparisons to the equivalent answers by Piro and Kytraan, and so in the way the history of each of the four was gradually revealed.

This conversation has been given to show how our friends carried out their journey. While they did so, their elders were concerned with the pursuit. Khaavren was always in the lead, head forward, nearly sniffing like a hound. Zerika walked next to him, at times appearing to hold him back: developing, one might say, a serenity quite Imperial in its character. Behind them came Aerich, Tazendra, and Pel—Aerich saying little and smiling much, Tazendra doing most of the talking, and Pel putting in an occasional remark. Next were those brigands who had, either from loyalty to the Empress or from coercion at the point of a sword, come over to our friends' side: Grassfog, Iatha, Belly, and Ritt; with the servants walking behind them, and the younger generation, as it were, bringing up the rear in the fashion we have already had the honor to describe.

Near the end of the day, they found a small village called Barleytown, which is in the southern portion of the district called Agate for reasons of which we must admit our ignorance, as it cannot be considered a rocky area by any means. Doubtless it was settled by someone who had taken his name from another region in which agates of various kinds are common, for this is how names often come to be associated with places; indeed, for every "Stonybrook" that was named for a nearby stream that was full of rocks, there may be two or three that are named because Lady Stonybrook first settled it, and another named in honor of Lord Stonybrook for some action he took that was meaningful to those who settled the new town. As there are so many places in our Empire in which agates might be found, and so many nobles who have taken their name from such places, there is no reliable way to ascertain the source of the name of this district, at least until some presently unknown records should come to light (this author does not, as a rule, accept oral tradition as a reliable source of historical data!). As we are, thus, unable to determine the origin of this name, we will avoid wasting the reader's time by discussing it.

There was not much to this village—that is to say, it consisted of what had once been a posting station but was now a sort of general indoor market shared by tradesmen who would gather there on Marketday, and a small inn marked by a sign depicting a bouquet of blue flowers which was painted every year and replaced every ten years so that it remained in good condition—better condition, in fact, than the inn itself, which was of crumbling stone that had sunk nearly a foot in front, and perhaps half a foot in back, so that the entire structure had a dramatic forward tilt. The insides of this inn were filled with Teckla and ingenious devices making use of the principle of the inclined plane to prevent drinks from following the slant of the building and arriving on the floor. And in addition to the Teckla and these various devices, the place was also filled with our friends, who had entered the inn within minutes of spotting it from the road.

After taking a moment to permit their eyes to adjust to the darkness within (there was only one window, far in the back, and but two lanterns hanging from the roof), our friends looked around, only to discover that everyone in the room was looking back at them, and that no conversation of any sort was taking place. To be sure, it was a sizable little troop that invaded this position, and, more than its size, it included, above all, Zerika herself, the Orb circling her head as it had the head of the Emperor from time immemorial, which would certainly be enough to attract notice, even without the company of sixteen persons who entered all in a troop, as if they were the occupying force of an army. And we must add that this troop entered an inn that was already crowded, this being Marketday, and the inn being the only one for fifty miles in any direction.

For a moment, no one spoke, and the silence may have become uncomfortable, perhaps even threatening, but then Zerika said, "Captain, speak to them."

Khaavren winced at this title, but he responded nevertheless, clearing his throat and saying, "Greetings. Are there horses to be purchased anywhere nearby? We have silver with which to pay for them."

There was murmuring, but, for a moment, no words could be distinguished. Then, at least, a burly woman with heavy eyebrows said, "I have several, but they are a trifle winded just now, and should rest."

"I should," said Khaavren, "very much like to see them."

"In that case, my lord," said the Teckla, "I shall be glad to show them to you, and this very minute, if you wish. Although—"

"Yes?"

"While you are here, you may wish to consider sampling the muskellunge."

"Muskellunge?"

"It is similar to the common pike, but with fewer bones and better flavor. Nowhere else in the world—"

"Just the horses, if you please."

"Of course, my lord."

Khaavren turned to to Zerika and raised an inquiring eyebrow.

"Yes," said the Empress. "We shall remain here, in the meantime; we can all use refreshment, I believe."

"As Your Majesty wishes," said Khaavren, bowing.

Soon, they were all sitting, occupying one small table and one very long one, with the locals moving aside to give them room. Piro found himself sitting across from Ibronka, with Röaana on one side of him, and Kytraan on the other. "Well, my friend," said Kytraan as they seated themselves, "it seems that we have, indeed, had an adventure."

"That is true," said Piro. "And yet, you speak as if it were over."

"Oh, not the least in the world, I assure you. On the contrary, it is clear that we are quite in the middle of it, and it is far too soon to say what will happen. Yet, already, it has been an experience to remember, has it not?"

"Oh, as to that, I cannot disagree with you. But yet, my mind is drawn to what will happen next to such a degree that I have some trouble considering where we have been."

"Come then," said Ibronka suddenly. "Tell my friend and me—" here she indicated the Tiassa, "what you have done, for you perceive your conversation has made us most curious, has it not, my dear Röaana?"

"Oh, as to that," said her friend, who glanced quickly at Kytraan, before flushing and lowering her eyes, "I do not deny that I should like to hear of it."

Ibronka frowned suddenly at her friend, but then quickly turned back toward Piro and Kytraan and smiled. Kytraan, who had not noticed this interaction, glanced at Piro, who had not understood it.

The Viscount said, "Well, you must understand that, for me, it was no small thing to meet the Enchantress of Dzur Mountain."

"How," said Ibronka, "you have seen the Enchantress?"

"Seen her?" said Piro. "I give you my word, I have been as close to her as I am to you at this moment."

"Well, but then, what is she like?" said the Dzur. "You must tell me."

Piro frowned, and, after opening his mouth and closing it again more than once, he turned to Kytraan and spread his hands.

"Oh, as to what she is like," said Kytraan, "well, she is very mysterious."

"How, mysterious?" said Röaana in a small voice. "In what way?"

"Why, in every way," said Kytraan, himself at a loss as to how to describe Sethra Lavode, a predicament in which he was not alone, as countless works of history and romance can bear witness—indeed, this author will confess freely that, of all the tasks he has set for himself in placing these events before the reader, those which touch upon Sethra Lavode are certainly the most difficult. In the event, Kytraan found that he had fallen silent, leaving the question unanswered.

"And then," said Piro, attempting to save his friend from the embarrassment that he, himself, had just felt, "we had the honor of assisting Zivra—that is to say, Zerika, the Empress, in arriving at Deathgate Falls."

"Oh, you were there?"

"There?" said Kytraan, back in the conversation once more. "I nearly think we were! And I will take my oath, there was hard steel involved in the mission!"

"You fought?"

"Fought? Almost! And, if you do not believe me, well, you may ask some of our ill-favored companions, at the far side of this table, because it was some of them who were on the other end of our blades."

"And yet," said Piro, "on that occasion they could get no advantage on us, and in this endeavor, my friend Kytraan played no small role."

"Ah, is that true?" said Röaana suddenly. "Was he, that is to say, Kytraan, much in the battle?"

"Nearly," said Piro.

"Well, I do not deny that my weapon tasted blood that day," said Kytraan modestly.

"Bah," said Piro. "He was everywhere at once, was my friend the Dragonlord. Even as was our friend the Dzurlord, Tazendra. Between them, well, they put matters to rest quickly enough, and settled all outstanding questions so that there was no room for argument."

Kytraan smiled. "I do not deny that I played my rôle, yet my friend leaves out that he, himself, was in command of our little band at the time of the engagement."

"How, you?" said Ibronka, startled. "You were in command during the melee?"

"Oh, as to that," said Piro. "Well, a decision was required, that is all. And, as Zerika was no longer there, and, in fact, as far as we knew, was now dead—"

"How," said Ibronka, looking at Piro with an expression full of interest. "You thought Her Majesty was dead?"

"Well, you perceive, at that time, she was not Her Majesty," said Piro, as if this intelligence explained everything.

"Nevertheless," said Ibronka, "how is it you thought she was dead?" We should note that the Dzurlord dropped her voice slightly when saying "she," proving that, to her at least, the Empress was most certainly the Empress.

"Oh," said Kytraan carelessly, "we all assumed this when she leapt from Deathgate Falls."

"How?" said Röaana. "She leapt from Deathgate Falls?"

"Not precisely," said Kytraan. "It would be more accurate to say that, at her command, her horse leapt from the Falls, and she was mounted upon the horse."

"But, how did she survive such a leap? Is it not said that the fall is three miles deep?"

"I have heard a quarter of a league," said Ibronka. "But, nevertheless—"

"We were never able to get the complete story from her," said Piro.

Kytraan nodded. "She does not appear to wish to discuss it. The last time I asked her, she only said, 'It killed my poor horse, alas.' And, as for us, well, it is difficult to insist, when she is the Empress."

"Yes," said Ibronka. "I understand that. But, nevertheless—"

"Yes," said Piro. "I should very much like to hear about it. Perhaps, someday, we shall. But first, well, it seems we must continue forward for a time, before we have the leisure to look back."

"That is true," cried Ibronka. "Whatever adventures we have had, well, I think there are considerably more to come. Do you not agree, Viscount?"

"Even if I did not," Piro found himself saying, "I could hardly find it in me to express disagreement with you."

Ibronka frowned. "Oh? And why is that?"

"Oh," said Piro, flushing suddenly. "Because, that is to say—"

"Yes?" said the Dzurlord, appearing genuinely confused.

"Well, I mean—but stay, is that not my father returning? Yes, yes there be no doubt. Perhaps he has found us horses. I confess, I should be glad to be mounted again; my feet have not enjoyed the last few days nearly as much as I should have liked them to, although do not think I complain."

"Well, yes," said Kytraan, rushing in to help his friend. "Perhaps he has. See, he is even now approaching the Empress, and is, no doubt, explaining to her the results of his mission."

"I am convinced that that is exactly what he is doing," said Piro.

"And yet," said Ibronka, "I wonder what you meant—"

"No doubt," said Kytraan, "we will soon discover the answer, and then, perhaps, we must be ready to leave quickly."

"You are right," said Piro. "I will pay the shot."

"No," said Ibronka, "permit me."

"Nonsense," said Kytraan. "I will—"

"No," said Röaana. "I insist that I—"

At this moment, Zerika, who had been sitting at the end of the table, speaking quietly with Pel and Tazendra, rose and announced, "We have acquired horses and equipment—to be precise, we have reacquired our own, which those we are pursuing traded for fresh ones two days ago. As this is Imperial business, I will arrange for certain supplies to be gathered, and will, in addition, settle the score with our host, after which we shall be on our way. I apologize to the brave captain, who has not been able to refresh himself as the rest of us have, but, nevertheless, I begrudge the time. And so, all of you, prepare to set out at once."

There was nothing to say to this except for some form or another of murmured agreement; wherefore they all rose and made their way out of the door, where they found, as Zerika had said, that their own horses were waiting for them on the street—in addition, of course, to a number of other horses, these being the ones originally belonging to Tsanaali's troop, and which he had traded for fresh mounts. In addition, the Empress had procured all the necessary equipage for those horses—simple leather, without decoration, but perfectly serviceable.

It took some time for each to find his horse, and to get reacquainted with it; and during this time Zerika, speaking directly to the servants, arranged for fodder and other provisions. When she had finished it was becoming dark, and there was some talk of remaining the night, but Zerika pretended that they could get two or three good hours of travel in, and declared that she begrudged every hour of delay, and so they set off as soon as they were ready, leaving the village of Barleytown, where the town annals recorded the event with no mention of the Orb circling the head of the visitors, and no apparent realization of the larger events of which this was, in fact, just a small part; indeed, one with which we should not have taken up the reader's time were it not for our desire to answer the question of how they managed to acquire horses, as well as our wish to describe, at least in passing, the conversation among our four young friends.

Chapter the Fiftieth

How Morrolan Attempted to Collect Certain Funds He Believed Were Due Him As Lord of Southmoor

Morrolan, who was traveling at the same time as those to whom we have just had the honor to allude, had no one to carry on a conversation with, save only his horse, who, though occasionally spoken to, did not reply.

The distance from Morrolan's encampment to Dzur Mountain was not long—only some forty or forty-five miles, which journey Morrolan managed to complete by easy stages, arriving in the middle of the morning of the day after setting out. By "arriving" in this case, we mean that at this time he found himself at the very foot of the mountain, straining his neck looking at the imposing height, whose peak was lost in the Enclouding, and wondering exactly what he ought to do next. He resolved to look for a road or a path, or at least some way to bring his horse further up the mountain, and, at length, he found one—not, in fact, the same road that, the reader may recall, our friends had traveled up earlier, but one that was, if not so steep, rather narrower.

Morrolan negotiated this path with a certain amount of care, being rather fond of his horse and anxious not to see it come to grief, and so it was well into the afternoon before he reached a level plateau near the top of Dzur Mountain and somewhat above the Enclouding. On either hand stood peaks rising several hundred additional feet. He looked out over the plateau, and away from the brightness of the Furnace at his back, casting a long shadow before him that reminded him of late afternoon in the Eastern lands where he was born and raised.

The Dragonlord frowned as he considered the two peaks, first looking at one, then the other. Eventually, it seemed that he descried motion from the one to his left, so he continued watching that direction, and soon was convinced that, indeed, there was someone or something alive, and that, moreover, it was slowly working its way toward him.

He checked that his sword was loose in its scabbard and turned his horse's head and began riding to meet it. It became clear that it was a human figure, slowly making its way down a path toward him. Soon the figure was close enough for him to see that it was a woman dressed all in black, save for something, perhaps a gem, that glittered blue at her waist. She did not, at first glance, appear to be armed. Morrolan dismounted and stood beside his horse, waiting. Presently, she stood before him, bowed slightly, and said, "My name is Sethra Lavode."

Morrolan returned the bow, saying, "I am Southmoor."

"Well, your name is Morrolan," said the Enchantress, "and I believe I shall call you that."

"You know my name?" said Morrolan.

"So it would seem."

"But how?"

"From the demon you know. She has communicated with me."

"Ah, I see."

"Come, Lord Morrolan, let us repair within my home, where it is more comfortable. I can provide stabling for your horse and wine that may suit your palate."

"Nevertheless —"

"How, have you some quarrel with this plan?"

"I, that is to say, well, none, in point of fact."

"Then it is agreed?"

"Very well, it is agreed."

"Follow me then, my lord."

"I am following."

"That is well, for I am leading."

"Ah, when put that way, well, as the Count, it seems that I should be leading."

"There is some justice in what you say, Lord Morrolan, only —"

"Well?"

"I know where we are going."

"Yes, your argument is full of logic."

"I am delighted that you think so."

"But then, where are you leading us? Because it seems that we have entered a cave, and my horse appears not entirely happy about it."

"Well, but soon we will reach a stable, with a manger, and your horse will be more pleased. And, as for where I am leading you, well, where do I appear to be leading you?"

"Into the mountain."

"That is exactly right, then."

"You live inside the mountain?"

"No, no. Only inside a portion of it."

"Still, you must have little problem with storage."

"Oh, as far as storage is concerned, you could not be more correct—I have as much space as I could wish."

"But, as for living quarters—"

"My living quarters are tolerably comfortable, as you will soon see."

"Well, if so, it will be very strange for the inside of a mountain."

"Indeed? Well, but how many mountains have you seen the inside of?"

Morrolan considered this for a moment, before saying, "I have taken refuge from storms in certain caves, but, in fact, it is true that I have never been inside of a mountain."

"And so, you perceive, you have nothing to judge against."

"That is true, and yet it seems—but here are the stables, just as you said."

"Does that astonish you, sir?"

"Not in the least, madam."

"Leave your horse here, then, and I shall arrange for her care."

"I no longer doubt you in anything."

"That is best, believe me."

"You perceive, I am following you once more."

"Very well."

"Are there many of these stairs?"

"Forgive me if I have never counted them, but, you see, we must come to a place very near to the mountain's peak, which is where I make my living area."

"I see. So that, yes, there may be many stairs. It is of no matter, for I should have had to climb this distance anyway, and stairs are easier than mountain paths."

"That is my opinion as well, which is why I had the steps cut into the rock."

"And it was well done."

"I am delighted that you think so. And here we are, arrived at my living area. Now, just a few more short steps, and you may sit at your ease."

"I will not deny that I shall be glad to do so."

"Apropos, have you a taste for wine?"

"Why yes, I rather like wine, if it is good."

"As to that, you must be the judge."

"Very well, I shall be happy to sample what you have."

"That is good, for, you perceive, I have plenty of space that is ideally suited for storing wine, and so I have devoted a considerable portion of it to that noble task."

"How, noble?"

"You do not the think the word well chosen?"

"I had not previously considered the word as it might be applied to the storing of wine."

"Well—ah, here we are. Please, sit. Well, it would seem to my mind that storing wine is far more noble than for large groups of strangers to come together on ground none of them care about for the purpose of slaughtering one another."

"I had not considered things in this way—but who is this?"

"You may call him Tukko; I have been calling him that more often than anything else of late. Tukko, bring the young Dragonlord some wine. Something peppery, I think, and rich. And I will have whatever you select for him."

The servant bowed and departed.

"Come, you were saying?" said the Enchantress.

Morrolan spent a brief moment looking around, considering where he was, and the quiet, dark elegance of the furnishings, and realized that he had, to some degree, lost control of the encounter from its very beginning, and, furthermore, that he had not the least idea with whom he was dealing, nor what her powers, resources, or abilities might be.

"I am here," he said without further preamble, "to discuss the matter of tribute."

"How," said Sethra in apparent confusion. "You wish to give me tribute?"

Morrolan cleared his throat. "That was not, in fact, precisely my meaning."

"Well, but then, explain further."

"I am about to do so."

"Very well, I am listening."

"This is it, then: I am the Count of Southmoor."

"I do not dispute that."

"You do not?"

"Not the least in the world, I assure you."

"That is well then."

"I am glad you think so."

"Oh, I do."

"And, as I am the Count of Southmoor—"

"Yes, as you are the Count?"

"And as, moreover, Dzur Mountain lies within the county of Southmoor—"

"Yes?"

"Well, then it would seem . . ."

"Yes?" said the Enchantress after a moment. "It would seem—? Ah, here is the wine."

"Yes, and I find it most excellent."

"Do you? Then I am gratified."

"I am glad you are."

"But then, you were saying? It would seem—?"

"Well, it would seem that you would owe me a certain tribute, as I am your liege."

"That I—?"

"Judging by your countenance, I beg to submit that I have astonished you."

"Nearly," said Sethra after a moment.

"That was not my intention."

"Nevertheless, I confess that you have done so. I am astonished."

"And yet, it would seem—"

"Well, but what sort of tribute would you imagine you are owed?"

"Oh," said Morrolan, suddenly confused, because he had not gotten that far in his calculations, "whatever is customary."

"Customary?"

"Yes. Excuse me, but a singular expression has crossed your countenance."

"And if it has?"

"It nearly seems as if you are trying to contain laughter."

"Well, that is not impossible."

Morrolan stood abruptly. "Come then, perhaps we ought to arrive at a place where there is sufficient space to laugh together."

At this, Sethra did laugh, albeit only briefly. "I do not believe, my dear liege lord, that you wish to duel with me. Besides, I am armed, as you see, only with a knife."

"Bah. You must have a sword about the place."

The Enchantress chuckled. "Come, come. Sit down and drink your wine, young Dragon."

"Sit down? I hardly think so. So far am I from sitting down, that I must beg you to arm yourself at once." And, as if to impress upon Sethra the sincerity of his feelings, he drew his sword.

Sethra sighed. "It seem you have drawn a weapon."

"Well, and if I have? Come, you must know that such a statement is not ambiguous, but, on the contrary, can only have one interpretation."

"Oh, I do not argue that, and yet—"

"Well?"

"I perceive you have not pointed it at me."

"Well, but I promise you I shall do so, the instant you have armed yourself."

"So then, you keep your weapon out of line because I am unarmed?"

"How, does this astonish you?"

"Nearly."

Morrolan frowned. "But why?"

"I begin to believe that you truly have no notion of with whom you are conversing."

Morrolan shrugged. "You have given me your name."

Sethra tilted her head to side, as if this view of the young Drag-onlord might provide a clue as to his character that would not be oth-erwise apparent. As she studied him, she idly tapped the blue hilt of the dagger at her waist. After a moment, she sighed and rose to her feet. "For some reason, Morrolan, I am loath to destroy you. And yet, you seem insistent—"

"Madam—" said someone from behind Morrolan.

Sethra's eyes focused on a spot over Morrolan's shoulder. Mor-rolan did not turn around, but, rather, moved to the side so that he could observe who had entered behind him without, even momentar-ily, losing sight of his opponent. In this way, he observed the strange wizened little man that the reader has met before.

"What is it, Tukko?" said Sethra.

"I beg you to recall what I told you some years ago."

"Tukko," said Sethra, who had still not drawn her dagger, "I must observe that you have told me a thousand thousand things over the years. Which do you have in mind."

"Need I repeat myself, madam?"

"I'm afraid you must," said Sethra.

Tukko's face seemed to twitch peculiarly, and he intoned slowly, "From the east shall he come, strong in ignorance, short in patience, hiding his wit beneath arrogance—"

Morrolan felt his eyes narrow, and he said in a low voice, "If this is to refer to me, sir, I must insist—"

Tukko continued, "And he shall be searching for blood, yet he shall find a black wand, and this wand in his hand will preserve a world."

Sethra stared at Tukko. "He—?"

Morrolan said, "Black wand?"

Tukko nodded to Sethra, turned on his heel, and left.

Sethra stared at Morrolan, who said, "Madam—"

Sethra shook her head and made a quick motion of her hand, and Morrolan's sword suddenly split lengthwise, from point to pommel, and fell to the floor with more of a tinkle than a crash.

Morrolan stared at the Enchantress. "Madam—"

Sethra seated herself once more, a singular expression on her countenance, as one who has just experienced an epiphany.

Morrolan said, "My sword—"

"We will attend to that by and by, my lord Morrolan."

"And yet, I insist—"

"Please," said Sethra. "Let us not fight. I promise you, I had not the least intention in the world of giving offense. Moreover, I believe I shall come to like you. As for a sword, it will be replaced. And, as for tribute, well, I shall, no doubt, find something suitable."

Morrolan stared at her, unable to decide precisely how to respond to these astonishing words. Before he was able to make a decision, Sethra was continuing as if nothing had happened.

"Please sit down," she said. "Tell me about yourself. From the way you attack your consonants as if they were an enemy swordsman and swallow your vowels as if they were a light snack, I would judge that you were raised in the East. Is it not so?"

Morrolan still hesitated, as if uncertain if he were being mocked, but at length he relented and sat down once more. "Yes, I was raised in the East."

"Should you meet my apprentice, she will, no doubt have many questions for you, as she has no small interest in the East."

"You have an apprentice?"

"Over the years, I have had several."

"But, what are they apprenticed to? That is, what do they learn?"

"Well, sorcery, for one thing."

"Sorcery?"

"Magic."

"I know of the Eastern magical arts. Is it, perhaps, another word for the same thing?"

"I do not believe so. Perhaps, now that the Orb has returned, I could show you something of sorcery, if you become a citizen."

"Citizen?"

"Of the Empire."

"You perceive, I know nothing about this."

"You will come to understand, I have no doubt. Where you lived in the East, was there not a kingdom?"

"There was a small principality where I lived, but then, in Blackchapel—"

"Blackchapel?"

"A village I came to. There was nothing in Blackchapel except Blackchapel."

Sethra frowned, as if there were something about the name, Blackchapel, that engaged her interest.

"You came to a village where they worshiped black?"

"Well, yes, you could say that."

"On foot?"

"I was, in fact, walking, yes."

"And you met there a fool?"

"How could you have known that?"

"And the fool led you to your name?"

"I . . . that is to say, well, that is one way to look at it."

"And then the fool brought you to a lady who rode in a coach?"

Morrolan frowned. "It was more complicated than that. There was one lady, and then the coach brought another, but that was a hundred years—"

"And the lady brought you to three sisters?"

"I—well, yes, but really only one of them. You see—"

"And you dreamed of a black staff?"

"That much is true."

"And of water that had never seen the light of day?"

"How do you know all of this?"

Sethra continued staring intently at Morrolan. "It is an old prophecy," she said. "Very old."

Morrolan shifted in his chair. "I am not," he said, "entirely certain I enjoy being in a prophecy."

"Well, but this will happen, if your soul-mate is a goddess."

Morrolan was now, without doubt, truly amazed. "How could you know—?"

"I am," she said, "the Enchantress of Dzur Mountain."

"But, madam, how is it that being the Enchantress of Dzur Mountain gives you this knowledge?"

"I read a great deal," said Sethra. "But come, tell me about this village of Blackchapel, for you perceive it interests me greatly."

Soon, without being entirely aware of how it happened, Morrolan was answering the Enchantress's questions as if it were the most natural thing in the world that he do so. Indeed, as the evening wore on, he found that he was answering questions about himself more fully than he had ever done before, and even that he was often required to stop and consider carefully in an effort to give his host the most truthful and complete answer he could to questions that from another he should have considered an impertinence at best, and a deadly insult at worst. And if she rarely said a word of herself, and then only in the most general terms, well, it did not occur to Morrolan to question this until much later when he was reviewing in his mind the remarkable events of the day.

Presently he found that he had accepted an invitation to stay for a meal; no small matter—for in the Eastern culture in which he had been raised, it was considered dishonorable to share food with an enemy. While he was never afterward able to recall exactly what was served, he did remember enjoying it at the time, although his attention was mostly on the conversation, in which Sethra continued to ask probing and personal questions which Morrolan answered fully and forthrightly. The conversation, we should add, continued for some hours.

It was early the next morning that Morrolan rode away from Dzur Mountain, on a horse which was no little refreshed, and with Sethra Lavode's "tribute" hanging from the scabbard at his side. We should say that at this time he was aware that there were unusual properties about this weapon, but he was not aware of what they were—the Enchantress had told him little, merely handing it to him with a wry remark as he prepared for his departure. He had, we should say, entirely forgotten the matter of the tribute he was supposed to have collected, and so accepted the offering with silent astonishment. "We shall meet again, I am certain" had been Sethra's final remark, to which Morrolan had replied with a bow.

During the return journey, Morrolan often let his hand come to rest on the pommel of the weapon while he considered the peculiar feelings that came over him when he touched it, yet he denied himself the pleasure of actually drawing it from its scabbard, which was of wood and iron, covered in leather, and decorated with a peculiar symbol. He slept under the open sky, and arrived the next day back at his encampment, where he was at once pleased by the visible progress that had been made in the temple during his absence. Moreover, it seemed that his small army had noticeably grown, and this could not help but delight him.

As he gave his horse into the care of a groom, he observed the Warlock standing near the temple, speaking with Lady Teldra. The dog and the cat lay near their feet, both looking about as if uncertain the area could yet be considered safe. Teldra and the Warlock both looked up and bowed, which salute Morrolan returned politely.

"Welcome back," said Teldra. "I hope your journey was pleasant."

"And," added the Warlock, "I hope that it was productive."

"Both," said Morrolan laconically. "But tell me, what has happened here while I was gone? Is there news?"

"In a sense," said the Warlock.

"In a sense?"

"That is to say, after a fashion."

"Come, I am certain you can speak more clearly than that."

"I mean only this: There is news of some kind, but I do not know it. I have observed scouts arriving, and consulting with your commander, Fentor, and being sent out again. But I do not know what they have reported."

"Ah, well, I understand perfectly, and I will speak with Fentor."

"An admirable plan, if I may be permitted an opinion," observed the Warlock.

"My lord," said the Issola, "would you permit me to bring you refreshment?"

"Why, yes, Teldra. That would be splendid."

"I shall do so at once."

"Inside, near the altar. And have Fentor and Arra sent to me, and we will consult."

"At once, my lord."

"And," added the Warlock, "please accept my compliments on your new weapon. Is there a story that comes with it?"

"There is, indeed, and once the others have arrived, I should be glad to tell you of it."

"And I shall be glad to listen. What of that Necromancer?"

Morrolan frowned. "Yes, let her come as well. It will be a full council of war. There may be much to consider."

Soon they had gathered together, and Morrolan studied his friends and companions. Fentor spoke first, however, saying, "I perceive you are armed differently than when you left. You had, then, a gift of the Enchantress?"

"A gift?" said Morrolan. "Well—" He paused. It had been on his mind to say that it was tribute, yet, in the event, he merely shrugged.

"Well," said the commander, "may I see it? Because, unless I am deceived, it is a Morganti weapon."

"A what?"

"It has certain properties."

"What kind of properties?"

"It will destroy the soul of anyone it kills."

Morrolan frowned. "I see. Are there many of these around?"

"Too many. But few, I think, as powerful as yours appears to be. Once it is clear of its sheath, we shall know for certain."

"Very well," said Morrolan, and drew the weapon for the first time—an event as monumental, in its own way, as the restoration of the Empire itself, not the least because it had no little to do with the preservation of that Empire; a fact which is not widely known, but which the author will demonstrate as our history unfolds.

In appearance, the sword was not unusual—of a good size for a Dragon warrior, of black metal that seemed not to reflect the light, with a simple crosspiece and a smooth black hilt.

The effect on those present of this apparently simple longsword was nothing less than profound. Teldra and Fentor, who had, perhaps, less sensitivity to psychic phenomena than the others, found themselves on their feet, back several paces, and were unaware of making the decision to move. It was, as Teldra described later, "as if Death itself had loomed over us all, holding out his arms in an invitation at once terrifying and nearly irresistible." Fentor, for his part, became aware that it was taking all of his strength to avoid trembling visibly, and he was utterly unable to keep the look of fear and horror from his countenance.

The Warlock gave a cry, almost a screech, and his familiars at once took their alternate forms, turning into a snarling dzur and a bristling wolf—the first time anyone had seen this transformation, and yet this went unnoticed in the turmoil of the moment. He spoke very rapidly in an Eastern language that not even Morrolan had ever heard pronounced, and made various gestures with the fingers of his right hand.

Arra also made gestures, although different ones, and those with both hand and arms—she seemed to be warding things from her, or putting a barrier between herself and Morrolan. And, while it is not possible to move from one place to another without traveling through the intervening space—at least, it is not possible using the arts of Eastern witchcraft—nevertheless it might have appeared that Arra had done so, so rapidly did she put a distance of several yards between herself and the naked weapon.

Even the Necromancer was visibly startled, and, with a couple of passes of her hands, built a sort of wavering, prismatic barrier between herself and Morrolan—a barrier which, after a few moments, she allowed to fade into the nothingness from which it had grown, but which left a certain impression in the minds of those who had seen it. As for how she felt, beyond her actions, we have no way of ascertaining this, but it seems clear that, like the others, she was startled and not a little frightened by the power emanating from Southmoor's hand.

To Morrolan, however, the result of his action was not only more profound, as the reader might expect, but was also entirely different, as we will detail at once: He felt, then, as if he had suddenly met again an old friend whom he had not seen in many years; simultaneously, it was as if seeing for the first time the person one knows will become one's lover. More than this, he felt flooded with well-being, as if, after a good night's sleep, one awoke to find klava ready and a day stretching out filled with only those things one wishes to do.

And above all of this, Morrolan was aware that, more than ever before, he would very much like to find something to kill. By preference, many things, all of them eager to fight back. How long they stood there, none of them was able afterward to say, but, after what seemed like hours, Morrolan at least pronounced the words, "My dream."

"Your dream?" said the Warlock.

"Ah," said Arra. "Yes, my lord. I remember it. I believe you must have been foresighted then; it was certainly a dream sent by the Goddess."

"A dream?" said the Warlock, in a tone indicating that he was only barely able to speak.

Morrolan turned to him and nodded. "Yes, I had a dream of holding a black wand."

"And this is your black wand?" said the Warlock.

"Yes," said Morrolan. "Yes, it is."

There seemed to be nothing to say to this, so the Warlock said nothing. Fentor was the next to catch his breath, as we might say, and he said, "My lord—"

"Well?"

"Give me ten weapons like that, and I shall fear no one."

"As for ten of them, I'm afraid that would be difficult. But, at any rate, we have one."

Gradually, hesitantly, they seated themselves, all of them looking warily at Morrolan's "black wand" as if it were a greensnake. After a moment, with some hesitation, he sheathed it, and found to his surprise—and pleasure—that he still maintained a certain sense of contact with it; the others were equally pleased that they were no longer aware of its presence, except in the dimmest, most distant way, feeling only a vague unease such as one feels on a journey when convinced one has failed to bring everything needed, but cannot remember what has been left behind.

"Well, then," said Morrolan, just as if nothing out of the ordinary course of events had occurred, "I gather, Fentor, that there were developments while I was away."

Fentor blinked twice, deliberately, as if doing so required concentration, then said, "Your pardon, my lord?"

"Developments. What has happened while I was gone?"

"Ah! Yes! The war!"

"Yes, the impending invasion of our home by a large army. I trust you have not forgotten about it?"

"In fact, for just a moment, I had."

"Well, but do you recall it now?"

"Oh, without doubt, my lord."

"Good, then. And, have there been developments concerning it?"

"Yes, my lord."

"And will you tell me what they are?"

"Whenever Your Lordship wishes."

"Whenever I wish? I think I have been wishing for nothing else for an hour!"

"Then, my lord, this is it: We have reports that the large army is moving more quickly, the still larger army more slowly, and the small troop is being pursued by a smaller troop. Moreover—"

"Yes, moreover?"

"I have calculated their destination more precisely."

"Well, and?"

"Yes, my lord?"

Morrolan groaned softly, clenched and unclenched his fist, then said, very carefully, "According to your calculation, what is their destination?"

"Dzur Mountain, my lord."

"Dzur Mountain," repeated Morrolan.

"Yes, my lord."

Morrolan looked at the others in the room, and met each of their eyes. "Well," he said after a moment. "They must certainly be stopped, then."

"Is Dzur Mountain important?" asked Arra. "That is, must it be defended."

"Yes," said Morrolan.

"Very well," said Fentor.

"How long until they reach us?"

"Three days, maybe four, certainly not more than a week unless they suddenly stop or change their destination."

"And our preparations?"

"As complete as we can make them."

Morrolan turned to the Necromancer. "Can you help?"

"My lord?"

"Sorcery. I have learned something of sorcery. I am told it can do amazing things. I don't know. Blast them with fire, or make stones fall on their heads, or create an illusion of giant butterflies with nine-inch teeth. Something."

"I know little of this sorcery, but—"

"Yes?"

"I can do something."

He nodded, and turned to Arra. "My witches?"

"There is little we can do, but what there is, we will. We will make the enemy afraid, and make our friends confident and strong."

"That is not so little," added Fentor.

Morrolan nodded and turned to the Warlock, who said, "I will be there, but I don't know what I can do—"

"Perhaps I do," said Morrolan. "I must give this matter more thought. Come back tonight, all of you, around the seventh hour, after I have had time to consider matters, and we will see what sort of plans we can make."

"Very well," said the others, and, with a last glance at the weapon hanging at Morrolan's side, they left him alone with his thoughts and certain maps which Fentor had caused to be prepared, in order to permit him to contemplate the forthcoming battle.

Having brought up this battle, before closing this chapter of our history, we should like to take the opportunity to say two words about this conflict in general.

The Ninth Battle of Dzur Mountain (or the Tenth, if the reader prefers) was not fought in the immediate environs of Dzur Mountain—on the contrary, the battlefield was some forty or forty-five miles south of it, fought for the most part along a small stream called Lostoar Brook, which ran generally east to west near to the southern border of the Southmoor County—indeed, it had at one time been the boundary, until it was observed that, over the centuries, the stream was creeping generally southward for reasons best known to itself, and this migration, though entirely approved of by the various Counts of Southmoor, was seen differently by the Counts of Iadim, and so, after the Fifteenth Issola Reign, the boundary was determined by certain hills and valleys which promised to hold their positions. But then, it should be remembered that, of the many battles called "the Battle of Dzur Mountain," at least three of them were fought at least twenty miles from the foot of the mountain, so to give it this name is merely to continue a tradition, as it were.

Morrolan's army—or Fentor's—was not prepared to Fentor's satisfaction, and, indeed, only the fact that a certain number of the recruits had military experience (these, of course, being at once made sergeants) saved it from, in Fentor's words, "an uncommon foul-up from the front to the back and from one end to the other." Instead, it was, in the view of this worthy commander, "just close enough to ready to permit itself to receive some amount of slaughter before dissolving utterly." Of course, holding this opinion in no way kept Fentor from doing everything he could to prevent it, and when word reached him that one of the armies—the smaller of the two—had made camp barely ten miles away, he at once began to arrange the details of supply and movement lines that he believed would be required by the battle he foresaw.

The morning after Morrolan's return from Dzur Mountain (that is to say, the very morning when Fentor learned of the proximity of the enemy troops), Fentor and Morrolan spoke, both of them on the roof of the temple (on which, we may add, construction had never halted), and both of them staring eastward, toward where the enemy was encamped.

"Then you agree," said Morrolan. "We must attack, and bring them to battle before the other army converges?"

Fentor sighed. "I can see no other way. And yet—"

"Well?"

"You perceive, we are outnumbered. And that by, well, by a great deal."

"Yes, I know that. However, they are not expecting to be attacked, and that must be good for something."

"That is true, they are not, and it is. But then—"

"Yes?"

"With an untrained corps, the movements required for defense are easier to execute than those required for attack."

"Bah! What is required? You say, charge, and they charge."

"My lord—"

"Well?"

"You must trust me, it is more complex than you pretend."

Morrolan appeared unconvinced.

"Shall I explain, my lord?"

Morrolan sighed. "I suppose you had better." As he prepared to listen and attempt to understand, he took a drink of water, a deep breath, and a glance in the opposite direction, at which time he suddenly frowned and said, "What is that?"

Fentor followed his glance, frowned, and said, "What?"

"There is something on this side of the temple that I had not observed before."

"Ah! Battlements, my lord."

"Battlements?"

"Yes. For defense."

"For—who had this done?"

"I did, while you were gone. You would have noticed them yesterday if you had not been distracted."

"Oh, I do not doubt that. But for what reason are they there?"

"My lord, if we are required to withstand a charge—which is very probable, even if we begin by making one ourselves—those few changes will permit our survival a longer time than—"

"And you made these changes in the temple—the temple dedicated to my patron Goddess—without asking me first?"

Fentor looked at him coolly. "My lord, you were away, and had I waited for your return, there would have been no time. Moreover, you told me to take charge. I had to make an abrupt decision, and I did so."

"You were wrong," said Morrolan.

A certain redness came into Fentor's countenance, and he gave Morrolan a stiff bow.

Morrolan studied him, and, for the first time, showed some signs of what he would become. He said, "You still believe you were right?"

Fentor remained mute.

"Answer!" said Morrolan.

"I do, my lord!" said Fentor, glaring now.

"Well, then explain to me why, and perhaps I will be convinced."

Fentor, who had no small amount of experience with commanders, not to mention generals, stared in surprise.

"You will?"

"Perhaps."

Fentor frowned, "I will explain my thinking, then."

"Do so," said Morrolan.

How Our Friends Prepared for Battle,
With Some Discussion of How Conversations
Can Be Overheard, and How This Might Lead
To the Transmission of Significant Messages

While Fentor attempts to explain to Morrolan certain principles of military science—principles which, we fear, could only interest a small fraction of our readers—we will turn our attention to a place some fifteen miles away—because even as Morrolan and Fentor were looking east, so Zerika and Khaavren were looking west.

"I confess," Zerika was saying, "that I should feel better if I knew how many of them there were."

"Well," said Khaavren. "Since you bring that up, so would I. It seems clear that those we pursue have either joined with a larger army, or are about to do so. I, like you, wish to know which it is, as well as the size and precise disposition of this larger army which is, at this moment, only theoretical."

"Is there a way to learn?"

"I could go there."

"I should rather you send someone. I wish you to stay nearby in order that I might have your advice."

"What advice can I give without knowing more about our enemy?"

"As to that, I do not know. But send someone else."

"Very well." Khaavren frowned, considered, and then gave instructions to Pel and Kytraan, who bowed and departed without comment. Khaavren turned to Zerika and said, "Well?"

"Yes?"

"You wished my advice?"

Zerika shook her head.

"How, you do not?"

"In fact, Captain, what I wish for is your companionship. I find that having you nearby reassures me."

Khaavren clenched his teeth severely against the display of any emotion, and gave the sort of grunt that he had been accustomed to make when, as Captain of the Phoenix Guard in what he thought of as his "old life," the Emperor had uttered some enormity to which he, Khaavren, had been unable to make any response that was both honest and respectful.

Zerika interpreted this grunt correctly and made the only possible response—that is to say, none at all. In this, her actions were as appropriate to her station as Khaavren's were appropriate to his. At this point, the reader may have observed that, in many ways, Zerika had fallen instantly into her rôle—she was acting more Imperial, one might say, with each passing day. Was this because she came from the House of the Phoenix, and, what is more, from a line that had produced many Emperors? Was it a chance matter of character? Was it from certain training she had received, perhaps unknowingly, during her youth?

Alas, this is not a question the historian can answer. We know how she acted, because all of the records are clear on this matter, as well as countless letters and journals that speak of interactions with her. But we cannot know why it is, and moreover, we must look with great suspicion upon anyone who claims to such knowledge.

An hour or two later, Pel and Kytraan returned and presented themselves, saying, "We beg permission to report on our mission."

Khaavren nodded, and Zerika said, "I should like nothing better. Did you learn anything?"

"Nearly," said Kytraan.

"The troop we fought with before is now scarcely two miles from us," said Pel.

"And what are they doing?" asked Zerika eagerly.

"As we are," said Kytraan. "That is to say, resting."

Zerika nodded. "Yes, we are close. If, indeed, their destination is Dzur Mountain, as it appears to be, then another two days will see us there, and they wish to be rested."

"No doubt Your Majesty is correct," said Pel, bowing slightly.

"Well," said Khaavren. "Come, let us hear. You were able to find them, I take it?"

"Nearly," said Kytraan. "That is, we were nearly as close to Grita as I am to—"

"Grita?" said Khaavren, glancing quickly at Aerich, then at Pel. "Grita was there?"

"We saw her speaking with them some days ago."

"That is true, but I had not known she was still with them."

The Yendi nodded. "She is. I recognized her from a distance away—you perceive, she has a distinctive posture."

"And so you went closer?"

"Closer?" said Kytraan. "He walked up to the camp as if he were invisible, and there were no danger of being seen, or, if there was, then no harm could come to us if they saw us."

"There were certain obstacles to their line of sight," said Pel. "It was possible to get very close without being seen. Their watch was lax."

Kytraan looked at Pel as if about to question this analysis, but, in the end, said nothing. Khaavren understood exactly, however, and said, "Tell us what was said, then."

Pel permitted a thin smile to cross his countenance. "You pretend I would listen in on a private conversation?"

"I believe you might," said Khaavren. "And I am nearly convinced that you did."

"Well, you are not far wrong."

"And then?"

"Grita explained to the young lieutenant that what she called the 'main army' was only ten or eleven miles away, and, moreover, that there was only one small garrison between them and Dzur Mountain."

"A garrison?"

"So Grita explained."

"What do we know of this garrison?"

"Grita said it numbered a few scant thousands, and had only the barest of defensive fortifications."

"Then it will not delay the main army for long," said Khaavren, "if the main army is, indeed, worthy of the name. Is there more?"

"There is indeed."

"Let us hear it, then."

"They spoke of us."

"Did they?" said Khaavren. "I am not startled. I ought to have noticed the back of my neck itching. My mother always said that if the back of your neck itches, someone is speaking ill of you."

"Yes?" said Kytraan. "I had not heard this. What if the back of your neck, rather than itching, hurts?"

"That means someone has stuck a knife into your neck."

Kytraan looked carefully at the captain, wondering if he were being made sport of; but Khaavren's attention was once more on Pel, who was saying, "Grita wants very much to do us harm, my friend."

"Well, that we had already known. But does she now have a plan for how to go about it?"

"Oh, that one is never without a plan. It is in the blood."

"Ah. The oven says the candle is hot? But go on, my friend. Let us hear this famous plan, for I have no doubt you crept close enough and stayed long enough to hear every detail."

"You are not far wrong," said Pel, permitting himself a thin smile.

As he spoke, the others gathered close to listen. Zerika frowned, as if considering whether this should be permitted, but in the end said nothing. Pel, for his part, quickly noted the audience, then turned his attention once more to the Empress and Khaavren.

"She wishes," said Pel without further preamble, "to have us caught between themselves and the army with whom we are all presently closing."

"Was that the plan?" said Kytraan, a look of astonishment crossing his countenance.

"Without question," said Pel.

"And yet, I heard no such thing."

"You heard, my friend," said Pel coolly. "However, you did not listen."

"How, I did not listen? Yet, I give you my word, my attention was concentrated upon nothing else in the world."

"Nevertheless, when Grita made that reference to being a hammer, what did you imagine she meant?"

"Why, I didn't know."

"And then, when that lieutenant remarked that the anvil had more pressing business?"

"Well—"

"And Grita spoke about waiting until the anvil was secure before striking?"

"Upon my word," murmured Zerika, "I believe I am beginning to understand, myself."

"Pel has remarkably good hearing," said Khaavren, also in a low murmur. "I have had occasion to make this observation before."

"But then," continued Kytraan, "did they say when and where?"

"They did indeed," said Pel, "and in terms that left no room for misunderstanding."

"Bah!" said Kytraan. "Impossible!"

"Not the least in the world," said Pel.

"And yet—"

"Listen, my young friend, and learn."

"Very well, I listen."

"As we sat—"

"Sat!"

"Very well, crouched then."

"I did not believe a man could be made to occupy such a small amount of space."

"Oh, it can be done, believe me—and, you perceive, we were not seen."

"That is true, nor heard—though I confess that, at the time, I was convinced the entire encampment would hear my heart pounding before they even discovered the gentleman whom we left sleeping at his post."

"Bah. There was no danger."

"So you have convinced me. But go on, then. As we were crouching while Grita and the lieutenant, Tseranok, were—"

"Tsanaali," corrected Pel gently.

"Yes, Tsanaali, were speaking."

"Exactly," said Pel.

"And I listened to what they said to each other."

"Bah!"

"Very well, then, I *heard* what they said."

"Yes, that I accept."

"And while I believe what you say about hammers and anvils—"

"And you are right to do so."

"—I give you my word they never mentioned times, or dates, or places."

"No, but they did speak of horses."

"Horses?"

"Yes, don't you recall?"

"Well, I remember Grita said something about horses, but she spoke of horses in general, not of specific horses."

"What is a specific horse but one of the general class of horse?"

"And yet—"

"So if one were to say something that is true of all horses, it follows, does it not, that this must be true of a specific horse?"

"Well, that is true," said Kytraan. Tazendra, though she looked doubtful at this proposition, did not venture to comment upon it.

"What," prompted Pel, "did she say of horses?"

"Why, very little. Only that they needed water."

"Exactly! She said that horses need water! By the Orb, there is nothing wrong with your ears!"

"You think not? That is good, then. I feel better in regards to my ears."

"And you are right to, for they function admirably."

"But, there may be a deficiency between them."

"You think so?"

"It is possible. Because, even though we agree about what my ears heard, well—"

"Yes?"

"I cannot conceive how the mention of horses requiring water—which the Gods know is true, because they were not built like clidogs to live for days without water, any more than clidogs were built like horses to be ridden—I cannot conceive of how this wisdom brings us any closer to knowing when and where they plan to bring us to battle."

"And yet," said Pel, "to me it explains everything."

"Impossible!"

"Nonsense."

"But then—"

"Come, Khaavren. Does it explain everything to you?"

"Nearly," said Khaavren. "That is, I could now point to the spot on the map where the attack is to take place, and name the precise hour at which it is to occur."

Kytraan now stared at Khaavren as if he were a specter emerging from Deathgate Falls. "And yet, I do not see —"

"That is all right," said Pel. "Our worthy Tazendra does not understand either, and yet she is our close friend."

"In fact," said Tazendra complacently, "I do not, but matters like this no longer disturb my peace of mind."

"They do not?" said Kytraan.

"No, because soon Pel will tire of his game, and point me at someone to fight, and then, well, I will fight, and all of this careful contemplation will be forgotten, and only the fight, and its results, will be remembered."

Kytraan now looked at Tazendra in wonder. "Do you know, I would never have thought a Dzur could have so well explained the heart of a Dragon."

Tazendra bowed, accepting this as the compliment it was. Kytraan bowed back, then turned toward Pel, who, if truth be told, was himself rather astonished at the exchange he had just witnessed. After a moment, however, he remembered the discussion in which he had been engaged and said, "It is not so difficult, my young friend. Consider, we have horses, do we not?"

"My mind is nearly convinced that we do," said Kytraan. "And there are other parts of me that have no doubt at all."

"Well then, as Grita pointed out, we must water them."

"Well, yes, that is but natural."

"Where, then, are we to do so?"

"I would imagine at a stream or a river."

"Those are few in this region."

"And yet, are we not at one now?"

"We are. And that is why we picked this place to rest for the day, even though it was not quite dark."

"Yes, and therefore?"

"Therefore, a careful examination of a good map will tell us where we must arrive at to-morrow, where the enemy army must be—for they also have horses, and where Tsanaali and Grita must be, for they have horses as well. And, as we are moving faster than the army, and, moreover, as we know that Tsanaali wishes to converge with them—"

"Ah! I comprehend. But, have we a map? I confess that I have not seen one."

"My dear," said Pel, "we have all the maps that have ever been made."

"How, we do?"

"Nearly. We have the Orb."

A look of wonder crossed Kytraan's countenance. "I had not thought of that," said Kytraan. He turned suddenly to Piro. "Had you understood?"

"In fact," said Piro, smiling, "were I not ashamed to admit it in front of the Count my father, well, I should have to confess to being as astonished as you."

Khaavren, for his part, permitted himself another smile, and, bowing, turned to Zerika. "If Your Majesty will condescend to draw us a map of the region, well, we will soon enough know where they plan their attack—or their ambuscade, if it please you."

Zerika, who had a fair hand, quickly sketched out a map (after causing the Orb to glow enough to see by—for it was becoming quite dark), and, as promised, they were soon able to determine that they would be likely to meet up with their enemies at a small stream called Lostoar near the southern border of a duchy called Southmoor.

"In the late afternoon, the day after to-morrow," said Pel.

"Or, rather, the morning of the day after; because I believe, knowing what we know, we may wish to delay the attack until the morning."

"That may be," said Pel, "only—"

"Yes?"

"What will we do for water for the horses if we stop short of Lostoar?"

"We will come near a small town, here, in the middle of the day to-morrow. There we will purchase casks and a wagon, and we will use the wagon to haul the casks, and we will fill the casks with water either in town, or—" He pointed at the map again. "—here, at this brook." As he said this, he looked at Zerika, who nodded her approval of the plan.

"If I may," said Aerich, speaking for the first time.

"Yes?" said Khaavren.

The Lyorn pointed one of his long, graceful fingers at a spot on the map. "Let us arrive here, to the south of the place they plan the engagement, so that, at least, we may arrive from an unexpected direction."

The others at once agreed with this plan, and, this decision made, they at last settled in for the night. As quiet settled over the camp, Piro, who had set up his pallet near Kytraan, said, "My dear friend, you seem agitated."

"Do I?"

"So it seems."

"Well, I confess I am disturbed."

"Tell me what troubles you, then, and perhaps together we will be able to ease your mind."

"Very well, I shall do as you suggest. This is it, then."

"I am listening."

"Pel sneaked into the enemy camp, and overheard Grita's conversation with Tsifalli."

"Tsanaali, my dear."

"Yes. Well, Pel overheard her—"

"As did you, in fact."

"—and, before that—"

"Yes? Before?"

"Grita, herself, it seems, approached our camp and succeeded in overhearing our plans."

"Well, I agree, I believe she did so, the wretch!"

"There, then. We have heard her plans, and she has heard ours."

"Yes, and then?"

"How do we know she has not overheard our plans this time?"

"What do you mean?"

"Well, it seems to me we have seen a great deal of this sneaking around and listening to people."

"But, Kytraan, we have guards."

"So did they, Piro. I know this, because it fell to me to knock one soundly on the head to prevent him from raising an alarm."

"There, you see? We have guards, and they have not been knocked on the head."

"Therefore?"

"Therefore, no one has been sneaking about listening to us."

Kytraan considered this for a moment, then said dubiously, "If you are convinced of it."

"Oh, I am, I assure you."

"Very well, that is good enough for me, then."

"I am glad it is."

"Thank you. I shall sleep the more soundly for our conversation."

"And you will be right to do so."

With this, Kytraan at once fell into a sound sleep. Some ten or fifteen minutes later, Piro rose and went to seek out his father.

BOOK FOUR

In Which the Ninth (or Tenth)
Battle of Dzur Mountain Is Fought
With Some Discussion of Its Results

How Those Unable to Think
The Thoughts of Others Are
Content to Think Their Own

W
e must now turn our attention to a place we have never
before visited—a place outside of the confines of the
Empire (although, to be strictly accurate, there was a
period of thirty or thirty-five years in the Ninth Dragon Reign when
the Empire claimed it)—a place that can be found some twenty-five
miles off the coast to the southwest.

It is, as the reader is well aware, the Island of Elde: some seventeen hundred square miles of rich, fertile plain in the central and
southeastern area; rocky coastline to make fishing a challenge to the
east, and a few modest mountains inhabited by a particularly bad-
tempered species of goat across the neck of the northern "staffhead,"
which effectively makes the northernmost section its own country,
although politically part of the Kingdom of Elde.

This northern region, about two hundred miles across and ninety
or ninety-five miles from the mountains to the coast, has only two
cities of any consequence. The first of these is the port of Salute,
named, we are told, from an ancient custom of waving flags at the
Imperial ships in the channel in a gesture of respect. The other city is
called Kripna, which, we are informed, means "dry spot" in a language of the island that is no longer used except on ceremonial occasions. Kripna is placed at the inner bend of a river (named Cideen,
which means "river") that runs from the mountains to Salute.

Kripna is a respectably sized city, boasting some eight or nine
thousands of permanent residents, as well as a considerable number
of peasants who work the nearby land, bargemen who facilitate trade
between the mountains and the coast, and a certain number of freshwater fishermen who work the river and are constant rivals of their
coastal counterparts.

No doubt, there was a great deal to be said on both sides—that is,

while the clams and culls of the northern coast of Elde (or the southern coast of the Empire) are justly famed, the longfish from the
Cideen have a reputation extending across the channel—a reputation
only bolstered by the number of shipments of this delicacy that fail to
reach their destination because of "accidents" to the transport ships
embarking from Salute.

There are as many ways to prepare the longfish as there are villages in the staffhead, from the spit-roasting common in the upper
reaches to spicy stews of the lower river—but perhaps the best is the
simplest: quick frying in butter with a bit of garlic, a few of the local
sweet onions, slivered, and the merest hint of juice from the bitter-
nut, the whole accompanied by goslingroot just barely steamed and
the delicate white Roolina wine from the mountains. It was, in the
event, this very meal that was being served at this moment by an inn,
some ten or twelve miles from Kripna, marked by the sign of the silver goblet.

The individual serving it was a certain Carnaro, a man of about
one thousand and three hundred years, with thin hair, a long face,
and a slight paunch—a testimony, perhaps, to the quality of his
comestibles. He had inherited the inn through a fortunate marriage,
after discovering that the hauling and lifting required as part of
working a river barge was not to his liking. The Silver Goblet had
been founded some two thousand years before, upon the discovery of
a way to distill liquor from the pea. The idea of the original founder
was that his pea-liquor, which was in some ways similar to the *oushka*
of the Easterners, would spread far and wide, and make him both
rich and renowned, and that he would reveal his recipe only on his
deathbed and to his chosen offspring.

In fact, it turned out that no one sampling this drink ever asked
for a second sample, and so, unable to live on the sales from his
drink, he ended up opening a hostelry and, fortunately, employed as
a cook someone more skilled in the culinary arts than he himself was
a distiller. But there was, nevertheless, always a jug or two of the pea-
liquor under the counter, to be used for cleaning or for practicing
upon strangers who asked to sample the specialties of the region.
Those who generally patronized the Goblet (which, in fact, had no

silver goblets anywhere within) generally made do with the wine to which we have already had the honor to refer, or to the heavy, dark stout that was brewed in the winter.

On this occasion, Carnaro, having just served dinner to a lady who wore a simple but well-cut gown of a yellow or golden color, observed a stranger enter his hostelry, and hastened to attend him.

The stranger was a young man of between six and seven hundred years, with hollowed-out cheeks, very deep eyes, curly hair, and long, elegant hands. He was dressed in a fashion that Carnaro recognized as a warrior's outfit, black and silver, from the old days of the Empire across the channel. All of this piqued our host's curiosity in no small measure, but he contained this emotion, and merely greeted the guest, asking how he could be of service.

"In the simplest possible way, my friend," was the answer.

"So much the better," said Carnaro.

"I am looking for someone, a woman, who arrived in this district seven or eight hundred years ago. She is noble of appearance, fair of skin and hair, with refined tastes and a pronounced noble's point. I would suggest that, though she has lived in this region for the entire span of time to which I have alluded, she has few friends, and keeps mostly to herself. Do you know of such a woman?"

"Indeed I do," said Carnaro at once, having no thought to dissemble. "In fact, she is in my establishment at this moment."

"Ah. You delight me. Here is a silver coin for your trouble. And here is another if you point her out to me."

"Nothing could be easier, because I have just this instant brought her a meal. Her name is Tresh, and she is in that corner, eating."

The stranger observed a woman sitting quietly in a corner, ignored by the peasants and tradesmen who frequented the inn. He at once determined that she matched the description he had given the host, and, moreover, matched the small drawing he carried with him.

Paying the host as promised, he approached the woman at the table, and, as she looked up, he gave her a courtesy and said, "I was told I should find you here. I am called Udaar."

"Well?" she said, as if wondering why his name should matter to her more than the food and wine set before her.

"I was sent to find you."

"That is unlikely," she said. "No one knows where I am, or that I live, or even my name."

"On Elde, I have just learned that you are called Tresh," said the one called Udaar. "But your name is Illista, and I was sent by His Imperial Majesty, Kâna."

The one addressed as Illista gave some signs of astonishment, but covered them up quickly. "You are correct, at any rate, about my name. At least, I was once called that, years ago. But I do not know of any Emperor, nor anyone named Kâna."

"Do you recall a Count from the west of the Empire called Skinter?"

She frowned, "Yes, I do seem recall such a young man. From the mountains, if I am not mistaken. A Dragonlord who was involved in a duel over who had the right to send flowers to a certain Maid of Honor to the Consort early in the last Phoenix reign."

Udaar bowed. "Your memory does you credit."

"Skinter is Kâna?"

"The same."

"And he now calls himself Emperor?"

"As do many, many thousands of others, my lady."

"Many thousands call themselves Emperor?"

"No, many thousands call Kâna Emperor. But I see you are pleased to jest. That is well, you may jest if you choose. But my mission here has nothing of the jest about it, and the proof is, I would not have made the journey across the channel, and then ridden all this way, merely for a jest, however much of wit it might display."

"I see. Well then, I shall treat you with all the seriousness you could wish. To begin, then, I will ask a serious question: What does this Skinter, or Kâna, wish of me?"

"As for that, perhaps after you have eaten we may find a place more private, and there I will explain my mission."

"Very well, I agree. I will finish eating, and, if you will acquire a cup, I will share with you the remainder of this excellent wine. Unless it chances that you are hungry yourself, in which case I can recommend the longfish without reservation."

"I am grateful for the wine, my lady. That will be more than sufficient."

"Very well."

Udaar signaled the host, and a cup was promptly supplied. He drank his wine and permitted Illista to enjoy her meal in silence. When she signified that she was finished, Udaar, still without saying anything, left a couple of coins on the table, a courtesy that elicited a bow from Illista. They left the darkness of the Silver Goblet, and he indicated a conveyance he had hired, consisting of two donkeys and as comfortable a cart as could be found in the region. She secured her horse to the rear and said, "This way for half a league, then—"

"Your pardon, my lady, but I know where your home is."

"Do you? That does not astonish me. Very well, then. What is your rôle? From the colors you choose, as well as certain features of your countenance, I would judge you to be of the House of the Dragon."

"You are perspicacious, my lady. And you, I know, to be a Phoenix. One of few that still live."

"Ah. That, then, is my value to this Kâna."

"You are perspicacious, my lady."

"When you say 'few,' just how many do you mean?"

"So far as we know—"

"Well?"

"You and one other."

"Who is the other?"

"We do not know, exactly. A child raised in secrecy, who has just recently revealed herself."

"Revealed herself? Then, she is challenging Kâna?"

"Yes, that would be one way of expressing it."

"Hmm. And what would be another?"

"Another way to put it would be to say that she has retrieved the Orb."

Illista stared at him in silent astonishment. Eventually she said, "Retrieved the Orb? And yet, the word that reached this island where I have been exiled for more than seven hundreds of years was that it had been destroyed."

"This is, it seems, not the case."

"Well, but what can I do? That is, if she has the Orb—"

"She has the Orb, but that is all."

"In my opinion, that is a great deal."

"She has, perhaps, twenty troops. Kâna has a hundred thousands of them."

"And is he bringing them to battle?"

"Even as we speak."

"So he will then have the Orb?"

"It seems likely."

"And then? What am I to do?"

"You are to show him obeisance. That is, you will be the representative of your House, and show the people that the House of the Phoenix agrees that the Cycle has turned, and that you acknowledge Kâna's legitimacy."

"And, in exchange for this?"

"A place at Court, and the title of Princess. Certain lands that the Empire took from you will be restored. An income of ten thousand Imperials."

"I wish more."

"More income?"

"No, an additional inducement."

"Name it."

"There are certain persons who inconvenienced me at one time. I wish for the privilege and the resources to dispose of them."

"That can be done."

"How, you answer without knowing who they are?"

"His Majesty knows who they are."

"How can he?"

"He has been told."

"By whom?"

"By the person who informed him of your existence."

"And that is?"

"Her name is Grita."

"You perceive, that tells me nothing."

"Alas, it is all that I know."

"Very well. But how did she come to tell this Kâna of my existence?"

"She managed to overhear certain conversations between this pretended Empress and her friends, as a result of which it occurred to her that you might be useful to His Majesty. Upon reaching this conclusion, she bespoke the Emperor, telling him of your existence."

"And what was your rôle in this?"

"I have the honor to be a member of His Majesty's household staff, a member of his Guard, and thus heard the entire conversation. His Majesty did me the honor of suggesting that I would be suitable for this errand."

"I now understand completely."

"And?"

"And—but here, we have now come to my home—this hovel is where I have been living since my exile."

"Yes, my lady."

"We must stop here."

"Of course."

"We must stop here long enough for me to pack up my belongings. I assume a ship is ready?"

"It is, Your Highness."

"I like the sound of that," said Illista.

Udaar bowed, but said, "We need not, however, leave at once."

"On the contrary," said Illista. "I do not wish to spend another night in this land of exile."

"Very well," said Udaar, bowing once more. "The ship and the conveyance on the mainland await, and there is no need to delay on that account."

"Then still less is there a reason to delay on mine."

"Then I take we have Your Highness's agreement?"

"I must still consider certain matters."

"If they are matters in which I can help in the consideration of, I stand ready to engage in such activity as may be beneficial to your endeavors."

"I beg your pardon?"

"I will help if I can."

"I ask for nothing more. For now, I must pack. Do you relax here two minutes while I make preparations to leave this accurséd house on this accurséd island."

In less than an hour, Illista had packed all of her belongings — or, at any rate, those she wished to keep — into three small trunks. She and her servant, a taciturn and rather stupid-looking man named Nywak who had been with her all of her life, climbed into the conveyance and, without a backward glance, began the journey to the harbor.

They stopped that evening at an inn which could have been a twin to the Silver Goblet, save that the longfish was prepared with lemon and capers, and, in Illista's opinion, over-cooked. The lodgings were, however, comfortable, with Illista and Udaar each having a room while Nywak slept in the stable, and no one asked any questions. The next day, around noon, they arrived in Salute, and from there, without stopping to see the city (which, though she had lived scarcely a day's journey away for hundreds of years, Illista had never visited), they at once procured a barque which took them to the ship Udaar had engaged. The arrangements had, as Udaar promised, been made satisfactorily: the captain was waiting, the ship ready, and before dark that night they had embarked across toward the mainland.

By chance, the waters of the channel were kind that night — or, to be more precise, they were not unusually surly — and so by the time morning shook her fair hair over the southern coast, Illista was not remarkably ill, and they had already reached a small natural harbor, which has no name that we know of, but is found some twenty or twenty-five miles southeast of Ridgly; which is to say, at one of the nearest places to Salute upon which to make landfall. They were met there by a wagon not dissimilar to the one upon which they had made the journey to Salute, and by a barrel-chested Dragonlord named Hirtrinkneff.

"Welcome home, Udaar, and welcome to you as well, Your Highness."

"Thanks, Rink."

Illista bowed.

"I take it," continued Hirtrinkneff, drawing Udaar aside as Nywak loaded the trunks onto the wagon, "that the crossing was not unpleasant, and that all is as His Majesty wished?"

"I have a certain soreness in my throat, but, beyond that, all is well."

"A soreness in your throat? I assume from the salt air, or the coolness of the vapors you inhaled?"

"Perhaps. But I suspect more because our guest required me to speak at every stage of the journey, explaining to her as much of the situation in the Empire as I could manage. She wished to know the extent of devastation caused by the plagues and by the Reavers, the numbers and strength of opposing forces, the attitudes of the Princes—many things which I could not have answered if I had wanted to, and many which I could only answer in guesses, and some of which I was required to evade; but at no time was I permitted to stop talking."

"Ah. Well, I have just thing for you. My grandmother taught me an infusion of herbs that is put into hot water along with lemon and honey that will, without question, remove any pain in the throat. I shall have it prepared when we make our first stop."

"Apropos, when will that be?"

"Almost at once. It is full night, and I should prefer travel by day; hence we will rest at the Cliffside, which is not five miles from here."

"Very well. And, as I perceive the trunks are now loaded, let us proceed."

"I agree."

They arrived within a few hours, and there passed the remainder of the night, as well as, after making special arrangements with the host, several hours the next day, after which they made their way further up the coast, stopping next, as chance would have it, at the town of Merinna. We hope the reader has had, or will have, the chance to visit this village—of course, we entertain no doubt that the reader has at least heard a great deal about it. In either case, there is no call to describe the low, trim multi-colored brick houses of the "berjeses," nor the elegant shops that attract so much attention, nor the famous smiling constabulary in their well-known yellow tunics and twirling their wands of authority. All of these things are real, so far as they go; and Merinna is, in the opinion of this author, every bit as pleasant a resort town as one could hope to find.

Indeed, the greatest point of interest is how Merinna survived the Interregnum so nearly intact—that is to say, how it suffered so little from the depredations suffered by those around it. The answer lies in the place we have just quitted: the Island of Elde. For six thousands of years before Adron's Disaster, Merinna had been under the unofficial protection of the Kings of Elde, who had, in many ways, created the village to have a hospitable landing site on the mainland for visits ceremonial and personal. The Kings of Elde, therefore, saw no reason to withdraw their protection from this little parcel of coast simply because of certain unpleasantness within the political confines of their large neighbor across the water. The royal court of Elde, therefore, let it be known to those Reavers who used the Interregnum and the harbors of Elde to launch excursions against the coast of Dragaera that Merinna and its environs should be left unharmed. They even went further, and would from time to time send over provisions to stave off the famines, and even medicines to provide some relief from the plagues.

So, as it was before the Interregnum, it was, in large part, during the Interregnum, and still is today—and the reader knows well enough of how very few things this can be said. They spent the night, then, in Porter's, and broke their fast on the fruit muffins for which that hostelry is so justly renowned, as well as klava, which Illista had not tasted since leaving the Empire.

"And now," said Illista, as she finished her repast, waited on by the ubiquitous Nywak, "I assume we at last leave the coast, and make our way inland to meet with His Majesty?"

"Soon," said Udaar. "There is a small matter to attend to first."

"A small matter? Well, then let us dispose of it at once; you perceive I am as impatient as a three-year-old at the pole."

"Then I will be as brief as the report of the starter's whip."

"I ask for nothing more."

"Before leaving the island—"

"Yes, before leaving?"

"—Your Highness did me the honor of mentioning that you had certain matters still to consider before accepting our proposal."

"You have a memory like an athyra."

"I must now, before bringing you further, ask whether Your Highness has completed these contemplations."

Illista looked at the Dragonlord carefully before saying, "You are more than a messenger, aren't you?"

Udaar bowed his assent.

"Very well," said Illista, when no other words were forthcoming. "I have completed my contemplations, and I have no objections to make to His Majesty's plan."

"Then we are agreed?"

"You have my word."

"I ask for no more. We may now set out at once."

"Do you know," remarked Illista, "I have always desired to see this town, for I have heard so much about it, both in the old days, and then again from the Court at Elde."

"You were, then, acquainted with the Court at Elde?"

"I came there first when I arrived upon the island, and I asked for sanctuary. I was told, 'We have a large island, madam, you my live where you choose.'"

"He said that?"

"His very words."

"Was he aware that you had been in the Imperial Court? That you were, moreover, a close relative of His Imperial Majesty then on the throne?"

"I had explained those matters upon arriving."

"Some might consider this an insult."

"Nearly."

"Indeed, an insult to the Empire itself."

"That is my opinion; I am glad it coincides with yours."

"Oh, it does. And, moreover—"

"Yes?"

"It is my opinion that His Majesty ought to be informed of this."

"It is no secret."

"And, once the details of securing the Empire are concluded, well, we shall see."

"Yes, that is—but wait."

"Yes?"

"Where are we going?"

"Going? Why, toward the Palace, of course."

"But—ah, I had forgotten. The Palace, the city is no more."

"You speak of the old Palace, the old city."

"Yes."

"You must understand, that was before my time."

"That is true. Your pardon, I was confused. Where is the new Palace to be, and the new Imperial city?"

"For now, Hartre, or, rather, a small village not far from Hartre, where you are to await the result of certain negotiations. That is where we are now going. Later, it will be moved to Adrilankha."

"Adrilankha? That is in the county of Whitecrest, and I do not think His Majesty will have the support the Countess of White-crest—we were on tolerably poor terms when I quitted the court."

"I perceive you have not been entirely out of touch with matters while you were away."

"Not entirely."

"She was later exiled from court herself."

"Was she? That does not displease me."

"And to answer your point—"

"Yes, the answer?"

"I believe that, when the time comes, the Countess of Whitecrest will not present a problem."

"Very well, I will accept that. Then we are now bound for Hartre. Well, that it is a tolerably long journey, and so I will prepare myself for it."

"That is best, I assure you."

"You have been to Hartre before, my dear Dragonlord?"

"Never. And Your Highness?"

"Yes, several times."

"Perhaps Your Highness would be good enough to tell me of it, as we travel."

"If you would like."

In this way, several hours passed in pleasant enough travel, because Udaar, in fact, truly wished to know about Hartre, whereas

Illista, for her part, truly enjoyed speaking before an attentive audience. They spent that evening at a run-down hostelry on the road, where the host, grateful for the custom, made every effort to make his guests comfortable in spite of the condition of the inn, and the next day they continued on the road.

"You seem lost in thought, my friend," said Illista.

"Well, I am."

"And might I inquire as to these thoughts?"

"Well, I will explain, and, once I have done so, you will see at once why I am thinking my own thoughts."

"Bah. As if you could think another's!"

"I mean that I am thinking thoughts that I do not wish to share, that is all."

"I understand that, only the expression is absurd."

"I do not deny that."

"Very well, explain then."

"Explain?"

"Explain what has caused you to think these thoughts you do not wish to share."

"Very well. If all is on schedule—"

"Yes? If all is on schedule?"

"Today is the day His Majesty's forces should be attacking Dzur Mountain, and, therefore, today is the day that the Orb will fall into his hands, and the Empire will be secured. Now do you see why I seem busy with my thoughts?"

"Yes, I understand completely. It will be annoying to have to wait several days for messengers to arrive with the results of the battle."

"It will not be so long. With the Favor, we should know quickly enough."

"How is this possible?"

"Can you be unaware that the Orb has returned?"

"You mentioned something of this fact, yes."

"Well, but can you be unaware of the sensation of its presence?"

"Nearly. I have had no sensation of citizenship since my exile."

"Ah. Well, His Majesty will remedy this situation."

"That is good."

"For now, you must understand that I am very much aware of my own citizenship, and there will be no difficulty to communicate with His Majesty on the results of the battle."

"Ah. I see what you mean. But then, if the battle is not successful—"

"Not hearing of the results will tell us the results."

"Yes, I understand. And then?"

"If that is case, you have been asked to remain at the hostelry toward which we now drive until we get a message to you."

"Very well. And do you know what this message will be?"

"Not precisely, Your Highness, but I have been given to understand that Habil—"

"Who?"

"Kâna's cousin."

"Very well."

"I have been given to understand that Habil has developed what she calls 'contingencies' and that you are part of these."

"It is good to have contingencies, and I have no objection to being included in them, provided, of course, that they do not preclude me from getting what I want."

"They will not, I am convinced of it."

"That is good," said Illista. Then she frowned, and said, "Contingencies."

"Madam?" said Udaar.

"If the attempt to take the Orb by military means should fail for some reason . . ."

"Yes, if it should?"

Illista shook her head, and didn't answer, being busy, for some time, with her own thoughts.

Chapter the Fifty-Third

How the Old Question of Whether The Ends Justify the Means Is Debated Again, This Time With the Unique Perspective Of the Lyorn Expounded Upon in Some Detail

This was the situation as the next day's morning filtered gently through the Enclouding: Kâna's forces, under General Brawre, had reached a position a hundred or a hundred and ten miles west of Dzur Mountain. Kâna's other army, led by Izak, was, at this time, camped just outside of the village of Nacine, which the reader may recall as being on the very doorstep, as it were, of where Morrolan was causing his temple to be built. Also in Izak's camp that morning was Kâna himself, and the small detachment under Tsanaali. Zerika and our friends had arrived where they had planned, in a place that was also just outside of Nacine, and, in point of fact, less than ten miles from Izak's outposts.

Morrolan stood upon the roof of the temple he was causing to be built and studied the work Fentor had done and listened patiently while his commander explained the use of the ditches, scaffoldings, buttresses, and other devices of modern military science that this worthy had arranged in only a few days. At last, the commander said, "Well, my lord? Is that sufficient?"

"For what?" asked Morrolan.

"For your understanding."

"Not the least in the world," said Morrolan. "But it is of no matter. You say it will do, and I believe you."

"I did not say it would do."

"Well, will it?"

"No, but it is the best that can be done."

"Very well."

"Then Your Lordship still intends to attack them?"

"I do. And if we must then retreat, well, we now have fortifications to retreat to."

Fentor bowed, accepting the inevitable. "And may I suggest—"

"Yes?"

"When the battle commences, this will be an excellent place from which to observe."

"Oh, as to that—"

"Well?"

"I think the front line will be better."

"My lord? You intend to lead the troops personally?"

"How not?"

Fentor hesitated. He could hardly explain that Morrolan was insufficiently skilled at generalship to be entrusted to make decisions in the field. He cleared his throat and said, "And yet, a position in the rear is better for receiving communications and making decisions."

"In that case, my dear Fentor—"

"Yes?"

"As you know this business better than I do, I would suggest that you position yourself here."

"How, me?"

"And why not?"

"Because, my lord, my place is with the men engaged in battle."

"Just so," said Morrolan.

"And yet, should you be killed—"

"Well? If I am killed, will that make you less able to make decisions? On the contrary, I should imagine that you might better be able to make decisions without my interference."

Fentor cleared his throat again, as this was uncomfortably close to his own thinking. He said, "If you believe that, my lord, why not—"

"Because it is my army, my fief, and my responsibility. Therefore, so long as I live, the mistakes will be mine."

"I hope there are none, my lord."

"I hope so too. Because, understand this: We are not setting out with the intention of fighting a gallant fight and losing. On the contrary, we are setting out with the intention of winning."

"My lord—"

"Well?"

"I do not know if this is possible."

"We will see. Be clear on this: I will do anything that is necessary to win. Anything."

"That is but natural, my lord."

"Then you agree?"

"We cannot fight with the intention of losing. And, if we wish to win, all else follows."

"I am glad we have an understanding on this matter. As you are insistent upon being at the battle, I will wish to have you next to me to advise me."

"Very well, my lord."

"Are we, then, prepared?"

"The men are ready to move, if that is Your Lordship's meaning."

"And we know where the enemy is?"

"We do."

"Then let us go there and fight him."

"I shall give the order, my lord."

"On your way, have Teldra, Arra, the Warlock, and the Necromancer sent to me, and have someone saddle my horse."

Fentor bowed and retired to carry out his orders. Presently, those Morrolan had named had joined him upon the roof of the temple. Morrolan studied them for a moment, as if searching for the words he required. He coughed in confusion, then said, "Arra, is everything arranged?"

"Everything," she said, "except that we do not know when we are to begin."

"As to that," said Morrolan, "word will reach you."

"Very well," she said. "We will be ready."

"And you," said Morrolan, addressing the Warlock. "You will travel with me?"

"Gladly."

"And be prepared to aid me as we discussed?"

"Certainly. I have nothing better to do."

Morrolan turned to the Necromancer and said, "Well?"

"Lord Morrolan?" said the addressed demon in tones simulating human curiosity.

"Will you aid me?"

"My lord, it was for this purpose that I was sent here."

"How, to aid me?"

"To aid in the restoration of the Empire. That is, the Gods sent me to aid Sethra Lavode, and she, in her turn, sent me here to aid you."

"You were sent by Sethra Lavode?"

The Necromancer bowed her assent.

"And she pretends that fighting this battle will aid in the restoration of the Empire?"

The Necromancer again indicated that this was, in fact, the case.

Morrolan considered these remarkable revelations, after which he said, "Then you are at my orders?"

"Entirely."

"That is well, then. I have nothing to say about this Empire, I have not given it full consideration. But I have no interest in bending my knee to this Kâna, whoever he is, and moreover, I feel a certain fondness for Sethra Lavode. So, then, do you recall our last conversation?"

"As if it had taken place yesterday, my lord."

"The Gods! I hope so, because it did take place yesterday."

"Ah. Did it, then? I beg your pardon; time sometimes confuses me."

"In any case, you remember the conversation, and that is all that matters."

"Yes, my lord."

"Good, then. As for you, my dear Teldra—"

"Well?"

"You will remain here, and see that all is in order, in case we must retreat."

"What must be in order?"

"Listen, and I will explain."

"Very well, I am listening."

"First, there must be fresh water in barrels every twenty feet along the entrenchments."

"The well is full, and, should it run low, the stream is tolerably close. Next?"

"There must be bags of biscuits next to the water barrels."

"I understand about the biscuits, we have been baking them for three days. What else?"

"Clean linen piled next to the biscuits, to dress wounds."

"I understand about the linen, and we have a good supply. What else?"

"That is all."

"I will make the arrangements."

"You understand what is required?"

"Your Lordship will judge: Water, biscuits, linen."

"That is it."

"Very good."

"All is then ready. I but await word that the army is ready to move."

Teldra bowed. "Then I have nothing left but to wish you all the best of fortune, my lord."

The others echoed this sentiment, and, as they were doing so, the signal came that Morrolan's horse was saddled, and his army was ready to march. In only a few minutes, with no ceremony whatsoever, Morrolan was mounted and leading his force—numbering, we are told, somewhere between three thousands and four thousands—toward their meeting with the forces of the self-styled Emperor Kâna.

Even as Morrolan, mounted, we should add, on a pure-white Megaslep mare, began his march, not far away Grita was leaving the small pavilion-tent that had been arranged for the comfort of him who called himself His Majesty, Kâna. On her way out, she happened to pass a familiar figure.

"Well, Lieutenant," she said, giving him an ironic bow. "I hope the day goes well for you, and that we will soon have the opportunity to meet again, as we have agreed."

For his part, Tsanaali returned both the bow and the irony. "I anxiously await the opportunity to do so—if, indeed, I survive the upcoming engagement."

"You say if you survive? You, then, fear this little band we face?"

"Them? Not the least in the world. But, rather, I do not consider it impossible that, while I am engaged in defending His Majesty, you will arrange to have me poniarded."

Grita chuckled. "Am I to be insulted by this?"

"There is no need to waste time with such pretense."

"You, however, would never do such a thing to an enemy—dispatching him with guile?"

"I would never achieve a victory at the cost of my honor; that is the difference between us."

"Is that it? Do you think, perhaps, that there is also this difference: I am determined?"

"And I am not?"

"You carry out your duties as well as you can, being certain that you are never required to do anything on a certain list, a list of things a nobleman wouldn't do. Whereas I—"

"Yes, you?"

"I intend to accomplish what I have set out to accomplish, and I do not let obstacles deter me—whether the obstacle is imposed from without, or is only in the mind."

Tsanaali shrugged. "You have only re-stated what I did you the honor to explain before."

"Have I? Well, Lieutenant, so long as there is a difference, I am content."

"I am glad that you are. Then, until we are able to meet under circumstances more to our liking, I bid you—"

"Ah, but a moment, before we conclude this charming conversation."

"Yes, madam?"

"I was bidden to find you by His Majesty, and to require you to wait upon him. As I find you so near to him, my task is thus made easier."

"I shall do so at once."

"So much the better, for it is now nearly full morning, and a fine time to finish the business."

"Yes. And afterward, our own business."

"We have already agreed upon that, Lieutenant; it is useless to repeat it. Besides, I think you will have other things to occupy your mind after you speak with His Majesty."

Tsanaali frowned. "Explain."

Grita shrugged. "I only mean that the Emperor will have some very specific instructions for you; instructions that will keep you busy enough not to worry about personal errands."

"And how is it you know so well His Majesty's intentions?"

"Because it was I who suggested to him the mission."

"Mission?"

"Yes."

"What is this mission?"

"There is a noble lady who must be protected, and brought to His Majesty."

"And you said that I should be the one to do this?"

"Not in the least. But, after explaining what would be required, he directed me to send for you. And now—"

"Well?"

"You are keeping him waiting, and that will not do at all, you know." And before the officer could say another word, she had continued past him and on her way.

As Tsanaali, still scowling, begged permission to come before His Majesty, some few miles away Tazendra was sitting in the shade of a droopy old willow sharpening her sword. This willow was at the top of a small hill—a very small hill, more of a mound—with something like a glen below it with a quite respectable stream or brook running at its feet, and some number of other deciduous trees, mostly willows, camped about to keep watch on the hill. Tazendra, and the rest of our friends, had made a sort of encampment on both sides of the brook.

Pel approached her as she was just completing her task and she looked up, saying, "Is it, then, time to move?"

"Nearly," said Pel.

"Bah. It has been nearly time for a hundred years."

"Well, you perceive there is no hurry. We know where they are, and—"

"Do we?"

"Assuredly. Khaavren and Piro did the scouting themselves."

"Ah! The father and the son. Well, that is good then. I sometimes regret that I have no son or daughter, you know. Do you have such regrets?"

"I? No, I have never given the matter any thought. But you know, it is not too late."

"For me? Oh, yes. There is only one man I should have considered marrying, and he is not of my House, so the matter is completely impossible."

"I did not know that. Is it someone I know?"

"Know him? I think you do. It is our friend, Aerich. But come, let us see what the others are doing. There will be some steel singing today, and, I shouldn't wonder, a bit of wizardry as well, so I will have my staff in one hand."

Without giving Pel time to respond to the astonishing announcement which she had made so casually, she rose and went over to where Grassfog and his friends had made a small fire and were drinking klava.

"Well," she said, addressing this worthy. "Are you and your compatriots ready for the day's festivities?"

"Ready?" said Grassfog. "Well, I imagine there is nothing that could make us more ready, so the answer, perforce, is yes."

"And are you eagerly awaiting the opening of the games?"

"My lady," said the recent bandit, "do you pretend it matters if I am eager?"

"Well, why should it not?"

"My lady, I was agreeably disappointed when, upon the defeat of our band, we were not all summarily killed, as is, you must admit, customary."

"Oh, I do not deny that; Her Majesty was merciful."

"I am aware of this."

"Well, and then?"

Grassfog shrugged. "And so we have been granted a few more days to live, and we are all grateful. If we should die today —"

"Well, if you should die?"

"Then so much the worse for us. We have gained several days, and we see each day of life, especially when one has been granted such a reprieve, as a gift. And so you see —"

"Yes?"

"We are not eager to play, but neither does it matter if we are eager. We will do as we are ordered to, and die when it is time to die, and be grateful for the time in between."

Tazendra shook her long hair and said, "My friend, we see things differently."

"The Gods! We should! Because, in the first place, I am not a Dzur."

"Well, that is true. And in the second?"

"In the second, you are not a bandit."

"Do you know, I believe you have hit upon a great truth there."

"A great truth? Bah. I only work in small truths. Small truths, small purses, small rewards. That was what our leader, Wadre, taught—because he pretended that small purses were less likely to lead to great chases. Great chases lead to captures, and captures, to a bandit, can never be pleasant. And, well, it seems that he was correct."

"You think so?"

"I think that the first time he deviated from this principle it led at once to his death."

"Certainly, that is an argument in favor of his principle."

"I think so, too."

"And yet, I have always been happier with grand enterprises."

"Then you should be eager for to-day's festivities to begin."

"Oh, I am, I am! And, moreover, I am sorry that you are not."

Grassfog shrugged. "We will fight all the same, and, when all is over, that is what matters, is it not?"

"Yes, I suppose it is."

"Well then, all is well."

Tazendra frowned and attempted to make sense of this conversation, but in the end, merely sketched Grassfog a hasty bow and a smile of friendship, and moved on to where Piro, Kytraan, Ibronka, and Röaana sat at their ease. As she approached, Kytraan looked up and said, "Do you think there will be much sorcery in to-day's battle?"

"Well," said Tazendra. "I fully intend to try out my new spell; I would imagine everyone who can will do the same. What makes you ask?"

"We have been talking," said Kytraan.

"That is right and proper," said Tazendra at once. "Many talk before a battle. Some sleep, but that is more unusual, and displays a coolness that, I freely confess, is beyond my powers. Others wish for silence and solitude, which I respect, although—"

"Yes," said Kytraan, "only we have been speaking on a certain subject."

"Oh, that is a different matter altogether. Then, to judge, it becomes a matter of knowing the subject."

"Well, then I shall I tell you."

"Certainly. I am listening."

"We have been considering sorcery, and its use in the upcoming battle."

"A worthy subject; I say so," pronounced Tazendra, without the least hesitation.

"I am glad you think so," said Kytraan.

"I have been wondering," said Röaana, "if the use of sorcery would be, well—"

"Yes?"

"Strictly honorable."

"Honorable? And yet, how could it not be?"

"Because we have the Orb on our side."

"Well, and if we do?"

"Our enemies do not. Hence, we are able to do things which they cannot do."

"And yet, could they not use the Orb as well, merely by choosing citizenship?"

"Certainly," said Röaana. "But then, if they did that, they would have surrendered."

"Well, there is something in what you say," admitted Tazendra. "And how does Piro feel about this?"

"Oh," said Piro, "as for me—"

"Well?"

"I am considering the matter."

"Yes, it is worth considering," agreed Tazendra. "But for myself—"

"Yes, for yourself?"

"I should like to hear Aerich's opinion on this matter."

"Then let us call him," said Ibronka. "I, too, am anxious to hear his opinion."

"Then," said Piro, "let us ask him."

"Very well," said Tazendra. "Aerich! Come, we wish to ask you a question."

The Lyorn had been sitting with his back to a tree, ankles crossed in front of him, and his eyes closed. Upon hearing his name, he opened them, smiled slightly, rose, approached Tazendra, and bowed. "You wish for something, my dear?" We should add that Khaavren, Pel, and Zerika, who had been speaking to one another quietly, observed this, and, without a word passing between them, agreed to follow Aerich and listen to the conversation.

"We are involved in a debate, and we would like you to settle the matter for us."

"I am at your service, as always. What is the subject?"

The matter was quickly explained to Aerich, who frowned and shrugged. "Well," he said, "I believe this is a matter that can be clarified easily enough. My dear young Tiassa is, I'm afraid, looking too much at the matter of the coming fight as simply a fight."

"Well, but is it not?" said Röaana, genuinely puzzled.

"It is more than a fight. It is a step in the restoration of the Empire."

"Well, and if it is?"

"The defense of the Empire is a gentleman's first duty, at all times. To attack the Empire, as those people are doing, is, well, it is to commit a grave crime. A grave moral crime, that is; which goes beyond a matter of statute. Any aristocrat can declare this or that thing illegal—but to commit a crime is to do something wrong, and to oppose the Empire is to commit a crime. This is not a matter of making a test of combat, but of preventing a great evil."

"And so the method by which this is accomplished is not important?" said the young Dzurlord, looking rather dubious.

"Important?" said Aerich. "Very! It is of supreme importance. It is through the means that the goal is accomplished. If the goal is important, how can the means not be?"

Röaana shook her head and glanced at Tazendra as if for help, but the Dzurlord ignored this silent plea, and merely frowning as if trying to work out for herself the Lyorn's logic; instead it was Piro who came to Röaana's aid, saying, "My lord, let me attempt to explain the issue in other terms, so that we may achieve some clarity in the matter."

"Very well," said Aerich. "Clarity is important at all times, but never as much as when one is about to risk one's life. I am listening."

"As I understand the lady's point, it is this: Are you actually saying that, if the goal to be achieved is noble, we are permitted to use ignoble means to accomplish it?"

"Not the least in the world," said Aerich.

"But then, what you have done us the honor of telling us could be interpreted in exactly this way."

"Then I trust you will permit me to clarify my position?"

"Permit you? My lord, I believe I speak for the others when I say I would like nothing better in the world."

"Very well, then, this is my belief: Those who say the ends justify the means, and those who say the ends do not justify the means, are both wrong."

"Both wrong?" said Tazendra, who had been following the conversation carefully. "Impossible! You perceive, they are saying opposite things, therefore, if one is right, the other must be wrong, and if one is wrong, the other must be right. Is that not logic?"

"It is logic, of a form," agreed Aerich.

"Well?"

"It is, however, incomplete. In this case, it is not the answer that is wrong, it is the question."

"Bah! How can a question be wrong?"

"Well, if I were to ask you whether you prefer to fight a battle empty-handed, or holding a piece of cloth, you might tell me that my question was wrong; that, in fact, you would rather be holding a certain length of tempered or folded steel."

"Not only might I, my dear Lyorn, but I most certainly would."

"Therefore, you perceive, in that case, the question would be wrong."

"Well, but—" Tazendra broke off, frowning.

Röaana spoke instead, saying, "Then, in the case which we are discussing, how is the question wrong?"

"Exactly what I wish to know!" cried Tazendra, delighted.

"In this way. There is a relationship between means and ends, but is neither one of justifying, nor of failing to justify."

"But then, what is it?" said Piro.

"It is one of prescribing and proscribing," said the Lyorn.

Röaana frowned, started to speak, but instead interrogated Aerich with a look, inviting him to continue. Aerich bowed. "Consider that, if I am at my home, and wish to visit a neighbor who is located along a road that runs to the east, I will not usually travel west. My decision to travel east is not *justified* by my goal of visiting my neighbor, but is rather *determined* by it."

"But is it not true," said Röaana, "that there are many roads to a destination?"

"Indeed, that has often been said," replied the Lyorn. "But one can only walk upon one. And the decision as to which road to take is determined by the goal. One must know one's destination, and perhaps be aware of other matters—dangers upon some roads, or a particular view one enjoys along another, or delays from flooding along a third. All of these matters, subordinate to the goal, influence our decision as to the road we choose."

"And so," said Piro, who had been closely following this reasoning, "if one finds oneself using dishonorable methods to achieve a goal, it would follow that the goal, itself, is dishonorable? Or, if not dishonorable, in some other way flawed?"

Aerich looked over at Khaavren and smiled. "Your son," he said, "has your quick comprehension. He listens, he understands, and then he takes the next step on his own."

The older Tiassa smiled proudly and bowed, while the younger one flushed slightly and could not restrain a quick glance at Ibronka—a glance the Dzurlord missed, as she happened to be looking down at the time.

"And is the young Tiassa satisfied with the answer?"

"My lord," said Röaana, "you have given me a great deal to think over, and I must do so."

"Very well," said Aerich. "And the Dragon?"

"It is clear enough to me," said Kytraan. "Her Majesty says fight, and so I fight."

"I believe I like this gentleman," murmured Tazendra.

"And what of the young Dzurlord, who has remained so uncharacteristically quiet?"

Ibronka smiled. "I admire your reasoning, my lord, and moreover, I believe I must do myself the honor of being in agreement with you on all points."

Aerich turned suddenly and said, "And I cannot help but wonder what our Yendi thinks of this reasoning."

Pel permitted himself a thin smile. "It is not new to me," he said. "I seem to recall many conversations on this subject sitting in the parlor of our house on the Street of the Glass Cutters. And my own opinion has not changed, nor do I see a need to re-state it now. Instead, I will content myself with an observation."

"And that is?" said Tazendra. "For my part, I always find your observations both interesting and apropos."

"My observation is this," said Pel, with a bow in Tazendra's direction. "It requires a certain bending of logic to consider that our use of sorcery might be dishonorable, when we are about to enter a battle outnumbered by something like a thousand to one."

"I like those odds!" cried Tazendra. "Will it really be that much?"

"At least," said Pel.

"That is better than when we faced odds of three against a thousand in the Pepperfields."

"I am glad that you are pleased," said the Yendi.

"Oh, I am, I assure you."

"That is good, then. But what does the Empress think of these odds? Is she as pleased as you?" Pel glanced at Zerika, giving her a thin smile.

"What does the Empress think?" asked Zerika, who had been listening to the conversation, but had not yet interjected her own opinion.

"If she would condescend to tell us."

"The Empress," said Zerika carefully, "thinks this—"

"Well?"

"It is time to mount up and go to battle."

"Ah!" cried Tazendra. "And that is the best opinion I have heard to-day!"

Chapter the Fifty-Fourth

How the Ninth (or Tenth, Depending Upon Which Historian is Consulted) Battle of Dzur Mountain Was Fought

It still lacked two hours of noon when the outriders of Morrolan's small army spotted what seemed to be a small force — perhaps twenty or twenty-five strong — who were either stationed or merely resting along the road that runs from Nacine to Gravely. This was reported to Morrolan, who, without a glance at Fentor, riding by his side, said simply, "Brush them aside."

Fentor gave no reaction except to turn to his aide and say, "Close up," and then, very soon after, "Advance."

The "brushing aside" of which Morrolan spoke was, in fact, accomplished easily enough; the soldiers, not having expected an attack, immediately upon being charged by the leading company, which had three times their numbers, retreated hastily a quarter of a mile back up the road, where they reported that they had been charged by ten times their number. This report was received coolly enough by the officer in charge, a certain Saakrew, who at once dispatched a messenger to his commander, saying that certain enemy forces had been encountered, and making a guess as to the strength which was not far from accurate — the officer being experienced enough to reduce by half the numbers that had been told him.

The commander, a certain cavalry colonel with, herself, no small amount of experience, dispatched forces sufficient to "Secure the road," and sent an errand runner to the brigadier who was responsible for that wing of Izak's army. The brigadier personally consulted Izak, as they happened to be speaking together when the message arrived, and Izak suggested pulling back until the army could be concentrated, rather than bringing on a full-scale engagement at that time. The concentration to which we have alluded was accordingly ordered, and begun in as efficient a manner as possible.

Morrolan, for his part, continued sedately up the road after it was cleared, until he came to sloping field, or rather a gentle hillside, that, before the Disaster, had been used to graze cattle. Upon seeing it, Fentor said, "This is a good place from which to make an observation, my lord."

"Very well, let us do so, then."

Morrolan signaled for the army to halt and, with Fentor, rode up to the top of the slope, where he and Fentor each took out a touch-it glass and looked around carefully. After a moment, Morrolan said, "Well?"

"Matters are going as we could have wished, my lord. They are not concentrated. We seem to have found a detachment that is well within our strength."

"Is there a reason not to spread out and attack them?"

"No reason that I can see."

"Then let us do so at once."

"I will give the order, my lord."

In only a few minutes, thanks to the training through which Fentor had put them, the companies and battalions were arranged across the field. Upon learning that all was ready, Morrolan, who had not yet learned the importance of ceremony, grandiloquence, and inspirational utterances in convincing the desperate to do the impossible, gave the order to advance, and himself led the way. (It should be added that none of the events which followed did anything to show Morrolan why he ought to use brave words to inspire his army, and so, as far as this historian can determine, he has never learned.) On Morrolan's left was the Warlock, on his right was Fentor, and near them also was the enigmatic Necromancer.

Observing this through his own touch-it glass was Saakrew, who, with more troops now available to him, instructed his aide to give the order to hold the position, remarking, "We must attempt to delay them until we receive either reinforcements, or orders to retreat."

And it was, according to the military historians, who have studied the matter with their classic thoroughness in order to support their habitual squabbling, at just about this time that Izak, who was far more interested in the diminutive band that included Zerika and the Orb than he was in the slightly larger force moving from the other direction, gave the order to sweep through the area where Zerika was, according to Grita, making camp. Izak, who, though young, was known as a careful commander, had arranged for a battalion of three or four thousand to sweep through this area, looking for an enemy force numbering less than a score—history records few such unequal contests, but the reader must recall that, in the first place, Izak was uncertain what the Orb could do, and, in the second place, he did not consider it a battle, but rather an action more after the fashion of what some number of officers of the police might do upon learning that a notorious bandit was hiding in a certain neighborhood of a city.

It should come as no surprise to the reader that, of all of them, it was Khaavren who first observed the approach of a well-disciplined troop, and coolly remarked to Zerika, "I believe they are coming for us."

"How many?"

"A hundred, or perhaps a hundred and fifty, with more on either flank."

"I see. This was not what we had anticipated."

"No," said Khaavren. "It is fewer."

"And that is all to the good," said Her Majesty.

"On the contrary."

"It is not fewer, or it is not all to the good?"

"It is not good. They are not attacking, they are searching."

"And this means?"

"That there are many, many more than we had thought."

"Ah. You do not appear startled."

"My son, Piro, warned me that we might have been overheard when making our plans."

"I see. And so they changed their plans?"

"Your Majesty has understood the situation exactly. It was for this reason that I had us leave the horses saddled and everything prepared for a sudden withdrawal."

"Well, what is your suggestion, Captain?"

"Let us withdraw."

"In what direction?"

"As they are approaching from the northeast, let us move southeast, in the hopes of finding their flank, and skirting it. Moreover, if I recall correctly the map which Your Majesty did us the honor of sketching, we may be so fortunate as to strike a small village, called Nacide, or Nacine, or Naciter, or something similar. In such a village it is possible that we will find places in which to conceal ourselves until we can formulate another plan."

Zerika frowned, evidently displeased at the notion of retreat, and more displeased at the notion of concealing herself. "What would be the alternative plan?" she said.

"The alternative would be to do what my friend Aerich is preparing to do."

"And that is?"

"To die gallantly in defense of the Orb."

"I see. Well. Those are the alternatives, as you see them?"

"They are, Your Majesty."

"Then I choose the first of them."

"Very well," said Khaavren coolly, as if the decision had been a matter of complete indifference to him.

And, with no more ceremony than Morrolan had indulged in when ordering his charge, they abandoned the plans they had made so carefully, mounted upon their horses, and set off at once in attempt to avoid the overwhelming force moving inexorably toward them. Khaavren led the way, with the sharp-eyed Pel next to him. Directly behind was Zerika, with Aerich on her right and Tazendra on her left. The others came behind, with Piro and Kytraan bringing up the rear.

Over the course of the next half hour, they twice very nearly ran into the enemy, but both times Pel warned them, and Khaavren was able to lead them in a direction that offered some concealment, and they were not found. At the expiration of thirty or thirty-five minutes they struck a narrow road that led into Nacine, and Khaavren at once set them on it.

By this time, Morrolan had been through his first engagement, which he had found to be, more than anything else, confusing. The reason for this confusion we will explain at once, because it was not, in fact, because of the usual confusion that can come about the battlefield, especially for a commander who has put himself directly on the lines—rather, it was because none of the enemy would come near him. On the contrary, the instant he drew his weapon—his "black wand"—from its sheath, every enemy he drew near turned on his heels and ran. In a skirmish on as small a scale as this, the effect was decisive.

"We seem to hold the field, my lord," reported Fentor.

"So we do," said Morrolan. "Casualties?"

"Nine injured, one perhaps fatally."

"Well, and enemy casualties?"

"We have taken a dozen prisoners, and there are six bodies which we have stripped according to custom. I cannot say how many of the enemy were wounded."

"Nevertheless," said Morrolan, "as you have said, we do hold the field."

"Yes."

"What do you think we ought to do with it?"

"My lord?"

"We have the field, well, shouldn't we do something with it?"

"According to your plan, my lord—"

"Well?"

"We should press forward at once."

"Very well, let us do so. Let us find where the enemy concentrates, and see if they react as these fellows have. That would be best for us, I think."

"Yes, my lord. I will give the orders."

And even as Fentor was giving his orders, Saakrew, who had observed the results of the engagement, was giving his. He summoned an aide and, through him, sent a message to his commander reporting on what had occurred, asking for instructions, and requesting reinforcements. This done, and anticipating that the enemy, having achieved a certain victory, would find no reason to stop, expected, on the contrary, that his troops were about to have the honor of receiving another attack. Accordingly, he arranged them as best he could in defensive positions, and had the drummer sound the call known informally as "Mind Your Manners," and officially as "Prepare to hold your position against an expected enemy attack."

The attack came without delay, with results we are about discover to the reader.

Morrolan, we should say, found himself transported into that
peculiar world of the Dragon warrior. It was a sensation he had
never before experienced, nor had any warning of, as he had, as the
reader recalls, been raised far from any other of his House, and so
had no one to tell him what to expect. But his blood was high, and his
vision at once narrowed and expanded, so that all he saw was the
battle around him, yet he saw that in its entirety; indeed, the oft-
repeated claim that a Dragonlord in battle grows "a crown of eyes
around his head" has never been more true. But even beyond this
was the experience of Morrolan discovering, as countless Dragonlords had discovered before him, that he was "made for battle."
There was his sword—that is to say, his black wand—which, itself,
was created for such moments. Morrolan was never aware of how he
came to be afoot: whether he dismounted, was thrown, or jumped
from a stumbling horse; but on foot he was, spinning and thrusting
and cutting and yelling like a veritable dragon of the mountains, at
length coming to a stop, frustrated by the gradually growing awareness that there was no one else to fight, for all of his enemies were
dead, or had left the field.

And the rest of the engagement? The reader may assume, from
the fact that Morrolan eventually ran out of enemies, that it was his
side which gained the victory, and in this the reader would be correct. The matter was more hotly contested than the first had been,
and casualties on both sides were accordingly higher, but in the end,
Saakrew's forces were unable to withstand the onslaught, and had to
give way, grudgingly, it is true, and without panic, but, when Morrolan was once more able to receive communications, Fentor, who
now looked at his liege with an expression of respect not unmixed
with fear, was able to report that the enemy had been driven away.

"Then we will continue at once," said Morrolan, with no hesitation. "What casualties have we taken?"

"Forty-one dead, perhaps three hundred wounded."

"Perhaps?"

"We are still gathering and regrouping those who were scattered
in the fighting."

"And the enemy?"

"We do not know. At least thirty dead—most of whom, my lord, fell to you personally—and nearly a hundred prisoners. Of course, we cannot know how many of the enemy sustained wounds, for they are unlikely to be polite enough to tell us."

"Very well."

"My lord—"

"Well?"

"It will take some time before we are able to move forward again."

"How much time?"

"An hour."

"That is too much."

"My lord—"

"We will advance in three-quarters of an hour. See to it."

"Yes, my lord."

Fentor went off to see to it, muttering under his breath about lack of cavalry.

By this time, it was nearly mid-day, and, as the reader has no doubt observed, the bulk of Izak's army had yet to become engaged in the conflict. Indeed, Morrolan's attack had an effect very similar to that of a buzzbirch flying about the ears of a dzur—and, though neither Morrolan nor Fentor were aware of it, they had by now quite flown into the dzur's mouth; that is to say, he had come forward so far that Izak's army, busily concentrating and preparing for battle, was now on three sides of his small battalion.

It must also be observed, however, that Saakrew had no knowledge of this either. This fact may, in part, account for his reaction when, as he was attempting to organize and rally his twice-defeated force, he received word, sent several hours before, to withdraw and avoid bringing on a general engagement.

"Avoid an engagement?" he cried, glaring at the messenger, who had had no part in the matter. "Now I am told to avoid an engagement? After all of this, my troops demoralized, more wounded than the field physickers are able to cope with, and all of our food and supplies in the hands of the enemy"—which was not true, but only because Morrolan's forces had not observed how close they were to Saakrew's encampment—"now he wishes me to avoid an engagement? The Gods! I should very much like to have avoided an engagement! But more, I should like to have the support I requested two hours ago!"

The messenger, who had some experience in running errands during a battle, listened patiently enough, serene in the knowledge that, eventually, he would be either given a message to deliver, or dismissed without any actual harm being done him. On this occasion, it was a message—to wit, Saakrew gave a brief summary of the engagement as he understood it, and requested relief, or, at any rate, instructions that would be more to the point. The messenger bowed and went on his way.

By the time Morrolan was ready to move forward again, Zerika had entered Nacine—the first village she is considered to have entered as Empress (the stop in Barleytown being either forgotten or ignored by most historians), which fact is not only noted in the town records, but much is still made of the event. Indeed, it is celebrated each year with a parade and a mock battle, with the Queen of the Harvest taking the role of the Empress and riding with great ceremony down the main street. On this occasion, the real Empress, instead of riding down the main street, crept in between a chandler's shop—unmistakable for its smell—and the abandoned dispatch station. There happened to be few people in town that day, and none of them aware of the battle outside, and so the Empress's party attracted no special notice—a fact which today's residents choose not acknowledge, and we apologize to anyone from that fair town who might read this, but we are unwilling to stray from the truth, however damaging that truth might be to the self-love of certain individuals or the civic pride of certain municipalities.

Khaavren was looking about for a place in which they could conceal themselves (he of course at once dismissed the dispatch station to which we have just alluded; he knew that nothing is as subject to immediate search as an abandoned building) when Aerich cleared his throat. Khaavren turned to him at once, giving a look of inquiry.

Without saying a word, Aerich gestured toward a place on the other side of the main street and rather far to the right, or east (our friends having entered the village from the south). Khaavren frowned, and said, "Well? I see only a few small houses and—ah! Yes. We are not so far ahead of pursuit as I had thought. There seem to be twenty or thirty of them, and there must, therefore, be many more at hand. We must either abandon our horses and attempt to hide somewhere in this town, or else attempt to outrun them."

"Well, Captain," said Zerika. "Which of those would you suggest?"

"I am no more partial to hiding than is Your Majesty," said Khaavren. "And, moreover, I have become rather fond of this horse."

"Very well," said the Empress, as if these reasons were sufficient. "As we have not yet dismounted, we need only turn the heads of horses, and continue on at whatever pace you, Captain, think is reasonable."

"The horses," said Khaavren, after taking a moment to study them, "are tired, but not yet exhausted—as, I might add, are we. Therefore, I will led us at a brisk trot. Come."

And with no further discussion, the captain (whose rôle, we are obliged to observe, is entirely neglected in the annual parade, replaced by some nameless general who seems to represent Morrolan, or Fentor, or both; neither of whom was present in the town) led them back out of Nacine. After only a few minutes, Khaavren called a halt, saying, "My dear Pel, would you be so good as to direct those sharp eyes of yours back behind us, and let us know if we are pursued?"

"With pleasure," said Pel.

Khaavren and Pel rode to the top of a bluff, dismounted, and, lying flat, studied the surrounding area with the aid of a touch-it glass, Khaavren looking forward, Pel looking back.

"As of now, I see nothing," said the Yendi.

"I wish I could say the same," remarked Khaavren. "More, I wish I had some understanding of the meaning of what I see."

"Well?" said the Empress. "Tell me what you see. It is possible that I can make some sense of it."

"Does Your Majesty think so?"

"Well, if you see what appears to be several thousand armed men in conflict, then, in fact, I have some idea of what it means."

Khaavren stared at the Empress in silent astonishment, until Zerika, smiling slightly, said, "Does my captain forget that his Empress has the Orb, and that, through the Orb, I am able to communicate?"

"The Horse," said Khaavren. "I *had* forgotten this circumstance. Then I take it Your Majesty has had a communication?"

"This very instant, and from none other than Sethra Lavode, who is, as you recall, more than a little concerned in these matters."

"I remember that very well. And will Your Majesty condescend to give me the gist of this communication, that I might be able to make better decisions as to our next tactical movement?"

"I will do so this very instant. In fact, I am about to."

"Then I am listening."

"The Enchantress tells me that the Lord Morrolan is engaged with Kâna's forces, even as we speak. If you have seen a battle—"

"I have."

"Then, no doubt, that is what it is."

"Very well, but—"

"Yes?"

"Who is Lord Morrolan?"

"Oh, as to that—"

"Well?"

"I have not the least idea in the world, I assure you."

"But he is on our side?"

"He is a Dragonlord who has chosen to defend the Empire, although whether from loyalty to me, to the Empire, to Sethra Lavode, or simply a dislike of Kâna, I do not know."

"That, then, is sufficient, I think. Is there more?"

"Nearly."

"Well?"

"He is terribly overmatched."

Khaavren nodded. "So it seemed, from my brief observation. Then we cannot expect him to gain the victory."

"That is true."

"However, perhaps we can use this battle to gain safety, at least temporarily."

"Yes. If we can reach Dzur Mountain, they will not find it easy to dislodge us."

"That, then, is the plan."

"Very well, Captain, let us then put it into practice at once."

"As Your Majesty wishes."

Khaavren led his small command, which included no less than the Empress herself, around the fighting, and as straight as he could toward Dzur Mountain, even as Morrolan was facing defeat for the first time in his career.

It had come about quite nearly by accident, although, to be sure, the disparity of forces had made something similar almost inevitable. But it was not, in fact, the brigades sent in response to Saakrew's urgent pleas, but, rather, some of a group of those who were searching for Zerika who came upon Saakrew's command just as Morrolan was advancing once more. Saakrew knew opportunity when he saw it, or, rather, he understood that if these four or five thousand additional troops were permitted to leave then there was nothing to stop his enemy from continuing his advance. He therefore, after a certain amount of discussion over precedence of orders and command, prevailed upon the leader of these companies to regroup them and fall upon the flank of those advancing.

This was done with considerable success, and it was only Fentor's quick realization of what had happened, and his ability to prevail upon Morrolan, even in the delirium of battle, that prevented his small army from being completely destroyed. Morrolan himself led the retreat, breaking through an opposing force attempting to complete the encirclement, and, after having done so, he returned to lead a delaying action to discourage the pursuit.

By the time he was able to rest, it was past the second hour after noon, and he ought, by all logic, to have been exhausted—yet, because of some strange power granted him by his Goddess, or because of some attribute of his remarkable weapon, or because of the peculiar nature of a Dragonlord in battle, or perhaps because of all of these things, he, according to all witnesses, showed no signs of fatigue as he consulted with Fentor upon what ought to be done next, as they regrouped on top of a hill not far from where they had launched their first attack (a hill which is today called Battle Hill under the mistaken impression that the battle was actually fought there).

Morrolan's first word was the simple question, "Casualties?"

"I don't know, my lord. We have suffered badly. Killed and captured, I should say at least two hundreds, with a similar number of wounded, though many of the wounds are light."

"Very well. How much time have we before we are attacked again?"

"Only minutes, I should think. There is no reason for them to delay longer than is required to organize a brigade or two."

"Then let us retreat to those fortifications you have so cleverly arranged. Do you agree with this plan?"

"Entirely."

"Then see to it, and there is no reason to hesitate."

"I understand, my lord."

"Fentor—"

"My lord?"

"You were right."

"Sir?"

"I had no conception of just how many they had. Or, to be more precise, I knew the numbers, but didn't know what they meant. You were right."

"Yes, my lord. As were you."

"As was I?"

"Indeed. We have delayed them considerably, and confused them more; your maneuver was far more successful than I'd have thought."

"Well, but—we cannot hold them, can we? Even in our fortifications?"

"That seems to be the case. But then, as I recall, you had some tricks which ought, at least, to delay them."

"Verra! I had forgotten those! Well, let us retreat at once, as we discussed, and I will consider matters. Apropos, where are the Necromancer and the Warlock?"

"Nearby. Neither has been hurt. I will send them to you."

"Very good."

The psychology of an army is a peculiar thing. After the first few victorious skirmishes, the entire force was filled with a spiritual fire, ready to fling itself at any enemy with no hesitation, whereas now they were slow, hesitant, fearful, and uncertain—yet not more than one out of three of Morrolan's troops had, as of yet, actually faced an enemy; many of the companies had been in reserve, others had been moving from one place to another, while others had been in positions where there was no enemy. Nevertheless, they were as one in mood and spirit, and Morrolan, even then, was sensitive enough to be aware of this, and wise enough to know he must take it into account in his future decisions.

His horse was brought to him at the same time as the Necromancer and the warlock arrived; he gestured to them to accompany him as he led the way back to the fortifications Fentor had labored so hard to prepare. These fortifications, to be sure, were not the sort of which a modern military engineer would be proud, consisting of little more than obstacles to make it difficult for an enemy to mount a strong charge, and some minimal protection against any sorcerous or projectile weapons that might be directed against them; yet, should the supposed military engineer to whom we have just referred be made aware of the lack of time or resources with which Fentor had had to work, he would, without question, have respectfully saluted the Dragonlord who had carried out this construction.

We will not draw out the retreat unnecessarily—though it was, in the unanimous opinion of those who made it, drawn out almost beyond human endurance—and simply say that Morrolan's forces made it back to their fortifications as dark was falling, where each soldier slept, arms in hand, at his post.

We must also add that, by this time, the small troop led by Khaavren and including the Empress had succeeded in making their way around the flank of Kâna's army, though, it is true, not without a certain amount of difficulty. The difficulty came only a mile outside of Nacine, when, in the course of avoiding a sizable body of the enemy, they stumbled upon an even more sizable body of the enemy—the most outlying edge of the massive search being conducted for Empress and Orb.

Zerika drew her thin weapon and said, as cool as any Drag-onlord, "How many are there?"

Khaavren, who already had his weapon in his hand, said, "Per-haps a hundred. Rather less, I fancy."

"There are ninety-four of them, including officers and those who may not be engaged," said Aerich.

Zerika smiled. "You count quickly."

"Your Majesty will forgive me if I do myself the honor of disput-ing with her, but I did not count them."

"You did not?"

"Not at all."

"Then how are you able to know the number?"

"In the simplest possible way. You see before you, arraying them-selves to charge, a dismounted cavalry company—as evidenced by the standard which is born by the lady in the middle—which consists of forty men-at-arms, four sergeants, a lieutenant, and a captain. This makes forty-six. For the rest, we see two platoons of light infantry, each of which consists of twenty soldiers, a corporal, and a subaltern. This brings our total to ninety. If we include the usual three errand runners and a physicker, all of whom can fight if the need is great enough, but will not be involved in the charge that, you perceive, they are even now beginning, we find that we are about to face ninety-four of them; or, rather, the ninety, if we assume that four will not participate in the charge, which, observe, is the case—those are the four remaining behind."

"Your Venerance seems quite certain," remarked the Empress.

"There is little doubt of the sorts of troops involved," said Aerich. "Your Majesty may observe the slight curve evident in the weapons of the dismounted cavalry, and how they do not charge in such an even, well-spaced formation as do the infantry—which infantry is proven to be light rather than heavy by the lack of pole weapons, as well as by the weapons they carry—either two swords, or sword and dagger. And you perceive their easy step, exact cadence—they have done a great deal of marching, and have often practiced this very charge—you see, in another moment, they will break into a run. Ah, you see, there it is. They really are well trained."

By the time the Lyorn had concluded this remarkable speech,

Khaavren had arrayed his small company in a line, curving back on both sides. He made no observations about the unfortunate aspects of the situation—that is, that he was facing odds of more than four to one in an open area where there were neither any obstacles to interfere with the charge, nor enough time to permit maneuvering. In other words, he had no choice but to simply face the organized troop of trained Dragon warriors.

Khaavren frowned, studying the enemy approach, then said, "My dear Tazendra."

"Well?" said the Dzurlord, who was in position only a few steps away.

"If you are able to do something, well, now would be a very good time."

"Oh, I am capable of doing something."

"That is good."

"And, in fact, I had been about to do so. Only—"

"Well?"

"I have been unable to select which spell would be the right spell. You perceive, I have been looking forward to such a moment for a long time, and there are so many choices that—"

"Bah! Can you give us something with smoke, fire, and loud sounds that will disrupt their attack?"

"Well, yes, I believe I can do something of that sort."

"Then, my dear, I beg you to do so at once. You perceive, they are nearly upon us."

"Very well, my dear. Fire and smoke and—but would lightning and thunder be appropriate as well?"

"Certainly, yes, all of that."

"Then let us—"

"Gently, however."

"Gently?"

"You recall how it was when you made that test."

"That is true. Well, gently then."

"Very well, proceed."

Tazendra acted, raising the long, heavy staff she held in her left hand, and making certain gestures with it, while murmuring under her breath.

"That had some effect," remarked Zerika.

"None too soon," observed Khaavren.

If the good captain was less than completely comfortable with how long it took Tazendra to cast her spell, he was, at least, entirely happy with the results—there was a flash that caused everyone present to shut his eyes, and to see spots when opening them, after which was revealed a long line of flame reaching to a height of ten or twelve feet, and, though it was a good twenty yards in front of them, the heat was sufficient to make them uncomfortable. These effects, spectacular as they were, were accompanied by lightning, which, as is the custom in sorcery and nature, was, in turn, accompanied by a thunderclap.

In point of fact, the effect of the spell was less than might be assumed—some five or six of the enemy were killed outright, and perhaps thirty more received burns sufficient to take them out of combat. But the reader can well understand that none of the rest had any interest in continuing the attack—nor, indeed, in doing anything except retreating as quickly as possible from the flames.

"That was well done, indeed," remarked Khaavren.

Tazendra bowed.

"It was," echoed Zerika. "Only—"

"Well?"

"Can you put the fire out?"

Tazendra frowned. "I'm not certain I know how to do that," she said.

"In that case," said Khaavren, "may I suggest this way as a direction, and that we move quickly? The wind is blowing toward us, and I have no doubt the fire will follow the wind, and I do not think I would appreciate the irony of being destroyed by our own spell."

"I agree," said Zerika.

"Then let us mount up again, if the fire has not scared away the horses."

"It has not," said Aerich. "The lackeys did a sufficient job of securing them to stakes; they are not happy, but they are still where they have been left."

"Then let us go."

Go they did, and quickly, so that, before their enemy had time to report their presence and ask for aid, they had gone some distance along what seemed to be a crude road, or perhaps a new but well-trod path, running west from Nacine.

As they rode, Tazendra said, "Well, are you satisfied?"

"More than satisfied, my dear friend," said Khaavren. "You have saved us."

"It was nothing," said Tazendra, smiling happily. "I could do the same a thousand times."

"Perhaps you will need to," said the Tiassa.

Zerika, overhearing this, said, "Excuse me, Captain, but you seem worried."

"Perhaps a little," said Khaavren.

"What, then, is the reason for this worry?"

"It is this. We cannot continue at this pace all night without killing the horses; yet I fear to stop. There is no question but that there is a pursuit. Should they catch up with us, well, even our skilled Dzur will be hard-pressed to save us."

"It will be dark soon," said the Empress. "Will we be able to hide in the darkness?"

"I am not certain. But it seems we must try, or else, at least, abandon the horses. We will kill them soon."

She nodded. "Another hour, then, and it will be dark. We will look for a place to hide."

"I dislike hiding," observed Tazendra.

"Then," said Khaavren, "do not think of it as hiding, but, rather consider it husbanding our forces for an attack on the morrow."

"I like that better," said Tazendra.

Chapter the Fifty-Fifth

How the Ninth (If One Considers Geography, Or the Tenth If One Considers Personality) Battle of Dzur Mountain Was Fought — Continued

Zerika and her escort were able to find a place between two hills some distance from the road, where ran a small brook, and they spent some nervous hours there, resting the horses, and themselves when they could, and keeping a constant and vigilant watch throughout the night—or, to be more precise, throughout much of the night, until a certain time when Röaana came to Khaavren where he was resting and said, "I hear something moving."

Khaavren was on his feet at once, listening (for it is well known that a Tiassa will listen better on his feet, whereas a Dzur will hear better with his ear near the ground).

"It is the enemy," he said in a whisper. "As I thought, they are searching for us even at night. This Kâna is more than a little anxious to possess the Orb. Come, let us wake the others, as quietly as we can, and saddle the horses."

By chance, this complex operation was performed, even in the nearly complete darkness, quickly and without undue noise or mishap. Very soon, they were traveling once more, Khaavren setting out in a northwesterly direction, hoping to stay parallel with the road, but fearing to ride on it before knowing if it was safe. After an hour or so, the captain decided they were secure for the moment, and called for a rest.

"Well, what do you think, Captain?" asked the Empress.

"Your Majesty, it is a difficult situation. We are still at least two days' ride from Dzur Mountain, and the forces arrayed against us are overwhelming. If they are now between us and the Enchantress, well, it could be difficult. If they come upon us, it could be unfortunate. But I see no alternative to our plan—that is, to continuing toward Dzur Mountain, avoiding the pursuit as best we can."

"Very well. How long shall we rest this time?"

"A few minutes only. Alas, I should have liked to rest until dawn, but the enemy is too close."

Zerika nodded. "We are in your hands, Captain."

At this expression, a certain shade passed across Khaavren's countenance, as if of a sudden pain, or a painful memory. Zerika affected not to notice, and soon it passed. A few minutes later, Khaavren gave the word, and they mounted up once more, picking their way carefully, according to Zerika's map and the few landmarks they could see, through fields parallel to the road.

As the first soft glow of morning began to spread itself through the gentle fields of Southmoor, Khaavren stopped, and said, "Come, my dear Pel. Bring those sharp eyes of yours here along with a touch-it glass, and tell me what you see."

After some moments, Pel replied, "Makeshift fortifications, defended by some few thousands of men."

"And the banner?"

"I do not recognize it."

"Aerich?"

The Lyorn took the glass, glanced through it, and said, "It is the sigil of the Counts of Southmoor."

"Who would raise that standard?" said Zerika.

"There are rumors," said Aerich, "that an offspring of Rollondar e'Drien survived the Disaster."

"Then that would be Morrolan."

"Very likely," said Aerich.

"Rollondar was always loyal; perhaps his offspring is, as well. In any case, he fights our enemies."

"I should like," said Zerika, "to be certain of his precise loyalties before we approach him, Sethra's remarks notwithstanding."

"I will go and ask," said Piro.

"I will accompany you," said Kytraan.

"That is a good plan," said Khaavren, himself now looking through the touch-it glass. "But, on reflection, I have a better."

"Then let us hear your plan, Captain."

"I propose we join them, for the simple reason that we have no other choice. His battles, yester-day and to-day, with our enemies, are sufficient, I think, to guarantee that we will have some welcome there."

"Can we," asked the Empress, "reach those fortifications before the enemy does?"

"I believe so," said Khaavren, taking the glass again. "But—what is this? There is now another force, a smaller one, directly in our path."

"Smaller? Small enough that we can make our way through them?"

"Perhaps," said Khaavren. "In any case, I should very much like to try. If I am not mistaken, there is someone in that troop I recognize."

"Who?"

Khaavren turned to the Empress, and, behind her, the rest of the small band, and permitted a slow, grim smile to spread over his countenance.

"An old friend," he said.

"Grita?" said Pel.

"You have named her."

"What forces does she have?"

"A mounted escort of perhaps a hundred and fifty."

"Those odds are not impossible," remarked Pel, "if our friend Tazendra can repeat her infernal performance."

"Why," said Tazendra, "I can do it a hundred times, if necessary." (The reader may observe that this estimate had been reduced by a factor of ten; we cannot say precisely why, and will not speculate.)

Khaavren continued looking through the glass.

"They are not moving," he said. "They have positioned themselves as if they knew where we are, and where we are going, and wish to prevent us from reaching it."

"Is it possible they know?" asked Zerika.

Khaavren shrugged. "I cannot imagine how," he said. "But who can say what is impossible?"

"I can," remarked Tazendra. "It is impossible for there to be a spell for which there is no counterspell. Sethra told me this is the case, and I believe she would know."

"But," said Zerika, "how does this affect our present situation?"

"Oh, it does not," said the Dzur. "But Khaavren asked who knew what is impossible, and so—"

"I comprehend," said the Empress.

She turned her attention back to Khaavren, and said, "Well?"

"Well," he said, without removing his eye from the glass, "I had been about to suggest that we charge them, counting on the skill of our friend who knows what is impossible. Only—"

"Yes, only?"

"Only if she repeats her performance exactly, we will find that we have barred our own way with fire, and we might find it problematical to convince our horses to ride through it. They may balk. And do you know, I do not believe I should blame them. Therefore, Tazendra, you must find a spell that will not prevent us from passing through the area now occupied by the enemy."

"I can do so," said Tazendra.

"Very well. But that is not all."

"What else?" said Zerika.

"The circumstances have changed, and we must consider how these changed circumstances affect our plan of action."

"What has changed about the circumstances?"

"The force that flies the banner of the Count of Southmoor—"

"Well?"

"They are now under attack by what appears to be an entire army."

"Yes, that does change the circumstances, doesn't it?" observed Zerika with all the coolness of a Lyorn.

"Yes, we cannot—ah. The enemy attacks."

"Well?"

"They are only committing a small portion of their force. Evidently, they are attempting to discover if a battle is actually required, or whether the defenders will simply yield."

"And the answer?"

"A fight will be required. There is a battle at the walls. Ah, the attacking force is withdrawing. Well, but it was not much of an attack at that."

"Then you think there will be another?"

"I am convinced of it."

"Might we have time to reach the fortifications before the attack begins?"

"It is possible," said Khaavren. "And yet, I cannot recommend such a course. Considering the disparity of forces, the defenders cannot long survive a determined attack. We are better here. We must find a way around this battle, and attempt to reach Dzur Mountain."

"Very well, then, if that is your advice, that is what we will do. When should we move?"

"When the battle is joined in earnest. And that will not be long. They are now moving in force. The Gods! Tens of thousands of them converging on those walls, defended by only a few valiant warriors. It will be frightful slaughter. However, we must—but that is peculiar."

"What is peculiar, Captain?"

But instead of giving an answer, Khaavren continued looking through the glass; and, as he looked, his mouth gradually fell open, which, as science has shown, will happen when the blood is drawn from the face to the liver, as in the case of the sudden onset of a strong emotion, such as surprise.

After a moment, the Empress said, "Captain? What is it?"

It became apparent that all of the blood had, indeed, gone to the captain's liver, because there seemed none at all in his face. When he still failed to answer the Empress (for such reaction cannot truly be considered an answer, when it was details she was after, and not merely the information that he was experiencing great emotion), she cried out, "By the Orb itself! What is going on out there? *Can't you see I am dying?*"

Khaavren swallowed and removed his eye from the glass. "I beg Your Majesty's pardon. I am not entirely certain as to what is going on."

Pel cleared his throat. They looked at him, and realized that he had his own touch-it glass, which he now offered to the Empress with a bow. "I believe," he said, "that I may recognize what is happening."

"Well? What is it?" said Khaavren and Zerika.

"Necromancy."

"Necromancy?" said Empress, frowning.

"The bodies of those who were killed in the first attack are being used as defenders, and, as more of them are killed, they, too, are re-animated to fight against their late comrades. It is not pretty, but it seems to be effective."

Khaavren returned the glass to his eye, even as Zerika said, "Impossible."

"Does Your Majesty truly hold this opinion?"

"Well, then, unlikely. Who could have such skill in that grey art?"

"As to that," said the Yendi, "I know of no one. But I believe, nevertheless, that that is what is taking place."

The frustration of those who had no glass can, we believe, be readily enough imagined. Each pushed forward in order to see as clearly as possible with naked eye and hoped, though no one asked, that one of the glasses would become available. Indeed, in their thirst for a better view of the remarkable sight of which they had heard, they would very possibly have continued forward into the presence of the very enemy force which stood in their path. They were saved from this, very likely, catastrophic event by Aerich, who, as always, kept his composure, and remarked, "If we wish to bring on an engagement, perhaps we ought to consider doing so with something like a plan."

Khaavren lowered the glass, looked up, and frowned. "Come now," he snapped. "Enough of this. Everyone remain behind these shrubs, and stay out of the path."

Zerika, without a word, handed the glass back to Pel, after which she calmly looked at Khaavren.

"In my opinion," said the captain, "we ought to do exactly what the good Aerich suggests."

"Attack?" said the Empress.

"Why not?"

"I can think of no reason."

Khaavren nodded. "Form up, all of you. We will charge. My dear Tazendra, are you prepared with more of your wizardry?"

"Oh, certainly. No preparation is required, I shall simply do it when you wish."

"Very good," said Khaavren. "With living corpses behind them, and the fires of creation before them, well, I believe we might be able to reach our objective."

"Our objective?" said the Empress. "But, what is our objective? Are we again back to attempting to the fortifications?"

"I think so. I have looked around, and there are no small number of the enemy around us. I fear we will not reach Dzur Mountain as matters now stand. Moreover, with the necromancy I see before us, and the spirited defense, I think that will be the best course."

"Well, I do not object, Captain, only—"

"Yes, Majesty?"

"I hope that, once we begin our charge for those fortifications we see yonder, you will not, once again, change your mind."

"Your Majesty, I hope I will not have cause to do so. Tazendra, are you ready?"

"You wish, then, the same spell, but without the fire?"

"Precisely, my love. The same spell without the fire. You perceive, we shall be riding through them, and it would be an embarrassment to me if we were to be burned in flames of our own creation."

"Yes, yes. I understand completely," said Tazendra.

"I hope so," said Khaavren.

The Empress looked over the troop: Khaavren, Aerich, Pel, and Tazendra; Röaana, Ibronka, Piro, and Kytraan; Grassfog, Iatha, Ritt, and Belly; and Clari, Mica, and Lar—not to mention the Empress herself. Zerika closed her eyes, and appeared to be concentrating for some few moments, after which she opened her eyes and said, "The Enchantress agrees. And, moreover, she says that what we observed is nothing less than the truth—the Lords of Judgment have sent the Enchantress a demon who is able to raise the dead, and Sethra has sent her to Southmoor."

"A demon," said Aerich, frowning.

Zerika glanced sharply at the Lyorn. "Yes. A demon. And a Necromancer. This is what we have to work with. Those are the tools given us by the Lords of Judgment with which to defend and reinstate the Empire. Have you anything to say to this, my lord?"

Aerich bowed his head. "Not in the least, Your Majesty."

Piro, for his part (for we do not wish the reader to completely lose sight of he for whom this history is named), watched this interaction with something like awe, and was very glad that he was not positioned directly between these giants—one of whom was his old friend, and the other of whom was an old friend of his father.

It was, we should add, one of those moments for the young Viscount when his view of the world changed in a small but significant way: it was driven in on him, yet again, that his friend truly was the Empress, and these feelings, as the reader can well imagine, involved elements of pride, as well as a certain sadness.

The Empress, for her part, nodded to Aerich. "Very well." She turned to the captain. "Lead us, then. We will attempt to join with this count and his necromantic demon, and may the Lords of Judgment watch over us."

Pel chuckled and gestured toward the battle. "It seems they have done so hitherto."

"Come then," said Khaavren. "Let us form up. This will not be easy. And remember, at all costs, we must protect the Empress."

Zerika began, "As to that—" but Khaavren interrupted her with a glance that reminded her that she was not simply Zerika, but she, herself, embodied the future of the Empire. She therefore bit back, if the reader will permit such an expression, the rest of what she had been going to say, and simply nodded.

"Pel, take Piro and Kytraan and guard the rear."

"Very well."

"Aerich, you on the right with Röaana and Ibronka. Grassfog, you and your band on the left. Tazendra, remain beside me."

"And me, Captain?" said the Empress.

"If Your Majesty will condescend to remain behind Aerich, well, it will permit me to concentrate on what must be done."

Zerika pressed her lips together, but said, "Very well. I trust that, if I am attacked, you will permit me to defend myself."

Khaavren bowed. "I would even encourage Your Majesty to do so as energetically as possible. Now, if we are ready, let us mount up, and prepare to charge."

Tazendra smiled. "And a fine charge it will be."

"Well," said Khaavren, shrugging.

He raised his hand, and something like twelve or thirteen swords were drawn in one motion from as many scabbards—which is to say nothing of a certain iron cook-pot, and a bar-stool made of good wood, that were now held at the ready.

Very soon the horses were in motion. Khaavren glanced to his left and right, and said, "At a walk, my loves. Do not get ahead of me."

In another moment; he said, "Let us trot," and did so, still making sure that no one was ahead of him. And then, "Are you ready, my dear Tazendra?"

"Yes, indeed, my good Captain. Only—"

"Yes?"

"Well, I had not realized how difficult it would be to hold my sword in one hand, my staff in another, and then attempt to find a means of holding these reins so that I may instruct my good horse as to its duties. It is a bother."

"Can you hold the reins in your teeth?"

"In my teeth? But then, how could I talk?"

"Well, it seems evident you must give up something, and I do not imagine you would wish to sheath your sword."

"No, that is true, I do not care to do that. Very well, in my teeth."

"But first, my dear, tell me if you are ready with your spell."

Tazendra made a grunting sound from around the reins, which Khaavren took as a yes. For his part, he then stood up in the stirrups for a moment and fixed his eye upon the enemy—who could now see them very well indeed and were scrambling to prepare their weapons to meet the attack.

"Charge!" cried Khaavren.

"Bother," said Tazendra. "I've lost the reins."

"Well," said Khaavren. "Can you still cast your spell?"

"Oh, certainly."

"Well then, do so."

"What, now?"

"This very instant, if you please."

"Very well, then."

Tazendra cast her spell with considerable success—whatever one might say of Tazendra, there is no question that she had, under the tutelage of Sethra Lavode, achieved no small skill as a wizard. Indeed, it would not be too much to say that Tazendra Lavode was the first of the great wizards who emerged after the Interregnum, and many who today stride the summits of skill ought to recall that it was this Dzurlord, all but unknown, who, with the Enchantress of Dzur Mountain as her guide, first found the path up the mountain.

But the reader, we are sure, does not wish to delay in learning the exact results of her spell, wherefore the author will indulge this impatience by explaining precisely what happened with sufficient detail to satisfy the most curious.

There was a crackling, as before, followed by several very loud claps of thunder—indeed, in those days, when sorcery on the battlefield was far from common, the sound itself would have been sufficient to have, at the very least, distracted anyone who did not have nerves of iron. All of which is to say nothing of the effect on the poor horses, an effect we are assured the reader may easily imagine.

But there was, the reader may be certain, considerably more to our Dzurlord's spell than loud sounds—there were several simultaneous flashes of light, each stemming from a short-lived whirling ball, giving the appearance of certain celebratory spells which are still employed on various holy days with which we are certain the reader is familiar. Each flash of light that struck one of the enemy laid him out, either dead, or, at the very least, hurt and insensible. As to the number of the enemy actually harmed, it was not great—perhaps ten or eleven. But the nature of the attack was so unexpected, and the onslaught so sudden, that Khaavren and his band were past them before they were aware. Indeed, so quickly were they past that there was no opportunity on either side for a clash of arms. All that happened was that Pel tipped his hat as he passed Grita, who was on her back after being thrown from her horse, and he said, "Another time, madam." For her part, Grita once again declined to test her sorcerous or wizardly abilities against those of Tazendra, although, with the power of the Orb now available to the Dzurlord, this was more understandable.

And then they were gone, riding as fast as they could drive their horses up the road toward where Morrolan was conducting his battle.

These events, we should add, had not gone unobserved from within the fortifications.

"My dear Teldra," remarked Morrolan, handing her the touch-it glass and pointing. "What do you make of that?"

"It seems to be sorcery," said the Issola after a moment. "Though I hardly qualify as an expert. But, after all, with the Orb having returned, we ought to have expected sorcery to make its appearance."

"Oh, I do not dispute that, only—"

"Yes, my lord?"

"Well, is it appearing against us, or on our behalf? You perceive, this is a matter of some concern to me. I had based my plans on the notion that, while we had access to certain magical abilities, our friends would be denied these resources."

"Yes, I understand that, my lord. Well, do you know, it would almost seem as if it were being used by a small band that seems determined to approach us."

"That is also my opinion. And, moreover, it seems this band has used sorcery in order to break through a force of our enemy, which inclines me to think they are friendly toward us."

"Yes, that is possible."

"And yet—"

"Yes, my lord? And yet?"

"I wonder if it might not be a ruse."

"That is possible, my lord. But, though I do not have a military mind, I do wonder why an enemy who outnumbers us by such a degree should think it necessary to use a ruse to bring a small band within our walls. It seems probable that, should they wish to bring an enemy within these walls, they need only continue as they are, and exercise a little patience."

Morrolan turned to Fentor, who stood next to him studying the progress of the battle and the effect of the undead upon the enemy. "Well?" said Morrolan. "And what do you think of this analysis?"

"My lord, I believe that I can do nothing to improve upon my lady's summary."

Morrolan grunted. "Very well. Let a break be made in the fortifications to let them through, if they make it that far. And then directly close them again."

"I will see to it," said Fentor.

Morrolan nodded and abruptly turned his attention back to the battle—even then he had that rare capacity to turn his full attention on one matter, and then, having made whatever decision it required, give his entire concentration to the next issue. Now the next issue, in fact, happened to be the conflict directly before his fortifications. There was no doubt, he decided, that the panic caused by the undead soldiers was spreading.

"Well," he said, addressing Fentor once more. "We have gained time, but I fear that is all. They will reorganize, and, now knowing what we can do, they will simply force their way through the undead soldiers as if they were living soldiers. Easier than living soldiers, for the undead do not actually fight as well."

"I agree," said Fentor. "We have gained time, but that is all."

"The question, then, is this: What shall we do with the time we have gained? For I perceive that, in battle, time becomes a most important resource, and, like men, horses, weapons, and supplies, it must be used as efficiently as possible."

Fentor bowed. "Permit me to say, my lord, that you have evidently learned in an hour things that some generals under whom I have served never learn in a lifetime, and I have no doubt that, in a very short time, it is you who will be instructing me in matters of warfare."

Morrolan permitted himself to smile to acknowledge this compliment—for there has yet to be an aristocrat born completely insensitive to flattery, especially when the flattery is heartfelt and sincere—before he said, "Well, but my friend, the question remains. What are we to do with the time?"

"Perhaps now is when we ought to speak with the Warlock. For, if I am not mistaken, you had made certain plans and arrangements with him."

"Yes, that is true. And yes, now might be the time—you see that the enemy has pulled back completely in response to the signals from their drum corps; that can only mean they are regrouping for a new attack."

"I do myself the honor to completely agree with Your Lordship."

"Then I will speak with him at once."

"Yes, but where is he?"

"I have not the least idea in the world."

"You don't know where he is? But then, how can Your Lordship speak to him?"

"He is a witch, and I am a witch."

"Well?"

"We are able to communicate, mind to mind, much as one speaks to another."

"You can do this?"

"With some, yes."

"In the old days, I am told, one could use the Orb for this sort of communication with anyone one knew well."

"Then you understand."

"Entirely."

"For this sort of communication, even between witches, one must be well acquainted with the other."

"That is but natural. And do you know him sufficiently well?"

"I nearly think so. In fact, I am convinced of it, for the reason that we made a test upon this before I returned to these walls, and he set off upon his errand."

"Then I have nothing more to say, my lord, except to suggest in the strongest terms that, whatever plan the two of you have, it should be acted upon at once—you see that the enemy is even now regrouping for another attack."

"I am doing so now, my friend."

A moment later Morrolan said, "Well, I have told him."

"And he said?"

"That he would commence his attack."

"And, do you know what form this attack will take?"

"I know that even less than I know his present location."

"Well, we must watch for it."

"We must first watch for this assault which seems about to break upon our forces, and it looks very much as if, this time, they will sweep past those whom the Necromancer has re-animated. And, after that, it will not be long before we are overwhelmed."

"That is true, that is true—but what is this? It seems that band we saw is now within our walls. Come, let us find out who they are."

"I shall lead," said Morrolan.

"I follow you, my lord."

Morrolan went down from the elevated position he had occupied (in fact, it was on the roof of the temple), and brought himself to where the small band stood on their sweating and blowing horses. Morrolan approached them without hesitation, inclined his head, and said, "I am Southmoor. Has your group a leader whom I ought specially to address?"

The answer came at once "I should imagine that would be me. My name is Zerika, and, as you may deduce from the Orb circling my head, I am your Empress."

"My Empress!" cried Morrolan, suddenly holding himself very still, and staring, first at Zerika, and then at the Orb.

"Kneeling may be appropriate," observed Zerika.

"My Empress?" repeated Morrolan, still with a look of consternation upon his countenance. "But, by what means did I acquire an Empress? I give you my word, three months ago I didn't have so much as an estate!"

"Do you do yourself the honor to jest with me, sir?"

"Perhaps a little," said Morrolan. "And yet, you may see—"

Teldra whispered in Morrolan's ear, "She should be addressed as Your Majesty," at exactly the same moment that Khaavren said the same thing, only not whispering in the least.

Morrolan responded to the one with a shrug, and to the other with a raised eyebrow, and it is possible that matters could have turned unpleasant, except that Zerika choose to smile—that smile that has been called irresistible by many a courtier and diplomatist—and said, "My lord Morrolan, if you do not recognize me, then, if I may ask, why do you do yourself the honor of fighting my battles? And very effectually, at that."

Morrolan bowed to acknowledge the compliment, and said, "I am fighting this battle for the simplest possible reason: Sethra Lavode asked me to, and she is my friend."

"Well then, my lord, perhaps I could be your friend as well, and then you could fight for me on my own behalf."

"Why, one can always use friends."

"I am glad you think so."

"Sethra Lavode, to prove her friendship, gave me this sword."

He touched the hilt of the weapon at his side—a weapon, we should add, that everyone had noticed.

Zerika laughed. "I believe you do yourself the honor of bargaining with me. Are you entirely certain you are a Dragon, my friend? For you begin to sound like a Chreotha."

"If you mean to insult me, madam, I fear I am too recently come to this land to comprehend. I beg you, in that case, to be more explicit."

"Ah, you were raised in the East?"

"I was."

"Much is, then, explained. My dear Morrolan, I ought to glower at you, as the brave captain does, or else give you a glance full of haughty disdain, as you perceive our good Lyorn is doing. But, do you know, I believe I like you. Therefore, I will prove my friendship to you by saying that, if the Empire survives, you shall be given the three counties to the north. Come, what do you say to that?"

"I say that Your Majesty's wish is my command."

Zerika laughed. "Yes, young Dragonlord, I *do* like you. And my wish, at this moment, is to remove myself from the back of this beast who must be as weary of my company as I am of his, and to walk around for a while under the power of my own legs while we decide what we are to do to earn you your three counties."

Morrolan bowed. "Very good, Your Majesty." Then he glanced first at Khaavren, then at Aerich. "And, should either of you wish to express to me in words what you have been saying so eloquently without them, then certainly we can make the opportunity to give these matters the discussion they merit."

Khaavren said, "Of course. I shall be only too glad to be at your service. But first, I would suggest we consider dispatching our common enemy, before we put so much effort into calculating how to reduce our own numbers."

Aerich shrugged.

"That is just as well," said the Empress. "For now, is there someone who can hold my stirrup?"

"With Your Majesty's permission," said Morrolan, "I should like to claim that honor for myself."

Zerika smiled, "With pleasure, my lord."

As Morrolan performed this service, the others in the band dismounted as best they could without the luxury of having their stirrups held. Khaavren, the first off his horse, bowed and said, "I am acting, for the moment, as Her Majesty's captain. My name is Khaavren, originally of Castle Rock, and now of Whitecrest."

"It is a pleasure indeed," said Morrolan, even as Zerika frowned, presumably in response to the phrase "acting for the moment," which the brave Tiassa had permitted to escape his lips.

"And this," said Morrolan, "is my seneschal, Lady Teldra. Over there is my general, whose name is Fentor, and who will, I am sure, be pleased to greet you when he is no longer quite so occupied with the ongoing battle."

Khaavren nodded, and the others were duly introduced. When this ceremony was completed, Morrolan instructed Lady Teldra to see to it that they were quartered as well as possible, especially Her Majesty, against the chance that they might survive the battle.

"Anything is possible," agreed the Empress. "At this moment, however, we should like to view the engagement."

"Very well," said Morrolan. "Although, at the moment, it is in a sort of lull. The enemy is about to launch another assault, and I—"

"Yes, and you?"

"I have given orders that I hope will gain us a respite, during which time, perhaps, we will manage to come up with another idea. But, in the meantime, may I suggest that the top of the temple—the large structure there—will provide Your Majesty a suitable place from which to observe?"

"Very well," said Zerika.

"If Your Majesty will permit," said Teldra, "I will show you the way up."

Zerika smiled and said, "Yes, please. It will be frustrating, and yet, also, undeniably a pleasure to witness a battle in which I am not required to take part."

"I will see to the horses," said Khaavren.

The Empress nodded. "When you are done, join me. And you others may accompany me as well."

Piro and Kytraan begged leave to assist Khaavren; the others followed Teldra and the Empress to the roof of the temple. As they walked, Röaana whispered to Ibronka, "There is no shortage of soldiers here, is there?"

"Indeed?" remarked the Dzur. "I had not observed."

"How, you had not noticed all these fine men in their black and silver?"

"Why no, I confess I had not remarked upon it."

"My dear, are you ill?"

"I? Not the least in the world, I assure you. And, truly, my friend, if you wish to be agreeable, you will not bring up the matter again."

"Why, if that is your wish—"

"Oh, it is, I promise."

"Very well, then we will not discuss it."

"You are adorable, my friend, and I thank you."

Röaana's bemusement, however, was short-lived, because even as they began climbing up to the temple roof, Ibronka was unable to prevent a sigh escaping her lips, and, at the same time, a glance backward in the direction of Piro, the Viscount of Adrilankha, and this glance and sigh were sufficient to answer all of the questions Röaana might have on this subject.

At this moment, the cry came up, "They are coming," and Röaana ran to look.

Chapter the Fifty-Sixth

How the Ninth (or the Tenth As It Is Sometimes Considered, Though Such Numbers Are, in Truth, Unimportant) Battle of Dzur Mountain Was Fought—Concluded

It is impossible to describe the feeling engendered by the charge of Izak's entire army on the small fortifications surrounding Morrolan's temple. To use numbers such as ten to one, or a hundred to one, conveys nothing of the emotions that course through one's being at the sight of an enemy charging with such overwhelming force. Along the lines, hearts pounded and hands gripped weapons, with countenances set in what could be considered masks of determination—for no one, whatever his reaction might be, wished to let the soldier next to him know what was passing in his heart.

The most common emotion was certainly fear. Yet not, in fact, fear of the enemy, so much as a fear of failing to do one's duty. It is safe to say that no one, from Morrolan on down to the lowest private soldier in his command, had ever before been in a situation so grim; yet the fear of death in battle paled beside the fear being thought cowardly or weak by the others on the line.

There is no doubt that many thought about the Empire at that moment. Indeed, while the desire for brevity has forced us to brush past the effect on Morrolan's army of seeing the Orb, the reader can be assured that this visible sign of what they fought for was, for many of the soldiers, like a powerful intoxicant, and the resolution to die in this noblest of causes held many of them steady who might otherwise have "wielded the leg," as soldiers put it. To others, it was simply a matter of personal pride. "I will not," a soldier might tell himself, "run an instant before the man to my left does the same." And this was, in many cases, sufficient.

The corps of sergeants held many in check—in some cases because the sergeant was loved, and the soldier did not wish to shame him, and in other cases because the sergeant was hated, and the soldier did not wish to give him the satisfaction of seeing weakness.

A few of them, to be sure, had entirely different feelings: some of them had long dreamed of the opportunity to die gloriously in battle, and this moment seemed to them to be the greatest moment of their lives; they feverishly willed the enemy closer, promising themselves to take at least three of the enemy with them.

But, whatever was passing in their hearts, they held steady as the foot soldiers of Kâna and his general, Izak, descended upon them as one of the "thunder waves" of Southpoint crashes onto the shore of that tropical village. But instead of particles of water, this wave was made of soldiers—many of them hardened Dragon warriors every bit as skilled as the defenders. And instead of breaking upon sand, this wave would break upon flimsy barricades scantily manned by Morrolan's quickly thrown together, exhausted, and defeated army. And instead of the thunder caused by the breaking of water upon water, the sounds would be those of metal upon metal, and the cries of the wounded.

One might suppose, under the circumstances, that all eyes would have been riveted upon this impending flood (if the reader will permit us to carry our metaphor a little further inland). In this supposition, the reader would be very nearly correct—nearly, but not completely. There was one pair of eyes—those belonging to Morrolan—which were not fixed upon the enemy, but, rather, were searching, attempting to see beyond the massed soldiery. Even as the enemy closed to within a few hundred meters, still Morrolan, from the temple roof, continued searching, as if he expected to see someone or something emerge suddenly.

The reader will, we believe, not be astonished to learn that, in fact, he found what he was seeking.

"There!" he cried, pointing to his left. "And there, too!" he said, looking now to his right. "Do you see them?"

"What is it?" said the Empress, now standing next to him, and following his gaze as best she could.

"Does Your Majesty not see? There, just beyond that rise!"

"The Gods! What are those?"

"Wolves."

"There are hundreds of them! And there, what are those?"

"Dzur. There seem to be ten or twelve there, and another nine or ten on this side."

"But—they are attacking the enemy!"

"I hope so! Should they attack us, well, our plan would not be nearly so good."

"But, how is this possible?"

"It was arranged," said Morrolan.

"Arranged? But, who arranged it?"

"I had that honor."

"But, who carried it out?"

"The Warlock," said Morrolan.

"Who is the Warlock?" said Zerika.

"A pleasant enough fellow whom we met upon our travels, and who is skilled in the arts of Eastern magic—which magic I hope Your Majesty will not disparage."

"Disparage? I? Not the least in the world. Even were I so inclined, I could hardly do so now, as these beasts fall upon our enemies, causing far more confusion among their ranks than mere numbers could account for. Do you see? The attack is faltering upon the right, before they have even reached our fortifications. And there, now it is falling back upon the left, as well. And those in the middle are now discovering that they are alone—you can nearly see the consternation upon the faces of the officers. We are saved!"

"For the moment," agreed Morrolan. "In any case, we have gained a certain amount of time. It now remains for us to make good use of it."

"Well, I agree entirely with your reasoning. And, have you a plan for making use of this gift of time?"

"Not yet, but I hope to discover one."

They watched as, for the third time, the attack receded before them. And, as before, there was a pause while the enemy regrouped.

"How long until darkness?" asked Morrolan.

"Plenty of time for them," said Khaavren.

"Yes."

"Ah!" said the Empress suddenly. "But, who is that?"

"Where?" said Khaavren and Morrolan.

"There, do you see? A rider seems determined to gain the fortifications by himself, where the masses of the enemy have failed. There seems to be a wolf and a dzur nipping at his horse's heels as he comes."

"Oh," said Morrolan. "That is the Warlock, and the wolf and the dzur you see are not nipping at his heels, but, rather, guarding and accompanying him."

"Impossible!" said the Empress.

"Your Majesty will shortly learn if I have spoken incorrectly, for he is very nearly here, and Fentor—that is my general—is causing a breach to be made in our defenses in order to permit his entry."

The opening was made, and the rider entered. The Empress's eyes were fixed upon him as he dismounted (by which time, though none of the onlookers had observed the transformation, his companions were once more a shabby-looking white dog, and a small black cat).

"Why, he is an Easterner," cried the Empress.

"Indeed," observed Morrolan. "Many of those who practice the arts of Eastern magic are Easterners."

Zerika turned her attention to him, as if she would reprimand him for daring to speak ironically to her, but in the end she said nothing, instead turning her eyes, now burning, back upon the figure of the Easterner, who was climbing up the rude wooden stairway. Indeed, it must be said (for it did not escape the quick eyes of Khaavren) that as she watched, there was even a certain trembling in her lip, and she uttered under her breath, "Oh, it is he! It is he! But how came he here?" in tones that escaped everyone's ears except those of our brave captain, who frowned to overhear it, and could not help but wonder. For this reason, when the Warlock came closer, Khaavren observed him carefully, and this observation was rewarded by catching the merest glimpse, as it were, of sudden shock upon the face of the Easterner, who at once covered up this surprise upon receiving a sign from the Empress—a sign that, like the murmur and the expression, were observed by no one except Khaavren. Our sharp-eyed Tiassa noticed more than this, however: the War-

lock's two companions, whom he was never seen without, upon seeing the Empress, seemed about to run directly to her, stopping only
when the Warlock gave them a sharp, whispered command.

In the meantime, Morrolan, who had noticed none of this, said,
"Your Majesty, this is the Warlock, a good friend, a brave companion, and a loyal ally. Warlock, this is Her Imperial Majesty Zerika."

At this point, Teldra, who had remained very much in the back-
ground, stepped forward and whispered into Morrolan's ear. Morrolan coughed, and said, "I beg your pardon. Her Majesty Zerika the
Fourth, Empress of Dragaera, Princess of the House of the Phoenix,
Duchess of Boxhills and Nerahwa, and so on, and so on." Upon con-
cluding this speech, Morrolan glanced at Teldra, who smiled fleet-
ingly, as if to tell Morrolan that he had performed his duty well.

"It is an honor, Your Majesty," said the Warlock.

"It is a pleasure, Warlock. But, come, that is no name for you.
Haven't you a title?"

"A title, Your Majesty? But then, I am not even a citizen."

"Well, but now you are, because I declare you to be one. And,
moreover, you may now call yourself Viscount of Brimford, which
title will be Imperial, as you are obviously of no House, but will be
considered hereditary. We hope you accept this gift as our thanks for
the service you have rendered the Empire."

The Warlock—that is to say, Lord Brimford—knelt quickly and
touched his lips to the proffered hand. Morrolan, observing this, was
astonished at how deeply the Warlock was affected by the honor—it
seemed as if the Easterner's hand actually trembled at the touch of
Her Majesty's.

Brimford rose once more, and bowed, and backed away several
steps, though his eyes remained fixed upon Zerika's face with an
intensity that could have been considered improper, had anyone
stopped to do any considering. The Empress herself, after a moment,
turned back to Morrolan and said, "Come. Our friend has gained us
some time; what are we to do with it?"

Morrolan shook his head slowly. "Your Majesty, I confess I do
not know. It astonishes me that we have held so long. But the enemy
still has overwhelming force, and seems determined to make yet
another charge. And now that the animals summoned by our friend

have been driven off, I do not know what is to stop them. In a moment, they will re-form, and break through our fortifications as if they were thinnest paper, and manned only by cut-out shapes, such as are used to represent crowds of people in theaters in the land of my birth."

"We had similar cut-outs," observed the warlock Brimford, who, it seemed to Khaavren, was only with great effort keeping his eyes from straying to the Empress.

"I have an idea," remarked Khaavren.

"Well then," said Zerika, "let us hear it."

"This is it: You are able to communicate with the Enchantress, are you not?"

"I am."

"Well, is it not the case that, at the time of the Disaster, she was able to save the Orb, in much the same manner that Adron himself preserved our lives, by causing us to move from one place to another?"

"I had not known about yourselves, but it is true that the Enchantress thus saved the Orb."

"Well then, in the same way, she can save you. She must sorcerously transport you to the safety of Dzur Mountain. That is my plan."

"That is your plan?" said Zerika. "But, what of the rest of you?"

"We mean nothing," said Khaavren. "You and the Orb must be preserved. The rest of us do not matter."

Morrolan, hearing this, looked at the warriors who had fought so hard over the last two days, but, if he had been about to make an observation, he was unable to do so, because before he could speak, Zerika said, "I reject this plan."

"And yet," said Khaavren, "consider—"

"No," said Zerika. "Now, has anyone else a plan?"

Khaavren, with some difficulty it is true, did not pursue the matter.

"Well then," said Tazendra, approaching suddenly. "I have a plan."

"I know your plan, my friend," said Khaavren.

"How, do you?"

"Of a certainty. And I shall prove by naming it in all its details. This is it: You wish us to man the defenses and all die gloriously for the Empire."

Tazendra stared at Khaavren in astonishment. "Have you learned, then, to read thoughts as if they were a letter already written and delivered?"

Khaavren shrugged.

"Has anyone else a plan?" said Zerika. "If not, well, I am not far from adopting Tazendra's."

"As to that—" said Khaavren.

"Ah, who is this who now approaches?" said the Empress.

Morrolan bowed. "A friend of the Eastern lands where I was raised. My high priestess, Arra. Arra, this is Her Majesty, the Empress. But tell me, why are you here?"

"To inquire, my lord," said the Easterner, after bowing respectfully to Her Majesty, "if there was anything you wished me to do."

Morrolan shook his head. "Not unless you can make the temple fly."

"No," said Arra. "Alas, we do not have the power to do that, nor will we until you can find me another five hundred witches in addition to those we have."

Morrolan stared at her. "Are you speaking seriously? If we had another five hundred witches, you could raise this temple?"

"Oh, certainly. With the Circle, in proper form, number, and alignment, it would be possible. Even now—"

"Yes, even now?"

"If you were, somehow, to make it levitate, we could hold it there, but—"

"You could?" said Morrolan.

"You could?" said the Empress.

"You could?" said Khaavren.

"You could?" said Tazendra.

"Oh, assuredly. We have, after all, the power of hundreds of us working together. Once it is raised, to maintain it is well within our power."

"But, for how long?"

"Oh indefinitely," said Arra. "It is not difficult. But to actually lift it—"

"Oh, I could manage that," said Tazendra, shrugging.

"You could?" said the Empress.

"Well, it is not a large structure. And, you recall, in the old days, why, all of the e'Driens had floating castles."

"Shards! That is true!" cried the others.

"Indeed," observed Morrolan, "this temple is built from the ruins of a castle that fell."

"It is, in fact, the falling part that concerns me," said the Empress, with a glance at Arra.

"I assure you, madam, that—"

"Address her as Your Majesty," said Khaavren.

"Very well. I assure you, Your Majesty, that we can manage this."

"We must talk, my dear," said Teldra softly in Arra's ear.

"Besides," said Tazendra, "if it fails—"

"Well, if it fails?" said Zerika.

"Think of how many of the enemy we will crush below us."

"I am consoled," said Khaavren dryly.

"How much area can you lift?" asked the Empress.

"Your Majesty," said Tazendra, "it is not a question of area, it is a question of weight."

"I understand that, my dear. But, you perceive, they are related. To begin, you have said you could lift the temple."

"Oh, the temple, certainly."

"And the stables?"

"Easily."

"And the fortifications?"

"Probably."

"Then we will confine ourselves to the temple and the stables, for I mislike probables when the matter at hand concerns great heights."

"Very well."

"And you could hold it there?"

"As to that—"

"Well?"

"I am certain that, once I have learned the proper spell, it will be a simple enough matter to cast it."

"It is a different spell to raise it than to hold it?"

"To raise it is simple levitation, though on a large scale. But, with the power now flowing through the Orb—"

"But holding it?"

"Someone must know that spell," said Tazendra.

"I believe," said the Empress, "that most of those who knew that spell died when it failed. And, of the rest, I should imagine most, if not all, were in Dragaera City. And, if there are any others, I do not know how to find them."

"And yet," said Tazendra, "if this lady," here she bowed to Arra with all the courtesy she would have given a human, "can use her powers to hold it—"

"They are forming again," observed Morrolan.

"Well?" said Tazendra.

"Well?" said Arra.

Zerika looked at Morrolan and Khaavren, then at Arra, and at last said, "Very well, let us do so."

"We shall be ready in two minutes," said Arra.

"And I," said Tazendra, "am ready now."

"In that case," said Zerika, "it would be best if you waited two minutes."

"Longer than that," said Morrolan.

"How so?" asked the Empress.

"I trust Your Majesty will give us time to get the troops into the temple, instead of leaving them where they are to be slaughtered or captured?"

"Ah! Yes, that is only just."

Morrolan bowed. "I am glad Your Majesty sees it that way."

"How long will it take?"

"Half an hour."

"And how long until the enemy attacks?"

"I cannot tell, but it will be soon."

"More than half an hour?"

"I hope so."

"As do I. Begin, then."

Shortly thereafter, General Izak appeared at Kâna's tent and begged permission to enter, which permission was quickly granted.

"Your Majesty," began Izak, bowing.

"Well, General? Is the attack prepared?"

"Nearly. But a strange thing is happening, and I mistrust strange things."

"Well, what is this strange thing? They have foiled us now three times, and you have promised that, this time, you will take the position without fail. If this strange thing interferes with that, I warn you, it will not go well with you."

"Your Majesty, it seems the enemy is deserting their position."

"Deserting it?"

"At least, it appears so."

"How can you account for this behavior?"

"Your Majesty, I cannot."

"How quickly can you attack?"

"The troops are nearly re-formed. We can launch the assault in twenty minutes."

"Do so, then."

"Yes, Your Majesty."

"And keep me apprised of any changes."

Izak bowed and left to give the orders. Twenty minutes later, he returned and, once more, was admitted into Kâna's presence.

"Well, General? Is the attack prepared?"

"The attack? Well, yes, so far as it goes, the attack is prepared."

"Then you have done right to come for me, because I wish to observe it personally."

"Your Majesty, there is certainly something to see, only—"

"Yes, yes, the attack will be something to see, I do not doubt it. Come, let us find a good vantage point. I do not forget that you promised me that this time you would take the position without fail."

"Oh, as to that—"

"Yes? Do not tell me, General, that you will not fulfill your promise. I am becoming impatient with this delay."

"So far as that goes, yes, I have no doubt we will take the position, and, moreover, do so with few or no casualties."

"Ah! So much the better!"

"Well, yes, but—"

"But what, General? You know that I do not like 'buts.' You can take the position, or you cannot. Earlier you said you could, and you have just repeated it."

"Yes, Your Majesty. There is no possible doubt about taking the position. I have said it, and I even repeat it. Only, I fear—"

"You fear? A general ought not to fear."

"Nevertheless, I fear."

"What do you fear?"

"I fear that taking the position will constitute only a hollow victory, if it will be victory at all."

Kâna frowned. "What are you telling me?"

"I'm telling you, or, rather, attempting to tell you—"

"Yes?"

"It is a difficult thing to say."

"Overcome the difficulty, General."

"Well, I will do so."

"And quickly, I hope."

"I have overcome it already."

"Splendid. Then you will tell me?"

"This very instant, if you wish."

"If I wish? And do you imagine there is anything else in life I have been wishing for this last hour?"

"This is it, then: They are all gone."

"Gone?"

"Gone."

"Yes, but, *gone*?"

"Exactly, Majesty. *Gone*."

"Well, but where have they gone?"

"Would Your Majesty like to know that?"

"How can you ask, obstinate man?"

"If Your Majesty will condescend to step out of this tent, well, I believe the answer will become apparent."

"That is all I must do to learn the answer, is to step outside?"

"Exactly."

"Well, then I will do so at once."

Kâna passed out of his tent, and, a moment later, returned.

"Well, I see where they have gone."

"Yes, Majesty."

"How high are they?"

"I cannot tell. Perhaps half a mile, perhaps more."

"Can they remain there long?"

"Before the Interregnum, there were castles that remained in the air for years at a time. And now that the Orb is back, our enemies have access to its power."

Kâna frowned. "It is hardly fair," he observed.

The general, having no reply prepared for this remark, made none.

As far as history is concerned, this concluded the Ninth (or the Tenth) Battle of Dzur Mountain, as there were no more offensive or defensive movements taking place in that district (which is, we pointed out at the beginning, some distance from Dzur Mountain). However, as the reader is no doubt aware, there is a great deal more left to consider. Therefore, we feel it incumbent upon us, before closing this chapter of our history, to say two words about what was occurring within the confines of the temple that now floated off the ground, as had certain castles before the Interregnum.

To say the temple was crowded would be to make what can only be called a lamentable understatement. Consider that the altar room had been designed by Morrolan (with, we should add, assistance from certain Chreotha) to hold, at the most, one thousand and one hundred worshipers, this size being determined by the skeleton of the structure as he found it. It is true that there were other rooms, and the roof, and a certain amount of ground outside of the temple itself. But there were, all in all, upward of five thousands of beings (human, equine, and Eastern) in this space, many of whom had taken wounds, more or less serious.

Most of the roof, in fact, was set aside as a sort of hospital, whereas another section was made the command center, where Morrolan, Fentor, Khaavren, and the Empress remained to consider matters and to make decisions. Of the smaller chambers within the temple structure, Arra claimed the one reserved for herself, but permitted Teldra and a few others to remain there as well. Arra's witches occupied the large basement room set aside for that purpose. These witches, according to their custom, held themselves in strict seclu-

"Oh, yes!" said Kytraan. "Let us, indeed, talk of the future. What could be a better subject?"

"Indeed," said Ibronka. "Consider that the possibilities are limitless. In the future, why, anything can happen."

"You think so?" said Kytraan. "Then, you do not believe that the paths which our feet are to tread are already laid out for us?"

"Not in the least," said Ibronka, who had recovered sufficiently to join the general discussion. "We make the future."

"That is true," said Piro. "We make the future, as the past makes us."

"But yet, we must have made the past as well," said Röaana.

And in this way, having passed from the specifics of fear to the generalities of philosophy, our four young friends passed the time, as Morrolan's temple to Verra floated in the skies above Kâna's army. And as they continued this discussion (which so effectually distracted them from their fear), over their heads, as it were, several others were also discussing the future, although in what might be called a less abstract sense.

"We have," Morrolan was saying, "what can be called a reprieve."

"Indeed," observed Khaavren. "But for how long? With four casks of water, two of wine, fifty boxes of biscuit, and whatever foodstuffs happened to be in the pantry, well, I do not think we have ultimately solved our problem."

"How long, then, Captain?" asked Zerika.

"Two days, then we begin to starve."

"Much can be done in two days," observed Zerika.

"By the enemy, as well as by ourselves," put in Fentor.

"This conversation begins to sound familiar," said the Empress.

"Can we move?" said Khaavren. "That is, Tazendra, can you cause this building to float in a certain direction?"

"Only slowly," said Tazendra.

"How slowly?" That is, how long will it take us to reach Dzur Mountain?"

"Five years, perhaps six."

"That is too long," suggested the Empress.

"We need a plan," said Morrolan.

"Well," observed Teldra, who happened to be standing nearby in case Morrolan or the Empress required anything, "if I may speak."

"If you have anything to say," said the Empress, "then, by all means, say it."

"I thank Your Majesty, and only wish to observe that, if we need a plan, I would point out that we have a Yendi with us."

"That is true!" said Khaavren. "He is there, in the corner, speaking with Aerich. Pel, my friend! Two minutes of your time!"

Pel approached with his habitual grace, bowed, and said, "My dear friend, you may have two hours."

"That is good. You understand our situation?"

"If you mean that we are floating above an enemy who vastly outnumbers us, and we have only a few days of food and supplies, well then, yes I understand the situation. If there is something else you mean, then I should have to be apprised of it."

"No, no," said Khaavren. "Your understanding, as always, is perfect."

"And then?"

"We need a plan."

"Ah," said the Yendi. "It is just as well, then, that I have one."

"Already?"

"I had just been discussing it with Aerich and the demon who is skilled at raising the dead, and with the Easterner whose pets are so entertaining. We have been discussing it, and we agree that it is a good one."

"Well then?" demanded the Empress. "Let us hear this famous plan."

"I shall relate it to Your Majesty at once, although I warn Your Majesty, it is not clever."

"It is not?"

"No, it is merely tedious."

"I accept that it is not clever. So long as it solves our problem, it may be as tedious as you like."

Pel bowed and explained his plan, with results that we shall, in due course, discover to the reader.

Chapter the Fifty-Seventh

How Pel's Plan Was Put Into Operation, And a Conversation Alluded to Some Time Ago Is, At Last, Revealed

At a certain time on the following day, Ibronka, her eyes wide, said to her friend Röaana, whose features also wore an expression of astonishment, "So, this is Dzur Mountain!"

"It is astonishing!"

"It is magnificent!"

"Just think at all that these walls have seen, think of the ages that have passed!"

"And our feet, Röaana, are walking through halls where Sethra Lavode—Sethra Lavode herself!—has walked. And still walks, come to that."

"Yes, it is wonderful!" said the Tiassa. "Do you think we shall meet the Enchantress?"

"It is possible."

"What ought one to say when meeting her?"

"Perhaps, 'How do you do?' would be appropriate."

"Do you think so?"

"It is all that occurs to my thoughts."

"We can ask Lady Teldra; I believe she has come over."

"How many of us have come over?"

"I have no idea, my dear Ibronka. But do you actually wish to know how many, or do you wish to know *who*?"

"Oh, as to that—"

"Well, I give you my word, I do not know yet whether a certain Tiassa has come over, so you may as well not ask; but permit me to say you blush most prettily whenever he is spoken of?"

"You are cruel, Röaana."

"Not the least in the world. I am merely trying to goad you."

"But why?"

"Because, my love, I am not his friend, therefore I cannot goad him."

"That is no reason. Besides, what is the hurry?"

"Hurry? Fate has thrown us together, and can just as easily tear us apart again. Suppose to-morrow he should receive an errand that takes him to Guinchen, where the girls are so pretty, or to the Sorannah, where they are so charming? What then?"

"Oh, stop this conversation; you can see it disturbs me."

"That is my intention."

"Please."

"Oh, very well."

In fact, it is the case that Piro and Kytraan had been teleported to Dzur Mountain some few hours before, and, being permitted, as friends of the Enchantress, to go where they would, were now sitting in Sethra's library, slowly consuming a bottle of Walking wine, or Traveling wine as it was known at one time, so named because it could, owing to how it was fermented, survive long journeys without undue harm.

"Well, my dear fellow," said Kytraan. "We are back, it seems, and we have seen a few things since we left."

"Indeed," said Piro. "And done a few things as well."

"Although to be sure, there is more to do—especially for you."

"Especially for me? Why do you say so? What is there for me to do that is not as much for you to do?"

"Pah, you know well enough what I mean."

"I have not the least idea in the world, I assure you."

"You imagine she will wait for-ever? That there will not be some dashing Dzurlord she might meet to-morrow or the next day who will carry her off?"

"Of whom can you be speaking, my friend?"

"My dear Tiassa, you are disingenuous. If you did not know of whom I spoke, there would not at this instant be so much color rising to your face."

"Let us not speak of it."

"On the contrary, let us speak of nothing else."

"Very well, if you will have it so, let us speak of it."

"Good. But, instead of speaking to me, you should speak to her."

"What should I tell her?"

"Tell her? You must have known girls before."

"Well, yes."

"And you must have known one with whom you desired to have conversation."

"Oh, without doubt."

"What did you tell her?"

"That I should like to get to know her better."

"Good."

"That I thought her most lovely."

"Good."

"That I have never before met another with whom I could speak so freely."

"I must remember that one."

"That it would be a great honor to be able to escort her for an evening of entertainment."

"And this has worked for you, has it not?"

"Certainly."

"Then what more is there to say?"

"My dear Kytraan—"

"Well?"

"I do not understand what you do me the honor of telling me."

"Merely that, if it worked before—"

"Shards! Those things? I cannot tell those things to Ibronka!"

"The Gods! Why not?"

"Why not? You ask me why not?"

"Indeed, I ask you why not. And if that is not enough, I ask you again. Why not?"

"Because—"

"Yes?"

"Because, well, because with Ibronka, they are true!"

"Ah!" said Kytraan after a moment. "I had not understood this circumstance."

"Well, but you understand now, do you not?"

"Oh, entirely, my poor friend. But then, speak to her of other things."

"What other things?"

"Oh, the usual things. Speak of her family, or talk about food, or about philosophy. You know she is interested in philosophy."

"Oh, I cannot. When I try to speak to her, my breath fails, and my throat closes."

"Ah, my poor friend. I understand entirely."

"Do you?"

"I promise that I do."

"Then have pity on me, and let us speak of other things."

"Very well, my friend, only—"

"Yes?"

"A caution."

"Very well, I will listen to your caution, since you insist upon it."

"Well, you know she is not a Tiassa."

"I think so! And I am not a Dzur!"

"Exactly."

"That is your caution?"

"In its entirety."

"Well, I have noted it."

"That was my only wish, Viscount."

As the reader has, no doubt, deduced, more and more of those who had been at the temple were arriving at Dzur Mountain, brought over by the sorcerous abilities of Tazendra, at times aided by the Enchantress herself. This could not be done at a great pace—as is well known, the casting of difficult spells requires a degree of concentration that cannot be maintained over long periods of time, and, moreover, the spell which permitted such movement was still clumsy and difficult, having not yet been refined by the Athyras Krimel and Thrace who would do such tremendous work at Twabridge University. However, it should be added that to transport non-living material was rather easier, and so, while only forty or forty-five persons had, as of yet, been brought to Dzur Mountain, a greater amount, at least in weight, and consisting mostly of food and fodder, had gone the other way.

Zerika, who occupied one of Sethra's sitting rooms, caused Pel to be sent for. The Yendi arrived and bowed, saying, "How may I serve the Empress?"

"I wish to tell you, Yendi, that your plan seems to be a good one.

As we bring the troops here, out of harm's way, and send supplies to them, Kâna's army is gradually melting away. Between the forces of the undead, the attacks by wolf and dzur, and the occasional spell with lightning and fire, they are becoming completely demoralized. Soon, Kâna must either turn around and march away, or he will have no army left at all."

"And if he chooses to march in this direction, to put Dzur Mountain under siege?"

"Then it will be a simple enough matter for us to return to the Lord Morrolan's keep, where they cannot touch us. Or, if they have been sufficiently weakened by that time, we may simply choose to engage them. You have done well."

"I am pleased, Your Majesty. Will that be all?"

"No, there is more."

"I remain at Your Majesty's service."

Zerika hesitated, then said, "I know something about you, Duke."

Pel bowed and waited for Her Majesty to continue.

"The Orb, you perceive, hears much, and remembers everything it hears."

"And if I may do myself the honor of questioning Your Majesty, may I ask what it is she knows of me, other than, it seems, my name and title, to which, as Your Majesty must know, I attach no great importance?"

"I know something of your activities before the Interregnum."

"Indeed?"

"Oh, you are a Yendi. I know that. There is no question that there are many things you have done of which I remain ignorant. But I know that, at the time of the Disaster, you were studying the art of Discretion."

"Your Majesty is not misinformed."

"You knew Wellborn?"

"I had that honor as a young man."

"I have heard that he epitomized all that could be asked for in a Discreet."

"I have heard the same. Moreover, I am convinced that it is the case. He was wise, and he knew how to listen, and he knew how to remain silent, and he knew how to say enough, but not too much. I know that he was a great comfort to His Late Majesty."

Zerika nodded. "Except for yourself, Duke, there were few students of Discretion who survived the Disaster. And of graduated, certified Discreets, I know of none at all."

"Nor do I, Your Majesty."

Zerika looked at Pel as if considering his character, or summoning her courage, or perhaps both. At length, with a sigh, she said, "My conscience stabs me, Your Discretion."

Pel took a step backward, and, for one of the few times in his life, an appearance of astonishment settled over his countenance. For a long moment he could say nothing, and, indeed, his hands were actually trembling. Who can know what thoughts and feelings were thundering through the ambitious and burning veins of the Yendi? Certainly, the Empress could not; because, at this instant, she was unable even to raise her eyes to meet his.

At length, Pel, or, as we should say, the Duke of Galstan, was able to master his emotions, and, in as steady a voice as he was capable of, pronounced the words, "I will bind the wounds, Sire."

And as he said these words, completing the ritual, falling into a pattern long established by training that was unused but not forgotten, he managed to keep from his features that which was in his heart—the fiery joy of unexpected triumph.

An hour later he left the presence of the Empress, followed in short order by the Empress herself, who at once found Tukko, and caused this worthy to lead her to Sethra Lavode.

"Your Majesty," said the Enchantress, bowing. "How may I serve you?"

"I must return to the temple."

"Very well," said Sethra, as if it were the most natural request in the world. "Now?"

"If you please."

In two minutes, the Empress stood on the roof of Morrolan's temple. Morrolan and Tazendra, who were engaged in conversation, bowed to her. She returned the salute and said, "My dear Tazendra, you seem fatigued. Could it be that you are straining too much?"

"Not at all. I was merely describing for the good Morrolan the processes of sorcery."

"Ah," said the Empress. "And you, Count, what do you think?"

"It is astonishing, Your Majesty. I had no idea so much could be done! And so easily!"

"He has," observed Tazendra, "something of a natural bent in this area."

"You are a good teacher," said Morrolan.

"So then," inquired the Empress, "you are serious about the study of this art, rather than the Eastern magic which, as I understand it, you have already studied?"

"I shall continue to delve into both, I think," said Morrolan. "But for now, after Your Majesty graciously granted me citizenship—" Zerika bowed. "—I find that I thirst to come to an understanding of this art as I have never thirsted before. Indeed, I have already begun casting a few small spells to aid in the discomfort of our enemies, and Tazendra assures me that, in a week, I will able to teleport inanimate objects to known locations."

"I do not doubt that, should you choose, you will become a most accomplished sorcerer," said Zerika, "or even a wizard, and that very quickly."

"I hope so, Majesty. The Enchantress has agreed to teach me as well, so, you perceive, I will have no shortage of skilled instructors. But forgive me, my enthusiasm has made me forget my courtesy. In what way can I serve Your Majesty?"

"Where is the warlock, Brimford?"

"Down on the surface, and out somewhere," said Morrolan. "Recruiting more beasts for the entertainment of our friends below. I tell Your Majesty that I should not enjoy being in their encampment; it is not a comfortable place. Thirty wolves descend on a camp, and the enemy all scrabble to find a new place to rest, and then a dzur attacks on the other side, and so another camp wishes to move, and then those killed in those attacks are re-animated, and so yet another camp is broken up. I do not believe any one in that army was able to sleep last night, nor will they to-night, nor for many nights to come."

"This army, yes. But, as you may remember, there is another army, even larger, that is still marching toward Dzur Mountain."

"What Your Majesty says is true," said Morrolan. "And we have been observing them, thanks again to more friends of Lord Brimford, but we have, as of yet, done nothing except observe."

"Very well. Morrolan, you have no small skill in the Eastern magical arts; are you able to reach Brimford by mind?"

"Am I? Of a certainty. But I should have thought Your Majesty could do so more easily."

"I? Why, I scarcely know the man."

"Yet, with the Orb—"

"My dear Dragon, through the Orb I have a mental link to some hundreds of thousands of people, with the number growing each minute. Can you imagine the difficulty of looking at each one, to see if it is he with whom I wish to converse? No, no. If you know his mind, you can reach him more easily than I."

"Very well," said Morrolan. "I am only too happy to be of service. But what would Your Majesty have me communicate to him?"

"To return here at once; it is my desire to speak with him."

"As Your Majesty wishes."

We should say that, while communicating with Brimford was not difficult, transporting him was not easy—it is well known that it is simpler to *send* someone than to *bring* him. But Tazendra and Morrolan between them managed the feat, receiving Zerika's solemn thanks.

As to the Warlock, upon being informed that it was the Empress who wished to speak with him, he gave her a bow and assured her that he was entirely at her service.

"That is well, my good Brimford. There are matters which I wish to discuss with you. Come, let us find a place where we can speak with one another without being disturbed."

Brimford appeared to experience a certain agitation at this suggestion, but made no argument; instead, after requiring the dog, Awtlá, and the cat, Sireng, to wait for him, he followed the Empress down into the temple, still crowded though it was, through the altar room, out through one of the wing doors, and so into the small alcove where a few days before Piro and his friends had carried on their philosophical discourse. This room happened to have a door, which the Empress shut, and then, turning to Brimford, she said, "The Gods! Laszló! It is you!"

The Warlock at once fell to his knees and, taking the Empress's hand, pressed his lips to it. "Zivra!" he said. "How came you here? And Empress? You, Empress? What does it mean? When I saw you, I thought surely I would die!"

Zerika smiled. "Then, you are not sorry to see me?"

"Sorry! Sorry! If live to be ten thousand, I will never be less sorry of anything. But why did you have that Dragonlord communicate with me, instead of doing so yourself?"

"It is useless to let everyone know that we are acquainted. And, moreover, it was my wish to give you an agreeable surprise. And did I do so?"

"I am enchanted! But what of you?"

"Oh, I?"

"Yes, are you glad to see me?"

"How can you ask? I am wounded!"

"I will cure your wound, if you but grant me leave!"

"Cure me? How? You alarm me, sir!"

"Ah, now you play the coquette? Oh, my sweet Zivra, if you knew what you do to me! Do you recall our last conversation?"

"Oh, can I ever forget it? In your little garret in South Adrilankha."

"Yes, yes. And you said you were going away, and didn't know if you would ever return."

"I was frightened that day. I had just said farewell to my friends, and I said farewell to you last of all. I feared it would be for-ever."

"It was a cruel day!"

"It was not easy for me, Laszló."

"Oh, you must not call me that. I renounced my name, and now you have given me a new one."

"Well, Brimford, then."

"But go on, go on. What happened next?"

"Next, Sethra Lavode discovered to me the secret of my birth, and said that I must travel to the Paths of the Dead and retrieve the Orb! And, do you know, with all I have been through, nothing was harder than taking my leave of you that day."

"You have suffered terribly, my love. Would that I could have spared you! And I—"

"Yes? And you?"

"I left that night, without even stopping to gather my meager belongings. I took the few coins I had, purchased a horse, and Awtlá and Sireng and I rode through the night, blind with grief."

"Oh!"

"I killed the horse before the night was out, and then I walked, and walked, and I found another roaming wild upon the plains, and so I rode more."

"Oh!"

"I thought, as I had no destination, perhaps, at last, I could complete my tasks and discover my name."

"And did you?"

"I believe now that I never will."

"Oh, do not say that!"

"Why? Do you imagine that I care?"

"How, you don't?"

"Now that I have found you again, I care about nothing else. Only—"

"Yes?"

"You are the Empress!"

"And if I am?"

"My dear Zivra—or Zerika, or Your Majesty, or whatever I am to call you—"

"To you, I hope I will always be Zivra."

"So then, you are Zivra. But—"

"Yes, but?"

"It is one thing for Zivra to have a subject and acquaintance who is an Easterner. It is quite another for the courtiers to say that the Empress's lover is an Easterner. What then?"

"Come, my friend! We will not announce it to the world! It is none of the world's concern. You perceive, I did not even tell those who just now brought you to me."

"Will you conceal it from the courtiers? I do not know what it is like in a Palace, but I cannot believe that such a secret can long be kept."

"Well, and if it isn't?"

"Then it will be known."

"Then let it be known."

"My dear Zivra, you cannot mean it! Think of the scandal!"

"I have thought of it. In fact, I have more than thought of it, I have asked someone about it."

"What? Who?"

"Who else is entitled to know such things but the Imperial Discreet."

"The Discreet? But there is no Discreet."

"There is now, because I have appointed one."

"Well, and he said?"

"He said that it is important—nay, vital—that, as Empress, my mind remains calm, and that I not permit strong emotion to interfere with my decisions."

"Well, that seems wise. And then?"

"He wondered how it might affect my decisions if I were spending my time weeping over a lover I could not have."

"Oh, would you weep?"

"Weep? Without you, my eyes would be red thirty hours a day! Don't you know that I cannot live without you?"

"Oh, say that again! You know how it makes my heart pound to hear it!"

"Ah! What are you doing? You know that I cannot repeat what I said when you are doing that!"

"Well, try."

"Ah, your whiskers tickle."

"Are they less welcome for that?"

"Oh, not in the least, only—"

"Yes?"

"You know that I must return to my duties at Dzur Mountain, and you must continue convincing Kâna's army to desert."

"What, now?"

"This very instant."

"But when will I see you again?"

"Tonight."

"Have I your word on it?"

"The word of the Empress of Dragaera. I hope that will be sufficient!"

"Oh, it is, it is!"

"Then you are happy?"

"Delirious. You know that I love you."

"And I love you, but we can spare no more time."

"Have I time to kiss your hand?"

"Here it is."

"Ah, I leave the happiest of men."

"And I bid you farewell, adoring you."

"Temptress!"

"My own Eastern devil!"

"My elf!"

"Farewell!"

"Farewell!"

Brimford fairly flew up the stairs, back to the roof, where, upon learning that Tazendra had retired to get some rest, and there was no one to transport him back down, found a corner, along with Awtlá and Sireng (who seemed especially happy, sensing the mood of their master), and settled down to take his ease for a few hours. Zerika, for her part, remained alone in the small chamber for a moment, smiling happily. "Well, it seems I must truly work to be a good Empress, if only so that I can deserve this happiness! Oh, if only it will last!"

Chapter the Fifty-Eighth

How Kâna Faced Defeat,
The Empress Faced Victory,
And Arra Faced Her Fear of Heights

So far, indeed, things seemed to be going the Empress's way: Even as she was speaking these words, Kâna had received the report of his general, Izak.

"Then," said Kâna, "desertions are increasing by the hour, and many of them are deserting directly into the camp of the enemy?"

Izak bowed his head.

"And we cannot stop these magical attacks?"

Izak signified his agreement once more.

Kâna nodded. "We march as soon as the army can be prepared."

"Very well," said Izak, speaking in the low, almost whispering tones of a general forced to face ignominious defeat. "Whither shall we march? Dzur Mountain?"

"Yes, though I hold no hope of taking it. But, still, we must rendezvous with Brawre's army, so that is where we must go. And there are other reasons as well."

"Your Majesty—"

Kâna waved him to silence. "Our attempt to take the Orb by direct means has failed. Well then, we will find another way. We must continue the pretense of military action, but, fortunately, I have other weapons in my arsenal."

Izak bowed and said, "I am gratified to hear it, Sire. Apropos, I know that the person—Grita—with whom you trusted certain messages has successfully passed Nacine, and is on her way west."

"Good. And the other matter? The artifact we had of her that I desired sent west some days ago?"

"It reached its destination, Sire. Word has come in that the matter progresses, though I do not know what this is."

"It isn't important that you know, General. That will be all."

After Izak had left, Kâna murmured softly to himself, "So this is how defeat feels. I cannot say I like it much. Fortunately, this cat has more than one whisker. Our attempt to take the Orb has failed—the Empress has reached or will soon reach Dzur Mountain. Very well. We will move forward, and be ready, because my other plans are already in motion."

By the time this conversation was concluded, Zerika was, with the aid of Sethra Lavode, once more in the bowels of Dzur Mountain, where she caused Khaavren to be sent to her.

"Well, Captain? How do matters progress?"

"All is, I think, satisfactory. So far as I can tell, the Pretender has lost nearly five thousands of troops to desertion."

"And how many of them have we recruited?"

"Nearly half. I should expect him to withdraw at any moment."

"And will he, then, march on Dzur Mountain?"

"It is very likely, either to put us under siege, or at least to combine with his other army."

"Even with our sorcery, our necromancy, and the witchcraft provided by Morrolan and the warlock, we are not yet in a position to face his army head-on."

"With this, I do myself the honor of agreeing with Your Majesty. Only—"

"Yes?"

"The wind, as the Orca say, has shifted. Now every hour that passes puts us in a better position. Thanks to Pel's agents who have been recruiting so industriously, we are gaining forces, and the Pretender is losing them."

"We are, then, winning."

"Yes, Majesty."

"I like winning."

"That does not astonish me. Your Majesty perceives, it is preferable to losing."

"I am convinced of it. I believe I could come to enjoy victory. But one thing I am curious about, Captain."

"If Your Majesty would deign to tell me, then, if I can, I will satisfy her curiosity."

"Whence come all of these agents of Galstan who are so industriously recruiting the deserters from the Pretender's army into our own?"

"From Kâna's intelligence service."

"From his intelligence service?"

"Exactly."

"But how is this possible?"

"In the most natural way: Pel—that is, the Duke of Galstan—was highly placed in this service before he shifted allegiance."

"What?"

"It is as I have the honor to inform Your Majesty. He worked for Kâna before you had retrieved the Orb. Your Majesty must know that there are many who had supported this pretender for lack of an alternative. But, when the Orb was returned—"

"Ah. I see. Well, it seems gaining his loyalty was a better stroke than I had thought."

Khaavren bowed.

"So then?" said the Empress. "What ought we to do now, in your opinion?"

"In my opinion, we must wait, and watch."

"The waiting I understand. But, for what are we watching?"

"His next stroke. He must know as well as we do what is happening. He cannot wait, but must, rather, do something. We must see what it is that he does, and be prepared to counter it."

"Is it difficult to counter an attack when one has no notion of what sort of attack it would be?"

Khaavren shrugged. "It is, to be sure, easier to parry a cut to the head when one's opponent announces that he is about to make one. But often, I have found, my opponents fail to inform me of their precise intentions in a timely manner. This has happened so frequently, in fact, that I have taken to keeping the nature of my own strokes a secret, as a sort of revenge."

"I take your point, Captain. But do not try my patience."

Khaavren bowed. "Will that be all, Your Majesty?"

"That will be all."

Khaavren bowed once more, backed away three steps, turned on his heel, and left in search of Pel, in order to learn the progress of the efforts at recruitment. At nearly this same time, Arra descended a small circular, iron stairway in the temple, entering the basement—a single, open structure with a floor of stone, and walls hung with black curtains filled with strange diagrams and designs that had meaning in the arcane world of Eastern magic.

As she entered, she saw before her, seated on the floor, several hundreds of Eastern witches, grouped in eighteen circles, each of which numbered thirty-four witches, and each circle being sealed by joined hands. Chanting was continuous from these circles, although often one of the witches would receive a tap on the shoulder and would rise, to be replaced by another. Arra looked upon this scene with a certain degree of discontent. As she watched, frowning, an Easterner dressed in a loose-fitting garment of dark brown with a hood over his head approached her, bowed, and touched his palms to his forehead.

"Priestess," he said, "you seem distraught."

"It is nothing new, Esteban; only that we are three Circles short of the number that a spell of this magnitude ought to require."

"And then?"

"I confess to you, Esteban, I should very much prefer not to fall."

"You have, then, some fear of it?"

"Two sorts of fear: rational, and irrational. But then, if we are able to dispel the rational fear, which is to say, my observation that our Circle is weaker than it ought to be, well, then I believe that my irrational fear would be sensibly reduced."

"You say the Circle is weak."

"Weaker than it ought to be, yes."

"And yet you know very well, Arra—Priestess, I mean—that we could fill those three Circles."

"Certainly, if no one became ill, and if everyone could hold the chant for four hours instead of three, and if everyone could survive with only two hours between sessions and six hours of sleep. How long could we survive under such conditions?"

"It would not have to be so bad, if—"

"No, Esteban. I know what you are going to say. If we were to cease our call."

"Exactly."

"But that, my friend, I will not do. We must have greater numbers."

"And yet, should the temple fall, will that not decrease our numbers? After all, if we should all die—"

"The temple will not fall."

"You know we are at the edge of our ability."

"Only a few hundred more witches, and we will be able to manage three more Circles and we will have achieved the magic numbers of twenty-one and thirty-four—that is to say, twenty-one circles, each with thirty-four witches. With this arrangement, I should undertake to maintain a structure with a hundred times this much weight, and to hold it up forever."

"I am aware of this."

"And so I will not stop calling for more witches."

"And yet, with what is going on below, even as more arrive, how will they get here?"

Arra smiled. "The army below is leaving."

"How, you have done a Seeing?"

"Exactly. Thirty hours from now, all we be clear."

Esteban bowed. "I yield, Priestess. You have been proven correct once more."

"And what of yourself, Esteban, my friend? Have you anything to say on your own behalf?"

"On my own behalf? What could I say?"

"How is it with Thea?"

"Ah, she is polite to me."

"And that is all?"

"Alas, that is all."

Arra smiled. "You will wear her down, in time. Who could resist you?"

"It would seem, Priestess, that you have done an admirable job of resisting me."

"You know very well that my position makes any liaison impossible."

"So you have explained, Priestess, and I must, perforce, believe you."

"Well, what else? How are the facilities?"

"Strained, but not unbearable."

"Cramped?"

"Oh, not in the least, though it would be good to see the outdoors from time to time."

"Yes, I have no doubt of that. Soon, I think."

"Yes, once the army below us is gone, we can return to the ground."

"We can, my dear Esteban, but I am not certain we will."

"Priestess? I do not not understand what you do me the honor to tell me."

"I was speaking with the Lord Morrolan, and he is considering leaving the temple here."

"Here? A mile in the air?"

"Oh, it is not that high, is it?"

"But he can't think to leave it here!"

"Why not? Can you be unaware, my dear Esteban, that those in his family lived for millennia in castles that floated?"

"How, and they never fell?"

"Oh yes, at the time of the Great Disaster of which you have heard the Lady Teldra speak, they all fell. It must have been a horrible catastrophe; I make no doubt that hundreds were killed. Undoubtedly, that is why it is called the Great Disaster."

"Well, and this is not sufficient to convince him that this is a bad idea?"

"Oh, but now he has us, you see. He says that he has been considering constructing an entire castle around this temple, and building it all without ever touching the ground."

"These elfs—they are strange people."

"I cannot dispute with you."

With this, Arra, giving a last look around, returned to the main floor of the temple.

Chapter the Fifty-Ninth

How the False Emperor,
As Well as the True,
Can Set Plans in Motion

The reader has, by now, received certain hints that, although having faced a military defeat, Kâna had by no means given up his ambition, but, on the contrary, had already set in motion plans that he hoped would secure him eventual victory. It now remains to begin our investigation of these plans, which require shifting our attention away from events happening in the environs of Dzur Mountain.

The place to which we now direct our reader is in the county of Merwin, along the Grand Canal—or as near to the geographical middle of the Empire as anywhere one could name. In the north-western corner of this county, actually touching the canal, is a barony, called Loraan, that has been under the domain of the House of the Athyra since the canal was built. The only significance of this barony, hitherto, had been the difficulty, recorded by many songs, some letters, and a few documents in the office of the county clerk, of cutting the canal through the solid rock of the district. It had required the combined effort of the Imperial engineers and the baron himself—an accomplished sorcerer—to dig the canal, and the barony had been that sorcerer's reward.

The first baron, upon being granted this all but worthless land, had thought to at least use it to build an interesting home, which he did by causing a keep to be carved out of the very rock itself. He had first intended to name the place Redrock, because the rock was, in fact, of a reddish color; but a distant cousin of his was already lord of a county far to the east called Redrocks; so, to avoid confusion, he named his home Sitria, after his mistress at the time.

To Sitria, then, came a certain person whom, though we have neglected her for some time, we hope the reader has not forgotten: this being Kâna's cousin, Habil. Upon reaching the door and pulling the clapper, she gave her name to the servants and desired that the Baron be asked if he could spare her two minutes of his time. The Baron, a quiet, studious man, who had been devoting himself to certain arcane magical studies, had no reason to be rude, and so took himself away from his work, with some regret it is true, and agreed to hold a conversation with his visitor.

They met in his parlor—windowless, like the rest of his keep, but with light provided by ingenious glowing bulbs spaced throughout the room.

"It is good of you to see me, Baron," said Habil. "I know that you must be busy."

"Think nothing of it, madam. May I ask what brings you to this region? For, if I am not mistaken, your home is far to the west, in the mountains, is it not?"

"Well, yes, but how is it you could have heard of me?"

"In the simplest way: My cousin is married to the youngest son of the Marquis of Mistyvale, who had the honor to attend a certain meeting in your home. This meeting, you must understand, has been the subject of no small amount of discussion, and in this discussion, your name was mentioned."

"You have a prodigious memory, Baron."

"It is kind of you to say so, madam. But tell me, what brings you here?"

"Why, I am here to see you, sir."

"Come, do not jest. You could not have made this journey of hundreds of leagues merely to see me!"

"And yet, that is exactly what I did."

"How, you made this journey only for this conversation in which we are now engaged?"

"I have said so, and I even insist upon it."

The baron frowned, and said, "Well, as I have no desire to give a lady the lie, I have no choice but to believe you."

"And as what I have told you is the truth, then that is yet another reason to believe me."

"My lady, I find myself overwhelmed with reasons, so that it leaves me only to inquire as to the *specific* reason for your journey. That is to say, about what did you wish to speak to me?"

"Since you ask so frankly, I will answer. I have come to offer you something that, unless I am misinformed, you will be gratified to have."

"You interest me exceedingly, madam. Pray say more."

"You then wish me to continue?"

"I wish it of all things."

"Then I will."

"I assure you, you have my complete attention."

"Then listen, my friend: We have heard that your studies have taken you in the direction of necromancy."

"Well, that is true; but is there something wrong with this study?"

"Not in the least. We have learned, moreover, that you have been researching the connection between the soul and the body."

"I admit that I have been curious about this matter ever since my late uncle, the Marquis of Blackvine, explained his researches to me in the course of my training."

"Then we were not misinformed. And, is it the case that, now that you have accepted citizenship, your researches are more productive?"

"Entirely. Access to the Orb is invaluable for a sorcerer."

"Yes, I understand that. Well, we find ourselves in need of a skilled Necromancer who is able to make use of the Orb."

"Why certainly, as long as it doesn't require betraying the Empire—"

"But what if it does?"

"Oh, in the case, I must decline."

"Are you certain, my dear Baron? Before you answer, permit me to show you something."

"What is it you wish to show me?"

"This staff."

"Well, but it seems very like an ordinary wizard's staff, only rather smaller."

"In fact, however, it is anything but ordinary."

"Indeed? In what way is it unusual? It does not appear in any way remarkable—white, with a reddish mark on one end. What makes it worthy of note?"

"Had you known that it was possible to capture a disembodied soul?"

"What? Such a thing cannot possibly be done! You perceive, I have studied this matter. Once the body has died, the soul clings to it for a certain length of time, after which time it either wakes up in the Paths of the Dead, or else at once enters the process that results in eventual reincarnation. There is no time when the soul wanders free of the body."

"But what if some force were to rip a soul from a still living body?"

"Impossible!"

"Not in the least."

"What could do such a thing?"

"Adron's Disaster."

The Baron stared, open-mouthed. At last he said, "But, who found such a thing?"

"Who? That is unimportant. An amateur sorceress, who was exploring in the area near Dzur Mountain."

Loraan's eyes dropped to the staff, and he spoke in a whisper. "To have such an artifact . . ."

"It can be yours, my friend, and easily."

"It can?"

"I will give it to you the instant I have your word that you will perform the simple task we require of you."

"A simple task, you say?"

"I give you my word, it is within your powers."

"And yet, the risk—"

"My lord, there is no risk if we succeed. But even if we were to fail, which I believe is unlikely, but no chance ought to be overlooked—"

"Yes, you are cautious, and that is a virtue."

"Even then, the chance that your rôle will be discovered is negligible."

"You are sure of this?"

"I swear it."

"You tempt me."

"I intend to. It is a simple task, and it is without danger to you, and, as for the reward—"

"Then name the task!" cried Loraan, his eyes still fixed on the staff.

Habil smiled the smile of any successful negotiator.

In a very short time, messengers began running from Canal, a near-by village that boasted a posting station set up by Kâna some time before, and which had proved useful to him more than once. To follow these messengers on their rapid but uneventful path cannot but prove wearisome to the reader, so instead we will direct our attention to Piro, the Viscount of Adrilankha, as he and his friend Kytraan pass through the unadorned yet somehow magnificent hall-ways of Dzur Mountain.

Chapter the Sixtieth

How Family, Food, and Philosophy
Provide Good Subjects for Discussion,
With Special Emphasis on the Pomegranate

Piro and Kytraan had, to this point, caught a glimpse of the Sorceress in Green (pointed out to them by Lar, who had learned the identity of this mysterious person from Tukko), but had not yet seen Sethra Lavode, who was, without doubt, still involved in sending supplies to Morrolan and bringing elements of the army to Dzur Mountain.

"I have not seen many of the soldiers brought over from Morrolan's temple," observed Kytraan. "Where do you suppose they are?"

"Oh, that is easily enough answered," said Piro. "Lar tells me that, as they arrive, they are sent out of doors, to a camp on the slopes of the mountain."

"A cold and uncomfortable camp, it would seem."

"Perhaps. But I am told that the Enchantress has done what she could to provide warmth, and whatever comforts are available."

"Still, I confess that I am glad to be in here, rather than out there."

"Oh, I quite agree, my dear Kytraan. There is nothing like travel in the wild to make one grateful for the comforts of a good shelter and warm food."

"I could not agree with you more, Viscount. Apropos—"

"Yes?"

"On the subject of warm food, well, I perceive the kitchen is only two steps down this hallway, and you know we were invited to partake of whatever is there."

"That is true, and it seems this Tukko is a tolerable cook."

"I have made the same observation."

"And then?"

"After you, my dear Viscount."

"I am leading the way, my lord."

Upon entering the kitchens, however, the Viscount stopped so abruptly that Kytraan could not help but run into him with a certain amount of force. The Dragonlord was just in the process of formulating a remark—some observation that would serve as both apology and gentle remonstrance, when he, that is, Kytraan, observed the reason for Piro's sudden halt.

Quickly deducing that his friend might be at a loss for words, Kytraan stepped around Piro, bowed, and said, "Ladies, this is an unexpected pleasure."

"Indeed it is," said Röaana. "We sent Clari for wine, and thought to procure ourselves some biscuits to accompany this repast. Would you care to join us?"

"A splendid notion," said Kytraan, "and one I subscribe to with all my heart. And, you, Viscount, do you agree?"

"What is that? Oh, certainly, certainly. Yes, wine and biscuits. A capital idea, upon my honor."

Clari appeared with wine, and was at once sent to fetch glasses, while Kytraan and Röaana found the biscuits. Piro, during this activity, made a careful study of a corner of the kitchen ceiling, perhaps to see if any arachnids had left webs there at any time; Ibronka, for her part, made an equally careful study of a lower corner, no doubt to see if there were signs of rodents.

When Clari returned, they marched at a good pace to the nearest sitting room. Upon reaching it, Clari, setting down the glasses, begged leave to run water out to the soldiers who were setting up camp outside.

"That is a good plan," observed Ibronka. "You should bring them water, lest they become overly dry in among the streams leading down from Dzur Mountain."

"Perhaps," said Clari, "I will, instead, bring them fresh fruit that I have observed in the kitchen."

"That might be better," said Ibronka. "You know how much danger there is of developing the toothfall to anyone in a mountain such as this, where only small-apples and redberries grow in abundance."

Clari suppressed any reply that might have sprung to her mind, bowed, and left. As Clari was leaving on this vital errand, Kytraan remarked, "My dear Röaana, there is a matter that I wish to discuss with you, having to do with the economy of certain districts of the Kanefthali Mountains."

"Oh, indeed, sir? Well, that falls out remarkably well, because there are certain matters concerning training for small engagements that I have been wondering about, and it seems there is no one like a Dragonlord to answer such questions."

"Well then, if you might be good enough to accompany me, we shall stroll together and discuss these matters."

"I should like nothing better."

"Your arm?"

"Here it is."

And, without another word, they made their exit, leaving Piro and Ibronka quite alone.

Piro studied an upper corner of this room as assiduously as he had inspected the kitchen a few minutes before; while Ibronka shifted her attention to the toes of her boots. This, of course, could go on only a certain amount of time without becoming intolerable. At length, Piro gave up his efforts to find a good excuse to leave, and, clearing his throat, said, "So, madam, do you have a brother?"

Ibronka looked up suddenly, as if she had been unaware of his presence. "No," she said.

"Ah," said Piro.

After another uncomfortable silence, he said, as if to be certain that he had understood, "No brother?"

"None."

Piro cleared his throat again, and ventured to say, "That must be a trial to you."

"Oh, you think so? Have you a brother?"

"No."

"Ah," said Ibronka.

Dzur Mountain was most remarkably silent, its dark stone shielding any conversation or other sounds that might penetrate thinner walls.

"Or sisters," added Piro.

"Nor have I sisters," said Ibronka.

"Ah, well."

Piro began drawing small circles in the arm of his chair with his forefinger. Ibronka, for her part, shifted her position slightly and cast an anxious glance at the door, as if hoping for rescue (a rescue, we should point out, that would not come, for the simple reason that Kytraan and Röaana, without a word spoken between them, had positioned themselves each at one end of the hallway to be certain no one entered the room).

For the third time, Piro cleared his throat, then said, "So, do you know of the twisted noodles, made from a decoction of whipped hen's eggs, prepared in the fashion of the Southern Coast?"

"Why yes, I had this in Hartre."

"And did you like it?"

"Well, yes, I must say I did."

Piro nodded, searching for something else to say, and at length fell silent.

Ibronka glanced up quickly and noticed perspiration on Piro's upper lip—perspiration that, in fact, matched a certain dampness on the palms of her hands.

"Well," said Piro. "Tell me this: If you had a brother—"

"Viscount," said Ibronka.

"Yes?" said Piro, eager for anything at all that might help him out of the conversational desert into which he had strayed. "Yes, what is it?"

"Come over here, Viscount, and kiss me, before I die of embarrassment."

As these events were occurring, Clari, faithful to her errand, was traveling through the camp on the slopes of the mountain, or, rather, what would become the camp as soon as more of the army had arrived. At present, there were only a few officers and men there, busy laying out the boundaries of where the latrines were to be dug, the bedrolls laid, the pavilions set up, the food stored, and the horses stabled. Clari traversed these grounds with the thoroughness of a cutpurse traversing a fair, making sure each of them had received a piece of fruit until at last her basket was empty.

The last piece of fruit, a pomegranate, happened to go to a certain Dragonlord of middle years distinguished by a large build, and a bright, animated face beneath a head full of unusually fair hair.

"Is this for me?" he said.

"Certainly," said Clari.

"Well, I thank you. Please, sit down."

"You aren't busy?"

"Oh, yes, there are things to do. But five minutes more or less will make no difference."

"This chair is very comfortable."

"I'm glad to hear it."

"Isn't it awkward to carry when marching?"

"It collapses by removing this pin and then pushing here."

"How clever!"

The Dragonlord bowed.

"You must have considerable experience as a soldier."

"Why, yes, if one numbers years, certainly. And if one counts armies, then I would also have to agree. If one were to number battles, then, perhaps, not so many."

"But you fought in the recent engagement, did you not?"

"Oh, yes, and I even bloodied my sword a little."

"Oh!"

"It was nothing. Someone attempted to separate my head from my shoulders, and I believe I may have scratched the impudent fellow on the arm as I ducked."

"It sounds exciting!"

"It was certainly unsettling. Although what happened the next day was even more unsettling, in its own way."

"Oh, and what was that?"

"In the first place, I am sorcerously transported from one place to another."

"Yes, I can imagine that would be unsettling. In fact, I had the same reaction."

"And in the second place, I suddenly find that I do not know what army I am in."

"Oh? How is that possible?"

"Well, we went into battle in the service of this fellow South-moor—"

"My lord Morrolan, yes."

"Yes. A good Dragonlord, so far as I can tell. I did some garrison duty for his father before the Interregnum. E'Drien, the same line as my esteemed mother, although I am inclined to think I take more after the e'Terics line of my father."

"Well, and?"

"And then to-day I am told that I am in the Imperial army, which is another matter altogether."

"How, you do not wish to be in the Imperial army?"

"Well, at least not without being asked."

"I understand. But are you in the Imperial army, or is it that you serve in Morrolan's army, and he has put his army into the service of the Empire?"

"Perhaps that is the case. You perceive, I am uncertain, and this vexes me."

"Well, at all events, you are fighting on behalf of the Lord Morrolan, and for the Empire. Is this bad?"

"Looked at that way, why, no. And, to be sure, when all is over, no doubt I will be able to discover which army I am in, and, if I am not then in Morrolan's service, I can enter it again."

"Perhaps by then you will be an officer."

"Never in life. I have no wish to be an officer. Too much is expected of officers."

"Then a sergeant?"

"Better to be an officer."

"But then, tell me, if it is not for advancement—"

"Oh, it is not, I assure you."

"Then why do you like being a soldier?"

"Why, because of all the charming people I meet."

"Well, certainly that is a reason that didn't occur to me."

"Oh, it is true. And, except for the annoyance of battles from time to time, I find the life most pleasurable. I value the companionship, the singing—"

"Singing?"

"Oh, certainly. We often sing around the fires at night. 'I Hate the Soldier's Life,' and, 'What an Officer Must Kiss,' and, 'Only a Fool Joins the Army,' and, 'What Girl Would Marry a Soldier?' and many others."

"I should very much admire to hear them."

"I shall sing them for you, when you wish."

"But living out of doors all the time—isn't it trying?"

"Have you ever done it?"

"Too much of late, I'm afraid. I have been following my mistress about from one end of the world to the other, and never a roof over our heads."

"Ah, well, but you see, I like it."

Clari nodded. "You should be a soldier."

"You think so?"

"I am convinced of it."

"Then it is decided. I shall be a soldier."

"You already are a soldier."

"Oh, so I am. Well, in that case—"

"Yes?"

"Would you like to share my pomegranate?"

"I should like nothing better."

Chapter the Sixty-First

How It Is Shown That When
Sethra Lavode Is Uneasy,
Everyone Is Uneasy

Morrolan's army—or, we should say, the Imperial army, for no one was entirely certain which it was at that moment—continued to grow. Even after Kâna's order making his army ready to move, the magical attacks continued, the demoralization became worse, and there were more desertions than ever—and of these deserters, many met with Pel's recruitment agents, and no small number of these agreed to serve Morrolan (or the Empire—the recruiting agents were not entirely clear on this point). And of each hundred who joined, one or two might know enough of sorcery that, having become citizens, and now with the power of the Orb at their disposal, they could learn to teleport well enough to aid in the transfer of supplies, which, in turn, gave Sethra Lavode, Sethra the Younger, the Sorceress in Green, and Tazendra more time to transfer troops—an operation that by now was nearing its completion.

"But," observed Morrolan, who had been studying sorcery with an intensity impossible to describe, "I cannot help but wonder what it is for."

"Some great purpose, it would seem," said Arra, "although, to be sure, as an Easterner, I know little of such things."

"And I, raised as an Easterner, know as little as you. Although," he added, considering, "three counties to the north seem like good things to have."

"Yes, my lord."

"And, as our army grows, the day comes nearer when I can take it back east, to attend to certain matters that I hate leaving undone."

Before Arra could respond, someone else spoke: "I beg your pardon, sir, but I could not help overhearing, and you speak of a project that interests me greatly."

Morrolan turned, frowned, and said, "And I beg *your* pardon, madam, but whom do I have the honor of addressing?"

"I am Sethra."

Morrolan frowned. "I beg your pardon once more, my lady, but I have had the honor of meeting Sethra Lavode, and—"

"I am her apprentice."

"Ah. It is, indeed, an honor, madam."

"The honor is mine, my lord."

"Permit me to name my friend, Arra."

"My lady," said the priestess, bowing.

Sethra the Younger gave her a nod, and, addressing Morrolan once more, said, "But I heard you speak of going east, with an army."

"Ah. Yes, that is a little project of mine. I was raised in the East, and was forced to leave in something of a hurry, without having punished certain persons who caused me some annoyance."

"So that you intend to return, at the head of an army, and set matters right?"

"That is exactly the case, my lady."

"When that time comes, I should very much admire to accompany you. It may be that I will prove of value to you in your endeavors. While I am not Sethra Lavode, I am at least her apprentice."

"What you say interests me greatly, madam," said Morrolan, "and we will certainly speak more of it."

"Yes, I eagerly anticipate doing so."

"And I as well. But first, there is the matter of this Whitestone, or Skinter, or Kâna, or whatever he calls himself." Morrolan brought himself to the edge of the roof and looked out. The movement of Kâna's army could be clearly discerned, like so many insects moving slowly along the road in a thin column, with many thousands still in their encampment waiting for their marching orders. "I find," continued Morrolan, "that this fellow irritates me. He ought to be suppressed."

"That is the project which engages us, my lord."

"And yet, once more we must wait." Morrolan sighed. "Come, tell me what you think. Could this temple not become an admirable ball-room?"

"A ball-room, my lord?"

"Yes. Should I build a castle here, I would think that this structure, now a temple, might be an admirable ball-room, already with
small alcoves for private conversation."

"It is now a temple?"

"Yes, dedicated to Verra, my patron Goddess."

"And you are, instead, considering making it a ball-room?"

"For my castle, yes."

"I think you ought to have a castle; you perceive it is traditional."

"Yes, and I am told that floating castles are traditional in my
family."

"That is true."

"And soon I shall be able to manage the levitation spells myself. I
can nearly do so now."

"But if this is to become a ball-room—"

"Well?"

"What then of your Goddess?"

"It is of the Goddess I have been thinking. You were raised here
in Faerie—that is, in the lands of the Empire; I should be grateful for
your advice."

"Whatever I know is at your disposal, my lord."

"Well, in the lands where I was raised, it was not uncommon to
have a place wherein people would gather to praise and commune
with the Gods. Yet here, it seems, this is done in private—here, it
seems, if one wishes to speak with one's God, one does so by one's
self. Is this not the case?"

"You have stated it admirably, my lord. In the large cities, there
are altars and shrines, and occasionally even small temples dedicated
to certain deities. But these are rarely attended by more than one or
two persons at a time, except, perhaps, on certain calendar days that
might be sacred to one or the other of them."

"Then instead of a structure where all may gather to worship the
Goddess, a smaller, more secluded room might be appropriate."

"Indeed, I know many who have such rooms. They use them
when they wish to remain undisturbed, to be alone with their
thoughts."

Morrolan nodded. "Then I shall cause such a room to be built.

Perhaps a high tower with no windows, reached by climbing a ladder. A place of solitude. I will consider the matter."

"The Easterners," said Sethra the Younger, "believe that a God feeds on worship, and thus the more worshipers, the greater the God is pleased. We believe that what passes between a man and a God is private, and only of concern to them, as a conversation between two men is no one else's concern."

Morrolan bowed. "You seem to know a great deal about Easterners."

"A hunter must know his prey."

Morrolan frowned, but chose not to take the conversation in this direction, so he said, "But then, if it is nothing more than a conversation between two men, well, why are they Gods? That is, why speak to them at all?"

"I have had many hours of conversation with Sethra Lavode on this very subject."

"And have you come to any conclusions?"

"To call them 'conclusions,' my lord, may be coming at it rather strong."

"Then, instead?"

"Perhaps 'suggestions' would be a more precise term."

"Oh, I am in favor of precision in all things."

"A good quality, my lord, and I applaud it in you."

"Well, but tell me these suggestions to which you have just alluded."

"You wish to hear them?"

"Indeed, I should like nothing better."

"It seems, then, that, laying aside the superstitions of ignorant Easterners"—Morrolan, though faintly irritated at this, let it pass out of a desire to hear the rest of what she had to say—"most of us feel the need to believe that our life, that what we do, has some use or purpose greater than ourselves."

"That may be true, I had not considered it. But, what has this to do with a man communing with a God?"

"Listen, and I will attempt to explain."

"Very well."

"To be a God, is to embody principles greater than life—that is, greater than day-to-day existence. So then, insofar as one acts in accordance with the wishes of a God, one acts for a purpose higher than one's self. Do you see?"

"Nearly," said Morrolan. "And yet—"

"Yes?"

"I am uncertain as to this higher purpose to which you do me the honor of speaking."

"In what way are you uncertain?"

"Is it true that men desire it?"

"Don't you?"

"No," said Morrolan.

Sethra the Younger smiled. "Well, but you are young. It may be that, someday, you will."

"I do not say that this is impossible, only—"

"Yes?"

"It seems to me it would be a better world if, instead of considering higher purposes, we all simply tended to our own affairs. Let the Teckla plow the fields, with his ox or his mule to serve him; let the lord provide him protection from brigands. Let the Empire, if there must be one, facilitate trade and insure that the roads are safe. It seems to me that serving a higher purpose has led to more trouble than benefit. Think about our enemy, Kâna. If he were not so committed to what is, no doubt, in his mind a higher purpose, well, he should have been content to let matters lie, and we would not be required to go through all of this work to suppress him."

"There is, no doubt, some truth in what you say. But then, consider that Her Majesty, also, is committed to what one might call a higher purpose. And, were she not, then we should have no Empire. Or else we should have an Empire ruled by the likes of Kâna, which I do not believe I, for one, should care for, as I do not believe he has the favor of the Gods, nor of the Cycle, and these are both necessary to rule without undue tyranny."

"You make a good argument, madam. I must consider this further."

"I am pleased, sir, to have given you something to think about. I believe that we shall have much pleasure in one another's company when this is over."

Morrolan bowed. "I look forward exceedingly to more conversation with you. But for now—"

"Yes, I must return to my tedious task of sending crates and casks one way, and people another. It should go faster now: I have enlisted the help of a friend, a sorceress who wears only green. No doubt you will meet her later."

"I shall be glad to. And I am going to give more consideration to the sort of structure in which I may wish to live after these irritations have passed."

Sethra the Younger shook her head. "You appear sanguine, my lord, about the ultimate defeat of this Kâna."

"Well, and should I not? Our army is growing, his is diminishing. We have the sorcerous power of the Orb, he does not. We have a necromantic demon, and Eastern witches, whereas he has only mundane means of attack and defense. What chance can he have?"

"All you say is true, but—"

"Well?"

"I am worried nevertheless."

"Have you a reason to be worried?"

"Yes, and, moreover, I think it a good reason."

"Then tell me what it is, and I will consider."

"It is simply this: I have just left Sethra Lavode."

"Well, and?"

"And she is worried."

Sethra the Younger bowed and went about her business. Morrolan watched her go, and anyone looking upon his countenance at that moment would have been convinced that Morrolan, too, was now worried.

Chapter the Sixty-Second

How Three Women Had a Conversation
That Is Far More Entertaining
Than the Laughter of Lovers

Piro and Ibronka emerged arm in arm and laughing. They were at once joined by Röaana and Kytraan, the latter of whom said, "Come, what is this laughter? You must tell us why you laugh, and, if it is funny, why, we will laugh with you."

"Why are we laughing?" said Piro, nearly controlling his mirth.

"Yes, yes," said Röaana. "You must tell us about it."

"Well," said Ibronka, "we are laughing because—"

"Yes?" said Kytraan. "Because—?"

"I do not believe," said Piro, speaking with some difficulty, "that I could possibly explain, or, that if I did, you would understand."

"Oh, but you must try," said Röaana.

"Then tell me," said Ibronka, tears of laughter running down her cheeks, "do you consider it amusing that he has hair on the back of his hand?"

Piro lifted his hand to demonstrate, in case this was doubted. This action on his part was, unaccountably, a source of even more merriment, to judge from the response it elicited from Piro and Ibronka.

"Why, I cannot say that this is amusing, in all conscience," said Kytraan. "You perceive, we all have hair on the backs of our hands."

"Well, and so it is proved," said Piro.

"What is proved?"

"That I was right: You do not comprehend."

Piro and Ibronka looked at each other once more and began laughing again. Kytraan looked at Röaana, who shrugged and said, "Perhaps we have made a mistake."

"That is very possible," agreed Kytraan.

"However, it is better than it was before," suggested Röaana.

"Perhaps," said Kytraan.

Even as this conversation was reaching its conclusion, Piro and Ibronka were ahead of them, continuing a discussion of their own — a discussion on certain subjects which included not only arm hair, but skillets, telepathic plants, and chips of masonry, all of which were, evidently, sources of boundless mirth. Kytraan and Röaana shrugged and followed them down the hallway.

"Perhaps," said Röaana, "Kâna will launch an assault on us with overwhelming force."

Kytraan nodded hopefully.

Piro and Ibronka led them on a chase throughout much of Sethra Lavode's lair, their uncontrollable mirth at last moderating to mere bubbling good spirits; they explored nooks and crannies, acting for a while as if they were children, and also now engaged in a secondary game, that being to find ways to distract their friends' attention long enough to steal a kiss without being observed.

This is, we hope, sufficient to give the reader an idea of what was transpiring with Piro and Ibronka — we have no doubt that should we continue in this vein the reader will soon feel as much annoyance as, in fact, was experienced by Kytraan and Röaana.

Wishing above all to do nothing that might distress or irritate our reader, therefore, we will turn our attention from the heady excitement of new love just revealed, to the cold intensity of old hatred carefully nurtured. From the east, then, we travel west to a place near the port city of Hartre, and three women, all united by a thirst for power and revenge, whose meeting cannot fail to be more entertaining for the reader than a continuation of the scene he has just witnessed.

They met in a small posting house less half a league east of Hartre. This was a charming house, often filled with music, and, in spite of its sign, which depicted a brown jug, was known far and wide as Peffa's for reasons of which we must confess our ignorance. Just a few steps from Peffa's was a small house that let rooms by the week or the year, and, as it was here that Illista was staying, she often passed her days at Peffa's, eating a little, drinking moderately, nursing her hatred and grievances, and awaiting word from Kâna.

On this day, she signaled for the attention of the hostess, a cheerful Chreotha with a dimpled chin and heavy eyebrows. On observing that her attention was requested, the hostess brought herself to Illista's table and inquired as to how she could be of service.

"My dear woman," she said, "I have been a guest in your fine house for several days now."

"Yes, my lady, and permit me to say how pleased we are with your patronage."

Illista bowed her head and said, "On the first day, I dined on a goose prepared with plums and oranges, which I found entirely satisfactory. On the next day, I sampled the stew that you keep cooking over the fire, and it was even better than the goose. The next day, it was a suckling pig being roasted over a spit—"

"Oh, yes, with the fat dripping into the stew. The stew is even better today."

"No doubt. What I wish to say, my dear hostess, is that I have been entirely satisfied with what you have served me, and yet—"

"Yes, my lady? And yet?"

"I cannot help but wonder if there is not something you would especially recommend."

"Oh, Your Ladyship inquires as to our specialty?"

"Yes, that is it exactly."

"Well, my lady, but that is the simplest thing. It is our fish."

"Your fish?"

"Yes. We are, after all, on the coast, and the fish are brought to us within minutes of being caught."

"But, what sort of fish?"

"Oh, can Your Ladyship ask? Here is the only place to find the true cryingfish, which is, as my lady must know, famed throughout the land."

"What sort of fish is it? For, upon my honor, I do not believe I have ever heard of it before."

"Well, my lady, that shows you how poor is our world without an Empire, for in the old days—but that is neither one place nor another. The cryingfish is rather like the saltwater pinkfish, but not so strongly flavored, and, when prepared with a few leaves of basil and a smattering of blackberries, has an almost nutty savor, for which it is renowned. Indeed, no other fish—"

"Very well, I shall have some, along with whatever wine you recommend."

"Excellent, my lady. It will be up directly."

"Ah, a moment."

"Yes?"

"Prepare two of them. Unless I mistake, the lady who has just entered will be joining me, and, if she is hungry, she will not have to watch me eat, which I am sure would be unpleasant for her."

"A friend of my lady, then?"

"No, I have never had the honor of seeing her before."

"But then, how do you know she will join you?"

"In the simplest manner, my good woman. I have been told that, sooner or later, a lady of the House of the Dragon would find me here. And, you see before you a lady of the House of the Dragon. Do you often see Dragonlords here?"

"Never, my lady."

"Well, there you have it."

And, indeed, even as she was speaking, Habil, having recognized Illista by her description, approached and begged to be permitted to join her.

"Of course," said the Phoenix. "I have been expecting you. So much so, in fact, that I have ordered you a fish in case you were hungry."

"Is the fish good?"

"So I am told."

"Well then, if two are good, three are better, for we are expecting another."

"Another?"

"Yes, and though I have not met her, I have been given a description which, if it is accurate, would indicate that it is the lady who is just now entering this charming house."

"Three then," said Illista coolly.

And, as the hostess ran to the kitchen to order the fish prepared, the third member of the party, Grita, came to the table and said, "You are Habil? Then I compliment you on the post system that you and your cousin have arranged, because, if you will credit it, three days ago I was in the county of Southmoor. And though I have not had much sleep, to be sure, I have made the journey."

"You must be Grita."

"I am."

"Then you are welcome," said Illista. "I have heard a great deal about you."

"None of it good, I hope."

"I have heard that you are determined."

"That is a polite manner of expressing it."

"And do you object to this?"

"Not in the least; let us be polite by all means."

"Then, my dear Marchioness, if we are to be polite—"

"Oh, let us be polite."

"—then introduce me to your friend."

"Ah. I beg your pardon. I had assumed you knew her."

"And why should I know her?"

"Because, my dear Grita, if I may call you that—"

"Certainly you may. Intimacy is even better than politesse."

"Then, dear Grita, I assumed you knew her because it was you who directed her to us, and us to her."

"Ah, then you must be Illista, as I ought to have known at once from the cut and color of your gown."

Illista, who had listened to this conversation with the greatest coolness, now nodded and said, "You have named me."

"And our charming Marchioness has named me," said Grita, "so it leaves only her to be named, and that is a name we both know, is it not? Cousin to the Emperor—if, indeed, he is the Emperor. I have heard no news. Has your cousin managed to acquire the Orb?"

"No," said Habil. "Our military efforts have failed."

"You said that was a possibility," observed Illista.

"Yes, and the possibility has become a reality. Fortunately, thanks to you ladies, we have other possibilities. I must say, my good Grita, that you have been more than helpful."

"I am glad to hear that I have been of service—the more-so as it gets me closer to my own goal."

"Well," said Illista, "but what is your goal?"

Grita smiled, and if the tree-viper were able to smile, it would have been just such a smile as curled Grita's lips as she said, "My goal is the same as your own, my lady."

"Ah! You speak, then, of vengeance?"

"Oh, yes, vengeance. But more, vengeance against a particular four persons."

"Four?"

"That is their number, yes."

"How oddly that falls out, my good Grita. Four is just my number."

"I know," said Grita, smiling a particularly disagreeable smile.

"Do you tell me—?"

"I do."

"Who are you?"

"I am the daughter of your old acquaintance, Lord Garland."

"Impossible!"

"I must insist upon it."

"Who is Lord Garland?" said Habil, frowning.

"No one of any importance to you," said Grita coolly. "He is dead."

Habil frowned and looked as if she would ask more questions, but, thinking better of it, she ended by saying, "So it seems, the two of you have common enemies."

"Exactly," said Grita.

"And they are your enemies as well," added Illista. "It is remarkable how well it all falls out."

"You perceive," said Grita, "that I have no special interest in this Empire of yours for its own sake. I aid you because, with your victory, my revenge will be easier."

"I understand," said Habil. "Whereas I have no interest in your revenge, but you have aided us, and we have made a bargain, and I will hold to it by aiding you in every way I can."

"And I," said Illista, "tell you frankly that I should be delighted to have my place in court once more, and so I am glad to aid you, but the thirst for vengeance drives me even more."

"Then we understand one another?" said Habil.

"Perfectly," said the others.

"Good, then," said Grita. "Khaavren, Aerich, Pel, and Tazendra. Those are their names."

"Pel," said Illista, "is the Duke of Galstan—a duke without a duchy. I recall him from the trial. And how I long to carve his face so that he can no longer sneer!"

"Oh, yes!" said Habil. "In his case, especially, I am pleased to give you all the help I can. He had our confidence, and he betrayed us. He must be made to suffer for this."

"That will not be difficult," observed Grita.

"How, not difficult?" said Illista. "I beg to observe that he is a Yendi."

"Well, and what of it?"

"It is rarely possible to gain advantage of a Yendi; their secrets are impenetrable, and their plans are too deep."

"I agree with Illista," said Habil. "If you attempt to cross the plan of a Yendi, well, you are likely to have done exactly what he wishes."

"It is true," said Grita, "that it is very difficult to surprise a secret from a Yendi."

"And then?"

"Well, I have not done so. I have, however, done something better."

"Come, what is it, then?" asked Habil.

"I have surprised a secret of Zerika."

"Well," said Habil, "I do not doubt that this could be useful."

"In particular," said Grita, "I know a secret that, insofar as Zerika knows, is known only to herself—and to our Yendi."

"You think so?" said Illista.

"You sound doubtful, my dear."

"I confess that I may be. I wonder, that is, how you can know for certain that the Yendi knows it?"

"In the simplest way: He has become Zerika's Discreet."

"Well, that is something, to be sure."

"And what better to speak to one's Discreet about than—"

"Yes?"

"A lover."

"Ah!" said both of the others.

"Moreover," said Grita with a malevolent smile, "a lover who is an Easterner."

"What do you say?" cried Habil.

"It is as I have the honor to tell you."

"And you learned of this?"

"You must understand that I have been planning my vengeance for many years."

"I understand that," said Habil.

"In the course of preparing my vengeance, I made close observations of our enemies."

"That is but natural."

"One of these enemies is Khaavren."

"To be sure."

"As I hate him above all, well, you may understand that I watched him more than any."

"That is true."

"He has a son."

"This we already know."

"This son had a group of friends."

"I do not question that."

"One of these friends was none other than Zerika, then living under an assumed name."

"Shards!"

"And I happened, in the course of learning what I could of Khaavren's son, to discover Zerika's lover. An Easterner, I swear it to you. She would go to South Adrilankha, where the Easterners live, and visit him, spending hours alone with him."

"But, where is this Easterner now?"

"With our enemies. It was he who embarrassed us at Dzur Mountain by calling out those appalling animals."

"He!"

"Exactly."

"You perceive," said Illista, "that I am not entirely certain of what you are referring to, but, nevertheless, I confess that I am entirely convinced."

"That is best," said Grita.

"We must now consider how best to use this information," said Habil.

"Oh, as to that," said Illista, "I know something of the ways of Court."

"Well?" said the others.

"You may leave that to me."

"I agree," said Grita.

"As do I," said Habil. "So then, we have a means of attack on the Yendi. I confess, that pleases me; as I have said, I hate him more than the others."

"For me," said Grita, "it is the Tiassa that I desire above all to have under my care for a few hours, or days. He is now Count of Whitecrest."

"A count?" said Illista. "He? Impossible!"

"He married into the title."

"Ah. Well, that I believe. He was not an unpleasant-looking man. But a fool. And Count of Whitecrest, forsooth? Well, my good Habil, that explains certain remarks you made, at all events, concerning the lack of difficulty in making Adrilankha the capital."

"Precisely," said Illista. "He and his family will be removed. As you have said, he is a fool."

"They are all fools."

"Not Temma," observed Illista.

"Yes. The Duke of Arylle. You are right, he is not a fool. We must eliminate him quickly and efficiently."

"Agreed. And the Dzur?"

"She is a Dzur," said Grita, shrugging. "Do not give her the chance to draw a weapon, and she will present no problem. Or, rather, a chance to cast a spell. She has become something of a wizard. But she remains a fool. I am not worried about her."

"Yes. Who else?"

"That is all."

"Let us try not to run afoul of Sethra Lavode."

"Is there a reason why we should?" asked Habil.

"None of which I am aware."

"Good, then."

"And I remind you both," said Habil, "that the Empire—that is, the forces my cousin commands—are only at your disposal for so long as you are working in our interests."

"Oh yes," said Grita. "We understand that entirely. And the reverse is true as well."

"Naturally."

"In that case," said Illista. "Let us make our plans."

"But can we make plans," said Grita, "without knowing the results of the engagements presently being fought in the east, not to mention the other matters—apropos, my good Habil, have you found a use for that staff?"

"Oh, indeed. And a good one, I think."

"Excellent. But, until we know what will happen—"

"Contingencies," said Illista.

"Contingencies?" said the others.

"Exactly. We make a set of plans that presume the good Kâna will succeed, another that presumes he will fail, and yet another that presumes the matter is undecided, and we are able to exert some influence upon it."

"Well," said Habil, "as much as I dislike contemplating the second of these, I understand the first two; but I do not understand the third."

"The third," observed Illista, "is the most likely. Consider, if you will: This Khaavren is now advising the Phoenix with the Orb, is he not? And the Dzur is assisting her as well. If these two, for example, should be eliminated, well, would it be helpful to your cousin's plans?"

"Oh, yes, certainly."

"Then that is the third contingency, and, indeed, the one that, as I have had the honor to tell you, I consider most likely."

"Well, I understand," said Habil.

"As do I," said Grita.

"Good," said Illista. "Then, if we are all in agreement, let us make our plans."

"Agreed," said Habil.

"Agreed," said Grita. "But first—"

"Yes?"

"There is the matter of the fish that, even now, the hostess is bringing us. I perceive three servings, which means that you have thought to order for all of us."

"Well," said Illista, "what of it?"

"Only that it was very thoughtful. I foresee much profit in our association."

"Let us drink to our association," said Habil.

"Let us, rather, drink to our enemies," said Grita.

"Our enemies?" said the others.

"Indeed. To our enemies—and may they die in torment."

The three women solemnly drained their glasses.

Chapter the Sixty-Third

How the Empress Felt a Certain Unease
That Would Have Been Even Greater
Had She Heard the Conversation
The Reader Has Just Witnessed

We are now pleased, and hope the reader is also pleased, to return at last to Khaavren, who is, just at this moment, riding up the slopes of Dzur Mountain. The reader, we have no doubt, is wondering how he came to be on this trail, when we had left him, only a few days ago, on the roof of Morrolan's temple; this question we will answer soon, waiting only for our friend to reach Zerika, which will permit us to learn the answer to our question as Khaavren explains the results of his mission to the Empress.

We must admit that it took Khaavren a certain amount of time to negotiate the passages of Dzur Mountain; indeed, he might still be wandering those passages, even as these lines are penned, had he not happened to encounter Sethra the Younger, who conducted him to the sitting room where Zerika was holding court. As he entered, she was engaged in conversation with Aerich, which conversation broke off abruptly. Aerich, observing that the matter was private, bowed and retired after giving Khaavren a friendly smile.

"Captain!" cried Zerika.

"Your Majesty," said Khaavren, bowing. "I came at once. If Your Majesty should prefer that I clean up first —"

"We can save those niceties, Captain, for a time when we hold court in a Palace. However hospitable and comfortable is Dzur Mountain, we may still consider ourselves to be in the field, and so it is useless to pretend to such formalities."

"Very good, Majesty. Do you wish for my report?"

"I wish for nothing else in the world."

"Then this is it: I remained near the head of Kâna's troop, although out of their sight—which is proved by the fact that I stand before you now—until I understood their line of march."

"Well, and then?"

"Once I was certain of their direction, I hastened along that path. I give you my word, I did not waste time, and I was able to travel considerably faster than marching troops. Therefore, in little more than a day, I found their destination."

"And this destination is?"

"Two days' march south of here, there lies the camp of the other army about which we had heard rumor from Southmoor, but been uncertain as to its precise location."

"And were you able to learn anything of its size?"

"At least fifty thousands of soldiers."

"So many!"

"Sixty thousands, when the remnants of the other army meet them."

"We will, then, be overmatched."

"Not impossibly, Your Majesty. If they wish to attack Dzur Mountain, we will only need to hold our position. Consider that we have the Orb, the Necromancer, Lord Brimford, and, as matters stand, perhaps nine thousands of troops—as well as whatever powers there are in Dzur Mountain itself, which, as Your Majesty is aware, has never been taken by an enemy. I believe we can hold them."

"Well, it is certainly the case that we must try."

"And there is more."

"Well?"

"I do not know how—one never knows—but word of what happened to Izak's army—"

"Izak?"

"The general in charge of the troops defeated by Your Majesty's forces."

"Well, go on."

"Word has reached the other army, commanded by someone named Brawre."

"And has this word had any effect?"

"Assuredly. There have been few desertions, but a great deal of glancing in the direction of Dzur Mountain, and no small amount of talk."

"So then?"

"Brawre's forces have no wish to make an assault upon Dzur Mountain."

"That is good, then. Is there more?"

"Just this: Kâna, whatever else he is, is not foolish. I do not believe he would risk an attack under such circumstances."

"Are you certain?"

Khaavren shrugged. "Nothing is certain, Majesty."

"Then we must prepare to defend this position. See to it."

"As Your Majesty wishes. Will there be anything else?"

"Only one thing."

"And that is?"

"If you are so sanguine about our chances—"

"Well?"

"Why is it that Sethra Lavode seems so disturbed?"

Khaavren frowned. "Does she, indeed?"

"So the Lord Morrolan has told me."

"I must admit that I have not the least idea in the world."

Upon leaving Her Majesty, Khaavren, guided once more by Sethra the Younger, made his way out of doors, where, amid the growing chaos of the encampment on the slopes of Dzur Mountain, he managed to find a face he recognized.

"Your name is Fentor, is it not?"

The other signified that this was, indeed, his name.

"And you have a cache of weapons?"

"A few, my lord. Most of them are not yet—"

"Any pikes?"

"Pikes?"

"Pikes."

"Well, yes, I believe there may be a score or so."

"Where?"

"I will show you."

"Lead on, then, and I will follow."

"Here, this is what we have."

"These will do nicely," said Khaavren, taking two of them. "And may I have the use of some of your troops?"

"As many as you wish."

Khaavren thanked the general (for this was now his rank,

although his actual position in the chain of command was, as yet, unclear) and, in a brisk walk through the camp, found two soldiers, whom he caused to follow him.

As they walked, he said, "Do you swear to serve the Empire, the Empress, and the Orb, to the extent of your lives, if need be, and to obey all orders from your superior officers that do not conflict with your duty to the Empire?"

"Well, that is to say, yes, my lord," said one.

"Certainly," said the other.

Khaavren nodded and, this time being able to find his way by himself, soon arrived once more at the door to the Empress's chamber. He gave a pike into the hand of each of them, accompanying it with these words: "Remain here until relieved, and let no one enter without permission of Her Majesty. I will arrange for a schedule of replacements, and a lieutenant or a sergeant. Until then, do your duty."

"Yes, Captain."

"Yes, Captain."

This accomplished, Khaavren set about the tasks he had just outlined, which tasks the reader may assume he accomplished with his usual efficiency.

Having now seen our friend Khaavren, the reader may be wondering about Sethra Lavode, from whom we have not heard in some time. What is passing in the mind of the Enchantress, now that we have, on two separate occasions, heard that she has certain concerns which indicate knowledge not shared by those around her?

It was to discover this, in fact, that she received a visit at nearly the same moment Khaavren was setting the guard for the Empress, this visit being from none other than our friend Tazendra—or, as we ought to call her now, Tazendra Lavode, dressed in the traditional Lavode uniform of severe black, without embroidery, ornament, or garnish.

Tazendra found her with no difficulty in one of the lower chambers of Dzur Mountain, a wide, cavernous room which showed every sign of its origin—that is, that it had been cut out of the very rock of the mountain. The Enchantress was, just at this moment, standing between two silvery stalagmites—or so, at least, they appeared—one hand on each. Her eyes were closed in concentration, though, to Tazendra's glance, she showed no signs of being engaged in any great effort. Nevertheless, effort or none, each of the stalagmites was progressing through subtle but unmistakable color changes: silvery, to a flatter grey, to a reddish tinge, and then to an orange which became stronger until it was unmistakable. As Tazendra had not the least notion of what these colors meant, nor, indeed, of the nature of these apparent stalagmites, we are unable to provide this information, about which we admit to as much curiosity as the most inquisitive of our readers.

Soon, the Enchantress became aware of a presence in the room, and she opened her eyes. The stalagmites at once lost their color, returning to the silvery sheen they had first emitted, and Sethra smiled at Tazendra, saying, "Ah, my friend, it is good to see you."

"I hope I am not disturbing something urgent, madam."

"Important it is, my dear Tazendra, but not urgent. I am plugging up certain ethereal holes, through which beings of whom we are both aware have been attempting to gain entry."

"I beg your pardon, my dear Sethra, but that sounds tolerably urgent."

"Not so much, now that the Orb is back. The Jenoine are strong, but slow."

"I bow to your knowledge, good Enchantress," said Tazendra, suiting her actions to her words.

"But what brings you here?"

"Something important," said Tazendra, "though not urgent."

"Ah, you are becoming a wit!"

"Do you think so?"

"I am convinced of it, my dear Dzurlord."

"Well, I give you my word, it was not done on purpose."

"Oh, I have no doubt of that. But you needn't worry, there is no harm in it."

"You are certain?"

"Entirely. Many people have become wits without the least unpleasant effect, many of them Dzur. Indeed, the exercise of wit has often led to the exchange of blows, and is, even when it has not, a happy precursor to singing steel."

"Well, if you assure me of this, I shall not be vexed at it."

"That is right. But tell me, what is this matter that is important but not urgent?"

"There have been rumors, my dear Sethra, that your words and countenance are not reassuring, in the matter of Kâna's plans, and this at a time when, it seems to many of us, we are on the verge of gaining a great victory."

"Well, and then?"

"Instead of listening to these rumors, and engaging in speculation that might create confusion and false impressions, I had the notion to come to you and frankly inquire about it—a notion which I have just this instant put into action, as you, no doubt, perceive."

"My dear Tazendra, that was well thought!"

"You think so?"

"I am convinced of it. You are turning into a wit, and, moreover, you are becoming clever."

"Well, but—"

"No, no. It is completely harmless, I promise you."

"It is good of you to reassure me."

"It is nothing. But whence come these rumors? That is, who has observed this supposed anxiety on my part?"

"Oh, I have heard it expressed by Morrolan, Lady Teldra, Pel, the Empress—"

"The Empress?"

"She made some remark to that effect, unless my understanding is at fault, which I confess may be possible."

"Come then, my friend, let us repair upwards to Her Majesty at once, and I will explain my thinking to her. If she has made this observation, then it would be best if she were aware of my thoughts on the matter, so that she is better able to make the decisions that, as Empress, she is required to make."

"Splendid, my dear Sethra. Lead, and I follow you."

"Very well."

The Empress was either unoccupied when they arrived, or else she decided that whatever was required by the Enchantress was of more moment than her activity; in any case, they were at once bid to enter by the guards whom Khaavren had posted at the door.

The Empress rose as they entered, acknowledged Tazendra, and bowed deeply to the Enchantress.

"My dear Sethra," said Zerika. "I am glad you are here. There is something on my mind, and it is exactly you who can answer my questions."

"You wish to know," said Sethra, "why, at this time when everything appears to be going so well, I seem to be more anxious than ever."

Zerika's eyes widened. "How could you have known that? Ah, but I forget who you are. But come, you have stated the question; please sit down, and, if you will, be so good as to answer it."

"I shall do so at once."

"But not before sitting down, I hope."

"I but await Your Majesty."

"There, I am sitting."

"As am I."

"And I," added Tazendra, not to be left out.

"This is it, then," said Sethra.

"I am listening," said the Empress.

"As am I," said Tazendra.

"It is, then, simply this: I have spent some hours closeted with our good Yendi."

"The Duke of Galstan?" said the Empress.

"Pel?" said Tazendra.

"Yes, that is how he may be called."

"Well, and what of it?"

"Of him, I have learned somewhat of the character of this pretender."

"Well, that seems time well spent. Indeed, I ought to have thought to do the same. But, what have you learned?"

"That he is a determined fellow, courageous, with a certain amount of skill in organization, but no imagination."

"Well, but that does not seem bad."

"It is not, insofar as it goes. But does it not raise a question in your mind?"

"No, it does not, except that I wonder how such a fellow could have been so successful up to this point."

"That was the question it raised in my mind."

"Well, but did you answer it?"

"The Duke of Galstan did, when I posed it to him."

"Ah!" cried Tazendra, admiringly. "That is Pel! I recognize him so well in that!"

"What was his answer?" asked the Empress.

"It is simply this: Kâna has a cousin."

"Very well," said Tazendra, unable to contain herself. "He has a cousin. But my dear Sethra, this is not remarkable. Many people have cousins. I had a cousin myself, only he was killed attempting to climb Dzu—that is to say, he died on a quest."

"Yes, but this cousin, the Marchioness of Habil, is everything that Kâna is not: she has foresight, a certain kind of wisdom that is able to see letters writ large, and she is not afraid to make plans another might consider daring, even grandiose."

"Well, attacking the Orb could be considered daring, and to rebuild the Empire without having it might be considered grandiose."

"Exactly. Moreover—"

"Yes?"

"She has imagination."

"Oh, from what you have said, that goes without saying."

"And, as Galstan spoke of her schemes, how she would conceive them, plan them, and execute them, I heard something in his voice that frightened me."

"Well, what did you hear?"

"Admiration."

"Ahh," said the Empress. And, after a moment's consideration, she added, "I see."

"I asked our good Yendi if this Habil was capable of launching— or causing her cousin to launch—an attack such as we have just withstood without having other schemes and alternatives in mind in case the attack failed. He replied that she could not."

"And therefore," said the Empress, "we may conclude that Kâna has alternate maneuvers, and that these alternatives are, even now, being prepared or executed."

"Exactly."

"And so we know of what some of these schemes might consist?"

"Your Majesty—"

"Well?"

"I have not even so much as a guess. And that is exactly what worries me."

Chapter the Sixty-Fourth

How Zerika Marched to Adrilankha

It was on a Farmday in the late winter that Zerika began her famous march to Adrilankha. To be precise, it did not begin as a march to Adrilankha at all. Instead, after having considered carefully what she had been told by the Enchantress, and after consultation with Khaavren, Morrolan, Fentor, and various other advisers, she made the decision (which Khaavren, for his part, heartily approved) to take the army, which was now, in its entirety, camped on Dzur Mountain, and attempt to brush aside the advanced elements of Brawre's forces that were, in her words, "close enough to our front door to give me the itch."

The expedition was far more successful than even Khaavren had hoped. Not only was the advanced brigade brushed aside (it was, after all, heavily outnumbered), but the efficiency and skill with which the advance was handled, and the speed of the advance, caused such fear and consternation among Kâna's army that he, being uncertain what he was up against, was forced to order a general retreat. Now Kâna had been, in a sense, far too successful until this point. That is to say, he had never, even in defeat, been forced to make a retreat, and therefore did not know how to carry one out. Moreover, his two generals, Izak and Brawre, were young, and inexperience is nowhere taxed more heavily than in attempting to pull back a large army in the face of a strong and determined enemy. The Necromancer and the warlock Brimford added their own skills, as did Sethra the Younger, Tazendra, the Sorceress in Green, and even Morrolan; the result, then, was that Izak very nearly lost his entire army. Khaavren, though at first worried about a trap (the victory had been too easy for his comfort), at length became convinced of the true state of affairs, and urged Morrolan (who had become, by this time, the commander of the foremost division) to press on. We need hardly add that Morrolan required very little urging on this point.

The second day, Zerika, upon learning what was happening, decided that she would accompany the army. When it was suggested to her by Khaavren that this might put her in a certain amount of danger, she observed that the presence of the Orb could not but serve to improve the morale of the army.

"I do not dispute Your Majesty on this point," said Khaavren. "And yet, it seems to have become my duty to protect you, and therefore I must make these observations."

"I understand, Captain. You have done your duty, and I have made my decision."

Khaavren bowed and accepted it. The Empress then summoned Morrolan to her. Morrolan brought himself to Dzur Mountain (having spent much of the last days in a determined study of sorcery, he was able to perform this thaumaturgical feat himself), where Zerika informed him that, as far as she could determine, and pending a meeting of his House, he was Dragon Heir to the throne, which meant that, as the Dragon was to be the next House, he had certain duties to fulfill in terms of making himself familiar with the Orb.

"Is it a position," he inquired, "that I am able to refuse?"

"No," she said. "But it is possible that my understanding is incomplete, and you are not next in line. But, from what the Orb tells me, of the four Dragonlords with a better claim than yours, three died in Adron's Disaster, and the fourth was disqualified by your House over some sort of impropriety."

"I will investigate, once matters become more stable."

"In the meantime, you can be addressed as 'Your Highness.'"

"Must I?"

"Well, not if you choose not to be, I suppose, save on certain occasions at court."

"A court which does not yet exist."

"That is true."

"I should much prefer, as I understand these matters from Lady Teldra, to be Warlord."

"I have offered that position to Sethra Lavode."

"Well, I cannot doubt her qualifications, but is it not true that she feels herself confined to Dzur Mountain for now?"

"For the most part. But I feel, nevertheless, she will make a better Warlord from Dzur Mountain than anyone else in the field."

Morrolan sighed and said, "Alas, I cannot dispute with you on this point."

"Then it is settled. And, as to there being a court—"

"Well?"

"I am now on my way to create one."

"Where?"

"I have settled on the port city of Adrilankha."

"Is it not subject to attack by reavers from Elde?"

"Perhaps. But our roads are in such poor condition that, for now, I believe it would be best to govern from a place where communication by sea is easy—that is to say, from a port on the ocean-sea."

Morrolan bowed, and said, "How do you intend to get there?"

"The army is marching now, and I do not believe that there is anything that can stop us."

Morrolan left Her Majesty's presence, and, upon leaving the room, found himself face-to-face with Khaavren, who bowed and said, "Two words with you, sir, if you please."

"Two words?" said Morrolan. "That is not so many. How are they divided?"

"Why, one each, upon two different subjects."

"Very well, then, let us hear the first word."

However sanguine the Empress may have been about her own safety, Khaavren was required by his post and by his sense of duty to be less so—there were, therefore, a thousand things to arrange, all of them focused on what was now his primary concern: the protection of the Empress.

With this in mind, he said, "The first word concerns the posting of my company of guardsmen, which I should like to place, for the most part, directly behind your division, but in front of Her Majesty. This will necessarily entail a gap in the ranks sufficient to permit the dust to settle—for, you perceive, Her Majesty cannot be expected to eat the dust kicked up by your infantry."

Morrolan, who had never previously considered this matter, said, "Very well, I see no trouble with this. What then?"

"Then it is only a question of insuring good communications between your division and my corps, so that this gap in the lines cannot be used by anyone thinking to make a direct attack upon Her Majesty, and also of providing certain mounted outriders to guard against the same thing."

"Very well, I will have Fentor speak with you on this subject. What is your second word?"

"My second word concerns certain looks I may have given you on the occasion of our first introduction. It occurs to me that you may have found these offensive, and, if so, I will observe that I should wish to delay any discussion of this matter until Her Majesty has arrived safely in Adrilankha."

"Ah. You wish to play, then?"

Khaavren shrugged. "In fact, I do not. I lost interest in such games several hundreds of years ago. But, if you wish to play, I will certainly agree to entertain you."

Morrolan frowned. "You must understand, good Captain, that I have not long been in these lands, and, where I was raised, matters are arranged in a rather simpler way."

"How, then, are they arranged?"

"If someone offends me, I pass my sword through his body, and then the issue is settled."

"Well, in fact, sir, I believe there is a great deal to be said in favor of such a custom. It saves time, and is easily managed, and anyone left standing is able to devote his energy to other concerns, rather than considering games to be played in the future. But then—"

"Well?"

"The fact that you did not, on that occasion, attempt to run your sword through my body—because, I give you my word, I would have noticed if you had—indicates that, perhaps, you did not consider there had been an offense."

"In fact, I did not. Ought I have?"

"As to that, I cannot say. Some would, some would not. But I assure you, it has not for an instant crossed my mind that you might be timid."

"I am glad of that. Because if you did think me timid, well, I should have to endeavor to change your mind. It would grieve me to have someone of your mettle have such an opinion of me, and the esteem in which I hold you would require me to dispatch you at once."

"I understand entirely, and permit me to thank you for the kind words you have directed to me."

"You are entirely welcome, sir. And so?"

"And so, it seems, there is no cause for a quarrel, and that pleases me, because of the admiration I have for all that you have done."

"You are too kind."

"Not at all."

"Farewell then, Count, and permit me to say that I look forward to speaking with you again."

"And I, you. Farewell for now."

And, with courteous bows, they took their leave, Morrolan to look for Fentor, Khaavren to set about arranging the guard for the Empress's place in the general movement toward Adrilankha.

Her Majesty's remark, which we have taken the liberty of quoting, to the effect that nothing could stop the march, proved to be correct. Kâna's army continued to fall back, shrinking as it did so, and, though supplying the advancing Imperial army was no easy task, it was handled by Sethra Lavode, who never stirred from Dzur Mountain, with as much skill and dexterity as has ever been displayed in the history of warfare, with the result that the march to Adrilankha was accomplished in an astonishingly short length of time.

But time, as everyone knows, has meaning only when associated with a particular event. That is to say, the hour spent waiting for one's lover is far longer than the hour spent after the lover has arrived. In the same way, what is, by the standards of military science, a very quick march from Dzur Mountain to Adrilankha is, from the standpoint of a conspirator preparing to put a plan into operation, all the time that could be required.

In all the march occupied some fourteen days at the end of which time the Empress stood, unopposed, at the head of her army (unless, indeed, it was Morrolan's army; history is unclear on this point) on the very road from which Piro had set out more than a year before. Piro was there, as were Ibronka, who rode next to him, and Kytraan and Röaana. Pel, in his role as Imperial Discreet, accompanied her, as did Khaavren, Captain of the Phoenix Guard (which now had swelled to some thirty or thirty-five guardsmen, taken from the ranks of soldiers). Tazendra had remained behind at Dzur Mountain, to aid the Enchantress; Aerich had returned to his home in Arylle, pretending that he had no interest in ceremony, and could be of no use to Her Majesty, but was prepared to return should he be required. Morrolan, for his part, had become so enchanted, if the reader will permit a small play on words, with the study of sorcery, in which Sethra Lavode and her apprentice were instructing him, that he could hardly be induced to tear himself away from it when his duty as division commander required it. The late brigands came along, far in the back of the army, in company with Brimford and the Necromancer, as none of them had any wish for recognition.

The Empress, then, in an elegant coach (requisitioned the day before in the village of Cambry and hastily festooned by certain artistically inclined Dragonlords), came to halt before what could be considered the gates of Adrilankha, had Adrilankha any gates to stop before. It was, to be sure, at the political boundary of the city of Adrilankha and the county of Whitecrest, and, at this point, word was given that Her Majesty desired conversation with Piro, who at once rode forward, dismounted, and bowed to Her Majesty.

"Well, my friend," said the Empress. "Or, as I should say, Viscount."

"Your Majesty?" said Piro. "In what way may I serve you?"

"In the simplest possible way, my dear friend, though in a way that, when I last left, I should never have imagined I should have had to ask of you."

"Well, and what is that? You know you have only to name it, and I will do what you wish, if not for the sake of our old friendship, than certainly for the sake of what I owe to my Empress."

"Well spoken, dear Piro. What I ask, then, is this: that you grant me permission to enter your city."

For an instant Piro was startled, for it had not entered his mind that, as Viscount of Adrilankha, he had certain official duties as well as a title that, until this moment, had been all but meaningless. He gave a glance to his father, in whose stern countenance he could now see the hint of a proud smile, and then Piro knelt before the Empress and said, "Your Majesty, I welcome you to Adrilankha with all my heart, and it is my only desire that, having left the city last year, you shall never regret having entered once more."

Zerika nodded her head in a manner quite regal, followed by a small smile in which Piro could not mistake her friendship. Then, as Piro backed away, she said, "Let the Countess of Whitecrest be summoned."

Daro, in fact, had been summoned the day before by messengers sent to her home, and it had been all that she could do to restrain her desire to mount a horse and dash directly to visit her husband and her son, both of whom, she was assured, were alive, well, and traveling with Her Majesty. She had relieved the ennui of waiting, at least to a degree, by spending a considerable amount of time upon her toilette: dressing in bright Lyorn red with gold trim that set her fair complexion off admirably, along with certain small but elegant gemstones in the form of ear-rings and necklace. Then she had been conveyed by carriage to the place where her presence had been requested—that is to say, the eastern edge of the city—and there she had waited.

Upon at last being summoned by messengers from Her Majesty, Daro at once came forward and, in spite of the dignity of the occasion, could not keep a delighted smile from her countenance; for, as promised, there they were, Piro and Khaavren, smiling back at her.

She responded to Zerika's request with words she could never afterward remember, although they appear to have been "the proper trim for the breeze," as the Orca say, because soon enough she was dismissed, and, as Zerika entered the city, Daro entered the arms of her husband and her son.

As to the entrance to the city itself, other than the ceremony to which we have just alluded, it was an astonishingly quiet affair. By Zerika's orders, no general announcement had been made, and so, although there had been rumors that the Empress was to visit the city, no one could say exactly when, or precisely which of the many roads into the city she might use. To be sure, word spread quickly, and eventually something like a crowd began to line the street for a look at the Empress, and Khaavren found himself required to call on the services of some of his guardsmen to insure that the Empress's passage was unobstructed; but if the degree of pomp is to be commensurate with the importance of the occasion, then it was lacking to no insignificant degree.

This lack, however, was not noticed at the time by any of the participants, for the simple reason that no thought had gone into it—indeed, it was only on entering the city that the Empress realized that that she had no notion of where she, not to mention the entire court, and not to mention the army (now boasting nearly twelve thousands of soldiers), would quarter herself.

Zerika was, belatedly, pondering these very questions as she rode in triumph along Cutter's Way, when Khaavren fell in next to her coach and said, "Your Majesty, I have been giving thought to where the army should make its camp."

Zerika laughed without affectation, and said, "Well, Captain, it is good that one of us has, for I give you my word, until this very instant, I had not given it a thought."

"It is hardly Your Majesty's duty to look to such trivial details."

"Well, my dear Captain, I do not say whether or not ten thousands of soldiers are trivial, but, in any case, I am glad you have given it thought. What then?"

"There are several places along the river where encampments could be made. And, apropos, would it be indiscreet to inquire where Your Majesty should wish to establish herself?"

"It would not be indiscreet, but, alas, it is a question which I am, at present, unable to answer. The home of my guardians is too small for such uses."

"In that case, may I do myself the honor of offering Your Majesty the use of Whitecrest Manor?"

"Are you certain it would not discommode you unduly, Captain?"

"I should consider it a great favor on Your Majesty's part."

"Very well, then, Captain. I must first return and see my dear guardians, but, after that, I shall establish the court at Whitecrest Manor until such a time as we can cause a Palace to be built. It is settled."

"I will see to it."

Khaavren at once found Piro, who was riding with his three companions, and said, "My dear son, a great honor has been done us: Her Majesty will remain at our home with her court. You must go at once to the Countess so that she can make the preparations."

"Ah, it is, indeed, a great honor."

"It is, and it is good that you are sensible of it."

"Oh, my dear father, I am indeed. But I wonder—"

"Well?"

"How many am I to say will be there?"

"Ah, as to that, I cannot say. Perhaps a score."

"A score! In the Manor?"

"Well, what of it? We have the space, have we not?"

"Yes, I am convinced that we have, only I wonder—"

"Yes?"

"Will there be room, perhaps, for another?"

"If you mean your friend, Kytraan, then there is no reason that we cannot find a place for him."

"In fact," said Piro, blushing, "that is not who I meant."

Khaavren, whose eyes had grown sharp indeed in the service of the Empire, did not miss this reddening of the Viscount's features.

"So," he said, smiling a little, "there is another you would have stay under the roof with us?"

"If it is possible, yes."

"But, you know, my son, if this someone were, by chance, to be a girl—"

"Yes, if it were?"

"Then it would hardly be proper, unless—"

"Yes, unless?"

"Well, unless such an arrangement were accompanied by a declaration of intent to marry."

"Ah!" said Piro, becoming more flushed than ever. "That is to say—"

"Yes?"

"With your permission, and that of my dear mother—"

"Well, with these permissions?"

"And, with the consent of her own mother—"

"Yes, of course, with this consent—"

"Then we should like to, at once, make this declaration of intent!"

"Ah, ah!" said Khaavren, smiling proudly. "So, you wish to marry?"

"Yes, my dear father. That is what I wish. It means everything to me."

"You know, I think, that I could do nothing to stand in the way of your happiness, my dear son; and I speak for your mother as well."

"Then you will consent?"

"Did you doubt it?"

"But, you do not even know whom I wish to marry!"

"You think I do not? Yet, for months now, you have been in the company of a pretty young Tiassa, who—"

"Oh, Röaana? Yes, yes. She is a nice girl, no doubt."

"Well, then? How could I not see—"

"But that is not whom I would marry."

"It is not?"

"Oh, not the least in the world."

Khaavren frowned a frown of bewilderment. "But, my dear Piro, if not Röaana, then whom?"

"Why, her friend Ibronka! Oh, I have never had such feelings! Have you not observed how her hair curls by her ear? And the arch of her neck? And how much passion, how much fire she brings to even the smallest action—"

"Ibronka?" said Khaavren, his eyes becoming wide.

"Why yes, father. Ibronka. Have you not seen—"

"You wish to marry this girl, Viscount?" he cried.

"There is nothing that I wish more."

Khaavren stared at his son, at length managing to say, in something like the croak of a frog, "What do you tell me?"

"Why, that Ibronka and I are in love with each other, and wish to be married. Therefore, you perceive, to live under the same roof—"

"Viscount!"

"Yes, Father?"

"Why, it is impossible!"

"Impossible?"

"It is infamous!"

"What do you tell me?" cried Piro. "But she is—"

"She is a Dzur!"

"Well?"

"Well, you are a Tiassa!"

"Of this I am aware, I give you my word. And yet—"

"How can you contemplate such a thing? I forbid it! I absolutely forbid it! What would your mother say?"

"And yet," said Piro, beginning to grow warm, "it seems to me—"

"No! There will be no more talk of this! I have given you an errand, now see to it at once, sir! Do you hear me? At once!"

We should say, lest the reader wonder, that Kytraan, Röaana, and Ibronka had all witnessed this scene, and had seen the fire in Khaavren's eye and the gestures of anger, but had been unable to hear what was said, wherefore they remained in worried ignorance, at least for a while. Piro, with some difficulty, bit back words of anger and tears of frustration, and, without another word, set off toward Whitecrest Manor, spurring his horse into a furious gallop. So fast did he travel that, although the Countess had left Her Majesty nearly an hour before, she had only arrived a few minutes before he entered behind her.

"Ah, Viscount!" she cried. "It is good to see you home."

"Madam," he said, bowing, "I am to inform you that Her Majesty has done us the honor to establish her court here in the Manor."

"That is wonderful news, and, indeed, a great honor, although it means that there is much to do. But, Viscount, why is there such a look on your face, and why do you not embrace your mother?"

"As to that, madam—"

"Well?"

"You must ask my father."

"Oh, Piro! What do you tell me?"

"I have nothing more to say, madam. Now please excuse me. My errand is completed, and now—"

"Yes, now? Where are you going?"

"I have not the least idea in the world, I assure you. But I must go somewhere, and it must be alone, for if not, I promise you I will commit some rash act that I should bitterly regret."

"Piro!"

"Farewell, Mother."

With this, Piro gave his mother a quick bow, and, without another word, turned and walked out of the house.

Grassfog had been riding with his fellows, positioned directly behind the place in the formation (for the army had formed itself into something like neat lines as it approached Adrilankha), and, as Piro rode off on the errand we have just described, he turned to Iatha, who rode next to him, and remarked, "Do you see, my friend? We do not belong here."

"I do not understand what you tell me," said Iatha. "In what way do we not belong here?"

"You did not observe the scene that just passed between the captain and his son?"

"Why, as it was none of my business, I paid it no mind."

"You would have been wiser to listen, because, in the first place, one can never have too much information; and in the second, it would have taught you something that now, in order for you to learn it, I must myself explain."

"Well, if there is something to be learned, then I will certainly be glad to hear all you care to say."

"The young man, Piro, has just broken from his family."

"You think so?"

"I am convinced of it. If you had heard the conversation, and seen the look on his countenance, or observed how he drove his horse, well, you would be as convinced as I."

"But why has he broken with his family?"

"Over a girl."

"The Dzurlord?"

"Naturally."

"His father does not approve of her?"

"His father does not realize that a flood of years—more than two hundred years of them constitutes a flood, I think—have washed away the social niceties of the old Empire."

"He thinks the social niceties must be observed?"

"So it seems."

"Perhaps he is right."

"Yes, Iatha, perhaps he is right at that."

"And if he is—"

"Yes?" said Grassfog. "If he is?"

"Then we do not belong here."

"As I have had the honor to tell you, my friend."

They continued riding through the streets of Adrilankha.

Chapter the Sixty-Fifth

How Morrolan Came to Decide
Upon the Name Castle Black
For the Home He Was Causing
To Be Built

L ord Morrolan e'Drien, Count of Southmoor and Commander of the First Division of the Imperial Army by the grace of Her Majesty Zerika the Fourth, was so astonished and delighted at his new abilities that he quite nearly killed himself on several occasions, merely by teleporting either without sufficient clarity of his destination, or by continuing to do so after his mind, distracted and discomposed by the casting of spell after spell after spell, was in too benumbed a state to carry out such a difficult and complex feat of magic.

After one of these attempts, in which he was only saved because Sethra Lavode happened to be attempting to psychically bespeak him at that moment and became aware of his predicament, he received, from this Enchantress, a stern discussion of the dangers of his activities.

"Come now," she said. "Suppose it were said of you that you had honorably created and led an army, but then, having done so, destroyed yourself through misadventure with a spell. Is that what you wish history to record?"

Morrolan explained that, so far as he was concerned, history could record whatever it liked and be damned to it.

"But then, what of your friends? How will they feel if you should come to such an end?"

"Oh, they will, no doubt, find other friends."

"And what of your enemies? What of those you intend to punish, especially in the East? Suppose word should reach their ears that they were now safe from your vengeance, because you had, in toying with powers you could not control, done yourself in?"

Morrolan frowned and considered. "Well, it is true, I should not care for that."

"Then I beg you, my friend, take your time. Do not push yourself so much. Consider that you have, without taking unusual measures to prolong your life, at least two thousands of years before you."

"You make a strong argument, madam."

"I am gratified that you think so."

"And yet, it is difficult. I so wish to learn —"

"There are other ways to learn."

"How?"

"You can read books."

"Read books?"

"Certainly."

"Books on sorcery? Do these exist?"

"Why, not above a million of them. There would be more, but, alas, some of the more rare were destroyed in the Disaster."

"Verra! I had not known this. How long do you suppose it will take me?"

"To read a million books? Well, as to that —"

"No, to learn to read this peculiar language of yours, in which one symbol may stand for ten different sounds, and two-symbol combinations may stand for a hundred."

"How, you do not read?"

"Oh, I read. That is, I am an accomplished reader in several languages. Only it happens that this one we are speaking now is not one of them."

"I believe that, in a week, you could be reading well enough to make some of my books useful to you."

"Then I must start at once. Can you teach me?"

"I shall get Tukko to teach you."

"Your servant?"

"I happen to know that he has certain skills in teaching of such things."

"Very well. I should like to start at once."

"Then you shall," said Sethra Lavode, and at once summoned Tukko to her.

In the event, it was rather less than a week before Morrolan was positively devouring Suivo's *Exercises for Mental Flexibility* and Bluedorn's *Basic Energy Transformations*. From this point on, and for some little time, Morrolan all but vanished to most of his friends. He remained within the structure that had once been intended for a temple but was then determined to be a ball-room, and split his time between reading, and running through sorcerous drills. Indeed, except for meals and sleeping, he would have done nothing else had it not been for the wise Suivo, who insists in his Foreword on the absolute necessity, when making an intense study of sorcery, of keeping the physical body in the utmost trim. Morrolan, having not yet the experience at reading to know that the reader of any book of instruction ought to ignore those lessons he finds inconvenient, took Suivo at his word and forced himself to spend at least an hour a day practicing swordsmanship with some of the dozen or so in his army (or the Imperial army, as the case may be) whom he had caused to remain behind as a sort of honor guard.

The other time he emerged was to discuss with the Vallista whom he had hired the castle he wished built. This project, once so vital to him, now became nearly an afterthought, and so he turned much of the decision-making over to Fentor and Teldra, except that he announced a desire for the central structure—that is, the one in which he made his living quarters—to no longer be intended as a ball-room, but now to be a library; the reaction to this of the Vallista who had been busily designing his castle is not recorded. It was also during this period that he caused word to be sent out among the peons of the region that any book on sorcery would be considered acceptable as a year's rent. This resulted in a flurry of books arriving, although, in fact, only two or three of them had anything to do with sorcery.

One of these, as it happened, was perhaps the most common of the pre-Interregnum publications for those, especially those Teckla who knew their symbols, who wished to have enough skill at the sorcerous arts to keep them from being victimized by cheaters at dice and curses from jealous neighbors. It is the anonymous *Fundamentals of Sorcerous Defense*, and contains not-inaccurate diagrams of certain runes and glyphs useful for making charms or wards. It was upon reading this that Morrolan, in one of his not-infrequent conversations with Sethra Lavode, asked why the book stressed in such unambiguous terms that all of these runes must be drawn in black.

"Why, to increase their efficacy," said Sethra. "Could it be that you are not aware that the color black has been associated with sorcery as long as the art has existed?"

"I had not known that at all. Why should this be the case?"

"For a very simple reason, my friend," said the Enchantress. "It is because all things that have true existence have color."

"But, what of untinted glass?"

"Untinted glass has the color of whatever is behind it."

"Well, water?"

"Water has the color of its container, or sometimes of what it reflects."

"Very well, then, I accept that all things have color."

"Not all things, my friend. All things that have true existence."

"Well, but—go on, then."

"Sorcery has to do with transformations and energies that have no true existence, and therefore it is represented as having no color. Black is the absence of color."

Morrolan frowned. "It seems to me," he said, "that something clear is much more the absence of color."

"There is something in what you say, but nevertheless—"

"Yes, I understand. Well then, I shall call my keep Castle Black, because I intend to make it a home of sorcery."

"I should like to make an observation."

"And that is?"

"There are many sorcerers who will consider such a name to be a challenge."

"Well," said Morrolan, shrugging. "Let them consider it however they wish. In any case—"

"Yes?"

"I do not think I should care to live in a place called Castle Clear."

"No, I can understand why you might not."

Most of the plans for what would become Castle Black were laid down, as the reader may have inferred, without Morrolan's direct participation, as he was much involved in his study of sorcery, wherefore they fell, as we have implied, to Lady Teldra, usually with agreement from Morrolan that came in the form of a distracted nod accompanied by the words "Yes, yes, certainly." Soon, Teldra was able to procure the services of Lord Carver, the Vallista who had designed the Hartre Port Authority, or "the Blue Needle" as it was informally called, which gave the illusion of so much more space inside than it appeared to contain outside. This worthy, who had had, of course, no commissions since the Interregnum, fairly leapt at the opportunity, and after careful study of many of the floating castles of the past, consulted heavily with Teldra, and considered carefully what it meant to be building a structure to be called "Castle Black."

Morrolan condescended to speak with the noble Carver on three occasions: the first time, to be certain Carver understood about the windowless tower which Morrolan desired to have built as a place where he might commune with his Goddess; the second time to inform him that he required an entire wing to house Arra and his Circle of Witches; and a third time to approve the final plans, which he did with the words "Yes, yes, of course. If Teldra thinks it is good, you may begin," after which he returned to his reading.

In this way, the construction of Castle Black was begun in earnest. The reader may perhaps be curious about where Morrolan acquired the funds necessary for such an ambitious project. The construction of a castle, even on the ground and without the services of an architect as eminent as Carver, is not a matter to be entered into without a great deal of money being readily available, and the silver coins discovered by Morrolan when he began his excavation could hardly last forever—indeed, Morrolan's funds were hardly sufficient to pay for the army with which the reader is already acquainted.

The answer is hinted at above: Morrolan, following the invariable tradition of all aristocrats, demanded rents, or at least payments of some form, from those Teckla who worked the land, as well as imposing a (modest, to be sure) tax on the various merchants who either lived in or traveled through his realm. In the event, the rents were rather easier to collect than the reader might have anticipated: the march of Kâna's army through the duchy, accompanied by the inevitable acts of thievery, rape, beating, and occasional murder that accompany the march of even the most disciplined army, were sufficient to convince the peasants that the relatively modest demands of the Count, blessed by tradition and the Empire, were, in fact, not at all unreasonable. Moreover, many of the older families recalled with something like longing the old days, remembering the ceremony and grandeur of serving a Dragonlord and conveniently forgetting the inconvenience and annoyance of the thievery, rape, beating, and occasional murder that accompanies the existence of a standing army by even the most benevolent of aristocrats.

These rents came in, then, in the form of grain, livestock, and copper pennies, as well as a certain number of books, to the extent that, even with the amount paid to and stolen by the tax collectors, Morrolan was able to maintain his army (or the Imperial army, as the case may be), cause his castle to be built, maintain and expand his Circle of Witches, and still live in such a way as to be able to entertain visiting nobles in a style that Lady Teldra found to be within acceptable limits.

He caused black marble and obsidian to be imported from the far north, white marble (for the interior) to be sent from the near north, silver from the Canthrip, brass and good steel from the forges and foundries of Tirenga to the east, glass from the south, and teak from Tree-by-the-Sea in the far northwest (this last being sent by ship to Adrilankha before coming overland, as it was still impossible to pass through the heartland owing to Kâna's continuing influence). Not only material, but builders were imported — Lord Carver knowing all the best artisans and specialists, and demanding that Morrolan (or, rather, Teldra) use only them, at least when they could be spared from their work on the Imperial Palace, which was also occurring at this same time.

And through all of this — the hauling of blocks, the hammering and shaping of copper and silver, the crafting and erection of scaffolding (all of this, be it understood, taking place well off the ground), Morrolan continued his studies of the sorcerous arts — reading, experimenting, and practicing.

And through all of this, the building of the castle, and Morrolan's study, the rest of the Empire was not standing still, although the details of Zerika's first year in power, in order to contribute to the elegant unfolding of our history, must be delayed while we devote our attention to that noble person for whom the history is named: the Viscount of Adrilankha.

Chapter the Sixty-Sixth

How Piro Made His Way Back East
Where He Failed to Be Alone

Piro rode northeast from Adrilankha with, it must be said, no very clear sense of where he was going. His entire conscious thought was devoted merely to the notion that, above all, he required to be alone. The idea of seeing his friend Kytraan, or above all Ibronka, but even of seeing anyone he knew, was strangely abhorrent to him. The reader may say that to leave thus precipitously was to treat Ibronka in a shabby way, and in this the author cannot disagree; but the reader ought to understand that the young viscount had never before been required to act in the face of such emotional turmoil, and, lacking experience, he was overwhelmed by his own feelings.

He continued, therefore, riding east, until, at last, his experience as a horseman penetrated his agitation and he realized that he was very close to killing his horse, whereupon he drew rein.

He was, by this time, well outside of the city, in a small forested dell between two low hills, and entirely out of sight of anyone, and it was by now fully dark. He dismounted and led his horse a short distance until he encountered a brook, where he watered her, then removed her saddle and brushed her down, spending a good, long time and making a thorough job of it. By the time he was done, his mind was calmer, and he was even able to engage, to some degree at least, in that strange human activity that we call "thinking."

At first, thoughts of Ibronka—the sound of her voice, the way she moved, the fire in her eye—came so strongly that he almost felt she was there with him; but he resolutely pushed these images aside. "I will have to make a decision, sooner or later," he told himself. "But I certainly cannot do so now." He looked around, hoping very much that he might suddenly be attacked by bandits—in his present mood, he thought it unlikely that anyone could stand up to him, and, if he were wrong, so much the better. But brigands are never known to appear when expected, for the obvious reason that those that do rarely last long in that occupation.

After some time, Piro at last rose, re-saddled his horse, and led her onward, at last reaching a small cabaret, set back from the road and nearly invisible, where he entered and secured an evening's lodging. He gave some consideration to whether he should should drink enough to forget his troubles for a while, decided that it would be best to avoid wine altogether, left his few possessions (he having nothing except what was in the pockets of his saddle), and went down to the jug-room and purchased a bottle of sharp, peppery, harsh wine.

A glance around the room told him that he would be unable to have a table to himself—the room was so crowded that most of the guests were standing, talking loudly in small groups—but he was able to procure a chair by finding a table in the corner and, with a look, requiring one of the Teckla to surrender his seat.

He sat down, pushing himself back into the corner, drained his cup in one motion, and refilled it from the bottle. He drank his second cup more slowly, and looked around a little. Everyone seemed to have a smile upon his lips, and all the voices were loud. The Teckla whose chair he had taken caught his eye, bowed respectfully, and lifted his goblet, saying, "It is a great day, is it not, my lord?"

"How, you think so?" said Piro.

"Oh, my lord! I am convinced of it!"

"What makes it good, my dear fellow?"

"My lord, can it be you have not heard the news?"

"Well, perhaps I have not. Tell me, and then, after you have done so, it will be certain that I have."

The Teckla appeared unable to find a flaw in this logic, and said, "This is it, then: The Orb has returned, and there is an Empire once more."

"Bah. That happened weeks ago."

"There were rumors, to be sure, and some old wives insisted they could feel the Orb once more. But now it is certain, because the Empress has entered Adrilankha."

"I am astonished," said Piro bitterly. "Who could have guessed?"

The Teckla, hearing the tone of his voice, became confused, but determined that this noblemen was not, perhaps, as congenial as some others might be; he therefore, with a polite bow, turned away. After that, Piro was able to drink quietly, which he did, finishing the bottle in good time. He asked himself if he were, in fact, going to get drunk, noting that, if he intended to stop, now would be the time. After giving it due consideration, the wine he had consumed to this point answered for him, and he began to rise to his feet in order to procure himself another bottle. Before he could do so, however, the intended bottle appeared, as if by magic, in front of him.

Piro frowned, looked at the bottle with its dark liquid contrasting so sharply with its light blue label, and, after considering for a moment, permitted his eyes to trace a path that started with the bottle, continued to the hand that held it, maintained its course up the arm and across the shoulder, rose abruptly at the associated neck, and at length came to rest upon the face. After the instant it took him to recognize this face, he leapt to his feet.

"Lar!" he cried.

"My lord, it seemed to me you were in need of another bottle."

"What are you doing here?"

"What am I doing here? I am getting you another bottle."

"Well, but—"

"Yes, my lord?"

For the first time in many hours, Piro felt a smile grow upon his lips, as he said, "Well, my friend, you have brought it; now you must help me drink it."

Lar bowed. "I shall be honored to do so."

Lar took from his pocket a small, ingenious collapsible tin cup, which Piro filled with wine, after which they silently toasted each other.

"Now tell me, good Lar, how did you happen to come here?"

"In the simplest way, my lord. I followed you."

"You followed me?"

Lar bowed his assent.

"From where?"

"First, from where you left us, and then from Whitecrest Manor."

"You followed me all the way?"

"Nearly. You perceive, you set out at such a pace from the Manor that I fell far behind. My horse cannot stay with yours for any length of time."

"And then?"

"Well, I found you again when you began leading your horse. Apropos, is she lame?"

"No, merely exhausted."

"Well, I do not blame her."

"Very well, Lar. I now understand how you found me. But now there is another thing I wish to know."

"If it is a question I can answer, well, I will do so."

"I wish to know why you followed me."

"Why? Well, because it is my duty."

This remark was made with such simple, matter-of-fact loyalty that Piro was rendered speechless.

The celebration around them continued for some few hours, but eventually the jug-room began to clear, and Piro invited Lar to sit. Some time later, Lar stood once more, and, hauling the Viscount over his shoulder, carried him to his room.

When Piro woke, Lar, without saying a word, handed him a steaming glass of klava, full of thick cream and honey, which Piro at once drank down, and if he did not say a word, his countenance expressed all the gratitude Lar could have wished for.

When the worthy Lar judged that Piro was again able to carry on conversation, he said, in as quiet a voice as he could manage, "Whither are we bound, my lord?"

"I don't know," said Piro, in a voice just as quiet, but one which, nevertheless, caused him to wince. He then observed, "I do not believe, my dear Lar, that I have been designed by the Lords of Judgment to become a drunkard. I appear not to have the constitution to sustain it."

"My lord," said Lar, falling back upon the single statement that a servant may always rely upon when any other response is fraught with peril.

Piro sighed and made an aimless gesture which Lar correctly interpreted as a request for more klava, which drink was supplied with silent alacrity.

With the second cup of klava inside of him, Piro was able to con-sider, and then reject, the notion of food. He was also able to ask him-self why he had consumed so very much wine, and, upon answering himself, the reasons came back with all of their force, and he bowed his head, momentarily overcome with emotion.

Lar said, "Master—"

Piro raised his head again and said, "It is nothing. Come, let us travel. Let us go back east. I will enlist in Morrolan's army, because he is a Dragonlord, and, sooner or later, he will fight someone, and I should enjoy a good skirmish of all things."

"Yes, my lord. But are you . . . that is, do you wish to travel now?"

"Yes, I wish to set out at once. Perhaps my head will fall from my shoulders as we ride. If it does, I swear to you by my right to Death-gate that I shall be delighted."

"Yes, my lord. I shall prepare the horses."

In the event, it took Piro rather longer than he would have thought to bring himself to the point where he was ready to mount, but at last they were both packed and ready to travel, albeit slowly, and they began the journey at a leisurely pace toward the county of Southmoor and Castle Black.

That night, they stayed in an inn that might have been the twin to the previous one, only this time Piro, only beginning to feel better after an entire day of exercise (for the reader ought to know, if he doesn't, that to sit upon a moving horse is to take exercise), limited himself to no more than a small glass of wine to accompany his mea-ger dinner of spit-roasted kethna and toast. He slept soundly that night, waking up once more with Ibronka's face and voice in his mind. He bit his lips till they bled to keep from moaning aloud (not wishing to display this weakness before Lar, who slept on the floor at his feet) and made himself think of other things.

They mounted once more and continued on the same road they had traveled more than a year before, on the way to Dzur Mountain. As they rode, Piro observed, "Do you know, my dear Lar, I have often heard talk of pains of the heart."

"Yes, my lord. I have heard this expression used before, often in songs."

"And yet, I had not considered that this sort of pain could be, well—"

"My lord?"

"—as *painful* as it is. Do you know, I should much prefer to be pierced with a few inches of good steel, if I could arrange for this pain to be replaced. Not, you understand, that I am making complaints. I merely point out an interesting phenomenon."

"Yes, young master, I understand."

"That is good. I believe we can ride a little faster now. Indeed, I should like, of all things, to feel the wind upon my face, and the excitement as this fine animal stretches itself out upon the road."

"My lord, I shall be happy to do so, but I beg to make two observations first."

"Very well, then, what are these famous observations?"

"The first is that your horse is able to run both faster and longer than mine, so that, sooner or later, you will be obliged to wait for me to catch up."

"Yes, I understand that. What is the second?"

"The second is that there is a horseman coming up behind us at a tremendous speed, so that we should, perhaps, wait for him to pass to avoid what might be an unfortunate meeting."

"Very well, I accept that we should wait for this horseman to pass."

The horseman, however, did not pass, but, rather, upon reaching Piro and Lar, instead drew rein.

"Ibronka!" cried Piro, standing up in his stirrups.

It was, indeed, the Dzurlord, who did not make a reply in words, but, rather, leapt from her saddle directly at Piro, knocking him, in turn, from his saddle, so that he landed on his back, breathless from the landing, and Ibronka on top of him, where she covered his face with kisses.

Piro, when he had recovered his breath, said, "Why, madam, there are tears on your cheeks."

"They are now tears of joy, Viscount."

"Now?"

"I have been attempting to bespeak you for two days!"

"Bespeak me? How?"

"Why, through the Orb."

"Ah. That is, no doubt, why I have, so often, heard your voice in my mind with such clarity. But I didn't know—"

"It doesn't matter. Now we are together."

"Together? Yes, but, my dear Ibronka, my father—"

"I know about your father; he spoke to me."

"He spoke to you?"

"He was—that is to say, he never failed in courtesy."

"Oh!"

"He was sufficiently cold, however, that I had to sit before a fire to become warm again. Of course, I at once took my leave of Her Majesty, and did not set foot in Whitecrest Manor."

"Oh!"

"Shall we rise? You perceive, we are lying in the road, and people are required to walk around us."

"Let them."

"And if one should step on us?"

"Lar will hit him in the head with an iron cook-pot."

"Very well. There is more."

"Tell me."

"I was able to use the power of the Orb to speak with my mother."

"And—?"

"She agrees with your father on all counts."

"Oh!"

Ibronka buried her head in Piro's shoulder. The Viscount stroked her hair and said, "It is wrong of them."

"It is."

"I thought I could tear myself away from you, and that it would be best for you if I did, that you would forget me, and—"

"It was wrong of you, Piro."

"Perhaps it was. I am glad you are here. But—"

"Yes?"

"What can we do?"

"Where were you going?"

"To offer my sword to Morrolan. Apropos—"

"Yes?"

"How did you find me?"

"I don't know."

"You don't know?"

"I simply knew where you would be."

"Well, that is love."

Ibronka smiled and held him closer. At length, she rose, and assisted him to his feet.

"Where is Clari?" he said as he stood up.

"She is behind me. My horse is rather faster than hers, and, if truth be told, she is not much of a horseman. But she will be along."

"Then let us continue at a walk."

"Yes, with this plan I agree."

They mounted their horses again, and, with the worthy Lar behind them, rode knee to knee in companionable silence. By the end of the day, they were close to the western border of Southmoor, and were looking for an inn.

"If my memory serves me well," observed Piro, "this is the Nacine road, and here is where it crosses the Shallowway Pike. Therefore, we should turn eastward here."

"Very well. But, what is that I hear? Horses. Perhaps it is Clari."

"Let us see, then."

"There are several horses. It is hard to tell in this fading light. Might it be road agents?"

"I hope so," said Piro, touching his sword.

"Well, now that you mention it, so do I. In all truth, I have nothing worth stealing except my horse and my sword; but I should welcome the attempt."

"I have a few coins, that would hardly be worth a bandit's effort, but I give you my word, I should welcome the attempt as well."

It was not, however, road agents, but instead the worthy Clari who appeared, and was given a friendly greeting by Piro, Ibronka, and Lar.

"But who is coming behind you?" asked Ibronka.

"How, you cannot guess?"

"Why it is we," said Kytraan, coming up at that moment. "It is Röaana and I. Come, you could not imagine that, after all we have gone through, we would leave you!"

"Oh, my friends!" cried Piro, tears coming to his eyes. "How did you find us?"

"Why, in the simplest possible way," said Röaana. "We followed the good Clari."

"But, Clari, how did *you* find us?"

"I promise you, my lord, it was not difficult. I merely had to ask passersby if they had seen a beautiful young Dzurlord mounted upon a dappled stallion and riding like the wind. Madam is difficult to miss."

"Yes, I believe that readily enough, my dear Clari. Only—" He turned to Kytraan and Röaana. "—why did you do so?"

"Why did we do what?" said Röaana.

"Why did you follow?"

"Why," said Kytraan, "in order to find you. You could not imagine that we could dissolve our little band, did you?"

"Indeed," said Piro. "I had thought I was alone."

"You will never be alone," said Ibronka.

"Well said," remarked Röaana. "And now, unless I am mistaken, you are even less alone."

"How, what do you mean?"

"Observe who is now riding up."

"I cannot tell. It is very nearly dark."

"That is true," said Kytraan. "But it happened that I saw them behind us some hours ago, and so I know who they are."

"Well then, who are they?"

"No one but ourselves," said Grassfog, riding up at that moment. "That is, it is I, and Iatha, Ritt, and Belly."

"But," cried Piro, "why are you here?"

"Oh, we did not care for the army. And now that, it seemed, we had fulfilled our duty in serving Her Majesty, why, we obtained a leave. We had nowhere else to go, so we thought we should join you, as you seem to be amiable enough companions. If, that is, you do not object to our presence."

"Not in the least," said Piro. "Only, how did you find us?"

"How else? We followed Kytraan and Röaana."

"The Gods! Is anyone else going to appear?"

"I do not believe so, my lord. So far as I know, no one came after us."

"That is just as well," observed Piro. "And I cannot but say that I am touched—" He broke off and fell silent, unable to continue his remarks for the emotion that washed over him.

Kytraan coughed to cover his confusion and said, "Come, let us find an inn and celebrate the re-uniting of our band."

"I agree that this is a good plan," said Piro, "only—"

"Yes?"

"Have you any money?"

Kytraan dug into his pockets, and was able to produce six copper pennies. Röaana had less, and, combined with what Piro had, they were scarcely able to arrive at an orb. As for Grassfog and his friends, they had nothing whatsoever.

"We have enough for a loaf of bread, some cheese, and few bottles of wine, in any case," said Kytraan. "And, for my part, I have no objection to sleeping out of doors. We have done it often enough in this last year."

"That is true," observed Röaana.

Piro said, "Yes, but—ah, who is this? A good evening to you, sir."

"And to you, young man," said a gentleman who had come up, driving a pony-cart. This gentleman, dressed in the simple yet tasteful garb favored by certain Chreotha merchants, stopped his trap and gave a polite bow of his head, accompanying this courtesy with the words "Have you heard that the Orb is back?"

"Yes," said Piro. "This fact has not escaped my attention."

"Oh," said the stranger, "but is it not the most wonderful thing? An Empire once more! The roads will be safe, money will flow from pockets again, and I—"

"Yes, and you?"

"I will become rich."

"Tell me, good sir, how you intend to become rich? You perceive, I am most curious, for I am too young to know how life changes with the coming of the Orb."

"Then I will explain to you in terms that leave no room for doubt."

"That will be best, I promise you."

"This is it, then: I travel with my little cart here to Nacine, and there I purchase items made from the good clay of the district, as well as glass bottles made from sand from the Great Sand Flats."

"Very well, you purchase pottery and glasswork."

"Exactly. And then, I take this pottery, and I travel to Rough-ground, where there is a winery, and a brewery, and a distillery. I then trade these pots and bottles, and, in exchange, I receive some of them back, filled with wine, beer, and spirits, as well as a certain amount of good money."

"So you have wine, beer, and spirits. What next?"

"I next take these to the Collier Hills, where they have little to drink, but a great deal of iron."

"So then, you get iron."

"Pots, pans, and even weapons now and then."

"I understand. But what do you do with these iron goods?"

"Why, I bring them to Nacine, where they are happy to pay for them with good coin, and where, in addition, I can purchase more glasswork and pottery."

"Why, that seems simple enough."

"Oh, it is. The only problem is—"

"Yes, what is the problem?"

"The roads are not safe. Indeed, the roads are fraught with peril for a merchant such as I. Or, that is to say, they *were*."

"They were?"

"Yes. Now there is an Empire again, and so no road agent would dare to appear on a main road for fear of meeting a detachment of Imperial troops, or else soldiers who serve the Count, who is now back as well."

"Ah, there, my dear sir, I must disagree, although I do so most respectfully."

"How, you disagree?"

"Respectfully."

"But, in what way do you disagree?"

"There are still road agents, bandits, and brigands on these roads."

"Oh, perhaps on the smaller roads, but here, on this fine avenue that runs between Roughground and Nacine, there will be no—but what are you doing?"

"I? I am drawing my sword."

"But why are you doing this?"

"In order to point it at your breast, my dear sir."

"You are going to do me an injury?"

"Oh, no. Believe me, I should be very sad if I were forced to injure you in any way. And I promise you that I will not, if—"

"Yes?" said the merchant, in a small voice that was nearly a squeak. "If?"

"Why, if you will hand your purse over to me."

"You wish my purse?"

"Certainly. You have no objection to giving it to me, do you?"

"Why . . . that is to say, none at all."

"Very good, then."

"Here it is."

"You are courteous. And now—"

"Yes, my lord? And now?"

"Why, now it leaves me with nothing to do except to wish you a very pleasant and peaceful good evening."

"You are most kind."

"It is good of you to say so."

The merchant, in spite of his still-shaking hands, was able to signal to the pony to resume his interrupted journey. Piro inspected the purse, and observed, "Six Imperials and a little more." Then, looking at his friends, he remarked. "Has anyone any observations to make? If so, I give you my word, now is the time to dis-associate yourself from what I have just done."

Kytraan studied the viscount and said softly, "You are, then, serious about this?"

"Entirely, my friend—for so I hope I may still call you. I have his purse, and have not the least intention of returning it. On the contrary, it is my hope to gain many others like it."

"As for me," said Grassfog, "I rather enjoyed the life I led, and I willingly accept you as leader."

"But what of you, Kytraan."

The Dragonlord frowned. "The Empire—"

"Well? What of the Empire?"

This question produced a silence that lasted a certain duration, while the young Dragonlord considered carefully. The reader can well imagine, with such a decision at stake, that he was permitted this time to reflect without any objection by Piro. The reader may also well imagine that both Röaana and Ibronka used the time in the same manner as did Kytraan—that is to say, for reflection.

At length, Kytraan said, "My dear Viscount, I am uncertain as to the wisdom of this thing, and I have grave doubts as to whether it is right, but—"

"Yes, but?" said Piro, pulling his cloak of Tiassa blue around his neck against the breeze.

"You are, you say, committed to this course of action?"

"Entirely, though I do not require anyone else to accompany me."

"Well, but I find, upon inquiring of my heart, that your friendship matters to me more than any of the other considerations."

"Very good," said Piro, accepting this reason without question or comment. "Anyone else?"

"You know," said Ibronka, "that I am with you, no matter what. You may turn bandit, you may rebel against the Empire we have just had the honor to help restore, or you may attempt to throw the Lords of Judgment from their thrones; I will still be with you."

"She speaks for me as well," said Röaana. "As, for that matter, does Kytraan."

"In that case," said Piro, "as our friend with whom we transacted business will soon be reporting us, we may as well take the little time that is available to us and find a good inn where we can refresh ourselves in peace for the last time."

"I know an inn," said Grassfog, "where they are friendly to highwaymen, and forces of the law were never used to coming, even in the days of the old Empire, and now it stands in the middle of eight counties that have reverted to the Empire, with nothing more than a scattered barony among them, so that the law, as you can imagine, is scarce in the entire district. Indeed, I had often suggested setting up there, as there are plenty of roads to choose from."

"Is it far from here?" said Piro.

"A few hours' ride at a steady clip will see us at the door."

"Lead the way," said Piro.

Chapter the Sixty-Seventh

How the Duke of Kâna Endured
Certain Indignities in Order
To Carry Out His Schemes

His Royal Majesty the Emperor of Dragaera, Duke of Kâna, Count of Skinter and Frond, Baron of Levy, Broadtide, and so and so on, entered Peffa's Inn dressed in a dingy brown cloak worn over plain black trousers and a shirt with pretensions toward white but none toward fashion; wearing tradeshoes instead of boots and not even so much as a dagger at his belt. A certain Issola minstrel occupied the front of the room, playing a cittern and singing popular songs in a sweet, lilting voice that sometimes achieved strikingly pure high notes. Near-by, in the best position to listen to the music, was a table occupied by two women, one of them obviously noble (wearing gold, no less, which color was by tradition reserved for the House of the Phoenix) and another who was hooded and cloaked, much as was His Majesty, so that her House was impossible to determine. Before the women were plates empty save for bits of bitterfruit and fish bones, and a single bottle of white wine, still holding more than half of its original contents.

As he approached the table, both of the women began to rise, but, with a gesture, he bade them remain seated. The woman in the hood spoke first, saying, "I am glad you have arrived without mishap, cousin. I was worried to learn that you traveled with no escort."

"The roads are tolerably safe, Habil," replied Kâna. "Especially for a poor man who appears to have nothing with him worth the effort to steal."

"Would Your Majesty care for wine?" asked the other.

"Yes, and I thank you, Illista. Wine would be most welcome after the journey. But do not address me as Your Majesty. It is useless to be overheard."

"As Your—that is to say, as you wish. But we shall hardly be heard over the singing."

Kâna sipped his wine and said, without further preamble, "Have we received word from Udaar?"

"Only that he arrived safely, and has been promised an audience."

"That is progress, then."

"Yes. But I do not anticipate learning the results of his mission for some days."

"Very well. Let us assume that his mission will be completed successfully, because, you perceive, there is no point in going on if he fails."

"Then," said Illista, "you believe that everything depends on his success, so that, if his mission should fail, all of our efforts come to nothing?"

"Not precisely," said Kâna. "But, should he fail, then, at the least, we will have to nearly start over from the beginning. But there is little that will keep me from making every effort—indeed, if it comes to it, I will, myself, march on Whitecrest Manor, where this Phoenix now holds court, and fight until I fall."

"Let us hope," said Habil, "that it will not come to that."

"I agree. And, moreover, let us hope Udaar is successful, and make our plans accordingly."

"Yes, let us do so," said the others.

"To begin, then," continued Kâna, "there is that baron—what was his name?"

"Loraan."

"Exactly. What of him?"

"He is ours, body and soul. You should have seen his gratitude when I placed the artifact into his hand. He would die for us."

"Excellent."

"If I may—" said Illista.

"By all means, if you have a question, now is the time to ask it."

"Then I will do so," said the Phoenix. "Have you heard from our friend the bastard?"

"Grita?" said Habil. "Yes. She says that her arrangements are complete as far as the Dzurlord goes, and that this will, necessarily, see to the Lyorn as well."

"Very good. What about the Tiassa?"

"She has found a way to separate him from the court, and, once this separation is made, he will be vulnerable in any number of ways."

"I agree. And the Yendi?"

"Grita says that he is the trickiest, and she is taking care with him."

"Well, that is good, so far as it goes. But has she found an avenue of approach?"

"He has become Imperial Discreet."

"So you have told me."

"And then?"

"Well, then he can be attacked that way."

"Precisely. And, moreover—"

"Well?"

"Without his friends, he becomes far less of a threat."

"Yes, I understand."

"Then," said His Majesty, "that leaves us with one remaining problem."

Habil nodded. "The influence of witchcraft in general, and that warlock in particular."

"You understand exactly, my dear cousin."

"Well, we discussed what needed to be done in that regard."

"Yes, we did, and we made an attempt, and our efforts came to nothing."

"We chose the wrong god, that is all."

"So you have said."

"Well, do you see another way?"

Kâna shook his head. "I do not. Do you, cousin?"

"None."

"Well, for my part, I am prepared."

"Then let us be about it."

"I see no reason to delay," said Habil. She rose, and, bowing to Illista, said, "Madam, I trust you will remain here?"

"I will."

"Good. Then I look forward exceedingly to speaking with you again, when we have something else to report."

"And I," she said, "of course wish you all the best of luck."

Kâna rose as well, bowed, and escorted Habil out of the inn. Illista, for her part, remained and listened to the music.

Kâna and his cousin took themselves to the same rooming house in which Illista had procured lodgings, where they entered a ground-floor suite that had the luxury of a private entrance. Upon entering, they first searched the three rooms that composed the suite—two bedrooms and a small parlor—to be certain that no one else was there. When they were satisfied, Kâna said, "You know what must be done?"

"I have studied the matter carefully, my dear cousin, and I am convinced that I will be able to give you precise instructions at every step."

"Very well, then. What is the first?"

"First, you must cleanse yourself. I have prepared this water with a mild soap and various herbs, and this sponge which is as fresh from the sea as could be found. After you are clean, you must dry yourself with equal care—here is a towel—after which you will apply this oil to your entire body."

"Oil?"

"It is very much like embalming oil."

"You perceive, this is not a thought that pleases me."

"It has a scent that is not unpleasant."

"That will help. This will be a lengthy process, I perceive."

"Tolerably long, and arduous. Perhaps you should have eaten."

"I had bread and cheese on the way. I believe I am sufficiently fortified."

"Very well."

After completing this ritual, Kâna stood naked in the middle of the room. "Well, what now?"

Habil produced a pot of blue paint and a brush, as well as a sheaf of paper on which she had written notes.

"Next, you must be decorated."

"In blue, for all love?"

"So I am informed."

"With what am I being decorated, then?"

"Various symbols about your body. This, upon your chest. Here, on your right buttock. This, upon your belly."

"There are a tolerably large number of them, all told."

"Yes, much of you is to be covered, and I am drawing small."

"This smacks of heathen worship."

"Raise your arms so that I can reach your sides."

"They are raised."

"Perhaps it does smack of heathen worship, cousin, but each god must be spoken to in his own language, and if we achieve the effect we wish, that is all that matters. There, you may lower your arms now."

"With this I agree. Those symbols," observed Kâna, dropping his arms, eyes, and dignity, "appear to be Serioli."

"Yes. They spell out his name in the peculiar alphabet of the Serioli, where each symbol indicates one sound, or what is, to us, part of a sound. And, moreover, should these symbols be played as musical notes—for the symbols that the Serioli use to denote sounds also represent musical notes, and we have taken their system in this regard—they will describe a certain melody that is sacred to this god."

"I know that melody. Am I to hum it?"

"Later. There, now you are prepared."

"I hope the paint will come off."

"It will. One advantage to covering you so thickly in oil is to lay the paint on it, rather than directly on your skin. It will wash off easily enough."

"I am heartily glad of that. What now?"

"Now we must plunge ourselves into darkness."

"The god, is, then, bashful?"

"Perhaps. Or it may be to remove distractions from your mind."

"I hope it is not that, because I give you my word the darkness is more distracting than anything I might see."

Habil put out all of the lamps, and using black naval cloth procured for the purpose, made certain no light could penetrate through the edges of the door or the single shuttered window. When the room was entirely dark, so that not even his own hand, passed back and forth in front of his eyes, made any perceptible difference, Kâna said, "What now, cousin?"

"Do you recall his name?"

"I do."

"And can you pronounce it?"

"The long version, or the short?"

"The long."

"Tristangrascalaticrunagore."

"Very good. I perceive you have been practicing it."

"It occupied my mind during the journey, along with humming that tune of which we have spoken."

"Did you also recall the symbol associated with his name?"

"It is a circle, and within the circle there is an arrow, pointing to the center, and an asymmetrical mark with four branches, a tetrahedron, and a crescent."

"I see you have done your work as well, cousin."

"What of this symbol?"

"You must hold the name firmly in your mind while you draw the symbol, and you must say it, very softly, over and over again."

"How large am I to draw it?"

"Large enough to stand fully within it."

"Very well. How am I to draw it when I cannot see?"

"Do the best you can. It may be that it is the act of drawing the symbol, not the actual representation, that matters."

"Perhaps that is the case. I shall, as you say, do the best I can. What shall I draw it with?"

"Your own blood."

"Very well. Then I shall require a knife."

"Here it is."

"Where?"

"Here."

"I cannot see — ouch."

"Are you hurt?"

"Not severely. I now have blood to draw it with."

"Very good. As you draw it—"

"Yes, as I draw it?"

"You must hold the name within your mind, and repeat it softly."

"So you have said. Very well. Shall I begin?"

"Yes, do so."

Habil listened carefully to the sound of her cousin drawing a complex symbol on the floor of the room, using his finger as a stylus and his own blood as the ink, and she heard him, as well, saying the god's name over and over as he worked. This took a certain length of time, which Habil filled by shifting from one foot to the other and hoping she was doing nothing wrong. At length, he said, very softly, "It is done. What next?"

"Now stand in the middle of the symbol you have drawn—"

"I am already doing so, insofar as I can tell in this darkness."

"You must hum or sing that melody of which we have spoken."

"Very well."

"And while you are doing so—are you still holding the knife?"

"Yes, in my left hand."

"Well, reach out with your other hand. Do not move; do not step outside of the symbol. I will move—there."

"What have you given me? It seems to be moving."

"It is a norska."

"What of it?"

"As you hum the melody, cut the norska's throat."

"The blood will necessarily blot out much of the symbol I have drawn."

"It doesn't matter."

"Very well. I am about to begin."

"May the god appear," said Habil.

"What if he does not?"

"That means our effort failed."

"And then?"

"Then we must try again."

"May the god appear," said Kâna fervently.

Chapter the Sixty-Eighth

How the Gods Puzzled Over
Some of Kâna's Actions

I n that hazy, dim, and confusing place where the minds of mortals lose all sense of what is real and what is dream, and where the Gods judge the fate of man in general and men in particular, and where *time* itself is a concept so dubious that its very existence becomes subject to reasonable dispute, that is, in the Halls of Judgment, the Gods considered the progress of the affairs of what they hoped would become, once more, the Dragaeran Empire.

Here the darkness seemed to have texture, and might ripple from one of the Gods to another in response to that deity's regard, and the occasional flicker of real light, from outside of the grand circle that made up the halls, might appear to flutter about the chamber, as if it were a living spark, searching for a way out before fading entirely; and so, in this place, a product of dreams from the minds of beings who pass our understanding, the conversation, as it turned to matters of the Empire, became general, absorbing the interest of all, or nearly all, of those present, even as a small figure, that of a little girl, slipped down from Verra's lap and quietly ran off, as will a child who knows that the adult conversation about to begin cannot but be wearisome.

"Your Phoenix has done nothing with the Orb," observed Ordwynac, "except play games. She and her companions flit hither and yon, and make pretty lights, and are no closer to closing our world from the Makers."

"More than that," observed Kelchor. "In the northwest, a dying man was saved."

"What of that?" said Ordwynac.

"He was so close to death that, even in the days of the old Empire, he would have been called a dead man. His heart had stopped, and there was little activity in his brain. Yet, an Athyra sorcerer —"

"So then," said Ordwynac, "the purification and enhancement of the Orb was successful. You perceive, this brings us no closer to our own goal, that of a functioning Empire which has the strength to bar the Makers."

"The demon," observed Kelchor, "has proven efficacious."

"And Kâna has proven desperate," said Moranthë.

"Desperate?" said Ordwynac.

"I think so."

"What has he done?"

"He has attempted to speak direct with me, desiring me to manifest. Presumably, he wished to bargain with me for my help—my help against myself, had he but realized it. I was half tempted to do so, and settle him at that moment."

"Why didn't you, sister?" asked Verra. "It would seem to be a remarkable opportunity."

"It would have ended him, but not his cousin, nor his organization. Indeed, it would have let them know that the Gods oppose them."

"And," said Nyssa, "if they knew this, might it not be sufficient to convince them to engage in other pursuits?"

"I think, in the case of his cousin," said Moranthë, "it would only have made her more cautious and more careful. The entire structure of the organization built up by Kâna must be dismantled, or else taken over; that is my opinion. The death of this Dragon by itself will not do."

"Yes," said Verra. "On reflection, I am inclined to agree with you."

"There is something to be said," observed Ordwynac, "for this Kâna. He is determined. Perhaps we should have supported his pretensions, rather than those of the Phoenix."

"And the Cycle," said Barlen. "What of that? Do we abandon it? For, I promise you, it will not abandon us. That is to say, it will continue to turn whether we approve of it or not."

Ordwynac sighed. "Yes, you are right, old god."

"As for taking it over," said Barlen, "the Phoenix has done exactly that as far as the post is concerned, or at least much of it. Many of the best elements of Empire created by Kâna are now in the Empress's hands, and she is working steadily to gain more. And the defection of the Duke of Galstan has crippled the Dragon's intelligence service; that was a heavy blow."

"Has he defected?" said Ordwynac.

"You didn't know?" said Verra.

"Well, that is good, I think."

"Oh, certainly."

Kéurana spoke, then, saying, "Moranthë, my love."

"Yes, dear sister?"

"You say that this Kâna desired you to manifest?"

"Certainly. And he had one of the older rituals, as well, and performed it admirably. I heard him call my name as clearly as I hear your words to me now."

"I understand that, but —"

"Yes?"

"Why would he have called you?"

"I should imagine," said Moranthë, "that he felt the assistance of a God would do him no harm. Perhaps I could have feigned to give him my assistance, and then betrayed him; but you know how difficult that is."

"Truly. But that is not my question."

"Well?"

"Why *you* of all of us?"

"Why not me? Am I not a goddess? Are you jealous at all, my love?"

"Not on this occasion, dearest one, though I have in the past been jealous of your beauty and skill; but who would not be?"

"Ah, you are kind."

"But on this occasion, I am curious. What attribute, that is to say, which of the many skills and talents that you possess, might he have wished for, so that he desired you of all of us?"

"Now that you ask, dearest of siblings, I begin to wonder myself. Most of my worshipers are in the East. Indeed," she said, addressing herself to Verra, "I was nearly hurt that you made a pact with that little Dragon of yours, as he was raised in the East, and studied the Eastern magical arts, which I am known to favor."

"Because, adored sister," said Verra, "I knew that he would go from the Eastern arts to those of the Empire —" Here she nodded at Kéurana. "— and that he will, someday, pass beyond those to the oldest of the magical arts, which are my province."

"And yet," observed Kéurana, "he has not the bloodlines to use such powers fully."

"As to that," said Verra, "we shall see."

"But," insisted Kéurana, "I say again, why you, Moranthë? What is he after?"

"I cannot guess," said the goddess after a moment's reflection. "And yet, since you introduce the subject—"

"Well?"

"I should very much like to know."

Afterword

A Book Review, Issued in the Form of a Circulating Document, Amplified and Enhanced with Observations from Life and Several Precepts for the Wise
By Ilen, a Magian

The material from the University Press which accompanies *A Mighty Thundering of Wisdom, Not One Word of Which Can Be Gainsaid: An Examination of the Failings, Ethical, Moral, Literary, Historical, Grammatical, Intellectual and Otherwise of the Work and Person of Paarfi of Roundwood, Formerly of this University—a Perfunctory Summary* makes it clear that, while the University Press has rushed this six-volume tome into print at the same time as the printing of the second volume of *The Viscount of Adrilankha*, it in no wise feels that such a book can or should be seen as a sad case of acidulated fruit; for, it points out, within the space of a mere 3,700 pages are gathered together over a dozen of Paarfi's former colleagues: professors of history, of literature, of viticulture, of folklore, of manners, and of several other disciplines, with one objective and one only, that being to demonstrate the failings of Paarfi of Roundwood.

Let it be said at the outset that, notwithstanding anything the University might say or refrain from saying, the overwhelming impression received by this reviewer is that the University, in publishing this volume, is convinced that the misguided souls who have been unfortunate enough to delude themselves into thinking that they enjoyed Paarfi of Roundwood's books, will, upon reading the first of these volumes, stand dumbfounded, the scales fallen from their eyes, determined to eschew such dubious pleasures in the future. That if a serving man were to read, say, Volume Two, Chapters XXIV–XL, which share the heading *On the Public Drunkenness of Paarfi*, he would henceforth regard *The Phoenix Guards* as anathema; while no serious reader (or one who considered herself such) could, after reading Volume Four Chapters XC–CXXXIII, *Common Historical Misconceptions Promulgated, Disseminated, Reinforced, or Permitted by Paarfi of Roundwood, with Additional Notes on Several Simple But Usual*

Misconceptions of Which Paarfi Failed to Use His Position of Trust and Responsibility to Disabuse the Public, and having learned that what Paarfi describes as "a polished exotic hardwood" has been conclusively demonstrated to be the wood of the blacknut tree, and thus neither exotic, nor, technically, a hardwood, nor polished (blacknut wood gains its patina and strength from being greased, buried in darkness, and greased once more), would henceforth swear a dark and binding oath that an author capable of perpetuating such dangerous fallacies is an author to be, in the future, avoided.

This reviewer's contact at the University Press declared that the University had confidently expected *A Mighty Thundering* to sell in numbers commensurate with Paarfi's own latest volume. Alas, the piles of unsold and unstolen volumes (except, curiously, Volume Five, *On the Lecherous Behavior of Paarfi of Roundwood, Profusely and Extensively Illustrated with Engraved Plates, Many of Them in Color, Depicting Each of the Actresses, Mannequins, Warriors, Courtesans, Hired Sluts, and Promising Young Female Writers with Whom Paarfi's Name Has Been Linked, Whether Conclusively Proved (Chapters I–LIV), or Merely Rumored, Either on Good Authority (Chapters LV–CIV) or Poor or No Authority at All (Chapters CV–CLX),* which had entirely sold out at several locations when this reviewer went for his morning walk through the booksellers' district) next to the depleted piles that were once towering stacks of the latest volume of *The Viscount of Adrilankha,* demonstrates that, while the reading public's appetite for the romances of Paarfi of Roundwood outstrips the capacity of the printing presses to keep up, their desire to learn of the failings of their author of choice is not similarly favored.

Thus, this reviewer believes it his duty to summarize and comment upon the University's volumes for those who shall not read them, that such prodigious (albeit, if the title is to be believed, preliminary) work may reach the audience for which it was intended. So. The thrust of the University's argument is that Paarfi has taken a discipline and reduced it to the petty crowd-pleasing antics of a fat man and his squirrel in the public square; that Paarfi has failed his training and education and is merely a mountebank, no longer capable of being considered in any way a respected or respectable historian. There.

Strangely, for a book which professes itself to exist purely for reasons of historical accuracy, *A Mighty Thundering* is at its best when dealing with naked rumor. My favorite moments were those scattered through the various volumes which attempt, not to prove, but to smear, to imply, or to force the reader to infer, that Paarfi's books were not written by Paarfi, but written by journeymen to Paarfi's specifications, due either to Paarfi's laziness or to his inability to write, and this latter probably caused by a misfortune of a venereal nature. There is no effort to prove this, beyond third-hand supposition. And yet, while it is manifestly false in all particulars, there are, each day, more and more young writers who write like Paarfi.

This reviewer's own encounters with Paarfi have been fewer and briefer than might have been hoped. Still, Paarfi of Roundwood gives his time unstintingly to those less fortunate than himself and in the advising of many on matters literary, and thus it was that this reviewer was, several days ago, able to encounter Paarfi at a gathering in this city of many artists and writers, in the upper room of a large tavern, and to overhear him in conversation with a young lady who had asked Paarfi if he would be willing to inspect and comment upon her manuscript, which she had with her. Following a most perfunctory inspection of the first page Paarfi announced that he could see that she was having difficulties with her conjunctions, and that there were several nouns both masculine-passive, feminine-active and (inclusive of a multiplicity of potential genders) *couchant*, that he saw immediately needed to be properly conjoined, perhaps with certain prepositions he had in mind. When the young lady suggested that they could repair to her chambers, with the manuscript, and *revise* her work together, Paarfi of Roundwood nodded his approval, and told her that while there was much to be said for that approach, he could not help but feel that her choice of verb was limiting and fundamentally incorrect, but that, with his help, together they would be able to find a verb that would prove perfectly satisfactory for both of them.

It was at this point, perceiving that Paarfi was preparing to leave the tavern, that this reviewer placed himself in front of the esteemed author and asked him directly about several of the matters alluded to in the *Mighty Thundering*—would Paarfi deign to respond to the accu-

sation that he no longer wrote his books, but employed several journeymen in different capacities to research, outline, describe, limn,
and revise the book, while he, for his part, merely oversaw the work;
or that *The Viscount of Adrilankha* was, at bottom, a direct and obvious
theft of, or at best an homage to, the bawdy street ballad, popular
several hundred years back, ". . . . And a Bandit's Never Parted from
His Sword."

"Well," boomed Paarfi, not looking one whit put out, "I have
heard such a song, it's true. I could even sing it to you, for I have what
is reckoned by many to be a fine and melodious voice, particularly
when accompanied on a stringed instrument that has been correctly
tuned. But of course I hear songs. Unless we were deaf, how could
we *not* hear songs?"

This reviewer agreed that this was so, and that indeed, the hearing of songs was something that none of us could avoid, try how we
might; and was preparing to ask him a further question, when Paarfi
ran a hand through his hair and looked around at those gathered
there in the upper room of that tavern. The room fell silent.

"I trust that you will permit me to say two words about the University, the University Press, and their so-called concerns with accuracy and what they term scholarly values. And the two words are
these: They are *not* and *now*, or conversely *now* and *not*. Does anyone
here have a copy of *The Phoenix Guards* with him tonight? Come on,
come on, I have scrawled my name in the front matter of several
copies. There. Good. Now, I shall find Chapter the Eighth, titled "In
Which it Is Shown That There Are No Police in Dragaera City," and
turn several pages until I find the place where our heroes find themselves outnumbered and in dire straits, but also in a disagreement
over their best course of action, whether it be to stay or to go. Ahem:

> *"The numbers, while still not equal, were at least a little more*
> *balanced, so that the Dragonlords, of whom perhaps a dozen remained,*
> *standing, hesitated before attacking.*
>
> *"'I think,' said Khaavren, 'that it is not time to withdraw.'*
>
> *"'Bah,' said Tazendra. 'The game is only beginning to grow*
> *warm.'*
>
> *"Aerich said, 'I, for one, agree with Khaavren.'"*

Then, his voice booming louder and louder, Paarfi said, *"Not time to withdraw? Not* time to withdraw? *Now* time to withdraw is what I wrote. *Now.* An obvious error, and one as easily repaired, or so we would think; and yet we would be mistaken, for as printing succeeded printing of *The Phoenix Guards,* and reader after reader was convinced of my own foolishness and of my deficiencies as a writer, I requested, I asked, I pleaded, I begged, I petitioned the University to change this, and to correct future printings. (I made no mention, I will have you know, of their stray comma in the first sentence I read to you, understanding that no publisher can fix every stray iota.) Each time I asked, they agreed; each time they did nothing. There are," Paarfi continued, his white garments flickering orange from the firelight, "authors who have slain publishers for putting a *not* where there should have been a *now* (and, doubtless, vice versa), and not a guard or officer or juror in the land would punish or even reprimand such an author. However, *we* have slain *nobody.* Instead we have merely withdrawn our labor and our person from their shallow lives of *nots* and *nows* and *not nows* and *not nots.*

"Well, and we say to you all, *now*! And if *not* now, then *when?*"

If he said aught else to the crowd in the tavern that night, it was drowned out by the cheers of the company assembled,

including your reviewer, who has the honour
to sign himself here,

Ilen, a Magian.